GHOSTFIRES

Keith Dixon

GHOSTFIRES

St. Martin's Press ❧ New York

www.stmartins.com

Design by Kathryn Parise

LIBRARY OF CONGRESS CATALOGING-IN-PUBLICATION DATA

Dixon, Keith, 1971–
    Ghostfires / Keith Dixon.—1st ed.
        p. cm.
    ISBN 0-312-31740-9
    1. Parent and adult child—Fiction. 2. Mothers—Death—Fiction. 3. Narcotic addicts—Fiction. 4. Fathers and sons—Fiction. 5. New York (N.Y.)—Fiction. 6. Physicians—Fiction. 7. Widowers—Fiction. I. Title.

PS3604.I95G47 2004
813'.6—dc22

                                                            2003058179

First Edition: January 2004

10 9 8 7 6 5 4 3 2 1

For M.A.

In short, you see, the essential is to cease being free and to obey, in repentance, a greater rogue than oneself.

—ALBERT CAMUS
The Fall

The evil that is in the world always comes of ignorance, and good intentions may do as much harm as malevolence, if they lack understanding. On the whole, men are more good than bad; that, however, isn't the real point.

—ALBERT CAMUS
The Plague

ONE

One

The shuttle bus came around the access road in the dark with its headlights scouring the pavement ahead. He watched it follow the long fence and turn into the entrance to the long-term parking lot. It passed under the raised gate and drove between the lines of parked cars to the blue kiosk halfway up the center row. The halogen lamps high overhead reflected brightly off the dark glass.

Please be on this one, he thought. Oh if you aren't on this one, Victor.

He'd been waiting here in his El Dorado for more than an hour, parked miles from the main terminals of Kennedy Airport, and it occurred to him now that among the many divisions of the human race lay a simple partition that overrode all others: there were those who were not in control of a particular situation and had to be on time, and those who were in control and could show up whenever they damn well pleased. He was always early, and not because he was punctual—he was early because he was comprehensively indebted to his addiction, and his addiction could not wait.

This past November he had turned sixty-eight. By any measurement, however kind, he was much too old to be waiting in this cold. It was supposed to be getting warmer all the time, wasn't it? Icebergs feeding the oceans. Antediluvian millennium. And still every winter the mercury fell further—that morning, the Channel Nine weatherman had predicted the *wintriest,* the *most Hyperion,* the *most hibernal* December second in recorded history. Now, with the mercury not just asleep but asleep and *dreaming* at six degrees below zero—and how demoralizing was that? to know that even mother nature could hit bottom, and penetrate, and keep going—even now, after an hour in this cold, the forecast made him think not of the temperature, but of other people. Cold he could handle. Wintry weather he could repel. Hyperion December frightened him not a bit. It was other people—dealers, sons, neighbors, informants, police, wives, two-bits, meter maids—who troubled him. It was they, with their wintry dispositions, with their squalls and advancing high-pressure fronts, who could really fuck up your day.

Please be on this one, Victor, he thought, and opened his car door. At the first lash of wind he felt a crazed arrhythmia in his chest: he realized he was not up for this. He, Warren Bascomb, was sixty-eight and a morphine addict, and his heart was not up for this.

Twenty yards away, the interior of the idling bus brightened suddenly. Passengers blinked up at the fluorescent light with childlike distress, then stood to take their bags down from the overhead rack. Warren spotted Victor, still dressed in his cobalt flight attendant's uniform, near the back of the line. A feeling not unlike love washed over him. Even from a distance, he reflected, you noticed the symmetry in his looks. You noticed the inevitable way his features converged with his reflexive manners, with his antigallantry. *After you. I insist.* And then that sharklike smile. He looked like the handsome killer from a B movie.

Warren waved to him. Victor set his flight bag on the pavement and began rolling it noisily toward Warren's car.

One hour late, he thought. Almost four thousand ticks of my watch, and still I go to pieces at the sight of him. Victor, he noted, had remained perfectly groomed, despite the turbulent in-flight drinks. His Latin good looks had probably seen him through a number of unpleasant moments. Or gotten him into some.

"For God's sake, Victor," Warren said. Victor had rolled his flight bag to a stop at the rear of the El Dorado. "One hour. I waited for one hour."

Victor made no explanation for his lateness. None was required. They both knew this was part of a structured, tedious foreplay that would lead, eventually, to a predetermined outcome. The only sign that Victor had even heard Warren was the sigh he expelled, suddenly and wearily, from between clenched teeth. His sigh suggested criss-crossed time zones, the detritus of persistent risk, and a failing patience. Warren let the matter drop. He fished his car keys from the pocket of his khakis and unlocked the El Dorado's trunk, then lifted out the steel jack and heavy toolbox. Victor, impatience suddenly all gone, coldly methodical now, scanned the lot for the white security minivan, then squatted down and unzipped the front of his bag. Inside was a locked steel case with WORLD HEALTH ORGANIZATION and the UN insignia stenciled on its face. Warren slipped the penlight off his key chain and twisted the end until the narrow beam sprang out, then placed the penlight between his teeth. He lifted the case from Victor's bag and set it on the pavement, then snapped the lock with a screwdriver.

The clear glass ampoules of Dilaudid, seated tightly together inside the case, reflected the beam of the penlight. They seemed to give off a gentle warmth. Whenever he looked at a full case he understood that the Dilaudid was stronger than he was. Accepting that had been difficult at first, but after a while it had been like having accepted gravity or time.

This case, Warren knew, wouldn't be missed. The three years he had spent in the Congo after medical school had taught him that lost medication was never missed. The bush doctors simply assumed the morphine had been used to bribe customs agents or soldiers at the local airfield. Whether you were in Kinshasa or Jakarta or Algiers, attrition was an accepted part of the humanitarian effort. Even in the business of kindness, dishonesty and empathy battled to dominate the human condition. "This is a rotten business," Warren said. The depression that was the hallmark of approaching withdrawal had begun to insinuate itself into his thoughts. "What we're doing."

"It's an unpleasant business. But it's no more or less rotten than what's already underway. Half the morphine we take comes in through the Russian mob, anyway."

"Still," he said. He hadn't explained himself well.

Victor had begun to shiver. He crossed his arms over his chest for warmth. "You need to adapt, Warren. You need to achieve a level of comfort with the unpleasantness."

"Unpleasant. That's how I used to describe the sensation of pain to my patients. 'This might feel a little unpleasant,' I'd say. Then I'd hack up their articular bursal wall. One of them once said to me, 'Doctor, you're like a politician with knives.' I was insulted."

"Of course you were. You're like those spineless reformists who sit in cafes and talk about change, but do nothing. You want something, but you're not willing to do the things you have to do to get it. All the dirty work gets left to someone else."

"It's not like that," Warren said. "I just get upset at night sometimes."

"Too much television." He turned and scanned the lot for the security van. "You've got to switch the set off after dark. Six o'clock, it's all laugh tracks and underwear models. But by midnight you've got jumpers and some guy who stuck his baby in the freezer." He yawned luxuriously. Warren heard his jaw crack. "Tomorrow could be big. Anthony says they've got four C-130s on the runway."

"Does he know where they're going?"

Victor shrugged. Warren sensed that the intended destination made no difference to him. He envied Victor's clean conscience. "The hangar's full of 463L pallets. Ben should clean out his trunk. Could be ten, twelve cases of morphine, depending on the shift foreman. Wes will be overjoyed."

"What time do you want him?"

"Eight o'clock. Which does not mean eight-ten, or eight-thirty, or nine o'clock. Has it occurred to you, Warren, that your son has a problem with lateness?"

Warren remarked that Victor should know a thing or two about late-ness. When Victor grimaced, Warren artlessly attempted to change the subject. "I'm surprised they airdrop with military hardware. The natives don't much like seeing stateside planes."

"They paint the fuselage gray, now. If they don't, they get the occa-sional grenade shot up from the canopy. Even if they do paint it some-times they get the RPG anyway. The stress is devastating. Most of the freelance pilots are speed freaks. Some fly twenty hours straight on nothing but Mars bars and diet pills. All for a thirty-second drop."

"It's a strange business," Warren said.

"You help other people. In return, you end up in rehab. The divorce rate is unbelievable. I think there's a lesson there somewhere."

Life, Warren reflected, was always about something else. There was always a human subtext fouling the works. He had gone to Africa specif-ically to irritate his father, in retaliation for being forced to go to medical school. Even the most selfless work of his life had ultimately been about satisfying a private agenda. Sometimes he wondered if everyone was that way. It depressed him to think so. He still harbored a faint hope that the world was a kind place.

Life had been simpler in Africa, and the return to America had been a catastrophic upheaval, his first encounter with true culture shock. His flight had landed in the middle of the night at Idlewild Airport, and, too exhausted to travel north to home, Warren had taken a room at one of the airport flophouses. The hot shower that the doctors had all fanta-sized about back in the bush had been nothing more than a miserly, scalding rain. The bed had been disquietingly, almost obscenely soft, and Warren had awakened in the dark later with the distinct impression that it was trying to devour him.

"I'll tell Ben to be here at eight," he said. "Anything else?"

"He should drive straight out to Wes's house after. We want to streamline things a bit."

Warren studied the razor wire that topped the parking lot fence. He hadn't decided yet if it was meant to keep things in or out. "You're not going with him?"

Victor shook his head.

"That's awfully trusting of you," Warren said.

"It's not a problem."

"Ben won't do anything without a paycheck, Victor."

Victor unzipped the front pocket of his flight bag and removed a taped envelope. "Six hundred there. If we do a double I'll have Anthony bring him the rest."

"I should count it."

"There's no need, Warren."

There wasn't, of course. There was never a question of absolute relative honesty between the three of them.

"You'll give it to him tonight?"

"He's at a dinner party. But I'll stop by later." After, he thought. After I've taken care of myself.

"Fine. I need you to drop me at the subway." With a rough twist of his hand, Victor removed his wedding ring and placed it in his pocket, then latched the lid of the toolbox and set it back in the trunk. He sat in the passenger seat and blew into his fists to warm them. Warren drove between the rows of parked cars to the exit gate and paid the four-dollar fee, then put the car in park. Victor asked the cashier if he could try to guess what perfume she was wearing. "Eternity?" he asked. He was stretched across Warren, straining toward her. His eyes were closed, his profile sleek and sharp in the halogen light. The woman opened the cash register and shook her head. Victor sat back in defeat. She seemed flattered by the attention. Unwilling to let the moment pass, she looked at Warren and asked, "What do you think it is?"

Thank you for choosing JFK, the raising barrier read. *Buckle up for safety.*

"Eternity," Warren said. "Not familiar with that one."

"Warren's favorite is Opium," Victor said.

Warren turned left out of the gate, then right at the corner of the employee parking lot and followed the long fence up the slight hill to the green sign for the Van Wyck. At the bottom of the on ramp, the traffic slowed and then stopped all at once where it fed left into the slowly rolling lanes of inbound cars. Taillights queued ahead like an endless string of Christmas lights. Cold sweat painted the back of his neck. It would be hours before he could fix again. Hours.

Some people, he knew, believed that he'd earned whatever suffering he encountered during years of vice. He rejected that. Vice, after all, wasn't an acquired taste. That was precisely what made it vice. Everyone knew that it came easily, and guiltily, and naturally. Warren didn't believe that he was flawed or selfish. He'd simply been less successful than others at holding weakness at bay. Virtually everyone he knew was addicted to one substance or another, to the nicotine he inhaled or the alcohol he swallowed; his was simply a less socially acceptable medium with which to entertain the same *need* that eventually consumed everyone. The needle, he believed, was what made people uneasy. It seemed strange to them that he could, without hesitation, feel a sort of love for an object they associated with explicit pain, with the chilly sterility of doctors' offices, with sickness.

And he believed the ascetics were wrong about what they were preparing for, their infinity of afterlife. In thirty years of performing surgery, Warren had seen no epiphanies in dying faces, no golden halos, no optical phenomena; nor had he sensed the presence of dead souls stirring about the operating table. Death—and he'd witnessed more than he could count—was neither transformative nor comforting. It was never pretty or dramatic. It was merely violent, and final, and often it was like something you'd expect to see in a stockyard.

"Easy, Warren," Victor said, looking ahead at the traffic. "Mind over matter."

Warren's hands, gripping the steering wheel, had gone pale from the pressure. He loosened his grip and flexed the joints. This was bad. Traffic was bad, yes—sitting here in traffic, unable to fix, with a full case of Dilaudid in the trunk, was a screaming agony of *almost*. But any amount of traffic was less bad than waiting for Ben's pickup tomorrow night. He would be all right. He would be all right soon. As he came to understand this, he felt a sudden wash of gratitude toward Victor. "Thanks for setting me up early," he said. "I didn't plan well this month."

"I prefer not to, you know? There's a reason why I use Ben and not you."

"I don't ask often."

"I guess not."

"Is it really such a problem?"

"No. And it does have its upside. The Dilaudid keeps you docile."

Warren didn't respond. It was true.

Victor removed his wedding ring from his pocket and polished it on his arm. "I don't know why you started in the first place, Warren. You of all people. You know what it does to people."

Warren prepared to trundle out his The Drug Chose Me argument, but stopped himself. Victor was a businessman. He wouldn't understand the premise of subjugation. It lacked the plottable geometry of a bottom line. "It really wasn't my fault, you know?"

"Everyone says that, Warren."

"Is that so?"

"Yes, that's so. Whether you were burned or not is beside the point."

"It didn't feel like it was beside the point. It felt like it was exactly the point."

"Lots of people get burned, Warren. How many of them become addicts? Lots of people get hurt and come out of it fine."

Warren recalled that his own wife hadn't come out of it fine. She had sickened and hadn't recovered, and near the end she had been an addict, too. Except, as a physician, you never openly called it a habit if the drugs were being used to manage pain. She had known her tolerance was up, and when she decided to end her life she'd taken enough MS Contin to kill ten people, so much that even the six milligrams of Naloxone he'd injected in her veins, enough to bring Jesus Christ himself back from heaven, hadn't saved her. Warren thought often of her silent departure. He often felt the merciless sting of regret. There were mistakes that could not be undone, he'd found, experiences that could only be put away or remembered differently or masked. Which was exactly why fixing was an act of mercy one took on oneself. Fixing removed you from that plane of existence where everything was charged with consequence.

His own habit had developed three years ago through the accident of his survival. He'd been burned very badly in a fire at his father's house, nearly killed. The burn specialist, noting his forty percent burn coverage, had expected him to expire within a few days, and had started him on Levorphanol for the pain. Nauseated by the Levorphanol, Warren was switched to Dilaudid the next day. Though his survival wasn't exactly miraculous, it was something of a surprise to everyone. Already, it was too late. Just a few weeks later, he began to sense that the daily injections were about something other than pain relief.

He assumed that eventually his affliction would be exposed, that he would be publicly humiliated and privately pitied, but the actual moment of discovery didn't happen until six months after the fire, when he lost his medical license, suddenly and catastrophically, for operating on a healthy knee while gliding along on six milligrams of Dilaudid. He remembered the day clearly, the sensation of glissading into the operating room on the slipstream of his high, unsure of himself after four months away for rehabilitation. The scalpel felt unfamiliar in his hand, almost awkward. He remembered a clash of steel on steel, and the sudden confusion that moved through the attendants in the room as he opened the knee and encountered an intact, elastic anterior cruciate ligament. For a terrifying moment he thought the Dilaudid was causing him to hallucinate. So he did what one does when one has a scalpel in one's hand—he began to cut.

"Not many people," Warren explained, "get burned as badly as I did." Or if they do, he thought, they're fortunate enough to die afterward.

"Let me see."

Warren rolled up his sleeve.

"Christ," Victor said. He turned away, revolted by the sight of the grafted skin.

"Don't go prima donna on me now, Victor."

"Warren, you should be dead."

"You should have seen it before it healed."

Victor was silent as he tried to picture Warren's burned limbs. "Ever try to stop?"

Warren looked over at him. He doubted that someone who had never tried it could understand.

"I'm guessing all you need is to go some place where you can't get it." He scratched his arm. "Maybe I should cut you off."

"Maybe I should cut your throat."

Victor sighed. He seemed bored. "You junkies. All the same. Make one joke about your supply and you're ready to pull a knife." He looked around the car. "You don't have a knife, do you?"

Warren blotted his upper lip with the cuff of his shirt. "No," he said.

"Then get one," Victor said. He looked away and tapped his fingernails against the glass, silent for a moment. "I'm getting worried about your son. Anthony says he's coming unglued."

"Ben has been unglued since his mother died."

Victor made a sound in his throat. "It could be bad for you."

"For me." A drop of sweat rolled down his ribcage.

"If there's trouble with Ben, this stops. You and me. No more rolling pharmacy."

"What sort of trouble are you worried about?"

"Maybe he's thinking of looking elsewhere for work. Wants to clean himself up. Or maybe he's thinking of flipping me."

Warren was thinking coldly and methodically, trying to figure out how to lead the conversation away from where it was headed. He had no money of his own to support his habit, and without this arrangement with Ben he'd be finished. "Ben needs you more than you need him."

"For now." Victor looked at him openly. "What do you think?"

"I think Ben has all the optimism of a kid out cutting his own switch. He needs a little positive reinforcement now and then."

"My father used to hit me with his belt, while he was still around. He called that positive reinforcement." He tapped his fingernails against the glass again. "You ever hit Ben when he was a kid?"

"Never."

"Why not?"

"I was always worried he'd hit me back."

Ben sometimes remarked that time turned things around; what he meant was that time took what was true and reversed it. He always managed to infuse the remark with his special brand of oblique menace. He seemed to be suggesting that Warren had been a hideous, tyrannical father, and that his time would come. Warren was glad he hadn't ever hit him.

"I was worried when my dad wasn't hitting me. After he left, it was all I could remember about him. The light bulb over the kitchen table swinging. The scars on his knuckles. His boots. Teeth. It was all flailing extremities with him."

Warren cracked his window. He was beginning to feel sick. Brake lights swam liquidly in his vision, doubling and trebling. His own father had never hit him, he recalled. He wondered if things would have turned out differently if he had.

Victor watched the traffic roll slowly north into Queens. He was still unsure of whether or not he had done the right thing by setting Warren up a day early. It was important to keep Warren supplied, he believed, because Warren, as a relatively crafty, well-educated man, seemed capable of causing more trouble than most. Almost as a rule, it was unwise to do favors for junkies. A favor conveyed two messages: first, that you were a friend, second, that you were a reasonable and perhaps even accommodating person. If you gave a junkie an inch they always wanted the proverbial mile, and any sign you gave them that they could mine the world any farther than they already had was, of course, a mistake. It was always more and more and more with them.

Ordinarily, he would have had nothing to do with someone like Warren. Victor preferred to leave all the unpleasant work of distribution to Wes. Trafficking narcotics made him feel unclean enough, but at least the trail seemed to end when the cases of morphine were handed over to Wes. Dealing directly with someone like Warren, who was obviously almost completely lost in his addiction, seemed to illustrate too clearly the end result of what he did. It was too real.

That was partly why he had decided, from now on, to have Ben drive straight out to Wes's and skip picking him up in Queens on the way. The three of them had been working together for two years, now, and it seemed to be the logical step. Warren had met Wes through another surgeon who'd become addicted to Percocet. At the time, Wes had been aggressively seeking to expand his mid-level operation into high-level dealing. At the time, he'd made most of his money dealing to rich high school kids from Garden City. Now, virtually his entire roster of customers was composed of defrocked physicians who had been caught dipping in the cabinet. There was safety in that sort of work, yes—but very little in the way of serious cash. Everyone knew that serious cash was in heroin, in Ecstasy. Pharmacists were the only ones who made money off the designer drugs Wes's customers were hooked on.

Ben, he was reasonably sure, could handle this, if he kept his head together. And it seemed best to leave as much of the immediate risk as possible to someone else. He hoped that Ben was too frightened by the inherent risks to gamble with changes to the basic plan; but still, Victor had found that people always became someone else when they were put under pressure. He would have to count on Ben's lack of initiative. The only thing required of him was that he appear to be an exhausted busi-nessman driving home from the airport to Long Island, and Ben did that better than anyone. And it wouldn't go on for much longer. If he, Victor, could avoid any problems, in another six months or maybe a year he would have saved enough to move back to Culebra. His life here had begun to make him feel diseased. People like Warren and Ben made him feel diseased.

Before he'd met Warren, Victor had been using his friend Theo as a courier. As a Queens Boulevard mercenary, Theo was well known for his sadistic tendencies, but he had a trenchant distaste for narcotics, and eventually he quit. Victor had moved the morphine himself for a while afterward, but narcotics gave him the cold sweats and the night horrors, because there was some serious jail time involved whenever you mixed narcotics and theft. He'd been pulled over twice on the LIE for not using his blinker. Yes, he was a bad driver, but it was obvious that the New York cops had him made from the moment he hit the on-ramp. As far as they were concerned, his black hair and dark complexion marked him as Puerto Rican, just another *cuchillero* with attitude. And he knew himself to be the sort who would never survive jail. It was true that he was a cheat, but he wasn't a criminal.

The problem of finding a suitable courier had been solved on the night he'd met Warren at Wes's house. "This guy," said Wes, pointing to Warren as the three of them stood in the front hall, "comes to us with a sterling resume. He's a newbie chipper." Victor took his hand back to wipe it on his pants, and replied that he hoped Wes was right—chippers, in his opinion, were entirely untrustworthy, because they lived with one foot in real life, one foot in their addiction. Victor preferred criminals, because criminals were predictable. Victor and Wes had gone out back and after they had finished their business, Warren, exultant with armfuls of morphine, volunteered to drive Victor to the train station. During the drive, Victor asked Warren if he knew anyone who could be trusted with some work.

"My son's looking for some money," Warren said. "He might be right for you."

"And what do you expect to get out of this?" Victor asked. Because that was how it worked: everyone had to get something. Or the whole system collapsed.

"I'm in a little trouble at work. Problem with a patient. If things go the way I think they'll go, I might need a cheaper source than Wes. Maybe you and I could make an agreement." Within ten stoplights it had all been worked out. The very next day, Victor met Ben. Since then, business had been good. So good that Victor almost felt obligated to worry.

Warren reached forward and switched on the dashboard radio. "You want me to take you into Queens? It's going to take me hours, anyway."

Warren had volunteered, Victor realized, because he intended to drive a few blocks north after dropping him off, and park on a residential side street to fix before he drove home.

"That's princely of you," Victor said. "Just make sure you lock the doors." It was amazing how easily and how quickly an addict could fuck things up. You had to watch them like children.

When Trina had given Victor a key to her Queens apartment months ago, she had asked that he use the intercom to let her know he was on his way up, but he almost never did. It was her apartment, but he felt that she owed him.

He let himself in the front door and found her wrapped in a quilt on the couch, watching television with all the lights off. The television cast her shadow against the back wall.

"Victor," Trina said. "I've told you about this."

"You're staying in?"

She sighed and adjusted the quilt. "I got my period this morning."

"Feeling all right?"

"It's not that. I just didn't feel like having anyone see me, you know?"

"I know. You want me to fix you something?"

She thought it over. "I want you to come over here."

He sat on the end of her couch and began to massage her feet. In a strange way, it made him feel good that she wasn't feeling well. Victor knew himself to be of the sort who needed to be needed. "What are you watching?"

"One of those bad movies."

"With the actors you know but you can't remember their names." But that was a stupid thing to say to her so he changed the subject. "How was class?" Trina was taking Expression Through Communication nights at a dance school on West Seventy-Fourth Street, in the hope that it would help her with her hand problem. She never knew what to do with her hands during readings, she said, and hadn't had a callback in months because of it. The classes were expensive, but Victor felt they were entirely worth it. The payoff was the same as meeting Warren a day early. He preferred both of them docile.

"It was strange. They had us lay on the mats in silence for ten minutes. All the lights off. No talking. And then one at a time we were supposed to say our name, loudly, as if we were introducing ourselves to God."

"To God."

"That's what she said."

"And this is supposed to help you with your hands."

"Victor," she said. "Please?"

"How was it?"

"Everyone used their stage name," she said.

"How was it for you?"

She flexed her ankle joint in his hand.

"It was kind of creepy," she said.

"Talking to God?"

"Hearing all those people use their stage names. It seemed—I don't know, like lying? So I used my real name. But it didn't sound like it was mine. It sounded like I was introducing someone I'd never met before."

"I'm sure it'll come back to you. You'll remember. You just need to be patient."

"I guess. If it didn't, would that be so bad?"

Six months ago, Trina's ex-boyfriend, a former associate of Victor's, struck her in the head with a lead pipe outside a Montauk bar and left her for dead. Victor was with them that night. Trina and her boyfriend had been arguing outside, and at some point Victor saw her boyfriend's car leave the parking lot. They left without saying goodbye before, so he thought nothing of it.

Later, with the line too long at the bathroom, he went outside to piss and found her prone in the weeds by the trash dumpster, moaning, her hair matted with blood. He took her to the hospital, where they learned that all she remembered about herself was her stage name, Trina Taylor, that she was a dancer and an actress, and that Victor was a friend. A few hours later, they allowed her—somewhat naïvely, Victor thought—to leave with him, on the condition that he take her back to her apartment and return with her the next day.

During the drive to her apartment, Victor told her nothing about her past. Are we friends? she asked. We are, he said. I've known you for a little while. But only in a peripheral way. I don't really know anything about you other than your name and that you never drink beer. That's strange, she said. You seem so nice. Strange that we weren't close friends. He turned on the radio to end the conversation, because he didn't want to lie to her any more than he already had. She had, before the accident, been a mediocre actress and had briefly worked as a high-priced call girl. A few weeks later, when they were in bed together for the first time, Victor found that her past work as a prostitute some-how excited him. As time went by, he occasionally fantasized during sex that he was a customer of hers.

To this day, he still remembered the resignation that crossed her face as she first entered her apartment after the hospital. A small part of her, he realized, had hoped that seeing her home would bring everything back. She walked around the apartment, studying the photographs and the architecture, getting her bearings for a few minutes in the way one does when staying in a hotel room or in the guest room in a stranger's home. The photographs, she said, even the photographs of herself, seemed like someone else's memories. Eventually, she removed them from the frames.

Her parents flew in from Oakland the next morning, but seeing them brought no more memories back. They left a week later, defeated, when her doctor suggested that it was possible there were psychological underpinnings to her memory loss. Soon after, her parents began to accuse her of trying to forget. That may have been true, she reasoned, but if it was, the forgetting was being done by someone other than her; thinking of this and its paradoxical implications gave her a headache. Whatever the reason, she said, her parents were strangers, and it made her feel odd when they told her they loved her.

She had stopped telephoning them three months ago, but they had continued to pay half her rent and her utilities. All in all, she said, it wasn't such a bad deal. Once you got used to the memory loss, you came to see that there was nothing to feel sad about. If you had forgotten completely, there was no sense of loss.

Privately, Victor didn't want her to remember what had happened. He had developed an elaborate explanation of how he had found her that night, not a word of which was true, and he worried that if she ever learned of his association with her earlier life and its sudden, violent end, she would leave him. It seemed obvious that he needed her more than she needed him.

"No," he said, "I guess it wouldn't be so bad if it didn't come back."

"I mean, I'm happy. Not remembering."

"I am too."

Under the blanket, he crossed his fingers.

Two
___

Emma Bascomb had been seated next to Jane Rhoden for five dinner parties in a row—a coincidence that was, she had recently learned, anything but coincidental. Jane lorded over a mysteriously inexhaustible supply of stories about airplane landings on crippled gear, steerage encounters during Atlantic crossings, fifth martinis, firearms discharged in the kitchen, and dogs loosed upon neighbors' garden parties. While waiting for the bathroom at the Skillmans' dinner party last Friday, Emma overheard one woman remark that as insufferable as Jane was, she always did a great job of carrying the boring corner of the dinner table.

I suppose, Emma thought, that money has had its revenge. When I had too much of it I was bored and restless, and now that I have none at all I'm a bore and I make others restless.

Her husband, seated across from her, was looking to his right with his chin in his fist, studying his twinned reflection in the dining-room window. She followed his gaze to the dark glass. In the candlelight, Ben's reflection was all chiaroscuro and bone structure, an image apportioned perfectly between pallor and shadow—his reflection seemed sickly and malnourished. For ten minutes, she'd been telegraphing time-to-go vibrations his way, but he hadn't noticed. He seemed, she thought, startled and frightened, as he sometimes did when he was in situations where people were drinking heavily and he wasn't doing well. Since they'd arrived, he'd been steadily drinking tomato juice with Tabasco and lots of ice, a drink he sometimes called, frighteningly enough, the White-Knuckle Express. He'd been sober ever since a drunken car accident one February morning three years ago. She had come downstairs and had found him in the living room, a bloody kitchen rag pressed to his forehead. He hadn't had a single drink since that day, and not a moment of his sobriety had been simple, or easy.

This candlelit tableau—this was the Lansing dinner-party scene. The word was, Emma felt, entirely appropriate, with its oblique suggestions of staging, of acting, of props and catwalks and ingénue. There wasn't much else available this far north, here in the relative wilds of Connecticut, nine exits north of New Haven—too far to city-trip. She wondered how much longer the two of them would be included, because they hadn't had a party of their own since the business failed.

Was it really five years already?

She certainly felt five years older, and more. But that was nothing unusual. As a mother, Emma was accustomed to the abuse of time. Sometimes a single day felt like five years: at breakfast, over scalding coffee, graced by seven hours' sleep, she was a still faintly hopeful thirty-five, but by dinnertime, after the coloring books had been painted full of their impressionist purple skies, maroon tree trunks, and green squirrels, after the knots in Sylva's stubborn curls had been unraveled with the typical Gordian delicacy, after the tampons had been shelved, the chipped dishes washed and dried, the fingernails clipped, the teeth luxuriously brushed, the stories read—after what, according to the round-trip clock, was nothing more than another exhaustingly utilized sixteen-hour swatch of time, she went into the bathroom to try on that new nightgown. And there, in the mirror, she encountered a woman who looked, and yes, who *felt,* forty, no —forty-five.

Their family had become decidedly less hip since they went broke and Ben began his business of repairing tractors and servicing old cars in their barn. It's impossible, he'd told her at the Skillmans, to be on equal footing with someone whose oil you changed last week. Eventually, she reflected, they'd be written off those invisible social lists and the telephone would fall silent. For now, she might as well enjoy it. She poured herself another glass of the excellent wine and decided she would try to fit one more in before they left.

Jane leaned over, closing the space between them to a conspiratorial distance of mere inches, and began whispering in Emma's right ear how *Phthirius Pubis,* as she called them, had come to infest her linen closet last week. "These little bastards," she said, "were what Lewis Carroll had in mind when he wrote *Through the Looking Glass.* Jaws that bite. Claws that catch. They struck like a German Panzer division. I could actually feel them running around my crotch. I had to burn the sheets in the yard Sunday night."

"Was Mick upset?" Emma asked. She imagined Jane standing before her linen bonfire at dusk, her face radiant in the firelight.

"He walks out to the yard and examines the fire. He nudges it with the toe of his loafer. 'Janet,' he says to me, 'why are you burning our linens?' 'I'm burning our linens,' I say, 'because that chippie who cuts your hair has given us the crabs. Our home is infested with an army that was born and raised in your girlfriend's cunt.' 'You're making a scene, Janet,' he says. And I say, 'Mick, when I take the carving fork from the block tonight and bury it up to the tang in your black heart, that will be a scene.'"

"You didn't do it, of course." She hadn't seen Mick in a week, and he was conspicuously absent tonight.

"Of course not," she said. "But he buried the fork in the yard to be sure."

"Couldn't you just dig it up?"

"I loathe gardening," she said, lighting a cigarette.

"I don't see how you can joke about it."

She exhaled smoke and glanced sideways at Emma. "How do you deal with it?"

"You mean how would I deal with it?" she asked. Because she didn't have to deal with that any more; that was in her past.

"No," Jane said, "I mean how do you deal with it?"

"I don't have to deal with it," she said, and turned away. Her mother and father had dealt with infidelity constantly, had been forced to address its crippling presence almost yearly, and Emma, the helpless witness, had promised herself before she was married that when she was married she never would deal with it, because whomever she married would be good to her and she would be good to him and the two of them, together, would get right all the things her parents had gotten wrong. But of course she and Ben hadn't gotten everything right and Emma had first broken her promise when Ben's business had gone bankrupt—they had nearly lost everything, and he began a six-month bout of drinking that nearly killed him. She had been unfaithful while he was drinking, partly because she was frightened and resentful, and partly because she needed someone to talk to. The sex had really been beside the point, an afterthought, a pantomime of the emotional intimacy she craved; but it had happened, and eventually the truth came out. When Ben realized that she was about to leave him, he cut out his drinking.

Eventually, he confessed that he had been unfaithful, too. The affair, he said, had seemed like a sign of life at the time, an attempt to grope his way back into the flesh-and-blood world. Now, they never joked about what she had done or what he had done, because joking about that subject seemed like cruelty of the lowest sort, the same as joking about a neighbor's dead child or a terminal disease. Ever since Emma discovered that Jane used jokes to shield the places where she was easily hurt, her funny stories all seemed sad and transparent. She never understood how people joked about terrible things because terrible things were never funny. At best they were ironic, which was another way of saying that the joke was on you.

But maybe it didn't have to be that way. Maybe it could be funny, even if it was funny in a sad way. Whether or not her jokes were sad and transparent, Jane seemed to have brokered a sense of peace with herself, at least outwardly. What Mick had done glanced off the outer shell of her dignity without leaving so much as a mark. She was the same Jane she had always been, and you could bet that she would be the next time her husband cheated, and the next. Whereas when it had happened to Emma, it had distorted her vision of herself so that what she had seen in the mirror the next day had seemed fractionally more imperfect than what she had seen the day before.

But then she'd always perceived herself as a person flawed in a fundamental, genetic way. She had suspected, from a young age, that her mother was sick, and not sick the way other mothers became sick—in their ovaries, in their joints, in their sinuses. No, her mother was sick in her *head*, and Emma had understood, even from a young age, that a portion of this sickness has been irretrievably passed on to her. Her suspicions about the sickness were confirmed in fifth grade, after an evening she'd spent skating at the mill pond over Christmas break. Darkness had already fallen as she turned the corner to walk up her street. Every home seemed alive that night with domestic electricity— upstairs lamps burned and televisions projected violet light onto windowpanes. Emma slipped the silver key into the lock, opened the front door with a combination twist and hip-push, and padded quietly up the stairs with her skates slung over her shoulder. As she turned the corner, she encountered her mother, or some bashed and benighted twin of her mother. Sarah was walking down the hall to the bathroom, weaving from side to side, pinballing from wall to wall like a drunken sailor on shore leave. She paused for a moment at the doorway to the guest bedroom and held the doorjamb to steady herself, hyperventilating. Then Emma's father opened the bedroom door and saw the two of them opposed at hall ends, polarized by space and the invisible canyons of mother-daughterdom.

He brought Emma downstairs and sat her at the kitchen table and told her all about the new medication her mother was taking. He assaulted her with medical terms that night, none of which eased her fears: she understood nothing of seratonin-selective reuptake inhibitors or free-floating sympathomimetic symptoms; nothing of cumulative side effects, of additive side effects, of residual side effects, of perceptual withdrawal symptoms. She understood only that her mother's strange behavior, dismissed for years as a symptom of a deep sadness or a baroque fugue that had been brought on by the weather, had been stripped of its emotional cloth. Beneath the basic sadness was an elemental depression that was a matter of perception, and not of mood.

The coffee cups were cleared and the candles were extinguished. Sleepy couples converged and exited. Jane lit another cigarette and asked Emma if she and Ben would be at the cocktail party she and Mick were giving next Sunday. Mick had taken Friday off from the club so they'd have time to set it up nicely. She made no mention of her earlier disgust.

Of course they would be there, Emma said. Her contact lenses had begun to irritate her eyes and she wanted nothing but to take them out immediately.

They would?

Well they would try, she said. But right now they had to go.

Were they sure they had to go? She had a story to tell them about her trip to Boston last weekend. She had been thrown out of the Brookstone in Faneuil Hall.

Yes they were absolutely sure that they had to leave now.

Would they drive carefully?

They would drive very carefully. No they didn't need a taxi. Ben was just fine to drive. Ben held her coat open for her, but she took it from him and put it on herself.

Ben drove home slowly, leaning forward over the steering wheel as if exhausted and fighting eyestrain.

"Christ," he said, and flexed his fingers, "it's *cold*."

"It is."

Not half an hour ago she'd been looking forward to this moment, to being alone with him so that she might share the latest Rhoden tale. But the recollection of her mother's illness had struck her dumb, as it always did. She had no idea how to articulate the complexity of the feelings she'd encountered, and neither of them spoke again. Although the trip was only a few miles, it seemed to take hours.

She paid the sitter and added a small tip. After she had watched the sitter's taillights turn onto Skylark Drive, Emma went to the sink and drank two glasses of water. There were two messages on the answering machine, but instinct told her they were not for her and that the information they conveyed would only irritate her more, so she left them alone. He'd be up long after her and would get them later. Ben had walked out to the barn and when he returned, pushing the front door shut with his foot, he had three logs stacked in his arms. A taped envelope was between his teeth.

"What's that?" she asked.

He let the envelope fall from his mouth onto the wood. "It was out in the barn," he said. "Something Warren left for me." He rolled his eyes in mock irritation, but Emma didn't bite. He could mince around the truth all he wanted, but she knew what was in the envelope. So why not ask him about it? she thought. Why not call him on it, Emma, and make tonight the night you finally pin him to the wall? They had been around and around on this wheel for two years—he pretended that the money didn't exist, and she pretended that she didn't know about it. They both knew that they needed it, but the possibility of discussing how he earned it seemed impolitic and unwise. It would just be another fight and another fight.

He placed the logs on the fire, and then opened the iron grate that sent the warm air up into the bedrooms. Emma hung her coat in the closet and turned out the lights. On her way upstairs through the dark house she found him sitting at the hallway desk in a nimbus of fluorescent light, a pencil held in one fist like a weapon, his other hand making a fist in his hair. A stack of twenty-dollar bills, seemingly produced out of thin air, lay at one elbow. The envelope from Warren he had carried inside lay in the trash. He was staring at some numbers he had just written on a yellow notepad, and seemed not to notice her watching him from the stairs. She instinctively moved toward him, thinking that she would somehow comfort him, but something stopped her. While this need to comfort him had tyrannically ruled her actions since the day she had spoken her wedding vows, lately the vows themselves had begun to seem abstract and indefinite. After all, she had already been unfaithful. So had he. They had undone the most serious promise one can make.

But although they had supposedly gotten past that, she couldn't bring herself to go to him, now, when that was so clearly what he, what they both, needed.

As she brushed her teeth, she realized that she hadn't gone to him because she resented him. She resented the fact that he knew she'd been unfaithful, that he knew she'd disgraced herself. The one thing we cannot forgive, she thought, is another person knowing all our terrible secrets. And I am disgusted that I did that; I am disgusted with that secret. Every time I was unfaithful I felt more unclean, and none of it has washed away since. She bent forward and violently spat the toothpaste in the sink, then lifted the washcloth from the hook and scrubbed off her makeup. When she was finished, her skin was satisfactorily abused.

Forty, she thought, and turned left and right to examine her profile in the mirror.

In the bedroom, she undressed without turning on the light and climbed into bed. As she lay in the dark with the heavy weight of the blanket over her, her mind began to examine the crevices and cavities of her doubts, and she began to worry. Somehow, during the last few years, she had lost control of her thoughts. They mercilessly reminded her of her steadily advancing age; they reminded her of the dwindling savings account; they reminded her that Ben had begun to struggle with sobriety. She loved Ben, yes. But all their pressing problems, their foregone infidelities, their nodding acquaintance with the humiliation of bankruptcy—all of it seemed wedded to his drinking. And one could only bear witness to so much destruction before one had to turn away. Not that turning away would solve anything. She was rapidly approaching forty, and if this family didn't work and she divorced him, it was too late for her to start over. She was still attractive and relatively young, and she knew that men desired her, but it seemed clear that if she remarried, it wouldn't be like starting over; it would be like picking up exactly where she had left off, but with a new, strange companion, and with a troubled sense that she had done all this before, that she had made these solemn promises to someone else. The women she knew who remarried too late sank into a conflicted fugue that surrounded them for the rest of their lives. They were conflicted because they had married the second time for much different reasons than they had the first. The first time they had married for love, and they had recited their vows out of love, but the second or third times they had married merely in the hope that they would see their initial vows through. If you didn't make the vows come true, that meant you had lied to God and to a priest, and that made you something else.

She lay on her side and watched the light from the desk lamp reflect off the landing wall. After her eyes had closed, she imagined that she heard his pencil scratch at the notepad. She thought, Ben, I can tell you how it ends. The anger was gone and she felt only the mourning you feel when something that was once very good has gone very bad. I can tell you the final result, because it's all subtraction, love. It's subtraction, doing its subtraction thing. We're working our way down to zero.

His numbers followed her down into sleep.

The window beside her was a gray scrim of predawn light. She was sitting up in the bed. Ben was beside the bed, quietly instructing her to wake up. He had shaken her awake, and she did not know why. His side of the bed was still made. Then she saw the bright smear of blood on his right temple and came awake all at once. She reached out to touch his head, and he pulled away. He pressed his index finger to his lips to silence her.

"Emma," he said softly. "I need you to check on the girls and call the police." He was naked, holding Nina's softball bat in his left fist. In the faint light, armed and bloodied, he seemed vaguely prehistoric.

"What happened? Ben, you're bleeding. Tell me."

A single drop of blood rolled down his temple. "They hit me with this. Call the police and get the girls up and hide under the bed." He blinked hard. "I think they're still in the house." He left the room silently and pulled the door shut behind him.

She listened carefully after he was gone, senses amplified, but heard nothing. They couldn't be in the house. They couldn't be. She lifted the cordless phone from the cradle and stepped onto the cold floorboards to move to the bedroom door, where she listened again. Silence. Then she opened the door and walked out into the hall. The absence of noise frightened her the most; it seemed alien in this house. Through the stairway landing window, she saw Ben, still naked, stumbling crazily across the driveway toward the barn. The head of Nina's bat dragged on the ground behind him. She went into the girls' room and shook each of them awake. "Wake up. Wake up, sweet." Nina sat up immediately; Sylva began to cry. "Sh. We're going in the bathroom for a moment until your dad gets back." Sylva closed her eyes and lay back on her pillow. Emma handed Nina the phone, lifted Sylva up, and carried her into the bathroom. When Nina was inside, she latched the door, lay Sylva on the floor, and was about to dial the police when she saw the towels, filthy with mud and sopping wet, that Ben had thrust into the hamper. She swept the shower curtain aside and saw long streak of mud that meandered into the drain; the cake of soap lay shrouded with earth-colored lather in its cradle.

You son of a bitch, she thought. So this was what you were trying to tell me last night.

"Nina," she said. "Take your sister back to bed."

Emma went downstairs to the kitchen and sat on one of the stools as she waited for him. You son of a bitch, she thought. I can't believe you had the audacity to hit yourself. If we needed money so badly, we could have asked my parents for it. It hurts me, too, when we have to ask them for help, but even that would be better than this. Anything would be better than this. You could go to jail for this and then where would we be?

She picked up the phone and dialed the police. "Could you send an ambulance? Ben's hurt." She knew the dispatcher, a slender young refugee from Jersey named Rickey whom she often saw around town. Rickey lived alone with her feathered hair and white lipstick in a one-bed apartment above the post office in downtown Lansing. If there was a stiff wind, Jane Rhoden liked to say, you could smell the spinsterhood on her at one hundred yards.

"Is he all right?" Rickey asked.

Ben opened the front door and rested the bat in the corner. He swayed slightly as he watched her, and she wondered if he'd hurt himself badly. "He fell down the stairs," she said. "He hit his head and he's confused."

Ben walked to her and took the receiver from her hand. "I'm fine. Just send the police. We were robbed."

Emma watched him in disbelief. She heard the muted tone of Rickey's reply.

"They're still in the house. Send the police right away." He pressed the END button and handed Emma the phone.

They watched each other in silence for a moment.

"I suppose you think you're being resourceful," she said. There in the moment, his nakedness seemed emblematic.

"I suppose I am."

"I'm going to tell them you fell and hit your head."

"If you do, this is all for nothing."

"You buried it?"

He didn't answer.

"What did you take?"

"Grandfather's things. From the attic."

"And what," she asked, "do you intend to do with it?"

"Sell it. All of it. And get the insurance."

"I thought the money from Warren was enough."

Another drop of blood rolled down his temple. He didn't answer.

"Ben. I know about it. I know what you do for him."

He walked out of the room. From the stairs, she heard him softly say, "No you don't. You don't know anything about it."

Overhead there was total silence. She wondered how much the girls had heard. What would she say to the police when they arrived? She'd have to say the same thing. *He fell down the attic stairs. He hit his head and I think he's in shock and he's acting strange and saying strange things.* She'd have to be gracious and slightly amused and very worried about him, and if she were all three of those things they'd believe her and they'd take Ben to the hospital and that would be the end of it. Gracious would have to come first. After setting the coffee maker, she went to the refrigerator and searched through the shelves for something to give the police when they arrived. She lifted a bag of pears that she had bought yesterday from the fruit drawer, and found that, somehow, they had already begun to brown and rot, as if the ravages of time and biology had mysteriously accelerated during the night. The first faint peal of a siren reached her, and she began to cut the fruit quickly. She would have to meet them as they came up the driveway and tell them everything was all right.

The point of the knife slipped easily through the ripened meat of the second pear and sliced the tip of her right index finger. She watched numbly as blood welled from the cut and began to drip on the counter, and then noticed Ben watching her from the doorway. He was dressed in a pair of khakis and was shirtless. The blood running down her arm had silenced him.

"God, Emma," he said, but as he reached for her she found that she didn't want him to touch her, didn't want him *near* her, so she held the finger tightly against her chest, the knife still held in her left hand. Her robe was spotted with patterns of blood.

"Emma," he asked, "what did you do to yourself?" He was trying to pull her hand free.

Before she could tell him, two uniformed policemen came through the front door with their guns drawn. One of them shouted at Ben. Emma turned in his grip and spoke to them. "I'm all right," she said, and then the officers raised their weapons. Emma saw both barrels flash, heard the earsplitting roar. The corner of Ben's right earlobe nicked away. The first bullet made a snapping sound as it passed inches from her face. The second punched through his left thigh and buried itself in the butcher block. Ben staggered back as if he'd been shoved. His feet crossed and he fell; his head struck the edge of the counter. As he collapsed to the floor, spent shell casings clattered musically on the kitchen tiles.

The first officer advanced with his sidearm pointed at the floor, "Ma'am," he said, "are there any others?" His scalp, through his clipped hair, was red. She counted two shaving nicks on his cheek.

"Two upstairs," she said. She bent down beside Ben, pinching her robe closed at her neck, and touched her index finger to his throat. His pulse was weak and rapid, the heartbeat of a frightened rabbit. A single drop of blood fell from his ragged earlobe.

"Are they armed?"

She looked up at the officer with disbelief. The second was watching Ben from the front hall, wide-eyed. "My kids," she said. They had nearly killed him. They had nearly killed him. "I'm talking about my kids."

"The perps," he said. "I want to know about the perps."

"There are no perps," she said. "There's only us."

"How many?" he asked.

Four, she thought. Four of us. And then subtraction did its subtraction thing.

Three

When Ben woke it was daylight and he was alone in a small hospital room. His entire body seemed connected by a web of pain that radiated outward from his spine. There was another bed in the room beside the window, a chair in the corner, and next to the chair a table with a vase of wilted flowers. As he sat up to look out the window, the room rolled under him and for a moment he thought he would be sick. He lay on his back and counted the tiles on the roof until the feeling had passed, and then pressed the call button twice. A nurse came into the room carrying two small paper cups.

"What are those?" Ben asked.

"A pill that will help you sleep and some water to swallow it."

"Do I have a concussion?"

"No," she said, "we took a CAT scan."

"I shouldn't be sleeping if I have a concussion."

"You don't have a concussion."

"It feels like I have a concussion." He had had a concussion in high school, and it had felt exactly like this.

She held the cup out to him with patient authority.

He swallowed the pill with the water, and the nurse dropped the cups in the trash and left. After the pill began to work, he found that if he moved slowly and gently he could look around the room. He had only the empty bed and the empty chair to look at, so he took the paper from the bedside table and began to read. Then he began to feel sleepy and the pages of the paper seemed to grow heavy in his hands. No one's coming to visit me, he thought. His mother had always visited him in the hospital, had slept in the chair beside his bed when he had his tonsils out at age ten, had spent hours reading at his bedside after Warren had scoped his knee in high school. Now his only company was this empty bed.

That was how life worked. Time turned things around; eventually, you swapped roles. First your mother came to see you in the hospital. Then she sickened, and you went to see her. And after the doctors told you that it was over (but not finished, no, because although everyone you spoke to knew that her life was over, he didn't know *when* it would end, because the finishing part was like a death scene from some Medean tragedy, a cruel Euripidean spectacle that went on for too long), after you were told that it was inoperable, she came home, and you and Warren circled about the house for three months after, shadowing each other like opposed suitors trying to win her attention.

Her death, he reflected, should have brought Warren and me together. Where did he put that love he had given her? It had to go somewhere, didn't it? Or could love sour and then spoil, become some curdled opposite number? With her gone, I was all he had. And he was all I had. Shouldn't the anger have been used up? Obviously it wasn't. Sometimes it felt as if the anger was the only thing we shared. It divided us, because it made us understand that we had loved her with two different kinds of love. Warren's love borrows but doesn't replace. It takes what's best from the other for its own sustenance and can't give anything back without starving itself. My kind of love makes an uneasy peace with life, because it knows the bill will always be paid in the end. It takes nothing but the happiness of the moment, and that sparingly and anxiously, knowing that every happy moment together assumes the cost of a sad moment apart later.

Love—real love—is wonderful deception. Because telling someone you love her implies that you'll *stick around*. And no one does.

My kind of love frightens me.

Ben had been out of college for eight months on the night his mother told him she wanted to die. At the time, he was living in a one-bedroom apartment in downtown Lansing and working as a foreman at Bascomb Centrifuge. He was hopelessly single, because ever since the doctors told her that the cancer was inoperable—*inoperable* in that the last X-ray looked as if someone had stood her up against the wall and taken target practice with a fucking tommy gun—ever since then his life had withdrawn into a narrow, pleasureless frequency. Food was necessary sustenance; sleep, rest. Nothing carried any sensory subtext. He was inaccessible to anyone.

He agreed to help her, because she wanted it. He agreed because it had already killed her—death was just taking its time getting its work done. He agreed because it was killing all of them.

After Warren fell asleep on the couch, Ben searched the house until he found the keys in the lapel pocket of his barn jacket. He took the keys upstairs and unlocked the lower right-hand desk drawer and the locked box inside that held the medication, the white bottles of MS Contin. He brought them to her, and she took them by the handful. After he watched her voice go slurry and her breathing slow and then stop, he kissed her, and then left and drove alone to the hospital, where he waited in the emergency room.

Forty minutes later, Warren's muddy Volvo sailed wildly into the ambulance bay and stopped with one wheel up on the curb. Two orderlies wheeled her in through the doors on a gurney, and as she was trundled by she looked, Ben thought, ancient and withered, all of her beauty drained;

she looked like a woman who had been broken by suffering. Warren spotted him sitting in the corner and their eyes locked. They shared a telegraphed instant of understanding before Warren wordlessly crossed the room and attacked him. It took three orderlies to pull him off. Ben's tooth was chipped by Warren's wedding ring. He hadn't defended himself at all.

He was very tired now, and he stopped thinking and put the paper over his face and fell asleep. When he woke, it was night. The room was dark, but the door was open to let light in from the hallway. Warren sat in the chair in the corner. He held a burning cigarette out through the opened window. In the hallway light he seemed more than ever to be a picture of depravity held at bay. Ben sat up carefully and turned on the bedside table lamp. Warren blinked in the fierce light and rubbed his eyes with his free hand. "How's your head?" he asked.

"I'm not so bad," Ben said. "But you look like Fagin from *Masterpiece Theater.*"

"Fuck off," Warren said. He took a drag off the cigarette and exhaled out the window. "Sick at all?"

"No."

"Seeing double?"

"No," Ben said. He considered his limbs. "I feel a little slow."

"That's Tylox. You've had it before. After your scope?"

"How lucky for me," Ben said. "Maybe I should have asked for Dilaudid."

Warren flicked his cigarette ash out the window and searched for a comeback. "You'd have to pay for it, though," he said. He grinned at Ben.

"They said I don't have a concussion."

"You don't."

"Dad," Ben asked, unable to suppress the feeling of irony that always accompanied his use of that word, "where are the girls?"

"Emma said they were going up to Boston."

"She talked to you?"

"She talked to another doctor. I talked to him. Information. Understand?"

"She won't leave without seeing me," Ben said. "She'll stop by first."

"Ben," Warren said, softly. It was impossible not to detect the note of victory in his voice. "She left, already."

Ben gathered the sheets in his fist. He wanted to smash Warren's smug face, to shatter every inch of his grin. He wanted Warren to know just how it felt to be the one in the hospital bed, the injured one. After thirty years of tinkering with knees and shoulders and ankles, of watching the weak and infirm beg for medication, of causing pain but feeling none himself, Warren had acquired a superior air. Even in the gutter, Ben thought, he believes he's better than everyone else. How little this intelligent man knows or understands. How little he matters, except in the troubles he causes. "What," he asked, "about the police?"

"They're scared of you. That could be a good thing for us."

"For me," Ben said.

"The five o'clock news said the two who shot you are on desk duty."

"What about the robbery?"

Warren shook his head. "What could they do? You haven't broken any laws, other than making what Emma effectively called a prank call. When she called for the ambulance, she said you'd fallen and hit your head. Then you picked up and said something else. So you were confused. It happens to lots of misguided kids like you."

"Then we're all right."

Warren watched him. "There's something else. Emma's worried about you. And she let the ER psychologist know it. Doctor named Sweet. They spoke for half an hour while she was waiting to get her finger looked at."

"And?"

"I think," Warren said, "he's going to admit you."

"Admit me where?"

Warren said nothing.

Ben stared at him in disbelief. "To one of those places where you color and paint all day and then take a little yellow pill with every meal? Fuck that, Warren."

"I've got nothing to do with it, kiddo."

"You must know someone who could step in," Ben said.

"I could talk to a few people. But I don't think it'll do any good. In fact it might make things worse for you if I did."

"So you won't help me."

"I'm saying I can't."

"You won't because you've got everything you need for the next month. You're all set up. Right now it's not such a problem if I'm inside, is it? But it will be in a month, Warren. I wonder how willing you'll be to help me when you start to run out?"

"I'd help you if I could," he said patiently.

"That's promising, Warren," Ben said. "Is that from the Hippocratic Oath? It's very sharp."

"You could learn a lot from that oath, Ben."

"Maybe you could teach it to me. Of course you'd have to learn it all over again yourself, first."

" 'The physician,' " Warren said angrily, pointing with his cigarette, " 'must not only be prepared to do what is right himself, but also to make the patient, the attendants and externals cooperate.' " He controlled himself and calmly sat back in his chair. " 'I swear by Apollo the physician and Æsculapius, and Health, and All-heal, and all the gods and goddesses, that, according to my ability and judgment, I will keep this Oath and this stipulation—to reckon him who taught me this Art equally dear to me as my parents, to share my substance with him, and relieve his necessities if required; to look upon his offspring in the same footing as my own brothers, and to teach them this art, if they shall wish to learn it, without fee or stipulation, and that by precept, lecture, and every other mode of instruction, I will impart a knowledge of the Art to my own sons . . .' " He trailed off to silence, as if he had suddenly forgotten or had lost his train of thought. He tried to regain his place. " 'I will impart a knowledge of the Art to my own sons . . .' " But it was gone. He seemed near tears at his inability to remember.

"That's lovely, Warren."

Warren shook his head, dispelling the sadness. "The laws are more interesting, anyway. 'Those things which are sacred are to be imparted only to sacred persons; and it is not lawful to impart them to the profane until they have been initiated into the mysteries of the science.' I like that. 'The mysteries of the science.' "

"Lovely Warren. We could sit here all day, waiting for you to connect the dots."

"It's harder than it looks."

"Well," Ben said, "it seems funny to me that the only parts you remember seem to fit your behavior."

Warren sat back in the chair. "I wouldn't expect you to understand," he said. "You're a businessman. And a bad one, at that. What would you know about the mystery of science?"

"I know that it's not yours to plumb anymore. How about that?"

"You're awfully tart for a guy who just got plugged twice. For a guy, I should remind you, who's about to go in The Box."

"This is ridiculous."

"You just about killed yourself, Ben. What'd you expect?"

"You," Ben said, "talking about me killing myself."

"I'm not killing myself."

"No," Ben said, "you're looking for a meaningful obliteration."

"Say what you want," Warren said calmly. "It changes nothing. You're there. I'm here. In a few minutes, I'm going to get up and walk out. If you did the same, you'd be stopped. Choice is a powerful thing."

"They can't make me stay."

"Of course they can. All they need is a court order."

"How long?"

"As long as the court thinks you present a danger to yourself." Warren tapped his cigarette ash out the window. "Or to your kids. I've asked around. Apparently Sweet thinks you're both."

"Oh for fuck's sake."

"Believe me," Warren said, "it's not good for either of us."

Ben rubbed the bandage on his ear. The wound itched. He longed to rip the gauze away and scratch and scratch. He didn't care if the ear bled or fell off, as long as the itch stopped.

"You were supposed to meet Anthony at the airport at eight o'clock to pick up the rest of the morphine," Warren said. "Or did you think that was just a tip I left in the barn for you last night?"

"Anthony," Ben said, "can fucking wait."

"I'm betting I'll go home to a very nasty phone message from Victor.

We've never been late before." The sarcastic note had faded from his voice. The thought of Victor seemed to trouble him.

"Why doesn't Victor have you go?"

"Would you," he asked, "trust me with eleven cases of morphine?"

Ben sighed. No wonder his business had gone bankrupt. Sometimes he missed what was most obvious. "Maybe Victor should learn some patience."

"He's got his own little world, you know? And I don't think that patience has a place in it. He's going to want that six hundred dollars back."

"If I know Emma," Ben said, "that six hundred is in Boston now. It's the only quick cash we have."

"Well you'd better look into that."

"There isn't much I can do while I'm here."

Warren looked around the room. "How will you pay for this?"

"I'm not sure."

Warren tapped his lighter against his teeth. "Maybe I could handle it."

"How? Sell your watch?"

"I could sell whatever it was of your grandfather's things you were going to sell. If you told me where you hid it all."

Ben thought of the things he had taken from the attic last night. He pictured the platinum pocket watch, the gold pen, his grandfather's scarred Rolex, the platinum brooch with four diamonds on its face, his grandmother's diamond earrings, the unused gold cigar clip. They lay buried now in the earth outside the barn, all of them items willed to him instead of Warren, denied Warren in deepest spite, items Ben's grandfather William had, in his will, forbidden him to sell. He remembered turning them over winking in the spectral shaft of moonlight, his wife and daughters sleeping sweetly one flight down. *I will do this,* he had thought, *if this is what I must do. But only if this is what I must do.* He had stood there gripping the brooch for a minute, eyes tightly shut, waiting for some sign that he should abandon the plan—he had waited for the barest ripple in his simple cosmogony, but none had come: it was just a cold piece of steel in his hands, and the bills were piled two hands high downstairs. There were three *women* in this house, two who shared his face and genes and one who shared his bed and his secrets. These women *needed* him, in their various women-ways—as lover or father or simple friend—but those simple links presupposed solvency. You could not parent while bankrupt. The beggar could not play the part. Money wasn't all he had to offer them. But he knew (with cold parenthetic certainty) that money was essentially the best of what he had to offer them.

"Tell Victor," Ben said, "that I'll be up and around in a few days. Then we'll get caught up."

"You're not going to be up and around in a few days. You're going to be in here, and he'll get more pissed off every minute. He's not so forgiving, you know?"

"Well then. You'll have to work that much harder to get me out." Ben was silent for a moment. "How's her finger?"

"Stitched up," Warren said. He seemed to come to a decision and dropped the cigarette out the window and then pulled the window shut. "I'll see what I can do. Can't make any promises."

"Of course you can't, Warren," Ben said.

After Warren was gone, he lay in the dark thinking. Victor was going to be upset for sure, and he had never seen Victor upset before. Anyway Warren was the one getting the free ride. Ben had been taking all the risks and getting only a few hundred dollars out of the arrangement. Warren had enough Dilaudid to get through the month. God only knew how much money Victor had made in the past two years. Both of them could fucking well wait until he had straightened his own problems out. If they couldn't wait, that was because they had planned poorly and that wasn't his fault. When he had decided for sure that what had happened wasn't his fault he rolled on his side and fell asleep.

He woke with early morning sunlight angling steeply into the room. With each movement, he felt a sharp stabbing pain where the bullet had passed through his thigh, but at least his headache was gone, and he was less nauseated than yesterday. His ear still itched, and he wondered if he had worried about it in his sleep.

The other bed was occupied now by a dark-haired, bearded young man who was reading Solzhenitsyn's *Invisible Allies* by the faint light of the window. He was scratching absently where his left thigh disappeared into a splint that extended to his ankle. The windowsill was lined with flowers and get-well cards. He seemed entirely absorbed by the book and didn't notice Ben watching him.

"My wife always wanted to read that," Ben said, "so I bought it for her last Christmas. But it just sits on her bedside table gathering dust."

When the man looked over from his book, Ben saw that the right side of his face, which had been turned away from him, was hideously bruised, his right eye nearly swollen shut. "I'm almost embarrassed to admit that I like it," the bruised man said. "Russians can be so dull."

"I wouldn't know."

"You were talking in your sleep." He lay the book down.

"What was I saying?" Ben asked.

The sight of the man's eye had startled him.

"Nothing really," he said.

"You must be very popular."

The man glanced at the flowers and cards. "Students," he explained. He seemed slightly embarrassed that Ben had none.

"Impressive," Ben said.

"To be liked?"

"To be liked by students. I always hated my teachers."

"If I taught economics," the man said, "things might be different." He scratched his thigh again.

"What happened?" Ben asked. He looked at the cast.

"I was attacked. Three kids with baseball bats. Aluminum bats, in fact."

Ben didn't know what to say.

"As far as I can tell," he said, "it was for sport."

"You seem calm about it."

"Well," the man said, "I'm pretty well sedated right now."

"Seems like your students are worried about you."

"I don't know. They arrested the three kids who did it this morning, and two of them, I was just told, are enrolled in my Freshmen Lit class."

"Had you failed them?"

"No," he said. "They just didn't like having a gay teacher." He was quiet for a moment. "The funny thing is, I haven't been laid in more than a year. It seems unfair to get punished for something you don't even get to practice."

"I guess you're right," Ben said.

"I've made you uneasy."

"No," Ben said, "violence makes me uneasy."

"How were you hurt?"

"I was shot. Can you believe that?"

"I don't know," he said. "Are you the sort of person who is occasionally shot?"

"Two policemen. In my own house. They thought I was a burglar."

"You're lucky to be alive."

"Lucky is the last thing I feel."

"I think the painkillers are making me talkative."

"They make me feel sick."

"They moved me in here because I was driving my other roommate up the wall."

"I don't mind listening," Ben said. He really didn't.

"That works out well for us."

"I've heard that anesthesia makes you talk even more."

"I'm getting that later today. That's why they won't let me eat anything. I can't even drink water. They're going to put a pin in my femur."

"You'll talk if you're not careful."

"I thought you just fell asleep."

"My father says that when you think you've gone under you're really awake for another minute or so and you talk and talk and make a fool of yourself. Everyone does. Once he was about to work on a teenager's wrist and as the kid was going under he told the anesthesiologist that he had lost his virginity to his daughter."

"No."

"Yes."

"That's fantastic."

"So watch what you say."

He scratched at the top of his splint. "I'm Raif."

"Raif?"

"Raif. Spelled like *naïf*, but with an *r*. My brother always reminds me of that."

"I'm Ben."

"I've always liked that name," Raif said.

"You don't think it's boring?"

"It's very past tense." He pinched the bridge of his nose. "That was a stupid thing to say. I told you the drugs were making me talkative."

There was a knock on the door. A slight, short man wearing a beeper and carrying a clipboard walked into the room. He looked very young and his clipped hair accentuated his youth. "You're Ben Bascomb?" he asked. They shook hands. "I'm Dr. Sweet."

Ben noticed a slight Jamaican lilt to his speech.

"You seem young for that beeper," Raif said.

"I had an early start," Sweet said. He smiled at Raif, showing twin rows of perfectly white teeth. Ben wondered if Raif found him attractive. Sweet looked back to him. "I'm wondering if we can talk soon, if you're feeling up to it."

"Anything in particular you want to talk about?"

"Your wife and I spoke. She seems a bit worried about your behavior."

"Apparently not that worried," Ben said. "She left the state."

Sweet removed his glasses and began to polish them on his shirt.

"Maybe we could talk Wednesday," he said. "If you're up to it?"

"If you're planning an interrogation," Ben said, "you'll have to take a number. The police have cornered the market."

"Not an interrogation," Sweet said. "Although I will confess that things are likely to get personal. It's unavoidable. I'd blame it on the situation if I didn't think it was necessary."

"I've just been shot twice," Ben said. "I'm not feeling particularly frightened of questions right now."

"Fine. I'll have the nurses bring you down to my office."

"I'm not very popular with them."

"He's right," Raif said. "They warned me. Bascomb has been labeled a nuisance."

"I think you'll be fine," Sweet said. "You're comfortable?"

"For now," Ben said.

They watched Sweet go. The doctor left the door open, and in the hallway the day seemed very much underway. "He's like a little kid," Raif said. He began to scratch at his splint.

After Ben had eaten breakfast, a bored orderly pushed a gurney into the room. He helped Raif onto the gurney and then gently loosened his splint. Beneath the splint the leg was swollen, the skin above the knee deeply bruised. The orderly carefully shaved Raif's leg with an electric razor, from the top of the thigh to midway down the shin, and then painted the bare skin around the knee with Betadine. Raif said goodbye, and as he was pushed out of the room Ben reminded him about not talking.

He slept during the afternoon and woke as a nurse brought in his dinner tray. "You had a visitor," she said. "Someone named Victor. He said he had come all the way from Queens, but I told him I wasn't allowed to wake you. He seemed upset."

Ben said that sometimes Victor got upset easily.

"He was very handsome," she said. "Is he married?"

Ben said that it didn't really matter, but yes, he was. He was listening to the nurse but he was a long way away, thinking clearly about Victor and the things he had heard that Victor had done to people who had crossed him.

"Well," she said. "He asked me to pass you a message. He says he hopes that you'll be out of here very soon. It must be nice to have someone so concerned about you."

Ben said that it must be.

The orderly wheeled Raif back in after dinner and helped him into bed. His leg was thickly wrapped in bandages. Two steel pins joined by a steel rod protruded from his leg, the first just above the kneecap, the second midway down his shin. Raif looked pale and sick, and he appeared to be in a lot of pain. "I threw up in recovery," he said after the orderly had left.

"You said you didn't eat."

"It was all bile. I was thrashing around in my sleep, and I shook the heart monitor loose. They thought I had gone into arrest."

"Did you talk?"

"I said absolutely nothing."

"We'll see."

Raif smiled and closed his eyes.

"Did they give you something for the pain?"

"They gave me morphine. I feel otherworldly." He lay silently for a moment. "That doctor was handsome."

"I was wondering about that."

"Have you had any visitors?"

"Just one," Ben said. "I was asleep."

"Your wife?"

"No."

"Sorry," he said. "I think I'll sleep."

"Do you mind if I read your book?"

"Not at all," he said. When he was asleep, Ben took the book from the night table and began to read. He read the first paragraph and then put the book back on the night table and watched the second hand on the wall clock. I wonder, he thought, if we are getting a divorce. I wonder if my presence has become as unbearable as her absence.

A year ago—less than one year past—they had been happy. He'd been sober, and having a tough time with it, but somehow the urge to drink had seemed less immediate, less lethal than it did now. Days before Christmas, he remembered, the four of them had driven into the city and had spent the night at Rockefeller Center, ice skating and having dinner—they had their picture taken in front of the tree. The photograph now hung in the front hall. Emma had put it there to remind him, he liked to think, why he stayed sober.

He closed his eyes now and envisioned the framed photograph, their family frozen in the flash instant: they are all dressed warmly, in black wool and wrapped scarves. He stands at the center of the frame. Emma is at his right in profile, her smile pressed against his jacketed shoulder. She holds his arm with both of hers, as if trying to pull him closer. Nina stands before him, facing the camera, visible from the waist up. Her head is tilted back so that she can look up at him, her mouth a perfect oval. His hands are in her hair. Sylva sits lightly on his shoulders, white-stockinged legs scissoring either side of his neck. He cannot see her face because she is twisting obliquely away to look at the tree behind them with one hand anchored under his chin for balance; the other is raised and pointing back toward the tree.

He is in the center of the frame. He is smiling, and he is happy.

This is why he is sober.

This is one year ago.

Four
_____

Warren often reflected that his life was similar, in structure and schedule, to that of an incontinent. His particular urge came to him slyly but suddenly, arriving in parking lots and supermarket lines, a need that couldn't be bargained with or reasoned away. When he couldn't wait until he was home, he sought out public restrooms. Sometimes the stall doors required coins that he didn't possess, so he crawled beneath them, the tile floors sticky with God knew what. Safely inside the sanctum of his affliction, he sought his unique form of relief, and then crawled out once again, a recast man, a furloughed junkie, only slightly filthier for the journey. He didn't so much mind the outer filthiness because the inner filthiness made crawling on a pissed-on tile floor seem like a minor transgression.

The world knew only as much about your addiction as you revealed, or rather as much as you allowed to slip through. Warren was a somewhat functional addict—a Chipper, the serious addicts at his YMCA group called him—and was still hopeful that only a handful of people knew about his dependency. Ned Strickland, the hospital's chief of staff, was one of the people who knew. He'd been a member of the hospital credentials committee that had fired Warren after he'd botched the knee operation.

You didn't botch anything, thought Warren as he waited now outside Strickland's office. The wrong knee had been prepped and shaved, and you simply operated on the one that was ready. A forty-five patient roster and you're expected to memorize each R and L?

More than a year had passed since he'd last spoken with Strickland. In November of last year, Warren had found a cancerous mole on his scalp one morning and had attempted to remove it himself that afternoon with his wife's antique silver thread cutters. The procedure hadn't gone well, and he'd ended up in the Emergency Room with an old t-shirt pressed to his forehead. He'd asked to see Ned, and Ned, he recalled, had made him wait then, too. Lateness was always a simple matter of establishing roles, as it was with Victor. Ned had wanted to make it clear that he was the Chief of Staff, while Warren was just a junkie and has-been malpractice surgeon.

It seemed clear that things would get complicated without Strickland's help. Rumor had it that Dan Sweet, the E.R. psychiatrist, was just off his residency, a real boy scout, and Ben, with his sad face and disturbed fatalism, was sure to say the wrong thing and provoke Sweet's inner hand-wringer. After that, everything would fall quickly into place. Sweet would get a court order, and Ben would end up in The Box. If he were hospitalized for more than a few weeks, Victor would follow through with his threat. He'd look elsewhere for what he needed, and the rolling pharmacy would close up its doors. But Strickland, with his downtown expense account, could stop Ben from going inside, if he wanted to. The older doctors, Warren recalled, willingly did favors for each other or covered for each others' mistakes, as long as patient care wasn't compromised. That was the unspoken rule. Their willingness to cover for each other, Warren believed, had something to do with the earnest, benighted, us-against-them language of The Oath. Hippocrates was rolled out at every med school graduation, at exactly the moment when every graduate, after three years of studying the cold facts of life and death, was ripe for some sort of seductive *ism* around which to re-establish his faith.

He looked at his watch and found that it was nearly six o'clock. It would be full midwinter dark outside, now. He'd been waiting for almost thirty minutes, and for almost two hours at Ben's bedside before that. So much to ask from someone whose only wish was to not rock the boat. His hands were beginning to tremble slightly, and he wondered if it might be best if he walked to the bathroom by the physical therapy wing to allow himself the indulgence of a pre-meeting fix. The Dilaudid would steady his hands and even his temperament, but Strickland would take one look at his pinpoint pupils and would know. His only choice, he realized, was to ride out the wait and hope it didn't go on much longer. He began to page through the stack of glossy magazines on the end table, and within a few minutes, embarrassingly enough, found himself three paragraphs into a column in a women's health magazine about PC muscles and sexual positions. Although open discussions of sex had always seemed odd to him—a queer, unpleasant level of honesty, akin to, say, open caskets—Warren had always been secretly fascinated by the textbook quality of the women's magazines. The amount of information they conveyed was staggering. It was no wonder women understood so much more than men. Forty years ago, he could have learned a lot from this one article. When he and his wife had first been married, a lot of the discussions about sex had been corseted and gagged. How times had changed. This article even featured a realistically drawn graphic of the act of copulation. His wife, he recalled, had always had orgasms very easily. Sometimes she had been able to have one by simply squeezing her pelvic muscles tightly for a few minutes. She had been much more experienced than he, and at first he had felt intimidated by her knowledge. On their wedding night, she had to show him what to do. Like this, she said, her hands on him, as he lay across her, quivering like a struck tuning fork, like that, she said, just like that, she said, yes that, she said, and then it was over, that quickly, and he lay breathing shallowly and happily with his nose pressed into the declivity just above her collarbone. They fell asleep together like that, and at the time it seemed like all he could ever want from life.

How times had changed. He couldn't stop his hands from trembling, and it seemed he could hear the pages rattle as he turned them. His legs began to cross and uncross, and he gripped each knee in a fist and willed himself to be still. He wanted to move; his limbs wanted to reach and grasp and strike. There was no use in pretending that he could wait for a fix. That's why he's making me wait, Warren thought. He knows that time will break me down and make me easier to deal with. What was it Victor said? Oh yes. Having Dilaudid makes me docile. I wonder what not having it makes me? Pliable, I suppose. So those are my two allotted states. Sober or stoned; pliable or docile. At your service, or incapable of service.

Warren had reluctantly reopened the early-fix debate when Strickland mercifully opened the door to his office. The smell of aftershave and freshly cleaned carpeting drifted out. Although Ned hadn't gained any weight since they had last met—his six-foot-two frame still carried his two-hundred plus pounds easily—Warren noted that his hair had surrendered the last of its color. "Warren," he said, "I was beginning to think that you were a figment of my imagination. You never return my calls. I had hoped we could hit a few some time." He meant, of course, golf balls, his famed obsession.

"Maybe next week," Warren said, pulling the door closed behind him. He could no sooner play golf than construct an atomic bomb, and Strickland knew this. Strickland was, Warren decided, truly postmodern in that he assessed the negative space of everyone he met, first. A row of trophies lined the wide flat windowsill behind his mahogany desk. Each trophy was topped by a brass golfer frozen in his follow-through, his brass eyes fixed hopefully on an invisible horizon. It occurred to Warren that with a little luck, the office might have been his. The idea of being chief of staff had never appealed to him in the years before the fire, but now he saw Strickland's office as an illustration of everything he was not. He thought fleetingly of his father's will, and its prescient expressions of doom. *A compromise, boys,* his father had written, *is not an independent act.*

It is a step from a high windy place. After that first step, forces of nature assume control, and then the fall is no longer the man's, but nature's itself.

Crackpot, Warren thought. No more or less complicated than your everyday crackpot. Someday, Ben might learn that.

"First," Strickland said, "I want you to know that I personally checked on Ben. He's comfortable, although we've had to manage his pain. He lost a corner of his right earlobe, and the thigh wound was through-and-through. Big knock on the head. Doing well, though. In six months he'll have nothing to show for it but a good scar or two. We took six stitches in Emma's finger."

Warren folded his hands and sat back in his chair. He noticed that his chair was slightly lower to the ground than Strickland's, accentuating the already vast difference in their sizes. Cheating bastard, he thought. Strickland, four years younger than he, had been his closest friend at Stanford, even when, during their third year, Warren had learned that Ned had stolen a set of lab keys and had begun sabotaging other students' projects to lower the curve. It was lucky for Strickland that he was a famously caring, thorough doctor, because his personality was, at best, acerbic, his absolute concern for patients his only apparent likeable quality. That quality had gotten him elected as chief of staff and his ruthlessness had kept him there. "Things have gotten complicated, Ned," Warren said. "Emma and the girls just left for Boston."

"I'd agree things are complicated. The police wanted to talk with Ben, but I held them off. They've got a guy clocking time down in the coffee shop."

"You think it's a problem for now?"

"I think," Strickland said, "that Ben has more important things to worry about right now."

Warren knew what was coming next. When Ned leaned forward to speak Warren cut him off. "Isn't there some way you can help us out?"

"That depends," Strickland said, "on how you define help."

"You want to admit him."

"Yes."

"For an evaluation."

"He nearly killed himself, Warren. We have the luxury of getting a second chance at this, and you know as well as I do that with a thirty-two-year-old man you're lucky to get any chance at all. Usually the first sign with someone his age and his past is a bullet in the mouth."

"I'm asking you for a favor, Ned."

Strickland sighed. "What exactly are you asking, Warren?"

"I'm asking you," Warren said, "not to admit him."

"And why should I do that?"

"Because his family needs him."

"His family needs him?"

"They're absolutely broke, Ned."

"You mean you need him."

"Ned," Warren said, knowing that Strickland hated when Warren used his first name, "I would know if something was about to go wrong."

"You didn't see this coming."

This wasn't going as well as he had hoped. "I think," he said, "it's the best option for everyone."

"I'm not sure I understand how that works for Ben, Warren. Anyone can see that he's in trouble. And considering the family history . . ." he trailed off and raised one eyebrow. "But you know all this. You know how quickly things can go bad for someone with a bad history."

"Ned," Warren said, "you know you owe me this."

Strickland sat back in his chair. Warren thought he could hear it strain beneath the weight. "We've known each other a long time, Warren," he said thoughtfully. "And whether or not you believe this, when I say no to you—and I am going to say no to you in a moment—I will do so with a clear conscience. Any debts between us have been paid by my willingness to be silent. The state medical board wanted to pursue you far beyond revoking your license, you know? I was interviewed four times. I conveniently forgot to tell them that you were raiding the cabinet when you ruined that kid's knee. Things could have turned out a lot worse for you."

"If you're expecting me to thank you," Warren said, "don't. You might even want to thank me. I was the one who got you this job."

"That's outrageous," Strickland said. But it was true; Warren had gotten him the job, simply by getting fired and getting out of his way. "I'm admitting Ben for forty-eight hours," he said, "by which time I expect to have a court order to admit him for a longer period of time. You'll just have to do without, Warren. Your son needs help. Whether or not it's convenient for you is another matter. Convenience can't be the deciding factor."

"I don't have to take this quietly," Warren said. "You and I have a history too, you'll recall. My credentials may be gone. But that doesn't prevent me from telling everyone what I know about yours." It was his last chip, and he spent it without hope.

Strickland seemed amused. "You're welcome to try to stir up trouble, Warren." He stood up and came around the desk to see Warren out. "But I'd have to do the same." He opened the office door and thanked Warren for his time and then firmly closed the door behind him. Ned's secretary watched Warren over the top rims of her glasses and then went back to typing. She seemed to understand, instinctively, what had just happened inside.

Warren sat on the bench outside Strickland's office and assessed the damage he'd done. He had threatened Ned, which meant he could expect the worst possible outcome. December would be a tough month, tough in its anticipation of a worse January. If Ben were still locked away at Christmas, the partnership would be dissolved. Victor was, after all, a businessman, however immoral his trade. Since Warren had never had to survive like most addicts, he had no idea where he'd even begin to search for another source. Until he found one, he'd have to show restraint, make what he had last. Restraint would be easy, now, with ampoules lined up in rows in his refrigerator. But he knew from experience that as their number thinned and became no more than a handful, the urge to devour what little was left would ratchet higher each day. It was impossible to bring restraint to bear on something you were about to lose. Anyone who had ever felt what it was like to lose someone he loved knew how it was. The losing made you hold on more tightly than ever, even though you knew that doing so drove them away more quickly. You knew but you couldn't help yourself. How had Eliot explained it? He closed his eyes and listened to the Brahms playing gently through a hidden speaker and strained to recall the exact words. He'd first read the words in high school. Even then, the passage had seemed troubling and prophetic.

> She gives when our attention is distracted
> And what she gives, gives with such supple confusions
> That the giving famishes the craving.

Before his wife had died, Warren had taken rolls of photographs of her in the hope that later, after she was gone, he'd be able to return to the moment in which he'd snapped the photo simply by holding it up and examining her face closely. The photos, which lived in messy disarray in a front hall drawer, captured her curled in bed, smiling in a shaft of backyard sunlight, wrapped before the fire in an itchy blanket. Too thin, pale-skinned, with a rictus of forced cheer. In all the pictures she was smoking an unfiltered cigarette—as blamelessly, she liked to say, as Nero setting fire to Rome. What do you think, Wren? she'd ask, while he snapped away with his Leica. She'd run her hands down the length of her wasted body. I'm going to burn it all down and rebuild it.

At first, the photographs were enough. On the night they buried her, he covered her side of the bed with the brightest portraits and lay down beside them. He was pleasantly surprised to discover that the bed still carried her particular smell, that of cigarette smoke sullying fastidiously clean laundry. In just a few weeks the clean-laundry smell faded, and he was left with only the photos to help him remember. In time, they yellowed and frayed. Later, it occurred to him that photographs were as synthetic as his Dilaudid high, a reaction of chemicals and light on photographic paper.

He rose from the bench and walked toward the physical therapy wing. The Brahms was still playing through the speakers, a gentle pizzicato lullaby. He pushed through the door to the men's room. Inside, he bent over and checked beneath the three white stall doors and found them all empty. While he had still had his license, he recalled, this tiled room had been his sanctum of choice. Hospital bathrooms were always spotless. He stepped into a stall and latched the door, hung his coat on the door-mounted hook, and set the worn leather case that held his works onto the back of the toilet. When he had unfastened his belt, he lowered his pants and sat on the toilet seat to begin what was—and, he was certain, always would be—the bleakest aspect of his addiction.

He really didn't need it any longer. He was an aging addict who didn't shower often and whose reputation seemed to precede him everywhere. There wasn't a woman in this world who would want him. He had neither the taste nor the money for prostitutes. It had been more than ten years, long before his first fix, since he had last been with a woman—his wife, the only woman he had ever made love to in his life. But still, it was hard to accept. Shooting in the dorsal vein of his penis seemed to have permanently destroyed the strange physiological processes that had taken place down there, so magically and effortlessly, in the glory of his twenties and thirties, and with the absence of that process had come an absence of his sense of manhood. Years ago, he had often listened with strained sympathy to his aging male patients' confessions that the Beta blockers they were taking for their hypertension had made them impotent, thinking all the while that the men should just be happy to be alive. As long as you were alive, he had reasoned, there were so many things other than sex that you could experience to make life worthwhile. Now he understood.

It was all part of the endless struggle to avoid tracks and infections. He had tried taking the oral Dilaudid for months, the little candy-colored two-, four-, and eight-milligram tablets. But the difference between taking it in the vein and swallowing those insubstantial pills was like the difference between a piccolo and an orchestra. It was a question that reached beyond amplitude into concerns of character. A thousand piccolos could merely shriek or be silent, but an orchestra had at its disposal dynamics and textures. A thousand eight-milligram pills, enough to kill you a hundred times over, could never match the richness of taking a single dose straight into your blood; a thousand eight-milligram pills could only shriek or be silent. But shooting meant tracks, and if you worried about tracks you shot up in places that no one would ever see. You rotated between the thigh, the calf, and, when it was time to rotate here, in this forgotten place, this one lonely, important vein.

He backtracked quickly, pulling the plunger infinitesimally and checking for the telltale backwash of blood into the syringe that told him the needle was seated correctly in the vein, then pushed the Dilaudid into his bloodstream and felt his body absorb and devour it. The knots relaxed and he sagged back against the water tank, knocking the leather case for his works onto the floor. He dissolved into himself, listening to the steady drip of a faucet. The room seemed to echo a distant, seismic roar.

Riding the roar were the sounds from the hall, the shrill voices of the bereaved or the injured, the pizzicato Brahms lullaby. Warren heard the sounds but was unable to draw any meaning from them; they seemed to compose a single tone of physical and spiritual anguish. Anguish was the common denominator, it was understood, zero interference, ten-four, loud and clear. As a surgeon, he'd seen enough of it for twenty lifetimes. He'd found you could put the anguish and the cold science away if you could bring your will fully to bear on it. Warren still hoped, despite a lifetime's evidence to the contrary, that absence was possible; he wanted freedom from anguish, but he didn't want to have to die to achieve it the way his wife had. At first he'd found the absence he sought by studying her photographs, but as the images had aged and had ceased to comfort him, he'd begun flailing about for hope, anesthetizing himself with alcohol and reading meandering Buddhist manifestos, seeking their particular form of peace. *Past deeds are like pictures in water,* he'd read in Rinbochay, *but afterwards they do not exist, so do not dwell on them later. To plan for the future is like fishing a dry ravine, so fall not into thought, but reduce wishes and desires. If you remember something, think of how unsure is the time of death.* For a while, the Rinbochay had only made things worse, as he'd tried to hash out the paradox of seeking absence for its own sake. Which really made no sense.

As the roar faded and the sounds from the hall untangled themselves, becoming voices and violins again, he understood that he was back in the moment and that it was time to gather up his things and go home. Someone could come into the bathroom any minute and find him; and yet he lacked the will to leave. It would, he reasoned, almost be better if he languished here until he were caught; if he were thrown in jail and forced to kick. Of course there was the chance that the cure would kill him, but then that was true with so many sicknesses.

He slid his works into his jacket pocket, and then searched through his remaining pockets for a quarter. Strickland's phone call had come early that morning, just after he had fixed up. He hadn't trusted himself to drive, so he'd taken a taxi downtown to the hospital. It had taken three tries to find a cab that would come out to Lasting Drive. He couldn't find any change for a pay phone. If he asked the nurse at the front desk to call him a taxi, she'd take one look at him and call for the doctor. No ride for him.

As he walked to the exit, Warren paused for a moment at the entrance to the hospital's chapel. In the thirty years he had spent walking the halls of this very hospital, he had never once been inside the chapel. Now, the empty pews inside seemed to reproach him. The organ music playing softly from a hidden speaker was chilling. Warren stepped inside and saw that he was alone. A small marble bowl of water stood in the corner, looking oddly like a bird-feeder that had been bought at a garage sale and refurbished for a nobler use. The soft light overhead was radiant on the water's surface. Warren stepped quietly to it, looked around once more for any sign of company, and then lifted a cupped palm full of water to his face. It ran down his neck and dampened his collar. The water was cold but soothing, and it tasted sweet. Warren allowed himself to take this as a sign that he had done the right thing with Ben, but then it occurred to him that perhaps the Dilaudid cruising his bloodstream had fooled him into thinking the water tasted sweet. He had blessed himself while stoned. His first religious act in ten years had been an act of blasphemy.

During the walk home it began to snow lightly. By the time a tow-truck picked him up, just outside of town where Main Street became Route Nine, his teeth were chattering and his collar had frozen stiffly. The driver, a young woman he often saw having coffee at the Silver-smith Diner downtown, asked where he had been. He had been at the hospital, he said, visiting his son, who had been shot unfairly by the police. It occurred to him that this was a sad event. Ben might have been killed, Nina and Sylva left fatherless, and yet somehow during the last six hours he had thought only of himself.

"Where should I drop you?" she asked.

"I live on Lasting Drive," he said.

"Right," she said. Lasting Drive was a weedy side road that dead-ended just past the train tracks outside of town. The locals liked to say that there was nothing lasting about it. If you lived there you were either on your way up or on your way down. Two miles out of town, the driver turned right off of Route Nine onto Lasting, and the tow truck bounced noisily over the train tracks. As they came around the bend before Warren's house, he saw a car parked at the end of his driveway.

"Stop," Warren said, "stop."

"Here?"

"Right here." She slowed the truck to a halt. The tow truck's headlights settled on the parked car. There were two people in the front seat. The person in the passenger seat turned and looked back at them, shading his eyes from the bright headlights with his left hand. It was Victor, waiting patiently. The headlights reflected on his wedding ring. Warren didn't know who the driver was. He had never seen him before.

She looked over at him. "Friends of yours?"

"Maybe we could go to Skylark Drive? My son lives there."

She looked at the parked car and back at Warren. "Look," she said, "I don't want to get involved in anything."

"If we leave now, you won't."

She made a sound in her throat and then did a U-turn and passed back over the train tracks. As they drove back into town Warren wondered if Victor would think to look for him at Ben and Emma's house.

It was late Sunday night and downtown Lansing was empty. They passed the darkened movie theater marquee and then rose steeply over a small hill before the road flattened out, grassy fields converging on either side of the pavement. She turned left onto Skylark Drive, downshifting out of each sharp bend in the road, and left him two miles in at the end of Ben and Emma's driveway.

He watched the truck's taillights disappear around the first bend. After it had gone, the drive was silent and windless and still, the neighbors' windows blank, as if the sudden cold had frozen all sound and light. His damp collar was stiff against his neck again, but he knew that in a moment he would be warm. The snow had cleared completely and now the sky was cloudless overhead, and as he walked up the crushed stone drive toward the barn the moon flickered brilliantly overhead through the tree branches. It really was a beautiful home, he reflected, exactly the sort of home a man who had just assumed control of a company would buy, a man who had an attractive wife and two beautiful daughters and had no sense of the fall that was nearly upon him.

Warren lifted the doormat and plucked the key from the cement. He unlocked the door and let himself in the front hall and then locked the front door behind him, pushing the bolt across. Intruder though he was, the familiarity of the front hall soothed him. For years, Emma had made him feel welcome here. She had insisted, despite Ben's simmering hostility, that he be a part of Nina's and Sylva's lives. Childhood, he guessed, had been less than perfect for her. While her welcoming nature had been charming and inviting, it had also been slightly desperate and sad, as if she had been trying to account for something in her past she herself had missed.

In the living room, he turned on the table lamp and went straight to the stone fireplace, where he built up a neat, miserly fire. The room warmed quickly, and Warren turned out the light again and undressed, hanging his damp shirt on a chair before the fire. Naked, he went to the window and looked out into the night. The moon revealed nothing but lifeless landscape. No one was parked at the end of the driveway. He went upstairs and turned on the hallway light at the top of the landing. In the bedroom, he dressed in a frayed pair of Ben's corduroys and an old flannel work shirt. After he was dressed, he noticed that he was comfortable here and that the silence surrounding him was entirely unlike the grating silence of his own home. As he was walking down the stairs, he caught sight of his reflection in the landing window. The blurred form that stared back at him in the glass seemed in every aspect to be an aged vision of his son. He reached up and snapped off the light, and Ben vanished in darkness.

Five

The bus drove into Springfield after dark on Sunday night. The downtown streets were nearly deserted, the windows of the department stores shuttered and blank. At the first red light, Emma opened her window and pushed her face out into the chilly air. She smelled damp cement and frying onions. The bus hadn't stopped during the four-hour trip, and she'd begun to feel claustrophobic. Her finger stung sharply, but she'd forgotten her pain pills, having left them on her vanity at home during the frenzied half-hour of packing, so she'd had to rely on chewable aspirin since Hartford.

You should have waited, Emma thought, for the later bus to Worcester. Even if you wanted to get away quickly, before you lost your nerve, you should have waited, because now you'll have to sit through the long ride home from Springfield, that crushing silence from the front seat. Mother, with the silver clasp of her purse pinched tightly between her fingers. Dad, fallen forward over the wheel, piloting the two-ton car with his index finger. No music or conversation. Just enmeshed silence.

The bus had turned onto a side street, then passed through an intersection and stopped at the curb before the bus station. The station, overrun by the Sunday night rush, was milling with students and senior citizens. Three bored prostitutes waited outside by the stand of pay phones, smoking and blowing into their hands for warmth. The entire lot suggested a shabbily festive tone that seemed out place in the empty downtown streets. Emma's parents were nowhere to be found, which, according to their tightly-monitored schedule, meant that they were either lost or dead. The lights went on suddenly inside the bus and everyone stood to lift bags from the overhead racks. Nina and Sylva awoke and looked up her. "We made it," she said, a little too optimistically, she thought.

"I'm hungry," Nina said.

"Just a little longer," Emma replied.

"I'm hungry, too," Sylva said.

"I'll get you something from the machines."

"I'm tired," Nina said.

"I'm tired, too," Sylva said.

"She always says everything I say," Nina said.

"You do," Sylva said.

"Enough," Emma said. She reached up with her good hand and lifted her bag from the rack. "I want you both right behind me." She was already ticking off the things she had forgotten as she stepped off the bus: Sylva's blanket; Nina's Ritalin. The two things essential to their emotional well being. Oh yes, one more thing: she'd forgotten to bring their father.

Enough, she thought. Enough.

The porter squinted at her baggage ticket and then dragged the two heavy suitcases from the belly of the bus and set them on the curb at her feet. Nina studied the prostitutes.

"Aren't they cold?" she asked.

One of the prostitutes yawned and waved to her.

"Let's go inside to wait," Emma said. She slung the small bag over her shoulder and lifted the heavier suitcase with her good hand. Nina and Sylva together carried the other suitcase and the three of them went inside to wait. Emma bought them each a diet soda without caffeine and some crackers from the machine with change scavenged from the bottom of her pocket book. Machine food was, of course, unacceptable, and she prayed they'd finish before her mother arrived and bestowed upon them one of her patented looks of nutritional disapproval. Or maybe her mother had given those up; it occurred to Emma that she really didn't know her parents well anymore. She hadn't lived at home in fifteen years, and had spent as little of that time with them as was reasonably possible. The resentment had carved itself too deeply into her personality. It was part of her, now.

She bought a two-pack of aspirin from the machine—her version of machine food—and chewed them both as she watched the sitcom playing on the wall-mounted television. When the girls had finished their snack, she threw out the wrappers and cans and told them not to tell their Nana about what she had given them.

Her father's dented silver Bronco pulled to a stop at the curb. He stepped out of the car and looked around the lot, his eyes lingering for a moment on the prostitutes. Her mother remained in her seat, the belt still fastened over her shoulder. Her mother, Emma reflected, was the sort who wanted everything strapped down, always belted in, prepared for the unexpected bash-and-roll. There was a tireless defensiveness in Sarah that seemed to spring from the spine. She'd stopped taking medication years ago and though giving up the drugs had brightened her personality, it had left her feeling unprotected. Aside from the occasional Valium, there was no real net to catch her fall other than the therapy, and what was that, really, but emotional groping? No wonder she stayed belted in.

When her father walked around to the passenger side, she lowered her window, and he spoke to her briefly. She loosened her seatbelt and then leaned across the seat to the driver's side. The red hazard lights began blinking. He spoke to her again, resting his head against the doorframe, and then walked wearily inside the bus station. As he searched the room for them he squinted in the bright fluorescent light. His tired features softened as soon as he saw her. He waved as he walked to her, and she realized that he had expected her, at the moment of initial contact, to dissolve into an ecstasy of daughterly tears, but she was far too tired for histrionics. She wanted sleep, not drama.

As he hugged her, she was reminded that her father was half a foot taller than Ben, a round-shouldered two-hundred pounds. It was strange to be held by someone who dwarfed her so. He smelled of tobacco and sawdust. After Carl had released her, he knelt down and kissed each of the girls and told them he had a surprise for them at home. The girls accepted this with guarded excitement. "Emma," he asked, lifting both suitcases, "are we going to talk about this?"

"There's no need to talk," Emma said. "Really."

"Pretend you're me," he said. "You'd want to know more." He held the station door open for her.

"I'm fine," she said. The blast of frigid air felt good on her face. "We just need some time apart."

"He needs more than that."

"He didn't hit me," she said, hurt, "if that's what you mean." Her mother, she noted bitterly, hadn't even unbelted herself to say hello. She merely reached down and grasped the girls' hands, and when Emma leaned in the window to kiss her, she turned her head slightly so the kiss fell on the coin of muscle where her jawbone met her neck. Her father put the suitcases in the back, pulled the driver's seat forward, and lifted the girls up into the back. Emma climbed in between them, and they immediately lay their heads in her lap. Their fine hair felt soft beneath her fingers. She was very scared and very glad they were there with her.

"I want to call dad," Nina said.

"We can call him when we get home," Carl said. He snapped off the hazard lights and watched Emma in the rearview mirror. "I'm sure he's fine."

"I want to call him, too," Sylva said.

"I want to call him, first," Nina said.

"It'll be too late to call," Sarah said.

"Why don't you two just lay quietly?" Emma asked.

"Us?" her mother asked.

"Sarah," Carl said. He did a U-turn and then passed through the stoplight, turned right onto Main Street, and drove past the shuttered department stores toward the turnpike.

Nina and Sylva slept during the entire trip and woke, restless and out of sorts, as they pulled into the driveway. They began arguing in the front hall. Four hours worth of bus ride came flooding out as Nina shoved Sylva and then Sylva, in an understandable retaliation, punched her sister in the shoulder. Carl told them if they were good and waited downstairs while he and their mom unpacked, he would give them the surprise he had gotten for them. Sarah had gone upstairs to bed without saying goodnight. The girls sat on the stairs. Emma followed him up to her old room and watched as he set her suitcase at the foot of her neatly made bed. Then she followed him down the hall to the guest room—the room where her mother had slept during her slack-jawed bad spells twenty years ago, those days when her father had to bathe her and feed her and comb her hair and beg her just to get out of bed in the morning.

I just can't sleep next to her when she's like that, she remembered him answering, when she had asked why they sometimes slept in different rooms. I feel like one of those men who. But he never finished the sentence. One of those men who *what*?

She began emptying the suitcase into the dresser drawers. Her father sat on the bed beneath the window.

"Is this okay for Syl and Nina?" he asked. "I thought you might want some privacy, so I made up the beds in here for them."

"This is fine." She opened the top dresser drawer and was startled to find a shoebox filled with her old swimming medals.

"He didn't hit you?"

"Never," she said, pushing the medals into the back of the drawer. "Absolutely not."

"Is he drinking again?"

"I'm not sure," she said. "That's not really it, anyway." She meant to hint at the seriousness of the problem without provoking alarm. Her parents were very practiced at alarm. They did it better than anyone.

"You don't want to talk about it," he said.

"I'm grateful, dad," she said. "But I never said I wanted to talk about it."

He left the room and she heard him take something from the hall closet and then walk downstairs. He told the girls they could have their surprise if they would eat some dinner first. Emma listened closely. Incredibly, as they were herded into the kitchen, neither of them said anything about their snack at the station. She finished unpacking, turned back the sheets, and plugged in the night light. In the bathroom, she locked the door and urinated for what seemed a long time, then went to the mirror to fix her hair. She found two new gray hairs and plucked them out mercilessly by their roots. When had she gotten so old?

She remembered the night on the beach in Westport, when she told Ben that Nina was inside of her, a small glowing ember in her belly. Ben had promised her they would be different than other parents who grew old and tired and used up; she had made promises to the same. They had agreed—that was the right word—that they wouldn't let having children change them. On that night, it had all seemed possible. What doesn't seem possible on a beach at night? But Nina arrived just as business worsened at the plant. Somehow, in the midst of all those hours devoted to composing exciting meals, folding laundry, signing bills, salaaming over scraped knees—somehow, in the midst of all that, romance, in its truly physical manifestation, became peripheral. They lost the desire to feel physically close to someone, because they were *always* physically close to someone—the children were like new appendages.

At first Emma felt sadness over the slow diminuendo of their love-making; she missed it in the way you miss a fond location you no longer visit or a favorite song you haven't heard in a long time. Then she felt a burgeoning fear, a sudden doubt about her attractiveness, his fidelity, their desire. In time, they began to fight about how, when, and why things had changed. Finally, and most frightening of all, there was no talk about it at all. Just an uneasy acceptance that a friendly, nearly sexless, parallel existence was the way things were meant to be. How young, she thought, how naïve the two of us were, making that promise. How young and naïve and in love. How surprised we were by the nature of the institution.

She pulled her hair back and flushed the toilet and went downstairs. Carl was sitting at the kitchen table, flanked by Nina and Sylva. Laid out before them was a game board, and he was reading the rules of the game to them from the box top. Emma recognized the name on the box top, *Epigenesis,* as that of the game that the school board had voted unanimously to ban from school grounds, just weeks ago.

"Dad," she said, "I've heard that's a little violent."

"It's not so bad," he said. He looked up from the box top. "You want me to get you something? Your mom made some bread today."

"I think I'll wait," she said.

"We called the hospital," he said.

"Dad went to bed," Sylva said.

Carl raised an eyebrow but didn't look up from the box top.

"We'll try again tomorrow when he's awake," Emma said. "I'll bet he'll want to hear about our trip."

"I want to play," Nina said.

"I want to play, too," Sylva said.

Emma sighed. Better that than get into a discussion about where Ben was. There were, she reflected, no safe honest answers. He was in the hospital because he'd willfully hurt himself. But why, one of the girls would surely ask, with their indisputable, kid-like logic, would anyone ever hurt themselves? It was the same question she'd asked the psychiatrist at the hospital that morning. What was his name? An adjective. Sweet. Daniel Sweet. She had asked him why anyone would hurt themselves, even though she had already known the answer; Ben had done it for her and the girls.

They had stood outside Ben's room for more than half an hour, exhaustion lining Sweet's face like a deep emotion, and she had told him everything.

Mrs. Bascomb, Sweet asked after she said her peace, do you really think he wanted to hurt just himself?

That was the crucial question, wasn't it? The question of who was to pay. The bills had always been left to him, but the emotional balance had always been extracted from her. She recalled how she had encountered him the night before, sitting there in the light of the desk lamp, the pencil held like a weapon in one fist. He had, in his typical Ben-like way, offered her only the tiniest glimpse of his thoughts, a glimpse she had ignored. In that missed opportunity lay the essence of his contradictions. He wanted help, but he wanted it on his terms.

If you're suggesting he was trying to punish me, she said, I think that's a possibility.

What sort of relationship do you have?

We're like everyone else.

Sweet removed his glasses and began to polish them on his shirt. Without the scrim of glass, his youthful face seemed even more haggard. She wondered when the last time was he had slept.

I'm not quite sure what that means, Sweet said.

It means that only a fraction of what's going on is up to us. We have good days and bad days.

How often does he have bad days?

She considered. *All the time* was the answer that leapt, reflexively, to her mind; but of course that was nothing more than marital jousting. Certainly every day was not a bad day. But when you were having a bad day it seemed that way.

I should explain some things, she said. He stopped drinking.

How long ago?

Three years.

Do you think it's hard on him?

I think it's fair to say that he's had some extraordinarily bad luck, she said. I think that when he dwells on that, yes, it's hard on him. Ben isn't like the rest of us. Most of us move in a straight line. Ben revolves.

Sweet replaced his glasses.

What I'm getting at, he said, is whether or not his behavior is a warning.

She blinked twice, recalling the image of him at the desk again. He'd sat there because he knew she would be on her way up to bed and would see him there. She pictured his face in the light of the desk lamp, the clenched jaw, the eyes tightly shut. Waiting for her to come to him and put her fingers in his hair.

I suppose it is, she said.

Then perhaps we need to take steps, Sweet said.

Now, sitting in the kitchen with the girls, it occurred to her for the first time that the doctor had been suggesting that they admit Ben to his care.

That can't be it, she thought. We can't have come to that. But had they? She imagined stock images of straitjackets and locked doors, of tiled, lighted halls where rough orderlies dispensed the same drugs that had turned her mother into something part-mannequin, part-drunk.

Please just be what you were, Ben. Please don't become what my mother was.

"It's your turn," Nina said.

"I think I'll watch," Emma said. Please, she thought. Please be what you were. If you leave me here, I have to be what I was.

She woke later, disoriented, and felt about madly in the darkness to get her bearings. Her fingers encountered a strange conical lamp and knocked over a photograph that stood on the side table. The slap of the falling frame startled her. Then she remembered where she was and why she was here. She sat up in bed, felt for the lamp chain and pulled it. The room brightened, and she shielded her eyes from the glare with one hand. Her heart was beating rapidly. The back of her neck was damp.

After her eyes had adjusted to the light, she went across the room and took her copy of *Dubliners* from her bag. When she had climbed back into bed and began to read, the words refused to connect. She read each sentence without remembering what the previous one had said. In frustration, she dropped the book on the side table and simply listened. Faintly, she heard her parents arguing in their bedroom. Her mother insisted that her father had gotten them lost in Springfield; he countered that the directions had been incomplete.

For as long as she could remember, she'd eavesdropped on their conversations at every possible opportunity—at keyholes, at windows, at upstairs phone lines. She'd listened to personal phone calls, tearful confessions, marital arguments, and—once—a startlingly, almost comically vocal act of copulation that occurred in the backyard during the neighbors' cocktail party. Emma had been silent witness to the thousand changes that composed any long marriage.

As a child, she had eavesdropped out of necessity. Her father had, despite his every intention, adopted his parents' habit of indirection in raising his own child. He'd been raised by Midwestern Jesuits who believed children ought to be seen and not heard, and that ugly truths ought to be left unsaid. Somehow, their parenting style had survived Carl's wholesale rejection of their religion and their way of life. When someone in the family died, Emma's father told her that person had *passed*; when a neighboring family was weathering a divorce, they were *going through a tough time*; when a town official was convicted of soliciting prostitution, *an unfortunate thing had happened* because *boys will be boys*. Because all things were implied and nothing was explained, it became necessary for Emma to learn the full truth in less than candid or open ways.

In time, by listening closely to phone conversations and reading his private letters, Emma learned that her father had been taught, from infancy, that sex was a filthy and debasing act that one undertook solely for the necessary purpose of procreation. It was never discussed in his home, except in dismissal or disdain, and he'd certainly never been taught anything about the mechanics of the act. As he grew older, Carl came to see himself as an emblem of embarrassment, a child who, through his very existence, was evidence of the fact that his parents had sampled Gomorrah. Their politeness, the academic seriousness with which they discussed marriage, their unwillingness to touch each other unless they were interlocking fingers to say grace, their parallel twin beds—always neatly, *severely* made, as if the coverlet were some sort of hood intended to cover unholy ground—all suggested to Carl the possibility that his parents had made love once and only once during their marriage. Reluctantly, dutifully, they'd surrendered their self-respect to create him. Although neither of them had ever stated this directly, their frigidity was implicit in their every word, in their every shared look. They didn't seem to resent him; quite the opposite, really. They seemed frightened of what he'd brought out of them.

Change came quickly and cataclysmically at eighteen. During his first semester at college, Carl broke no fewer than six commandments, obliterated a full three-fifths of the Decalogue in a scant three months, and by his senior year he completed all but one, *Thou shalt not kill*, which he nearly completed one April night while driving his friend Ash, drunk, from Montgomery to a party in Union Springs in Ash's convertible. Those were the days, Carl footnoted in one particularly rambling letter, when drunk driving drew nothing more than a stern warning from state cops to drive carefully. Ash was drunker than he that night, asleep by the Montgomery line, and Carl, nodding himself, somehow fell asleep halfway to Union Springs.

It seemed likely to him that they had cruised pilotlessly along the deserted, arrow-straight roads for as much as a half mile. The trip ended suddenly and violently when the right tires slipped off the pavement, noisily tearing up the hardscrabble breakdown. Carl came awake as the steering wheel was ripped from his hands. The sky and ground, he wrote, swapped places, and then swapped again. The lights of Montgomery burned in the distance.

He came awake facedown in a cornfield, two rows in from the road, bloodied but nearly unhurt. A cricket climbed atop his elbow and examined his face for a moment before it leapt powerfully away. Ash's car was a full fifty yards down the road, upside down, tires spinning lazily. Carl hunted around for fifteen minutes before he found what had been Ash laying on his back beyond the wreckage of the convertible. It appeared to be crushed. What had been Ash's arm was now an appendage bent at what seemed to be a new joint. His ear was now a planed-down swath of skin. What had been Ash's face was stove in on one side, the jaw collapsed as if by a sledgehammer blow.

It asked for help. It asked for its mother and for mercy, but neither showed.

Her father, Emma read on, went to jail for thirty days. Ash never spoke to him again. His face was reconstructed, but the friendship remained obliterated. Twice yearly, letters of apology were sent, and twice yearly those letters were returned, unopened and unread by Ash, to be first reread by her father and then filed on the top shelf of his study, where they were then read by Emma. It wasn't until she herself was ready to go off to college that Emma realized her father had opened them not because he had wanted to read them, but because he'd wanted her to read them. He'd had it both ways: nothing unpleasant had been discussed, and yet the truth had come out.

I feel like one of those men who.

The rest of the sentence seemed clear enough to her, now: *one of those men who sleep beside dead women.* A commandment that even God had thought implicit and unnecessary: *Thou shalt not sleep beside lifeless women.* You needn't worry about that, dad, she thought. You've broken no more commandments. By anyone's definition, you're a good man. You stayed with her through twenty bad years, which is admirable. You cared for her. We both cared for her, but unlike you I hadn't done anything to earn that punishment. I never felt that I deserved it, whereas you sought it out as penance for what you did to Ash—you rolled in it, bathed richly and willingly in it. I feel only like *one of those women who:* one of those women who constantly settle others' accounts. One of those women who serve someone else's conscience. Even your conscience, dad. I bear witness— I was forced to bear witness so that someone would *know* for all time that you were and are good.

That you were, and are, good.

I remember the first time we went to look for her. I remember that morning, that not-yet-morning—you stood black in the white square of doorway-light. In your pajamas and overcoat, your boots pulled over your bare feet.

She's gone again, Em, you said.

You handed me a flashlight and my coat and boots, you watched me dress, and then we walked outside and it still wasn't morning. I remember the way our flashlights played across the meadow. I remember that I ran my palm over the tops of the tall grass and found that it was stiff with frost. We crossed the back field and walked into the forest and down the sloped bank toward the creek. A thin shell of ice had formed around the edges of the deep pools.

We found her nightdress at the water's edge, abandoned like an afterbirth. And you were there, mother. You were there. You weren't far away. You were naked and covered with mud, shivering and curled into a ball on the bank. Dad stood you up and put his coat around you and led you home. He led *us* home. Because I was there, right behind you, and I remember that I wasn't worried about you—no. I was only worried about myself, wondering if it was too late, if someone would see us, if today would be the day I went to school and found out that everyone knew.

Say it.

Dad took you upstairs and washed you and toweled you dry and put you to bed. I went to the laundry room sink and scrubbed at that dress. The stains wouldn't come out.

Say My mother's crazy.

The next day you came out of the laundry room with the nightdress held in your fist, and you said, Carl, we need a new well.

He looked up from his game of solitaire.

I remember the steady tick of the grandfather clock as you stood there with the dress in your fist, your hair unpinned. No one spoke, and finally you said, Carl, the iron in the water is ruining my nightdress. You looked terrified. It occurred to me that, although you didn't know exactly what had happened, you *knew.*

Say it.

Of course, Sarah, he said. We can't have stains.

But it happened again. And again. There were more stains. And eventually someone saw us.

Say it. Say My mother's crazy.

"My mother's . . ." Emma said, but she couldn't complete the sentence because the word *crazy* hitched in her throat, as if the word didn't want itself to be heard. And then, maddeningly, the tears started. She gathered the sheet in her fist, furious with herself, but the tears wouldn't stop; she let them go, silently, into the pillow, here where no one could see them.

Tears never help, she thought, and turned out the light.

It's too late for tears. At night, alone—it's *always* too late for tears.

Six

Ben was alone in the short-term care unit's television room Wednesday afternoon, listening to the afternoon game shows with his eyes closed, when the nurse touched his shoulder lightly and told him he had a visitor. He watched her for a moment and then stood up and picked up his crutches and followed her to the nurses' station by the locked front door of the ward, his heart going lightly in his chest. He hoped the visitor was Emma, feared it was Victor, and resigned himself to an argument with either one. He was surprised to find Raif waiting for him at the door, sitting in a wheelchair, his propped-up left leg wrapped from thigh to ankle in bandages. He had shaved his beard and although his face was still bruised, he looked much younger. Ben was terribly relieved and embarrassed to see him.

"Why did you shave?" Ben asked.

"I needed a change," Raif said. He followed Ben into the television room and stopped under the window. "Will I be in anyone's way here?"

"You'll be fine there. You need some sunlight." Ben sat across from him. He needed sunlight himself. "How's the leg?"

"It doesn't hurt as much as I had thought."

"Are you still on morphine?"

"I may try aspirin tomorrow."

Ben folded his hands and looked around the room. On the television, a broad-shouldered Germanic woman was leaping up and down, a giant dollar sign flashing on a lighted screen behind her. As he watched the flashing symbol, it occurred to Ben that although he was essentially broke, he had never shed his New Money propensity for measuring himself by the people he associated with. For the last twenty-four hours he had been surrounded by crackups and nurses, and the fact that Raif had visited made him feel momentarily civilized and academic. He wished he had something intelligent to say.

"So," Raif said, "I guess you're here."

"I meet with that doctor this afternoon. I'll get it sorted out then."

"I brought you my book." Raif reached behind him and handed over his copy of *Invisible Allies*. "Smuggled it in, as it were. I didn't know if there was a policy. I finished it last night. Did you read any while I was sleeping?"

"I read the first paragraph."

"That's a good first paragraph."

"I've forgotten what it said." The Zoloft had blunted his short-term memory and he had spent the last two days adjusting to the nervous stupor of medication. "What was it about?"

"Why don't you read some tonight and we'll talk about it tomorrow?"

"I haven't read in years. I used to read to impress my wife. She brings a book everywhere she goes."

"I'd like to meet her."

"So would I," Ben said.

Raif looked at the television for a while. His fists were clenched on the armrests. When they had relaxed he turned back. "I can't think of anything to say."

"I guess we don't really know each other that well."

"You'd think we'd be able to work around that."

"It's my fault. I'll read this tonight, and then we'll have something to talk about. Nothing really happens here that you can talk about." Although the moment was awkward, he was grateful that he had a visitor. He didn't want Raif to leave. In the next room the two wards playing Ping-Pong began arguing about the score.

"It must be kind of nice having some time off."

"I guess it is," Ben said. He noticed that he had been snapping his fingers and forced himself to stop.

"What do you do with yourself?"

Ben spent his afternoons high on Zoloft and television game shows, the sound of the shows refracting faintly through the pharmaceutical shell that surrounded him. At night he worried. "I talk to the others," he said, "as little as possible."

"What are they like?"

"They're nice, of course," Ben said. He noticed that his voice was getting louder and his good leg was bouncing up and down. He was suddenly very upset. "Terribly nice and pathetic. Somehow the doctor thinks I belong here. Do I seem terribly nice and pathetic to you?"

"You're not pathetic at all," Raif said.

"I feel pathetic."

"It's not like that," Raif said.

"In the movies, the crazy people are all nice, and you root for them because it doesn't seem to be their fault that they are the way they are. But when you're here, you see how pathetic they are." He stood up.

"Take it easy," Raif said.

"Well, what the hell do you know about it?"

The nurse looked in the room. "Is everything all right in here?"

"We're fine," Raif said.

"Get lost," Ben said.

The nurse rolled her eyes and left.

"I can't help but bait her," Ben said. He sat down. "She reminds me of those teenage counter girls at fast food places."

"She reminds me of my sister," Raif said. "So your wife still hasn't visited."

"She hasn't even called. My daughters called me again yesterday morning, and she wouldn't come to the phone."

"She's angry with you?"

"She's probably angry with herself for marrying me," Ben said. "We tried to break up once. Way back. But neither of us had the guts to go through with it. I think she regrets it now." He noticed that Raif was turning pale. "Is it your leg?"

"It hurts a little to have it propped up like this."

"I'm sorry I acted this way. I'm glad you came, and it would make me happy if you would come by tomorrow."

"It's really okay," Raif said. "I wasn't doing so well sitting on my own either."

"I'll do some reading tonight, and we'll talk about that." He hopped on his good leg out into the hall and held onto the door jamb as he watched Raif go. He found that he was almost in tears. Raif twisted in his chair and waved to him as he was wheeled out and then pointed to Ben and mimicked turning pages before the door to the ward was closed and locked.

"Mr. Bascomb?" The nurse pointed to the public phone in the corner. "You have a phone call." He hopped down the hall and took the receiver off the shelf, then sat in the folding chair beneath it.

"Hello, Westchester," Victor said.

"Don't start," Ben said.

"Kidding. Warren told me Anthony has been getting under your skin."

"He's a rodent."

"He lifts baggage for a living. Have a heart."

"Victor," Ben asked, "what do you want?"

"Busy, are you? Places to go. Locked doors to pick. Ouch. That one was in the dirt."

Ben was silent. He watched his good leg bounce up and down. He didn't think he had the will required to sit and listen to Victor's self-indulgent wit.

"Clearly," Victor said, "our relationship has suffered a setback. Warren dodged me for a few days. You'll never guess where I found him."

"Rehab."

"You're getting warm."

"Maybe we should have this talk tomorrow."

"At your house," Victor said. In the background Ben clearly heard the frenzied uptempo of *Straight, No Chaser.*

"And?"

"He seems to think that you're going to be in the—in the place you're in for quite some time."

"He's paranoid." Victor didn't respond so he went on. "I need a few days to get things cleared up with the doctor. Emma put some ideas in his head."

"A baseball bat, huh?" The admiration in his voice was unmistakable. Ben heard the gentle clang of pans. "You don't kid around, Westchester."

"Softball bat, actually."

"A few days?"

"One or two at the most."

"You'll have to smooth things over with Anthony. He was less than thrilled to be stranded in the long-term parking lot with two flight bags of schwag. You could have called me."

"I was unconscious. And Anthony needs a little humility. It probably did him some good."

"Ben," Victor said quietly, "it was bad for business."

Ben picked at the chipped paint on the wall with his fingernail.

"Warren suggested that he and I locate the items you appropriated from yourself and sell them to reimburse me your advance. And his scag. I'm wondering if we might have your blessing on that."

"Absolutely not."

"And your guidance. That's a big back yard, Westchester. A lot of digging."

"Absolutely not. It's not my problem you gave Warren his share in advance. Work it out with him."

"What about yours?"

"When I'm out you'll get it back. Or I'll make up the lost work."

"So you're telling me no."

"I'm telling you no on all accounts." He had never said no to Victor before, and it occurred to him that Victor was not the sort to take refusals lightly. "Victor, he's got you all worked up. I'll be out of here in a few days and I'll take Anthony out for a beer and I'll smooth things over and then everything'll be fine. Just fine."

Victor was silent for a moment. "All right," he said. "If you say things will be fine, things will be fine. I want to hear from you in a few days, because I have to make some alternate plans. It doesn't end with me, you know? Wes has very little patience."

Ben hung up the phone and leaned his head against the wall, closing his eyes. Suddenly he felt sleepy. He drifted off briefly, sitting there, and awoke suddenly when another ward, a college-age girl who was clearly more of an addict than a head case, began complaining loudly to the hallway staff that Ben was always on the phone and never let anyone else use it. "Fuck off," Ben said.

"Mr. Bascomb," the nurse said, "you know our rules on language."

"You too," he said, and hopped into the television room. He sat on the couch and watched the television. He wondered if the nurse would summon one of the orderlies to intimidate him. Technically he hadn't cursed at her, but he had a feeling that technicalities didn't wash here. Presence on the ward was sufficient evidence of guilt. In the end, the orderlies would be summoned. That was how every story ended here.

He sat and watched the game show, waiting for the orderlies to arrive. Warren would find what he had buried in the garden, for sure. There was a shallow hole of freshly turned earth by the perennials, marked by a notch in the wood on the outside of the barn. In the hole, wrapped carefully in a drop sheet, were the pocket watch, the pen, his grandfather William's Rolex, the brooch with the diamonds on its face, his grandmother's diamond earrings, and an unused gold cigar clip. He'd found them, he recalled, on the day of William's funeral. After the service he had driven across town alone to what remained of William's destroyed home, had stripped off his shirt and shoes and socks and had placed them on the front seat of the car, and then had crawled around the front lawn, beneath the blackened timber, in a pair of shorts. He had spent more than four hours crawling in parallel lines from the edge of the house to the road, parting the ashy grass as sweetly as he would his daughters' hair.

His grandmother's flatware and the N. C. Wyeth sketch, *Study for Siege of the Round-House,* were safe. Warren wouldn't think to look between the two stacks of wood in the barn, where he had hidden them. But then again, Ben realized, it didn't matter if they found them or not—either way, he would need Victor's help to sell them. Warren would get something in the end, because he and Victor were together in this. But God bless the two-bits, he thought. God bless the Victors and the Warrens and the Weses. He reached over and snapped off the television set and looked out the window. For all of their posturing and their threats, bless them. They financed a cozy ten thousand dollars of my home. God bless the two-bits, for without them I would have no income besides changing spark plugs and replacing stripped flywheels. God bless them, because I think I may have become one of them.

Victor had let himself into Trina's apartment two hours ago. She had gone into Manhattan for a callback and would be home soon, and he wanted to have dinner ready for her. Most likely she hadn't gotten the part, and she'd be distraught. Losing a part always crushed her for a few days. He knew that until she was feeling better she'd be affectionate and wounded and receptive to attention. And anyway, if she didn't want him to let himself in, why had she given him a key?

Wes had phoned him that afternoon on his cell phone while Victor was at the supermarket. Call me back on the land line, he said.

Victor found a pay phone in the back of the store and made the call collect just to affect a pose of cool indifference. The truth was that he was scared shitless of Wes. He'd heard that Wes had stabbed a guy in the neck with a pair of poultry shears for cheating at seven-card hi-low.

It's just a minor hang-up, Victor said. I'll have it sorted out in a few hours.

A few hours! Wes shouted into the phone. I've got six chippers phoning me night and day, Victor! A day late isn't much for us, but for them it's like something out of Revelations. One of them came to my fucking house last night, Victor. Banged on my door in the middle of the night, scratching at his forearms. Did the Haldol shuffle up and down my yard, and kicked over my trash cans when I told him to come back tomorrow. Every one of my neighbors stuck their head out the bedroom window and had a look.

I've got another driver, he said, and checked his watch. She's in Manhattan, but she'll be back in a few hours.

Not Trina.

Of course Trina, Victor said. He had decided that afternoon to use her and had already arranged everything with Anthony. He hadn't checked with her first. That was why he was making a nice dinner. *Where I come from,* she liked to say, *you don't get something for nothing.* It was one of the things that had survived from her Other Life. It had crossed the invisible divide. How the hell did she know where she was from?

Victor, Wes said, I don't think a rental's a good idea.

He knew that. And it cost damn near a hundred dollars, so could they just get on with it? We'll be fine, Wes.

We? You'll be fine, Victor. But how do you think Trina's going to act when they shove her in central booking for twelve hours? You know what that's like? I've been there, twice. I can assure you it's unpleasant. And I don't like the fact that she knows my name, where I live and, most importantly, what we've been doing. I don't want you using her, understand?

After this time, Victor said, patiently. He just wanted to be done with this. He wanted to be back home.

Wes was silent for a moment as he weighed the risk of using Trina versus the likelihood of another midnight visit from one of his customers.

All right, he said. This time. And that's it. No more changes. The fewer people involved, the less risk there is. Get Ben back in line for the next trip, or I'm looking elsewhere.

Good, Victor said. Really, it's not going to be a problem.

I need someone dependable.

I do, too, Victor wanted to say, but checked himself. After he hung up the phone he went back to the grocery store and bought everything he'd need for a nice dinner, because it occurred to him that if Trina refused, he'd have to call Theo. He'd have to beg. The phone call to Ben had made it clear that Ben was not to be counted on. Victor had capitulated only to end the conversation.

As Trina's key slid into the lock, he hoped that he had done enough. He had set the table and had even chilled a bottle of that revolting blush wine she liked. "What's the occasion?" she asked, apparently deciding not to mention that he'd let himself in. She seemed tired and worn out by her day. Definitely didn't get the part, he decided. She was young, but disappointment always made her look old.

"No reason," he said. "How'd it go?"

"Same as always," she said and came into the kitchen. She pressed the cold tip of her nose against the back of his neck. "Too short, too tall, too blonde, too happy, too sad. It hurts to get rejected for what you are. It's worse than being rejected for what you aren't." She stood on tiptoe and looked over his shoulder at the stovetop. "I've never seen that before."

"Black bean stew," he said. He'd made it with pork shoulder and hoped it had cooked long enough. If the meat was tough she'd eat it anyway. She was sweet like that.

"Your mom's recipe?"

"Straight from the island."

"Maybe you should open a restaurant here," she said. She sat at the table.

He stopped himself from telling her that was a bad idea. It was in her nature to think of the hopelessly unachievable as genuine possibility. And the last thing he wanted was to be chained here.

Trina poured herself a glass of wine. He noticed that she hadn't even taken her jacket off. Was she that tired? "My mother called me today," she said. "God I hate calling her that. This must be what it's like for newlyweds. Trying to call their spouse's parents mom and dad."

"What'd she want?" He left the stove and sat beside her at the table. The silence in the apartment seemed strangely disappointing.

"She said everyone wants me to come home for Christmas."

"That might be odd."

"Said they'd get me a hotel room if I didn't feel comfortable."

"What'd you say?"

"I said I didn't know if I could do that. Then she broke down again. Just crying and crying. She said, 'Abby, we love you. We love you so much.'"

"That must have felt strange, them calling you by your old name!"

"It was embarrassing. Like when a stranger cries to you."

"Do you think you might go?"

She watched him.

"Maybe," she said, "we could go somewhere together."

It occurred to him that she had been hinting at that for weeks, and, having grown tired of waiting, had deliberately led the conversation there tonight.

"Where would we go?" he asked.

"You said you were thinking of going down to Culebra. I've never been to Puerto Rico myself."

He hadn't expected that, and he realized that in reply he'd have to step lightly around the truth. She didn't understand that he wanted his life here separate from his life there, and he didn't think he could tell her that without hurting her feelings. The truth was that down there she was just another *gringa rubia,* an artifact of his cultural sellout, and one who'd lost her history at that, a flaw that would be regarded as a sin in his culture. Here, he was just another operator and pathological liar; he'd failed to bring his good qualities with him across the ocean. His only real comfort was knowing that when he moved back down to Culebra, he'd leave all of this behind, including her. Her presence would be too strong a reminder of what he had done. It would be too real. "That's an idea," he said. He needed her to drive tonight and didn't want to have to fight two battles.

"I'll bet the weather's nice."

"Hurricanes," he said, tapping the tabletop. "Waterspouts."

"But warm."

"And rainy."

Something moved across her face, and he tried a different tack.

"Maybe seeing your parents would be a good thing. It might bring something back."

"Maybe," she said. "I think I'd take that hotel room, though."

"I would, too," he said.

"Should we eat?"

"We should," he said. He went into the kitchen and began to dish the stew out. "Trina," he said, "I need a favor."

"I know," she said, now just another weary, disappointed girl of the many girls Victor had left weary and disappointed. "Just let's eat first, okay?" The tone of her voice suggested that she knew exactly what he was going ask. She had known, he realized, from the moment she had walked in. He wondered what else she knew.

Seven

Ned Strickland was almost never alone. While he enjoyed the constant distraction, he had come to learn over the years that the greatest burden a doctor faced was that he was constantly being asked for an opinion on this or that matter, and that these opinions were forever being interpreted as facts. If the moral and intellectual status of his position was significant, it was also constant, and it was fair to say that the unceasing probity had flayed his conscience raw. The subject of right and wrong had come to possess an astringent sting.

In deference to the burnout that visited so many physicians, he did very little work when alone. Instead, he spent much of the time inspecting the frames of his many diplomas for dust, endlessly rearranging the trophies on his windowsill, or gazing out the window. Although he'd been in this office for years, he'd failed to make it entirely his; sometimes, during silent moments, he experienced a blind rush of vertigo, and a certainty that another man was hiding somewhere in the room. Nights, he dreamed of this man. He was very old, with red eyes and pale skin, and he never spoke. It was understood that Ned had supplanted him. The regularity of these nightmares had caused Ned's wife to wonder aloud if he should seek therapy, or at least some minor-league sort of medication.

It was late afternoon, and raining. He would have preferred to spend these fifteen minutes (a staff meeting approaching) reading the paper, or walking barefoot on the carpet (as he often did to relieve stress), but instead he was reading a file he had been avoiding. His verdict could not wait. The first page read

Patient Ben William Bascomb
Patient No 165-61-1251
Evaluation Sweet/mtk
Date Wednesday, December 6, 2000

Notes Social and physical withdrawal, anhedonia, feelings of hope-lessness and guilt. Rapid cycler? Signs of self-destructive behavior. Family history of depression, suicide, alcoholism, drug abuse noted. Should remain hospitalized with further observation. Zoloft 50 mg PO qhs / Zoloft 100 mg PO qam.

All of this neatly typed, but handwritten immediately below it

Ned what's the deal with Warren??

Strickland deliberately ignored the last sentence—it was Ben's health that was at issue here, and not Warren's—and turned the page to read the transcript. It was a hefty, comprehensive evaluation, not unusual for Dan Sweet. In a field full of overachievers (and, Ned noted, hopeless manic depressives who killed themselves at a staggering rate, six times the normal rate, last he had checked), Sweet had perhaps the most impressive *curriculum vitae* he had ever seen. The youngest Rhodes Scholar in history. Chief Resident. Published a book of poetry at twenty-four. And all this despite being abandoned by his father at birth. Or because of it?

Emma told me you've been having financial troubles. She's very upset. Very frightened. I think she was worried about your daughters, and she wanted to get them out of this, ah, environment for a while.

[Pause] I guess I can understand why she did that. We've had trouble. Since the business—[Patient falls silent]

Since your business failed.

I dislike the word fail. Fail is a word stamped on your spelling test. It falls short of the truth. Other words seem so much more appropriate, words like *crash, bomb, flop. Fold. Collapse.* I lost twelve contracts my first year, almost as many the second. By the third year there weren't any left to lose. We've had trouble ever since.

Ned had met Ben's wife at least twice. Black hair and green eyes. Yes, a very attractive woman, but one somehow not quite self-possessed enough to realize it. Whenever she was happy, she would blink rapidly and occasionally blush. You sensed that she had her thumbs pressed firmly to more than a few cracks in the emotional dike. Life, Ned guessed, had been difficult for her. Yes, she was a complicated woman. He was sure of it. But she certainly wasn't the sort of woman who cost a lot. Clearly. Ned understood women who cost a lot—he had married one—and he was certain that Emma was not one of them.

When did that happen? Your business, ah, failing. I remember—

Five years ago.

I remember that. It was in the papers. I even knew some people who worked there.

I'm sorry they lost their jobs.

Everyone's doing all right, if that's what you mean.

[Patient is silent]

You dislike talking about it?

Of course he dislikes it, Ned thought.

Of course I dislike it. We're talking about lost jobs here. Lost livelihood. I feel responsible. I wonder sometimes, How many divorces? How many bankruptcies? Dear God, how many suicides? How many people who lost their job and headed straight down and never came out of it?

Maybe you need to reevaluate, Ben. This wasn't something you engineered, right? I doubt that it happened because you didn't try hard enough. What might you have done differently?

I wish that I had gone to business school. I wish that I'd armed myself with some experience before I took control of the ship.

Why didn't you go to business school?

Grandfather wouldn't allow it.

He felt that strongly about it?

He suggested a few times that his experience at Harvard was not so good.

Anything in particular?

He didn't like the atmosphere. We talked about that a lot. He liked to say that the professors were the purveyors of an American dream gone berserk. That they had infected the students with the disease of postwar greed. And William, you understand, was a child of the Depression. He had been raised to think that sharing, even with one's enemies, was the only way to survive hardship. So when the profs talked of raising businesses from the ashes of Eastern Europe, he was horrified. He saw that as perversion. An enslavement.

I don't understand.

What don't you understand?

I've talked to people who knew him. Every one of them said that he wasn't so forgiving.

You're right. The man I knew was about as forgiving as a butcher block.

And that was William—everyone had known William, with his Gatsbyesque cachet: William the New Money manic-depressive alcoholic Faustian seriocomic et cetera. Three years dead. A man, Ned thought, of singular strangeness, possessed of more emotional tics than a narcissist's convention. Ned had had more than a few conversations with him, and all had careened from basic turpitude to a Grand Guignol of baroque self-pity. Ned had always thought of him as an emotional time-bomb, but the sort that went off one or two generations later. And here I am, Ned, he thought. Here I am, my finger on the tripwire.

What changed him?

[Long pause] His classmates. They, ah—

You don't—you don't want to talk about it?

The richest kids in the class singled him out because he was poor. He was hazed pretty badly, worse than most. One of them even pissed in his mouthwash.

He didn't use it.

He did. [Pause] For a few days after that, he was Piss Mouth. Then he was Mr. Piss. And finally, he was Piss-puss, which unfortunately stuck. It got so he couldn't go to a bar without someone shouting out, Hey Piss-puss, want a drink? William considered himself a dignified man, you understand. But when he told me about what they had called him. [Pause]

After he got out of business school, he was put in charge of quality control at his father's laundry equipment factory. His father wanted to retire in a few years. As soon as William took over quality control, the new lines of washers began failing, the wiring melting, and the engineers couldn't seem to figure out why. The problem got worse and they started to lose contracts. One night his father threatens to fire him. William is distraught. A failure at something that's been handed to him, see? He drinks some Bushmill's, starts feeling angry, drinks some more and starts feeling enraged, starts tasting the piss that he had drunk, and then his rage turns into something else and he grabs a claw-hammer from his toolbox and goes out to his car. He's never amounted to anything more than "Piss-puss," so he decides he's going to find Hunter Haskell, the man rumored to be the defiler of his mouthwash, and pound his skull until the red meat shows.

He drives across town and pulls up to the front entrance of Haskell Electric and waits until dark. Hunter comes out and sees him and shouts, "Hey, Piss-puss! How have you been?" and Hunter's end is all but sealed. William is about to grease his ass. But as Hunter walks up to the car, he says that he's been meaning to call William with an idea his brother-in-law, a biological researcher, gave him. He steps into the car and sits right next to the angel of death himself. Six months later, Haskell drops dead of a heart attack. William takes the idea for himself, Bascomb Laundry becomes Bascomb Centrifuge, and William becomes a rich man making machines that separate blood. And William had the business patent, so for seven years he was the only one who could make money off it.

Such a remarkable discovery for such a tainted family, Ned thought. Though in truth the discovery hadn't been William's. It had been someone else's, and he had taken it as his own as payback for all the humiliation. The family, he reflected, had profited from intellectual theft. The Bascombs were living on a bedrock of counterfeit respectability.

And this changed him?

He intended to kill a man. I've been angry with many people in my life. Furious. But never once have I gone to find someone with the actual intent to kill them. I think it frightened William to have been pushed so far. And yet he didn't blame himself. He blamed Hunter.

Sometimes we would be sitting out on his porch after dinner and he would look around at his land and say, "Hunter Haskell owes me this, Ben." He would rock in his chair and say it over and over. It soothed him. I think he came to believe it. Eventually he started using it as an excuse. If he had to fire good workers, good men with families, just to cut his payroll costs, he would say, "Hunter Haskell owes me this, Ben." Eventually, he tried to draw me into it. He started to say, "Hunter Haskell owes *us* this, Ben."

I tried to understand. This was a man who had been raised in poverty. His father had started the laundry factory with a loan from his uncle, and William had had no choice but to take it over and learn to make it work. It was that or starve. So he went to business school. And at business school, the most important thing he learned was that the poor will always have to drink the piss of the rich. The weak will always drink the piss of the strong. He never wanted to forget that, and he never wanted me to forget that. He even gave me his Harvard ring so that I would remember what had happened to him every time I signed a check, started the car, took out my dick to piss. *Veritas.* Truth. As long as the business worked, he said, he'd never have to drink any-one's piss again. And he had the benefit of blaming every ounce of the cruelty that success required on Haskell.

The story had achieved the status of local legend, in the way the lives of the very strange always do. Disillusioned William attempts to correct his own mistakes by having a son. Warren. Unfortunately, son kills mother in childbirth. Family of two soldiers on. Son is never quite forgiven for assassinating mother through his existence, and is constantly reminded of this. Is forced through medical school, where he is expected to collapse under the pressure of his own emotional debt. Instead, he flourishes—not

to the degree of a Dan Sweet, but does achieve notoriety as a gifted surgeon. Spends three years in Africa, just to irk father. Father attempts to
irk son by taking grandson Ben under his wing, except grandson Ben
has neither the talent nor the disposition for business. Carefully cultivated,
successful business collapses lickety-split. Son Warren remains traitor.
Grandson Ben is labeled Samson. All blame is neatly removed from now
alcoholic, severely depressed grandfather, who later sets the fire that will
be his demise—as an insurance scheme, or out of sheer madness, no one
knows. Curtain.

Ned skipped ahead two pages and read

How soon after all of this was the fire?

About two years after the business failed for good. Three years and a
few months back.

How much do you remember about it?

Late August. The neighbor called and said William's house was on fire.
I stepped outside with the phone and could see the smoke drifting
over the tops of the trees.

Emma and I pulled into William's driveway just behind the fire
trucks. William was four stories up in the attic, shouting for help
and throwing boxes and paintings and pieces of furniture out the window. The problem was, it was such a long drop that everything he was
trying to save splintered when it hit the lawn. There were broken
pieces of furniture everywhere. The flames had leaped over to the
barn and it was burning furiously. The old man had ignored his horses
to save his furniture. He had ignored living, feeling things for inani-
mate objects. You could smell the burning flesh and hair from the
barn, the burning leather, burning manure.

One of the firemen broke open the barn door with an axe and a
horse broke out in a long white streak of flame. It galloped across the
back field, trailing fire and setting the brush alight, zigzagging around
until one of the policemen took out his sidearm and tried to put it out
of its misery. The first shot missed, but I think the horse got the idea

because it froze, and I saw it standing there in flames, shivering and waiting for the kill-shot. He put a bullet right through its heart, right behind the front legs, and the thing went over in a flaming heap. He ran up to it and shot it twice more in the head to be sure, and then two firemen ran over with shovels to put out the brush that had started up around it.

By this time the first two floors of the house were engulfed in flames. You could feel the heat from thirty yards away. The bricks in the chimney began to explode. The attic windows vented streams of black smoke. Every now and then you saw the old man as he pitched something out the window. He was still shouting for help, and I realized that he didn't mean help for him. He meant for us to help him save his *things.* The firemen were trying to get a ladder up to him, and all of us started shouting for him to jump.

Then Warren came running down the driveway. Still in his pajamas. Never hesitated. He ran right by us, in through the front door, and then he was gone. The old man was still pitching furniture out the window. The last thing he threw out was the Wyeth, *Study for Siege of the Round-House.* It hadn't been harmed by the smoke, but the frame cracked when it hit the lawn. Then the roof collapsed and a huge gout of that black smoke boiled out into the sky, and in a few moments Warren came back out the front door and he was on fire. Like the horse. He was screaming in this very high voice, almost womanly, it was. I can still hear it. He was running around just like that horse, setting the grass alight, and I thought to myself, If I had a pistol I'd put one in him, too. I could smell burning hair and cloth and the burning horses. They fell on him with a blanket and put him out, but he went on crying out.

Ned vividly remembered that day. He remembered visiting Warren in the burn unit the following morning, and thinking, What a sad, frail thing is the human body. How repugnant in sickness. How sad and frail your wife was, when you brought her to us. Pinpoint pupils. Lips and fingernails blue. When I saw her I thought, Christ is that woman dead. That is the deadest woman I ever saw, Warren, and I hope you haven't brought her here thinking we'd revive her. And now look at you. You're essentially dead, too, so let's be merciful about this. Let's make this quick.

And on the way out of the unit, Ned put the idea in the specialist's head that perhaps Warren should be skating on a larger dose of Levorphanol. He had never intended for Warren to end up as an addict—but he had, admittedly, been open to the possibility. Awake to it. He had seen it happen before.

How did all of this affect Warren?

It happened so fast. Even at the reading of the will—you could already smell the disease on him. Like something he couldn't wash off. This was only a few months after the fire, and he already had a habit. They say addicts are genetically predisposed to dependence, and Warren certainly fit the bill. He has this exquisite talent for redirecting blame.

What about the will?

I think we both stepped into that office with expectations. I expected a dignified and merciful signoff by a man whose life had sadly gone off track. I think Warren expected a final jab from the grave.

Which one of you was right?

We were both wrong, and we knew it as soon as the attorney started reading. "Even in signing the record of my death, I find myself charged with the preservation of the family's dignity." Et cetera. A lot of portentous talk, some really heavy-handed stuff from beyond the grave. To distill: Everything is yours, Ben. Warren gets nothing. Had you been less headstrong you might have reaped the fruits of my labor, et cetera. He talked in six different directions, you know? But the subtext was clear: your birth—your delivery, your very act of coming to exist—killed my wife, your mother, and I do not forgive you.

What else did he say?

I don't remember much. The last few lines did stick with me. He said, "A compromise, boys, is not an independent act. It is a step from a high windy place. After that first step, forces of nature assume control, and then the fall is no longer the man's, but nature's itself."

What hopeless self-absorption, Ned thought. What lavish self-aggrandizement. How terrible he must have been alive, this man who was so insufferable dead. He still exerts power over these two. Three years in the ground, and he is still enforcing his will.

Was he right?

He was paranoid. But yes, to a point I think he was right.

But you've said a few times that what happened with the business wasn't your fault. That it seemed to be out of your hands. How do you explain that?

I guess I got what I deserved.

Here was the time bomb. Here was the end of the fuse. *I guess I got what I deserved.* A shred of self-pity, yes. But also a sense of terrible punishment withheld. Genuine guilt. Everyone knew what had really happened when Ben's mother died. An accidental overdose? Please. Ben's silence on the matter here was so very eloquent. Everyone knew what had happened (everyone, apparently, except Sweet—or had the doctor decided to pursue the matter later?), and here was the evidence. Not this transcript, but this—situation. This downward revision.

You think you deserve punishment.

Yes.

What sort of punishment?

I'm not sure yet. But getting shot certainly didn't do the trick. I have a feeling it'll be up to me.

Is that why you were stealing from yourself?

[Patient declines to answer.]

I mean, do you think that getting caught was the punishment you were after?

Of course not. I never intended to get caught. We're about to lose the house and I had to do something. I had hoped to sell what I took and collect the insurance money, too.

Couldn't you find another job?

You have to keep in mind that my resume is composed entirely of the financial ruin of a single company. Not much call for a person with that sort of experience.

You said your father has wealth.

Had. Addiction has a way of ending medical careers. He lost everything. So now he comes to me. We have an arrangement with a friend of his that gets both of us what we need. He gets Dilaudid and I get house payments.

Addiction usually didn't end medical careers. Usually the addict was rehabilitated. Usually. But Warren was not. Warren was served up publicly, and by Ned himself. His credentials destroyed, his license revoked. In medical school, where the two had met, Ned and Warren had been the best of friends. But there had been a downward revision there, too.

If you found another way to make your house payments, it might help him get well. And it might be good for your feelings of guilt.

You have to understand, I need this more than he does. And it's an all or nothing deal.

What do you think will happen when you leave here? I mean these problems won't just go away.

[Pause] Honestly? I think more of the same. These are the things I'm not supposed to tell you, right? But truthfully it scares me a little bit. That there would be more of the same. I haven't enough cash to pay the February mortgage. We could be on the street by March or April.

Why don't you sell the house?

Sure. I'll sell it, and then I'll get a job fixing cars at the local gas station for minimum wage. You can't fix cars from an apartment. I need the barn for my business. Without it we're bankrupt. First we go bankrupt. Then we move in with Emma's parents. And then they find me hanging in the closet.

Let's hope not.

Let's.

And that was where the conversation ended—not with the breakdown, the emotional release that marked so many of these confessions, but with genuine dread for what lay ahead.

Ned turned back to the front page, intending to close the file, where again he saw Sweet's apposite question

Ned what's the deal with Warren??

Ned checked his watch; he was more than ten minutes late for the staff meeting. In his mind, he pictured the chatter of the assembled doctors, women and men not used to having their time wasted. *This,* he reflected, was what he was good at. The distillation and distribution of his will. He thought of the hospital staff as an extension of his family, as his children, and in many ways the staff had all the requisite players—the adult equivalent of the sullen teenager, the squalling infant, the willful two-year-old. Too, Warren had once been part of that family. Widowed Warren, orphaned, exiled by his one-time best friend, and only now beginning to understand the true nature of his disease.

Eight

A lthough more than thirty years had passed since he had left the Congo, Warren still thought often of a friend he made there, a medical anthropologist named Rhazi. They had met his second year in, and had spent the next year trying to get around the chilly indifference most men use to mask the pleasure they find in the company of other like men. Rhazi had come to Africa to write a book about the anti-malarial genesis of the sickle-cell gene, but he confessed on his last night in country that he'd wasted all his time writing a book that developed a new theory of human ecology.

I didn't think it was possible to have a new theory anymore, Warren said. He'd smoked far too much of Rhazi's hydroponic dope, and his thoughts had begun to achieve the circular logic of paradox.

Of course, Rhazi said. He dipped a new joint in his mouth and held the tip to the flame of his butane hurricane lighter. You lack imagination, Warren.

It's not my imagination. It's that nothing surprises me anymore.

Rhazi exhaled thoughtfully.

Bipedal parasites, he said.

Where?

Here. Rhazi snapped his lighter shut. Us. We're the parasites. The world cures itself of us with disease.

The next morning, Warren had awakened to a note taped to his watch. *Warren,* Rhazi had written, *I think you should stay in this little slice of heaven. R.* Heaven? he wondered. He wanted to believe it existed. But why here? Too hot, disease-ridden, filthy, dangerous. Machetes, malaria, lockjaw, parasites. How could this be heaven? He'd turned the note over and had found Rhazi's simple postscript, a sentence that had stayed with him always.

Heaven, Warren, is a place with no memory.

Perhaps Rhazi was right, he thought. Perhaps heaven was not such an unattainable thing. Perhaps it was only that our imagination had failed us. We lacked the vision necessary to dream a better place for ourselves.

Warren had decided that morning that he would drive to see Ned Strickland at home, where he would plead once again for Ben's release. Strickland lived just outside Lansing on Route Nine, in a neighborhood where all the homes were new, the in-ground pools deep and wide and brimming with still black water. Warren had convinced himself that morning that Ned would be more receptive to his pleas outside the stern environment of the hospital. He was prepared to humiliate, willing to threaten, and balanced in a state of resignation somewhere between.

Though the homes were new, each affected the architecture and sprawling leisure of Old Money. In late August, one resident had sprayed a chemical on his stone wall that caused moss to grow over the rocks in a single weekend. The following weekend, his neighbors followed suit. Driving into town that weekend, one received the disquieting impression that the town was being devoured by foliage. Whatever the immediate effect, the property value of all the homes had doubled and then tripled soon after, and passing Strickland's home with that knowledge never failed to inspire bitterness. It seemed unfair that one man should hoard such overarching luck. How, Warren wondered, could a man like Ned Strickland—the sort of man who was always snapping people with his wet towel in the hospital locker room—become such a success? It seemed undignified for someone so disliked to achieve a position of distinction. The answer to the question, he guessed, was that sometimes all you needed was to be very good at what you did. If you were, people respected you at the very least. Strickland was an excellent physician who possessed a banker's attention to the bottom line. His ability to pare the fat from the budget without compromising patient care was drawing him offers from the urban hospitals two hours south. He was on his way up.

And that wife. Twenty years his junior. Her stage name, the rumors went, had been Esmeralda. No last name. No Miss or Lady before it. Just Esmeralda. And the swapped out y at the end of her given name, Warren thought, revealed a great deal about her roots. The swapped out y in Cindi suggested trailer parks in suburban Las Vegas, hardscrabble yards teeming with dirty white faces and bad teeth. Virtually every man Warren knew publicly denigrated her and privately lusted after her. Warren had met her many times and had always found her to be vibrant and charming and utterly undeserved by Ned. She was every bit the lengthy showgirl of Warren's grimy teenage fantasies. Still, always friendly and certainly never snobbish. Never. Perhaps because of her humble beginnings? Strangely quiet for an attractive woman with such charisma. Some sort of verbal abuse going on there? A tyrant like Strickland, Warren thought, a man so at home in the linear push and shove of his professional life, might easily find himself stymied by the revolving complexities of a marital relationship. Likely, he simply mentioned now and then that if she didn't remember how lucky she was, he could jog her memory by exercising that pre-nup and sending her, penniless and divorced, back to her glorious job of singing topless before half-cocked businessmen.

She received Warren at the door, looking markedly tired for a Monday afternoon. Definitely some sort of abuse going on. "Hi, Warren," she said. "Ned said you might be stopping by this week."

A good sign. "Is he in?" The smell of her perfume caused him to shiver pleasurably.

"He's chipping out back," she said. "I was just having some coffee. Would you like some?"

Warren suddenly discovered an overpowering thirst. "I think I could use a five-minute breather before I take on Ned." As he watched her stretch to take a second coffee mug down from the top shelf of the cabinet, he wondered, What was it truly like to be her? Armored by her looks.

"I know what you mean," she said, bringing his coffee to the kitchen table. "He's been manic lately with the bills piling up. The putting green went in a few months ago and I haven't seen him for five minutes since. He says that while he's out there he can't think. Which, I gather, is the way he likes things." Her raised eyebrow invited Warren to join her in a slight dig at her husband, but Warren declined. Spousal attacks, in his opinion, were undignified. And one didn't enter a doorway simply because it was open. Over her shoulder, through the kitchen window, Warren saw Ned standing out on the green, lining up a putt. A gust of wind snapped his collar up, but his concentration remained unbroken. Held in his large hands, the putter looked insubstantial and almost comic. With a single smooth stroke he sent the ball twenty feet across the deceptively wavy green and dropped it neatly in the hole. *Presto.*

"Exactly how bad," Warren asked casually, "are the bills?" Is it possible, he thought, that Ned Strickland, so attentive to the hospital's bottom line, has overextended himself at home? Couldn't you simply have built yourself a smaller palace, Ned? Not as if you've got ten kids to house.

"The garage cost twice as much to build as we thought it would, and the contractors who built the house filed for bankruptcy this summer, so when the roof began to leak, we couldn't go after them. And I'll tell you, Warren, the new roof cost about half of what I thought the house was worth in the first place. And then the budget committee clipped a bit off the top of Ned's salary—I mean, I think he could have fought that, but in fact he supported it . . ." She trailed off. "But I'm boring you. Poor little rich girl, right?"

"Everyone's entitled to a few minutes of feeling sorry for herself." He was beginning to feel sorry for himself. If he had known Ned was overextended, he might have approached things differently from the start.

"I don't mean to go on," she said. She warmed her palms against her coffee cup. "You hear about families who stretch themselves too thin, and when they hit a tough spot, everything collapses. The next thing you know the bank is auctioning off their house. I don't want that to be us. I don't want to be a cautionary tale you tell to your grandchildren. I was always happy having less, you know. But Ned has this opinion about the appearance of . . ."

The back door slid open, and a cold draft swept the kitchen. Ned stormed the room, dropping his putter on the counter with a jarring clatter. Cindi winced. "Hi Warren," he said. "What's the occasion?"

"I was just telling Warren your views on keeping up appearances," Cindi said.

Ned's back was turned as he poured himself a cup of coffee. He was silent for a moment. "Warren," he said, "should know quite a bit about that already."

"And what is your opinion, Ned?" Warren asked.

"My opinion," he said, walking to the table and giving Cindi an ironic kiss on the top of her head, "is that nothing is so expensive as wealth. So why not get it at a discount?"

"Ned has so many angles," Cindi said, "he's often mistaken for a rhombus."

"Darling," Ned cautioned, sitting beside her.

"I'm sorry about your roof," Warren said smugly. Ned's face pinched so tightly that it seemed as if under the table Warren had kicked him squarely in the crotch.

"I guess we'll know come the first snowfall if the new people did it right," Cindi said. "You should have seen us this summer. That first night they removed the tarp we had a few inches of rain. I came awake suddenly in the middle of the night. Water is dripping on my face. Next thing you know Ned and I are running around the attic naked, waving mops and slinging buckets and knowing it's not doing a bit of good.

The rain's coming in from twenty different places, and there's an inch of water on the attic floor." She laughed and squeezed Ned's hand. Warren imagined Cindi running naked with a mop.

Inside the garage, Ned selected a putter from his stash of secondhand clubs leaning in the corner and handed it to Warren. The pendulous head of the putter swung easily in his grip as he followed Ned up the crushed stone path to the green. "What are you going to do when there's snow on the ground?"

"Shovel," Ned answered grimly.

"I've got to hand it to you, Ned. I think you've fooled everyone. I always assumed this home was tip money to you. Must be rough, being broke."

"Count on Cindi," he said, "to confuse forthrightness with honesty." He lobbed a handful of golf balls around the green.

"In her defense, I was asking about the bills at the hospital, and she misunderstood." He watched silently as Strickland lined up a fifteen-foot shot. The putt seemed to be headed toward a spot three feet to the left of the hole, but a slight groove at the edge of the hole angled the ball sharply to the right, and it sunk into the cup with a sound like a marble rattling in a jar. "You know," Warren went on, "I was thinking as we were walking up here that you remind me quite a bit of my son."

"If you truly believe that," Ned said, "then you have sadly misjudged the seriousness of Ben's situation."

"You both hide debt as skillfully as my wife used to hide blemishes. You both consider wealth to be the solution to your problems. You both show a facility with objects that strike other objects. You both have wonderful wives who are unappreciated yet, for reasons even they don't understand, continue to support you. Both of you, one might think, would have it made if you would just pull your heads out of your asses."

Ned's putter flicked out and the head struck Warren just below the right kneecap. The superior tibial crest. Warren collapsed in pain. He held the spot with both hands for a moment, his entire body trembling, his face pressed into the maternal softness of the clipped green. He tasted the sweet grass and the slightly bitter chemicals that sustained its brilliant emerald color. When he rolled onto his back his hat fell off and he was suddenly aware of the cold wind on his bald spot. Strickland was standing over him.

"Don't ever talk down to me, Warren," he said. Definitely some sort of abuse going on there. He dangled the putter over Warren's face, let the chilly steel head slide across the lines of his mouth, his jaw line, the bridge of his nose. "I could crack you like a boiled lobster. Any time I want. Understand?"

Warren said he understood.

"You may think," Strickland added, "that your son and I have quite a bit in common—perhaps we do—but as of now all those similarities are qualified by the single fact that he is on the inside and I am on the outside. I'm sure you would agree that this is a small problem with your theory?"

Warren nodded. The steel head of the putter felt very cold against his left eyelid.

Strickland dropped the putter and squatted down next to him. "Here's what I'm guessing. I'm guessing that Ben funds your Dilaudid habit. I'm guessing that he refuses to support it further until you get him released. And I'm guessing that you're about to ask me once again to spring him so that you can both continue in your fucked-up ways."

"Something like that," Warren said. He sat up and replaced his hat. He tried to stand and for the moment could not.

Strickland grew pale at the sight of Warren trying to stand. A dismay that was entirely unlike him moved across his face. He stretched out his hand to help Warren stand but Warren ignored it. Strickland put his elbows on his knees and folded his hands. "What I'm doing, Warren, makes sense to everyone not involved. I don't doubt that you believe things would get better if I would just leave you and Ben to your own designs. But I don't trust you at all, Warren. I don't think you can trust yourself. You may intend to clean yourself up, you may intend to pilot your son into a steadier emotional state, but tomorrow, the next day— something could come up, right? Some unexpected need could arrive. Because when you get down to it, there's only one thing a man with your affliction has to do with his day. His intentions are meaningless. It's not, I think, that being an addict is so terribly important to you. It's just that everything else is so terribly unimportant. And I will not facilitate that. Your son is a relatively young man with a family, and I will not orphan his two daughters to support an old man's—a nearly finished old man's—addiction."

"Would it help if I threatened you?"

"You could give it a shot. Everyone can be gotten to. Everyone has one thing he mistakenly believes he can't live without."

"And what's the thing you can't live without?" Warren asked. He bent down and retrieved the ball from the cup. The thought occurred to him that in medical school he had considered this man to be his closest friend in the world.

Strickland gave him a quizzical look. "You have to ask?"

Victor was asleep on the couch when Warren got back to the house. He'd built a fire but hadn't opened the flue and the living room was filled with smoke. Warren opened the flue and threw open the windows and cold air rushed into the room. "Wake up, shithead."

Victor lowered his boots to the floor and sat up, rubbing his eyes with his index fingers. "Any luck?"

"None. In fact I may have made things worse. Where did you learn to build a fire?" Warren stabbed at the coals with the iron poker. The fire didn't really need to be stirred, but he thought he might need some sort of weapon in the next few moments.

"I guessed. It's just fire and wood, right?" He went into the hallway bathroom and threw water on his face. "I called Ben again."

"That so?" Warren sat on the couch and lay the poker against the arm of the chair. "I didn't think they could take outside calls."

"It's not prison, Warren." He came back into the room, wiping his face on a hand towel. "Anyway, he didn't go for it. Said what's buried stays buried until he gets out."

Warren pinched the fabric on the arm of the couch between his index finger and thumb. "Then we've both done what we can. We'll have to wait."

"But it doesn't work that way, Warren." Victor walked over to the couch and stood over him. He picked up the iron poker and set its tip on the floor before him, resting his palms on top of the handle. Warren thought that getting hit by it would feel a lot like getting hit by a golf club. "We'll never catch up. Wes doesn't want Trina driving any more. Theo has his scag hang-up. And Wes is getting upset. So we have two problems. I need a reliable driver, and I need that six hundred dollars back. And I should get reimbursed for that shit going up your arm. No freebies here, Warren."

"I could drive."

"That El Dorado," Victor said, "is a rolling felony. And I don't trust you."

"It's our only option, Victor."

"If I were to repossess your precious analgesic, I'm guessing you'd think of something else quickly. You'd think of something very quickly."

"Is that where we are?"

"That's where we are." Victor stepped back and took a golf swing with the poker.

"Well then," Warren said. "I guess we dig."

Victor walked into the kitchen and began to search around in the refrigerator. He was whistling—badly—an old Brubeck tune, *Kathy's Waltz* or *Pick Up Sticks,* and because Brubeck melodies always made him think of the time he'd taken Linda to see their quartet in Boston, Warren walked outside to study Emma's garden. His knee had stiffened noticeably and he knew it would be very bad tonight. Tomorrow, after they had spent the night digging, it would be worse.

They waited until it was completely dark outside. Warren located two flashlights in the hall closet and they carried them out to the barn, where Warren found Victor a pick and selected a shovel for himself. They went out to the garden and began to dig at the earth. There was a layer of frost just below the topsoil and it was hard going and as Victor began to work and then sweat, he recalled how much he had always hated physical labor. He hated it because he knew that most people thought of physical labor as being beneath everyone but his sort. The immigrant. Never mind how long he had been here. He also hated it because his mother had labored for much of her life for these same people who looked down on him, and he had begun to worry that the work was killing her. He hacked at the earth with his pick as he thought about her. She had raised him alone on a small island named Culebra perched twenty miles off the Eastern coast of Puerto Rico. He planned to visit her a few days after Christmas, and the thought of seeing her made him feel happy.

The only affordable way to get to the island was the ferry, a hellish one-hour ride across open ocean. It was always packed with islanders returning to their *municipio* from visits to relatives in Old San Juan and with tourists who had flown south to see the beaches on the west side of Culebra, rumored to be among the most beautiful and the most deserted beaches in the world. During the ferry ride back to Fajardo, the tourists would agree that rumors they had heard about the beaches were true, but that the ride had not been worth it because there was always a strong headwind and the three-story ferry would roll and roll. As soon as the boat hit the open ocean the honeymooners and families would all move to the rail, but the strong wind and their sickness and the drenching seaspray would conspire to make their aim untrue. Within fifteen minutes of leaving Fajardo, the gutters of the ferry ran with vomit. On the mainland, Victor would wait by the ticket stand in Fajardo reading the paper. If he ever heard a family talking about getting breakfast while waiting for the ferry, he would encourage them not to, but of course they didn't trust him and would never listen. He always waited in the front of the line, even when it was raining, so that he could get a seat on the benches on the ferry's deck, because at least that way there was open air. Below in the hold, the heat and the stench quickly became unbearable.

The temptation was to feel scorn for the sick vacationers. It was easy to resent their money and their silly new clothes and their hand-holding solicitude. Victor's mother had labored for these people all her life and had failed to make enough money with her tiny restaurant to retire, even in old age. But Victor still felt sorry for them. There were two bars by the dock in Culebra. In the evenings Victor and his friends would sit on the sidewalk outside the bars and drink inexpensive beers and watch the families preparing for the trip back to the mainland. The fathers and mothers of these families often had shell-shocked, thousand-yard stares. They would refuse to get the children anything to eat and would somberly hand out Dramamine pills and inspect the childrens' tongues to ensure that they had swallowed them. They seemed to be preparing the children for something they themselves were not ready for. Victor's friends would laugh and whistle and shout insults in Spanish, but Victor never taunted them. If the parents ever came close enough, he would tell them in English that they had nothing to fear because there was always a tailwind on the ride back to Fajardo—this was true, the ride home was as calm as a cruise along a glassy lake—because he couldn't bear the look of absolute dread on their faces. The act of bringing relief made him feel like a benevolent force in the world.

He had moved to New York ten years ago, expecting to encounter, quite innocently, someone exactly like himself, a native who would sense that he had been displaced in this city and who would dole out the same small bits of kindness that he once had. It took him more than a year to accept that he was waiting for something that was not coming. He had met many New Yorkers who were kind, but theirs was a kindness crossed by an armature of steely urban mistrust. They would lend you a dollar from their wallet but would not step close as they handed it to you lest you try to rob them of the rest. Was it because he was Puerto Rican? Or was suspicion simply embedded in their nature? What is wrong with you *payasos*? he would think, as someone refused to give him directions or rudely elbowed him out of the way on the subway platform.

And then one day he thought, *¿O me piensa el payaso?*

That was fine, if it was true. If they thought of him as a clown, as a joke, as the comical summary of every immigrant they'd ever met. People's self-importance, he'd found, could be used against them—it blinded them to their vulnerabilities. He would use it to make enough money to move back to Fajardo and relieve his mother of her burden. She would sell the restaurant and live off his money and finally she would have some rest. Most of his friends had stayed in Fajardo. While speaking with them on the phone, he often felt a stab of homesickness. He worried that if he didn't return home soon his mother would die. She was sixty-three and worked six days a week with only a local boy to help her wash the dishes every night before bed.

He stole joylessly and without anger and, laying in bed at night, his body tensing at the sound of each passing siren, he sought absolution in the image of his mother and the boy washing dishes. There was so much waste, she often said. The tourists never ate much.

Nine

———

Smoke," Emma repeated. She twined the telephone cord around her finger.

"From the chimney," Lila Schecter said. "I can see it right now."

"How long has it been going on?" Emma asked. She was sure that Ben was still in the hospital. The nightside nurse had just informed her, for the third time in three days, that Ben was deeply asleep and was not to be disturbed.

"Days. Maybe two, three days. Maybe more. We thought it was you."

"I've been gone for more than a week."

"Well," Lila said, "we did think it was a little strange that your car was gone."

The Schecters' twelve-year-old son, Gavin, had died four years ago after falling through the ice at Shrill Pond. He had been taking a short cut home from school and had dropped into the water only fifteen feet from shore. When the police arrived in Lila's driveway with the news, Paul and Ben were away at work, so Emma went with Lila to the pond, holding her hand in the back seat of the police cruiser as it slipped and bounced its way along the dirt road leading into the woods. Emma remembered very clearly how silent the woods around the pond had been that evening, and how sharp the edge of the ice seemed around the square of black water where Gavin had fallen through.

"You're sure you want to be here for this?" the fire chief asked. Lila said yes, so the fire department lifted him out with a crane, the frozen body twirling on the end of the rope like a dancer with arms outstretched, passing overhead dripping and then lowering to the upraised hands of the waiting firemen. As bad as things get, Emma thought, watching the body being lowered stiffly to the bank, at least I'm not Lila.

She wondered now if Lila felt that same way about her. "Have you seen anyone in the house?"

Lila was silent for a moment. "To tell the truth, we haven't. But there's been an awful lot of noise going on up there after dark. Last night Paul calls me over to the bedroom window about midnight. 'Lila,' he says, 'you have to see this.' Across the meadow I see two flashlight beams in the dark, bobbing around behind the barn near your garden. I just thought it was you and Ben getting your pipes unfrozen or something. But Paul says to me, 'Lila, their pipes are under the house. We ought to call the police.' And I told him to mind his own business and get back in bed. But then the McGraws phoned today and asked if we'd seen Ben lately, because they needed their front-loader and couldn't seem to find him. Well, I didn't want to spread any rumors, so I just told them Ben was away for a few days, and I'd have him call them as soon as he was back. So tonight after dinner Paul says to me, 'They're out there again. I'm going over to have a look.' He bundles up and takes the flashlight from the kitchen drawer and he's gone for ten minutes. When he gets back he says, 'Lila, you won't believe it. I went around behind the barn and wouldn't you know it? That garden is so torn up it looks like they're digging a new foundation out there.' You aren't digging a new foundation are you, Emma?"

"What else did he say?"

"'Someone's been using the McGraw's front-loader to turn every inch of the garden,' he says. 'Except whoever was using it didn't know the first thing about front-loaders, and now they've got it stuck. So they've started in with the picks and shovels, and it looks like it's slow going.' Have you got someone doing some work for you, Emma?"

"What else did he say?"

"'Well,' he says, 'I've seen a lot from the Bascombs, but for the life of me I can't tell what they're doing in the garden at midnight.' Should we have called the police, Emma?"

"No. In fact I don't want you to worry about it one bit, Lila."

Emma faintly heard Lila ascending her stairs, and a rasp of cloth as she pulled aside the drapes. "I can see them out there right now. Two flashlights in the dark. It makes me want to lock the door."

"I don't want you to worry, Lila," Emma said. "I'm coming back down in a few days, and I'll make sure everything's in order."

"But who is it?"

"It's Warren," she said. "Warren and a friend."

After she had hung up, Emma sat staring at the phone for a moment. The house was silent except for the tick of the grandfather clock. So Warren was out in her garden with someone else, certainly not Ben, out there this very moment rooting about the small square of earth that she had always thought of as her one place to hide. The garden was the one place where she felt a sense of control, of orderly cultivation—and Warren was tearing it apart. It was as if she had caught Warren searching through her birth control pills or her underwear drawer. She felt violated, and helpless to stop it, from this distance. She picked up the phone again and dialed information to get the number for the Lansing police department. The dispatcher who answered wasn't Rickey. "Look, lady," he said, "I've had two crank calls tonight. I can see you're calling from Massachusetts."

"Forty-two Skylark," she said. "There's a prowler."

"You must have good eyesight to see him from there."

"Couldn't you at least look?"

"You bet," he said. "We'll send our best guy right over."

In a rage, she hung up and then dialed her home number. Warren, slurring and disoriented, answered just as the answering machine picked up. "What?" he said loudly. "Who is it?" He sounded, she thought, just like Ben when he had been drinking.

We're not in right now, the fuzzy recording of Ben's voice said.

"I'd like to speak to Ben Bascomb," Emma said.

Warren paused for a moment. There was a loud beep as the machine began recording. "Speaking," he said, and she hung up.

Ten

————

B en was sitting on his bed reading his release forms by the bedside
table lamp when someone knocked softly on the door. The night
nurse opened the door and then wheeled Raif into the room. "He can
stay for a half hour," she said.

"I'm late for visiting hours," Raif said.

"It's not as if I make the rules," she said. "I'm just the one who has
to be the bad guy." She seemed genuinely sorry.

"Thank you for letting me stay."

Her face softened almost imperceptibly and then hardened again.
"One half hour," she said. "And then—" She drew her finger across her
throat and then closed the door firmly behind her.

Raif rolled his eyes. "She means it. What are you reading?"

"Release papers."

"How about that? When can you go?"

"First thing tomorrow. What does *in toto* mean?"

"*In the whole.* Why so suddenly?"

"I'm not sure," Ben said. "I haven't done anything but argue with them."

"You think your father might have pulled some strings?"

"He must have."

"Even with my handsome doctor?"

"Even with him."

"Too bad," Raif said, and sighed. "He seemed so earnest and uncorrupt. Well. Never look a gift horse, et cetera. All the better. We can use this to celebrate your parole." He unbuttoned his shirt and reached inside and pulled out a bottle he had hidden in his belt.

"I can't read the label from here," Ben said. He set the release forms on the bed. He was looking at the bottle. A small shiver moved through him, not a shiver of cold or of revulsion but of the sort he experienced when Emma's hair brushed lightly across his neck.

"This is called Aquavit." He held up the clear glass bottle and shook it lightly.

"I've never heard of it."

"Scandinavian. My mother used to drink it straight at dinner."

"Used to? What does it taste like?"

"Scented vodka." He turned the bottle under the bedside table lamp.

Ben had never explained to Raif that he was a white-knuckle drunk, but whether he had done this by design or simply because the subject had never come up, he didn't know. Either way it was too late now, and it seemed clear that only an intensely embarrassing moment would save him. This was, he reflected, how it happened—the grand backslide: you constructed situations where it became impossible for you to not have a drink. Afterward, you consoled yourself with the lie that there had been no choice but to drink. It was a pretty lie and like all pretty things it possessed the strange ability to destroy as it comforted. "I haven't had any hard stuff in years," he said.

"They'll smell it out in the hall if we're not careful." Raif grunted as he twisted in the chair to reach deep into his pocket. He pulled out two slender shot glasses and set them on the bedside table. When they were each filled to the brim with the Aquavit he capped the bottle and hid it in his shirt again. "I wonder what the penalty is for drinking here?"

Ben limped to the window and opened it all the way and cold air rushed into the room. For a moment he watched the faint pulse of a lighthouse far across Long Island Sound. He shivered again and pinched the neck of his sweater together as he walked back to the bed. Is this, he thought as he sat down, the way we give in? Not in despair or in hopelessness, but in celebration? Why do I feel as if I'm embracing something? He lifted the shot glass. Some of the Aquavit spilled, and he transferred the glass to his other hand and sucked the alcohol from his index finger. The taste brought tears to his eyes.

"Well," Raif said. "What do we drink to?"

"I don't know."

"Should we drink to your being ambulatory again?"

"Surrender," Ben said around his index finger.

"Surrender sounds nice."

They drank the shots down and then sat in silence for a moment. Ben counted the floorboards and tried to keep it down. He recalled that he had never liked the medicinal quality of vodka, not even when he had been a drunk.

"You look a little pale," Raif said. He was laughing.

"I feel like a teenager." He was frightened by how good it felt to drink again.

"Feeling like a teenager is a good thing."

Oh yes, it is good, Ben thought. He felt the alcohol begin its work. It was too late now, already in him. Past tense. Three years of sobriety, obliterated in an instant. But he hadn't felt like a teenager in such a long, long time. When was the last time he had felt like a teenager? Not since he had been a teenager, of course. Should they have another? he asked. Don't answer that, teach. Of course we should have another. Let me see that bottle. He took the bottle and uncapped it.

No, don't smell it, Westchester, Raif said.

I hate when you call me that. Never should have told you Anthony calls me that.

I know you hate it. So just drink it down. Don't bite it off. Hell and gore.

Hell and what?

I don't know, something like that. Hee-lawn gore. A little song my mother sang before she drank. It means take it all down, I think. See? That's no problem for you. We'll make a Norwegian out of you yet.

Is that Norwegian? Ben asked. Helling gore.

I can't remember. I can never remember what she is.

Your hair's dark though.

Yes, the old man's Italian through and through.

Where are they now?

She's dead. Sad. Rickety Baltic ferry. Can't swim. Blub-blub.

Yes, mine too.

I'm sorry.

I'm sorry, too. Nothing to be done about it. Helped her. The big cee.

Big sea?

Yes, big sea.

Just like mine. Let's have another.

Yes, another.

Sh. Someone's out in the hall. This one will be quiet. We just tap the glasses. Should we turn the little lamp out? No? You're afraid I'll try to kiss you in the dark. Ah, that was a joke, Westchester. I just like to see you turn pale. The truth is that I don't find you attractive.

Not attractive? Why the hell not?

You're too sad in the face. You seem so sad and frightened.

The hell I am. I've never felt better. I feel better now than you've ever felt in your pathetic life, teachey. Let's have another. I want to keep feeling this way.

But tomorrow you'll feel rotten if you do.

Save tomorrow for tomorrow. Are you with me?

Of course I'm with you, Westchester.

You're all right, teachey, Ben said. I've never had a drink with a Mo. What's a Mo? Raif asked. I'm not sure. I think it means homo. That's what the guys at the hardware store say. See, now I've made you mad. I'm not mad, Westchester, Raif said. I just don't understand you straight white guys. Finish another with me, teachey, and then tell me why you don't understand us. That's it. Ouch. All right. So tell me. Tell me you don't understand. I don't understand the jokes you make. What jokes, teach? You think that when you make friends with someone you can make fun of what they are. But I don't mean it seriously, Ben said. No, but you must never make jokes, Westchester. Never. You straight white guys should never joke. Well why not. Because the joke is never on you. Don't you read your Freud? You're laughing at me but I'm serious. There is aggression in every joke, Westchester. A joke presses a perceived advantage. The only person who can call me Mo and not be aggressive is another Mo. You white guys, you make a black friend and you can't wait until you can call him My Nigger. You get the essential thing all wrong. You think you are saying, I like you enough to call you this and not mean it. You think you are being ironic. When what you are really saying is, I am Westchester and you are My Nigger. I am Westchester and you are Raif the Mo. You see? Now we're all serious and not having fun. That is why you should never make jokes. It's better to be serious and let life make the jokes. Like my fucked up leg. Yes like your silly fucked up leg. That's a good joke life had on you. Nothing's funnier than a useless appendage, flapping. Now look what I've done. Don't be upset. I'm sorry, Bennie. Don't be upset. I'm not upset, teachey. I'm sorry. I don't think of you as Raif the Mo. I know. That's why I visick you. Visit you. Come on let's have another. All right, one more. Yes, one more and then I must go. What shall we drink to? Let's drink to being serious. All right, very serious-like. Hell and gore. Ouch. Yes, time to go. Of course I'll leave the bottle. The bottle is for you. Don't be sad, Westchester. You'll look even more unattractive to me. Now I'm making jokes. All right. A kiss on each cheek. No harm in that. See I left the lamp on for you. Good bye, Westchester. Make sure you call me because now we're friends. Yes, I forgive you. Of course. Goodbye. Goodbye.

After the nurse closed the door, Ben lay down and closed his eyes but the room began to whirl away without him so he sat up and closed one eye and tried to count the knots in the floorboards. The cold air from the window felt very good on the back of his neck. He couldn't remember how many drinks he had had. Six or Seven. Seven. Maybe

Eight. Christ it was strong. Big shots. No dinner. Too bad about his mother. Rickety ferry. Deck-sprawled. Quick though.

In the bathroom, he turned on the cold tap and ran the water over his head. The cold water felt very good even though he was shivering now. He sat on the tile floor and felt his damp hair drip down his back, wetting the collar of his sweater. One more drink before bed. He was glad that he was sleepy. Not like the old days. In the old days the drink had pushed him and pushed him and had sometimes kept him awake for days. Now he had it under control. After three years away, he had achieved a deep respect for its fearful power.

He must have fallen asleep, because some time later he opened his eyes with his forehead resting against the tile wall. In the bedroom, he lay down without undressing and pulled the coverlet over him. His hair was still wet. He remembered the bottle and the drink he had promised himself, so he picked up the bottle and had one drink and then replaced it behind the bed. Then he picked the bottle up again and uncapped it and had a second drink, tipping the bottle all the way up so he could watch the bubbles roll behind the glass. Then he capped it with authority and walked unsteadily across the room and heaved the bottle out through the open window with all his might. The bottle tumbled brightly through space for a moment and then vanished in the darkness. There was silence and then a small splash of sound from below by the train tracks.

Things could not continue this way. He could not keep driving for Victor. If he did, Emma would leave him, and now she and the girls were the only sane, focused things in his life. Without them he would start drinking again, and the whole thing would play out over and over, like a dull looped tragedy with far too many acts and very little poignancy. Because that was how life went—first you compromised a little. Then you compromised a lot. First things went a little wrong. Then they went a lot wrong. And then your only option was to keep going down.

He left the window open and went back to bed, where he pulled the lamp's brass chain. Then the room was dark with the faint square of light from the window.

Ben woke later in the dark with the room spinning around him. A notion came to him that cold air would clear his head, so he went to the window. He listened: the hall was silent, a locked and bolted mother-ship of chemical sleep, adrift. The lighthouse had vanished from the horizon. He was certain he had found it earlier, but now the light was gone, obscured by a cataract of fog.

In the morning Sweet offered to give him a ride home. No one had come to pick him up. "I'm sorry," the doctor said. He seemed very concerned. "I tried to contact your wife, but the number she left doesn't pick up. We get the answering machine every time."

"She must still be in Boston," Ben said. The bright sunlight hurt his eyes; he blinked tears. They watched two men repair one of the big white rigs. The hood of the rig was propped open, and some parts from the engine were laid out on a blanket they had spread on the ground before it. One of the men crouched and selected a small tube from the blanket, then held it up to the light and blew sharply into it. "Anyway, I don't mind walking. It's nice being able to go where I want."

"You shouldn't walk home on that leg. You'll freeze to death."

"No. I'll walk into town and get a taxi."

"But you have no money." Sweet took two twenty-dollar bills from his wallet and handed them to Ben.

"I can't take this." Looking at the bills made his throat ache.

"Of course you can. You'll pay me back."

"When?"

"I think we should talk next week. Here at my office."

Ben pocketed the bills and put out his hand awkwardly. "Thanks for your help," he said. They shook hands. He had been resentful, but now that he was outside in the sunlight he seemed to have a different understanding of what had happened. "You don't think I'm ready to leave, do you?"

"No," Sweet said. "I think it's too soon."

"I told you about Warren," Ben said. "When he wants something—"

"Forget about Warren," Sweet said.

"I'll try," Ben said. In his mind he had resolved to stop driving for Victor. They shook hands again, and then Ben began to walk. He turned to look back at the far end of the lot and saw that Sweet was watching him go. His leg ached but it felt good to be moving on his own, and the cold air helped his hangover. He wondered if tonight he would drink again. He didn't want to, but of course a thought you have on a cold, sunny morning is one thing. Once night falls, it's another thing altogether.

Eleven

As she brushed the morning sleep taste from her mouth, Emma tried to dismiss the heavy sourness in her stomach as a first-rate hangover, her penance for the three gin and tonics she'd drunk last night after her parents had gone to bed and left her alone with her copy of *Dubliners*. She always drank before going to bed now, a habit she'd developed after that awful first night here. After dinner, she downed at least three drinks while reading in her father's study and, when properly anesthetized, padded off to bed, often too tired even to brush her teeth. For the last week, she'd woken every morning feeling sick and foul-tempered, a sharp pain bisecting the back of her neck as she first sat up in bed, her mouth cottony. Drinking two glasses of water usually brought about a miraculous recovery. Today it did not. She sat on the edge of the tub and held a third glass of water with both hands but couldn't bring herself to finish it. Even water seemed to disagree with her.

The five of them had planned to drive to the mall before lunch, so she fought through the nausea and decided to eat a light breakfast. Her usual two cups of sweetened, amber coffee were cut to one, black; she stared at the ebony surface for a few moments before she was able to force herself to take a sip. Half a slice of lightly buttered toast, but no eggs—God no. God no.

"You all right, Em?" her mother asked, because she missed nothing. She'd noticed Emma's less-than-usual breakfast, just as, earlier, she'd noticed the sticky highball glass stashed in the back of the top rack of the dishwasher. She'd noticed the absent ice cubes, the grin of the quartered lime in the vegetable drawer, the sinking level of the handle of cabinet-gin. What she was really asking was, Enjoy yourself last night, Emma?

Have to get myself a spare, Emma thought. What Ben used to do. Beginning to see the logic in that one. Can't expect someone who cherishes sobriety to understand the need for a drink. Especially if you need the drink because of her. "I'm fine," she said, and rolled her warm coffee mug between her palms.

A few minutes later, as she was upstairs watching Nina and Sylva get dressed, something seemed to cavitate beneath her solar plexus, to flutter and collapse in on itself, and she realized suddenly that eating anything at all had been a fatal mistake. A cold sweat broke on the back of her neck. She left the girls and walked down the hall to the bathroom to stand before the toilet bowl for a few moments. At first she thought it was a false alarm, and she moved to the sink to splash water on her face, but then—in a sudden, audible heave—the small bits of toast and coffee she'd eaten came up. The sight of her breakfast crowding the drain, undigested, made her throw up again. The taste was vile.

"Sounds like a wicked bug, Em," her mother said, standing in the doorway.

Emma spat in the sink and waited to see if her stomach would seize again. She hadn't heard the word *bug* used that way in a long time. It fell squarely in her mother's lexicon of catchall words, alongside *tizzik* and *whosit* and the hundred other words she used when the right word was momentarily out of reach. *Emma, would you get me my car keys? I left them out in your father's workshop, on the—out on the whatsit. The whosit. The what, mom? The whirly-thing. You mean the lathe, mom? Yes, of course that's what I mean. The lathe.* Of course. Another of her parents' maxims she'd forgotten: if the right word isn't available, make one up. "I haven't felt well since I woke," she said. Truth is, she thought, I haven't felt well since I got here. Ergo, the three nightly *Dubliner*-drinks, which are usually sufficient to eradicate the night-think, the eavesdrop. They're better than Sominex, a warm bath, a good lay. They put me right to sleep. As bad as I feel now, mom, it's been a fair trade-off. But how could I ever hope to explain that to you?

"You want to stay home?"

"I think I should," Emma said. "Would you mind?"

"I think we could manage."

Emma ran the water to clean out the sink and then brushed her teeth. Now that she'd gotten everything out, she was, strangely, hungry. She pulled her hair back and checked her face in the mirror and went down the hall to get the girls ready. The floorboards were chilly beneath her bare feet. Her parents had always kept the house cold at night, a miserly Yankee attempt to forestall the startling winter heating bill, something Emma had obstinately rebelled against in her adult life. Even on balmy spring nights, she asked Ben to stoke the wood-burning stove and open the vents to the bedrooms. On more than a few occasions, the heat had sent him reeling from their bed to the couch and an open window.

Sylva was dressed, but had climbed back into bed under the covers. Since their first night here, she'd been having nightmares that the monsters from the *Epigenesis* board game were hiding in the closet. The two weeks of bad dreams had brought her to the brink of mutiny: every night, she stalled the light switch with glasses of water and bedtime stories; every morning, she was a zombie. Emma had summarily banned the game, and in the process had ended up as the Bad Guy. "Let's go, baby girl," she said. Sylva sat up and yawned expansively. Twice last night, she had left her bed and had walked down the hall to climb under the sheets with Emma. Which meant that Emma had probably picked up whatever it was that Sylva had. It would be a long night.

Emma spent what seemed five minutes helping the girls into the Bronco and fastening their seatbelts, a task that should have been relatively simple but never was. The bulky, fleeced cold-weather clothing made every task more difficult than it should have been, turning their mittened hands into useless appendages. When the maddening latching and tightening was done, Emma, arms crossed for warmth, backed away from the car to watch them drive away. The early morning sun reflected liquidly off the Bronco's waxed silver paint as it drove down the lane. She wished, suddenly, just an instant too late, that she could go with them—she was always realizing the simple things too late: alone, she'd waste the sunny morning. Since it was too cold to go for a walk outside, she went up the front steps and into the house, shivering now, and walked room to room downstairs, stopping occasionally to pick up and examine the picture frames and glass artifacts that crowded every tabletop in the house.

In the front hall, Emma considered the old black dial phone, the dynamic of its silence. Although Nina and Sylva talked to Ben almost every night, she hadn't spoken with him since the day they'd left. It was longest they'd gone without speaking in their almost ten years of marriage, and she wondered if avoiding him while he was hospitalized might qualify as abandonment in divorce court. She hadn't always been this stubbornly resentful. Even when he'd been drinking, she recalled, she'd watched over him in her own maternal way, and he'd been grateful, had returned her affection with his own sad, clumsy ploys: with bunches of flowers yanked out by their roots, with burned dinners, with a typically right-on-the-money birthday gift. The message he'd been trying to broadcast had been clear: *I don't want to be this way. Please wait for me to be what I was again.* As frightening an experience as that had been, they'd somehow gone through it together. After six months, his drinking had suddenly stopped. She had come downstairs on a blindingly sunny February morning and had found him sitting alone in the living room, a bloody rag held to his gashed hairline, scared sober by a car accident that had introduced the front end of his Saab to the guardrail and his forehead, violently, to the steering wheel.

Whatever Ben does on those Sunday nights, she thought, wherever it is that he goes, I know that it has more to do with Warren than it does with the cash he brings back. I will guarantee that what he does pushes Warren further down. That's exactly why he does it. He's not a risk taker. He's never been a thrill seeker. Accidents scare him. Violence scares him. *I think you like seeing him diseased like this,* she often said to Ben when the subject of Warren came up, and Ben never disagreed. The absence of a disagreement didn't necessarily worry her; she was content to leave Warren to his own vices. But it occurred to her now that Warren's disease had become contagious, and now they were all at risk.

She walked upstairs to her father's study to retrieve her copy of *Dubliners*. The book was face-down on the arm of the rocking chair—she'd been so looped she'd forgotten to mark her place and close it before bed. As she picked it up, she noticed a bound stack of her father's old leaflets laying on the center of his desk. They hadn't been there on the desk last night, which meant that he'd brought them down that morning. She sat at the desk and picked up the stack and removed the rubber band that bound them together. The first leaflet in the stack was one that she had seen many times before, handwritten in pencil with no artwork.

Hey VC, do you KNOW what your beloved is doing now? As you dig your foxhole to hide from the righteous BULLETS do you know what she is doing? As the MORTARS rain down on you do you know what she is doing? As you wait for NIGHT and the patrols of AMERICANS approaching in the darkness do you know what she is doing? As you risk your life for a GOVERNMENT being run by people who do not care for YOU, do you know what she is DOING? She is home with ANOTHER MAN who comforts her. She lets him comfort her because she knows he is not going to leave her and give his LIFE for a failing regime. Because that is what YOU are doing.

maybe drawing here could be vc in his foxhole scared shitless being shelled—or drawing of the wife—with another man yes i think that bc it's the image of her we want him to think about.

The leaflets, propaganda he'd designed during the late sixties for the National Security Agency, had been airdropped by the tens of thousands, a pastel storm that had fluttered down from the sky, mostly in Cambodia and north of the 20th parallel in Vietnam. As far as she could tell, they'd been intended to cause nothing less than deep moral and emotional turmoil. Considering the context, she guessed he'd succeeded on all counts. In the jungle at night, flares flickering through the trees, the simplest question must have assumed a crushing finality.

Occasionally he had—somewhat naïvely, Emma thought—appealed to the logic of the politicals.

Countryman, Prince Sihanouk needs YOU to repel the communist Red Khmer! The Khmer want to use YOUR country as an outpost of the Communist Party of Kampuchea. Countryman, they will ascribe ownership of your home to the STATE!

All his earnest capitalization. She wondered how well the emotion had translated. The writing seemed stiff and crude, even funny, until you considered what had happened just a few years later. More than a million dead. The educated and the skilled, anyone cursed with enough intelligence to pose a real threat, lined up in the killing fields and shot. On the sole occasion that they'd discussed his work for the NSA, during the short-lived pacifist stage she'd undertaken her freshman year at college, he'd told her that he sometimes dreamed of the people he'd failed to save, saw their faces, saw the bloody razor grass and the burning fields. But you can't save lives with words, dad, she thought. Peace doesn't evolve out of reason. It's a turning away. Peace is disgrace's antidote. Peace is what we're trying to find, now, the three of us.

She rebound the stack and walked into the bathroom, where she opened the mirrored cabinet to take down her mother's Valium. The white bottle was there on the top shelf—it hadn't been moved since she had arrived here with the girls. She twisted off the cap and shook two tablets into her palm. After she'd placed them on her tongue, she bent to drink from the faucet. The drain still smelled unpleasantly of the tang of bile.

Downstairs, she stretched out on the couch, where she hoped to get at least an hour of sleep. As the Valium began its work, gentle fireworks flared behind her closed eyelids and the sick feeling seemed to fall away.

In moments like this, she could almost identify with Warren. Almost.

She woke, feeling dull and slow, to the sound of the front door banging open. As she sat up, the girls spilled into the living room, exultant with sugar and caffeine, the festivity of their return marred only by her father's news that Nina had used a swear word when she had been told it was time to leave.

"Which one?" she asked.

"It begins with an *s*," Sarah said. "Ends with a *t*. The middle says *hi*." She hung her jacket on the closet hook and walked into the kitchen to put the groceries in the refrigerator.

Nina sat on the armchair, crossed her arms and began to cry.

"Nina," Emma said, "what do you say?"

Nina pulled her knit cap down over her face.

"I think that means she's sorry." She gestured to Nina and gave her father a look that she hoped said, *That's enough*.

He walked over to the chair and scratched Nina's head through the cap. She turned away from him and lay over the arm of the chair.

"Nina," Emma said wearily. "It's okay."

Nina sat up and took her hat off. Her eyes were red and the hollows beneath were dark. "When are we going home?" she asked.

"I don't know," Emma said. She tried not to consider the larger implications of redefining the word *home* for her daughter. Someday soon, *home* might mean an apartment. *Home* might be Portland or Atlanta. "Do you want to go home?"

"Don't you?"

She struggled for an answer. *Of course* was what was required, but it seemed like a half-truth. It occurred to her that Nina had never spent more than one night in a row here in her life. Emma had, from the day Nina had been born, willfully chosen to distance her children from her parents, and now that distance had collapsed. Nina had intuitively sensed that something was wrong. "I do," she said, "just not right now."

"What about dad?"

"Dad has some things to work out. He has to work them out by himself. We all have things to work out."

"But why do we have to be here?"

"What's wrong with here?"

"You don't even like it here."

"Of course I do." Which was the truth. It was a safe harbor. Right?

"No you don't," Nina said.

Nina was, Emma realized, angry with her. She was trying to articulate the fact that she suspected her mother was lying. "What don't I like?"

"You don't like gramma."

"I do too," she said. Suddenly she found herself near tears. Language had failed her, but only because you couldn't explain an entire childhood in a single conversation. "I do love her," she explained. "But I love her in a different way."

"No you don't. You treat her like Tilly."

Emma's cousin Tilly was a Manhattan ambulance-chaser with an icy disposition. At the Christmas party Jane and Mick Rhoden had thrown four years ago, Emma had offered a drunken impression of Tilly having sex, complete with objections and cross-examination. She had stopped when she spied Nina watching her from the stairs. It seemed incredible that Nina had remembered it. "That was a mean thing I did," she said. "I shouldn't have done that, and I owe Tilly an apology."

"I don't care about Tilly," Nina said. "I want to go home."

"Can you hang on a little longer? For me?"

"No," Nina said. She got up off the chair and walked upstairs. Emma debated letting her go and decided to follow her.

"What do you mean, no?"

"I'm going home now," Nina said.

"How are you getting there?"

"I'll go on a plane or a train."

"You don't like to fly."

"I'll go on a train."

"And where will you get the money for the ticket? A ticket costs a lot of money."

"Grampa will give it to me."

"You'll have to pay him back."

"I'll ask him," Nina said, "to give it to me as a Christmas present." She opened the closet door and dragged one of the large suitcases over to the bed. Sylva was laying on the floor with her *Toy Story* coloring book open before her. Nina began to pack her clothes into the suitcase.

"And what will you do when you get home?" she asked.

"I'll go see dad." Nina seemed resolute on this point.

"What will you tell him?"

She stopped packing for moment and thought about it. "I'll tell him," she said, "that I want to go to New York and see the tree."

She meant, Emma realized, the tree at Rockefeller Center. Almost a year ago to the day, the four of them had had an oddly perfect night there, getting their picture taken with the tree in the background and then having dinner and going ice skating after. There had been no fights and dinner had been fun.

The photograph hung now in the front hall at home. Emma had always thought of it as a sort of trophy. It was the last thing you saw before you left the house.

"Your father's not going to see the tree," Emma said. "He's in the hospital, and he won't be out for a long time."

"I'll tell them to let him out," she said. She began stuffing clothes in her bag again. Sylva had stopped coloring and was watching them with her mouth open.

"They won't let him out. He's sick," Emma said. She had meant to use *sick* as meaning unwell, as a pleasant euphemism for *deranged* or *misguided* or *depressed,* but had realized, too late, that in Nina's universe *sick* sounded even worse, even more judgmental. *Sick,* in Nina's vocabulary, meant *repellant. Sick* was what Emma had deposited in the sink a few hours ago. "The doctors want him to get better."

"He doesn't need to get better."

"He does," Emma said.

Nina abruptly zipped the bag shut, only half full, and then dragged it out into the hall. Emma followed her and found her mother standing in the bathroom doorway, the open Valium bottle in one hand, the cap in the other. Sarah glanced down at Nina, noted the packed bag, and seemed about to speak until Emma silenced her with a single look. Her mother went back into the bathroom and closed the door. As they passed the doorway, Emma heard the sound of the bathtub faucet turning and water coursing down the drain. Nina seemed momentarily stymied by the stairs, and then began dragging the bag down, a single step at a time.

"You're going to carry this the whole way to the train station?"

"No," Nina said, "Grampa's going to drive me."

Emma was waiting for the fury to crack. It had to happen any second. It had to. "Grampa won't drive you. He wants you to stay."

"How do you know?"

"He told me."

"When did he tell you."

"Just now. He said he wasn't mad at you for swearing and he wants you to stay."

She stopped at the bottom step to rest and then, incredibly, opened the front door and dragged the bag out onto the front porch.

"Now what will you do? Carry it?"

"No," Nina said. "You'll drive me." She dragged the bag down the front steps onto the front lawn. Across the street, a postal worker, heavy jacket zipped to his chin, stopped to watch them.

Emma stopped on the porch and crossed her arms. "I won't drive you."

"Yes, you will."

"No, I won't."

Nina dropped the bag. "You will."

"No," Emma said, "I won't. And there's nothing you can do about it."

Nina's lower lip began to quiver and a single tear slipped down her cheek. She turned and sat on her bag and put her face in her hands.

Congratulations, Emma thought, feeling sick for her daughter. You've just won an argument with a ten-year-old, and made her feel more confused than ever. You've made your point by obliterating hers. It occurred to Emma that she had brought the girls here to satisfy her own needs. She hadn't thought about what it would do to them. "Nina," she asked, "do you want to come inside?"

Nina shook her head.

She walked down the steps and knelt on the grass behind Nina and put her hand in her daughter's hair. "Are you mad at me?"

"Yes," Nina said.

"If we go home soon, will you stop being mad at me?"

"Yes," Nina said.

"I want to go see the tree, too."

"When we get back," Nina said.

I doubt it, Emma thought, and sat beside her on the suitcase. I doubt anything will be the same.

After dinner, Emma went upstairs to her father's study. The leaflets, she noted, had neatly vanished during the afternoon. Like her mother, her father missed nothing. He'd noted the skewed angle of the stack, the slightly turned rubber band. He knew immediately that she read them and had whisked them away, the deed done.

She dialed the number for the hospital and spent five minutes on hold listening to elevator music while the operator connected her to the short-term care ward. A nurse with a light Russian accent answered and Emma asked to speak with Ben.

"Are you a friend or relative?"

"I'm his wife."

"I see," she said. "Weren't you supposed to pick him up this morning?"

"Has he left?"

"This morning," she said.

"Is he—" Emma thought for a moment, "—is he better?" She wasn't exactly sure what that meant.

"Well," the nurse said, "it was kind of sudden. And we didn't appreciate the way he acted last night."

"What happened last night?"

"His friend showed up. The good-looking one with the dark hair?"

Warren's friend, she thought. "And what happened?"

"His friend smuggled something in, and they got drunk as the four horsemen."

Emma didn't answer.

"The friend—" she made a clucking sound with her tongue, "—he's not so good, you know? My husband would say he needs a bullet for a cure."

"You may be right," Emma said. She hung up and dialed the number for the house. Ben didn't answer and the phone rang and rang and the answering machine didn't pick up. She placed the receiver back in its cradle and sat back in the chair. From downstairs, she heard the cheerful murmur of the animated Christmas special the girls were watching with her parents. So we've both started in again, she thought. We'll try this one more time.

Her father knocked on the door jamb. "Any news?" he asked. He looked bored and hungry for conversation.

"Ben's home," she said. "At least, I think he's home. He's not at the hospital anymore." She debated telling him that Ben had drank and decided not to. It would only complicate things.

"I guess that's good news," he said.

"I guess so. If they discharged him they must have decided he was all right."

"Do you think he's all right?"

It occurred to her that Ben might be at a bar this very moment. She thought of the bloody rag he'd held to his forehead on that sunny winter morning. "I hope so," she said.

"There's not much you can do," he said. "I've been there, you know?"

"I know. I've been there, too."

"You have. But not the way I was. Now you see. You have to be a wife and a mother. It's not enough to be one or the other."

"Seems like an awfully dated way to define a woman."

He shrugged. He didn't mean it as an insult and she knew that. "Nina seems a little better," he said.

"She wants us to go home."

"I'll bet she wants a lot of things. But kids don't always want what's best for them."

Emma wondered if he wanted them to stay. She was about to ask him something to this effect when the girls were herded up the stairs by her mother.

"Carl," her mother asked, "could you rig a night light in the closet for Sylva?"

"I think I could manage that," he said. He looked back at Emma and then went downstairs. She heard him open and then close the door to the basement.

Emma followed her mother and the girls into the bathroom and sat on the edge of the bathtub and watched them brush their teeth. Nina, she wanted to say. Nina, your father's started drinking again. He's there and I'm here and there's nothing I can do about it. I'm sorry I made you feel bad today, baby girl. I'm sorry I made you feel that way because I think we're all about to feel a lot worse.

"You missed a good show," her mother said. She bent and spat in the sink and Emma realized she'd forgotten to clean it.

Nina and Sylva put their toothbrushes in the coffee mug on the back of the sink and walked down the hall. The mug said, YOU'D DRINK TOO IF YOU HAD MY JOB.

"You can have five minutes of quiet time with the lights out," Sarah called after them. She finished brushing and placed her toothbrush in the mug.

"Ben's out of the hospital," Emma said.

Her mother turned and leaned against the sink. "Did you talk to him?"

"I called home. But he didn't answer. I'm a little worried."

"He's probably out working," Sarah said. "I bet he's really backed up."

She hadn't thought of that. Her mind had immediately fixed itself to the worst possible alternative. "You may be right," she said.

"That was quite a fight with Nina," she said. "You want to talk about it?"

"It was nothing," she said, which came out sounding like *None of your business* or *It doesn't concern you.* When of course what had happened had concerned her, in every way. "She wants to go home. I haven't really told them much. Without her Ritalin, I think she gets upset a little more easily. A little more quickly."

"I can understand how she feels."

"I guess I can, too." She thought for a moment. "I guess I feel that way, too."

"You want to go home?"

Emma rubbed the back of her neck. "It seems like the right thing to do. I mean I brought them here because I didn't think it would be good for them to see him that way. Keeping them out of school isn't helping. Nina's falling even further behind." This was, she reflected, the most civil conversation she'd had with her mother in a decade, and she wondered how much of it belonged to the guilt she felt over Nina's Tilly comment from earlier. Of course she liked her mother. Of course she did. Of course she did.

"You may be right," Sarah said. "Maybe that'd be best for them."

Her father walked past the bathroom and into the main bedroom.

Emma realized that, unlike her father, her mother didn't necessarily need them here. She wasn't being spiteful or cold; it was just that she had, however late in life, achieved a degree of comfort with herself. She was happy without them. "So what do we do now?"

"You think on it for a few days," Sarah said. "You see it. Then you do it."

"About those pills," Emma said.

"I understand," Sarah said. "Believe me." She stepped close to Emma and, incredibly, kissed the top of her head, then crossed the hall to the bedroom and shut the door behind her.

Emma watched her own shadow that stretched across the hallway floor and wall, at rest on its bathtub perch. For a moment, she listened to the drip of the faucets, the tick of clocks—the human sounds had been absorbed by night. Houses at night, she thought, do this: they absorb the people you love. Houses at night subtract and isolate with sleep.

She debated taking another Valium—it was that or the handle of gin—when Sylva suddenly presented her with another option: she called from her bed to ask if her mother would check the closet. She decided that she would allow herself to accidentally fall asleep with one of them. After she had snapped off the bathroom light, she walked down the hall and pulled the chain to show Sylva the nearly empty closet—coathangers shone on the rack. An ancient vacuum cleaner stood guard over the empty suitcases.

"Mom," Nina whispered, "do you think Leelee looks like Tilly?"

Emma lay down, uninvited, beside Sylva and watched the ceiling. Nina was speaking of Mick and Jane's daughter Ellie. Both she and Tilly were strikingly beautiful. "I guess so," she said. "I've never really thought about it."

Sylva rolled close and placed one splayed hand on Emma's stomach.

"Leelee still believes in Santa Claus," Nina said. The disdain in her voice was impossible to miss.

"Give her time," Emma said.

Twelve

A subway train rolled by on the elevated tracks outside the window and brought Warren fully awake. He had been gliding in and out of hallucinatory dreams for the last hour, and now that he was awake he didn't know where he was. Looking around the room, he remembered that he was at Victor's odd, spare Queens apartment. For some reason, the shelves and walls were adorned with empty picture frames.

How and exactly when he had gotten here was a mystery. He sat up in bed and lit a cigarette but pitched it out the window when the first drag sent his head spinning. Thirst drove him to the kitchen sink, where he drank with his head tilted beneath the faucet for what seemed an eternity. He vaguely remembered going to a bar down the street with Victor. The two of them had driven all the way to Garden City yesterday evening, where they had passed off the silver they had found in

Ben's barn with a friend of Victor who worked for a wholesaler. The deal had paid off the Dilaudid Victor had fronted him.

During the drive back to Queens, Victor—being Victor—had nagged him about the six hundred he fronted Ben. You're sure of this, he had said. You're positive?

They shot him twice, Victor. In his own home. After his wife nearly lost the tip of her finger. In front of the kids. He had begun to notice the way money brought forth all of Victor's irritating qualities at once.

You're sure? Because you know I took a hit on this.

Scout's honor, Warren replied. He had hated boy scouts. This is exactly what you've waited for.

What about the hospital?

Nothing yet.

Victor's brow creased. What if they keep him there? Six months. A year.

Ben's too smart for that, Warren said. Ben wasn't, of course, but he had tried to make his voice sound soothing. He needs to convince them they made a mistake, and that can take time. There's a court order that has to be overturned. Victor seemed unconvinced, and felt compelled to continue with the lie. He'll be back with us after he's out. Lie. We're totally on the same page on this one. Lie. There's no reason for him to stop. Lie.

Victor drove with one hand, held the glowing dash lighter to the tip of his cigarette with the other. He seemed worried, which made Warren worried. January was rapidly approaching, and if there were any unresolved problems when it arrived, there would be no more Dilaudid. How had Victor put it? No more rolling pharmacy.

It'll work out, Warren said. You'll see.

Victor seemed skeptical. How much do you think he'll get?

Warren replied that it was hard to guess with something like that, but that it was bound to be a lot. He believed nothing of what he told Victor. Not a dime, he thought. Not one dime. For either of us. I wonder how you'll react when you find out. I wonder, Victor, what you're like when you're upset?

But Victor had been more or less convinced, and suggested they go to a bar in Queens to cement the deal. Warren decided that it would be wise if he accepted. Forty minutes later, he had found himself under the elevated R train in a bar so moorishly smoky, so poorly lighted, and so loudly jukeboxed that it was impossible for him to tell if the person seated next to him at the bar whose hand was on his thigh was a man or a woman. Although, he reflected, that's probably the idea. He caught sight of himself in the mirror and was stunned to see himself smiling.

How many more happy times? he'd wondered, studying his face. How many more good moments? He'll find out soon that you've been working him. How many more happy times?

He resigned himself to whatever would happen and placed his own hand on her thigh. When in Rome and all that. But he lost her, just before last call an hour later, to a bearded pool shark. Disgusted by his failure—and even more disgusted that he had placed his hand on the leg of what might have been another man—he pounded the bar with his fist and ordered two shots of tequila, and that was exactly the point at which his memory of the night stopped.

It was plain enough, now, what had happened after that. Apparently he'd gotten the keys from Victor, had returned here, and had shed his clothes in a roundabout path that led from the door to the bed. Now, as he retraced that path in reverse, gathering up the clothes, he saw that he had taken a small detour into the bathroom. As he retrieved his shoes from the doorway he saw vomit spattered and dried on the tile, a red exclamation of bile slashed on the filthy tub. Red? He opened the window and breathed deeply of the fresh air. As he urinated pleasurably into the bowl, he wondered if he had time to fix before Victor returned.

Warren heard the front door open and slam shut as another train rumbled by. "This place stinks, Warren," Victor said from the kitchen. Keys were thrown into a bowl.

"Jesus," a woman's voice agreed. A window was opened.

Warren hastily kicked the door shut. He scrubbed the tiles with a dampened hand towel and then, unsure of where to hide it, crammed the towel into the space behind the porcelain toilet. The smell of bile still filled the room but that couldn't be helped. He dressed quickly and then dunked his head under the faucet, slicking his wet hair back with his hands.

When he emerged from the bathroom, dripping and shivering, he immediately noticed the woman sitting on the couch. What drew his attention in particular was the way she sat back with no concern for keeping her legs closed, as if such necessities were beside the point for her. Warren sat in the chair across from her and willed himself not to look down. In the kitchen, Victor was making breakfast.

"Is this him?" the woman asked Victor.

"Is this he," Victor said. He walked into the room with two coffee mugs and handed one to each of them. Warren took a sip and winced. The woman set the mug on her belly and wrapped her hands around it for warmth.

"Mister," she said, "from what I hear, you tied one on last night."

"Look in the bathroom," Warren said, "and you'll know it."

Victor groaned. "You mean I have to call the maid?"

Warren decided that he was relieved. You always expected Victor to take things as they came, but you never could tell how deeply you had to mine his sort before you encountered the unexpected. That was how these people were. Nothing and then everything. "You said you wanted to celebrate. I was following orders."

"Restraint, Warren," Victor said. "You lack restraint."

Warren shrugged. It was true.

"I wouldn't get too far ahead of myself, you know? Ben's bound to be a little pissed. If you sold off my silver, I would be. These two," Victor said, turning to the woman, "are insufferable together. I had to drive them to JFK one time, and it was like parenting Jacob and Esau. Needling each other every chance they got. For sport."

"It's just the way we are."

"I'm not so sure," Victor said. "Seems like there's something else there. And I doubt that selling his silver's going to help." He considered the bathroom door. "I ought to make you clean it with your toothbrush."

"I could use yours," Warren said.

Victor groaned again. "Well," he said, "it wouldn't be the first time."

"Yuck," the woman said.

"My thoughts exactly," Warren said. She smiled and Warren took the bait. He sat forward in the chair and allowed himself a glance down. Not as if you could do anything about it, he thought. "Don't you like coffee?"

"I hate it," she said. She didn't seem to mind that he had looked. "You don't like it either."

"I don't."

"Then why have it?"

"I'm not sure," Warren said. "I think because it's worse not having it?"

"That's because you're used to it. If you'd never had it in the first place you wouldn't miss it."

"Hey Victor," Warren said. "She thinks I'm addicted to coffee."

"You should be so lucky," Victor said from the kitchen. "Imagine the money you'd save."

"What's he talking about?" she asked.

"I'm addicted to Dilaudid." And how, he reflected. The coffee mug chattered slightly as he set it on the side-table. Might have to exit stage left and take care of things.

"What's Dilaudid?"

"It's the junky equivalent," Warren said, "of dinner and a movie."

She sat forward. "Can I try some?"

"Of course," he said.

He had never shared any before, but it seemed like a good place to start.

"Trina," Victor said, "you don't want that shit. Have a Bloody Mary instead."

She gave Victor an evil look.

"He can be such a Calvinist, sometimes," Warren said quietly.

"Maybe after he's gone," she said.

Before Warren could interpret that, Victor walked into the room with three plates balanced on his arms. For the moment, he looked like a flight stew, minus uniform. It was amazing that someone could live so comfortably in two completely separate worlds. Warren took his plate and ate a single bite of what turned out to be a strikingly good if slightly mangled omelet. "Victor," he said, "I get the feeling you've done this before."

"This was tough," Victor said. "Breakfast for two is my specialty."

Trina rolled her eyes. "Victor's the Don of Ditmars."

"That's right," he said, "the Casanova of Queens."

"That doesn't work," she said. "That's a C and a Q."

"Not if you can't spell," Victor said.

"How did you meet Victor, Ms.—"

"Trina Taylor," Victor said. "The, uh, Wastrel of Woodside."

"That's not my real name," she said. "That's my stage name."

Warren placed his fork on his plate. He wasn't hungry at all. "And your real name?"

"Abigail," she said.

"You don't use that?"

"Amnesia," she explained. She twirled one finger by her temple.

"We were in Montauk one day," Victor said. "I went out back of a bar to piss and there she was. All bloodied up. Can't remember a thing. So I take her to the hospital, bring her home, give her something to eat, get her cleaned up. Show him your scar, sweet."

Trina lifted her bangs and showed Warren a squarish patch of scar tissue on her forehead. The color and shine of the scar reminded Warren of the grafts on his forearms.

"I've got some of those," Warren said.

"Not now, Warren," Victor said. "We're eating."

"At the hospital," she said, "they asked me my name. But all I could remember was my stage name. I mean everything was right there in my wallet, on my driver's license, but it was like reading about a stranger. They took me to my apartment and the first night it felt like I was house-sitting."

"I don't know much about amnesia," Victor said, "but I'm guessing that something very unpleasant happened to our little Trina." He seemed uneasy.

"The good thing," she said, "is that I don't have to remember it."

"Well that's a plus," Warren said.

"I was telling her that you might be able to help her," Victor said.

"I'm not much for dissociative disorders," Warren said. "Especially today."

Victor gave him an evil look as Trina set her half-finished plate on the side-table and excused herself. After she had closed the bathroom door, Victor said quietly, "I need you to talk to her." He picked up her plate and began to pick at what was left of her omelet.

"And say what?" Warren asked. He was beginning to sweat through his shirt, and the idea of performing a half-assed psychological evaluation seemed futile. From behind the bathroom door, he heard a muted but still audible *yuck*.

"Think of it as a favor. If you help her, I look like the good guy."

"Since when are you the good guy?"

"If she remembers everything," he said, "without my help, do you think she'll want to have anything to do with me?"

"You know, Victor," Warren said, "I'm guessing she's been through something exceptionally ugly. Traumatic amnesia tends to be limited and temporary. When it's sustained there are bound to be severe emotional factors. I wouldn't even know where to begin."

Victor looked at him skeptically. "You've got to be joking."

"She's not a lab rat. She's a human being. I think it's disgusting that you've got her caged up like this."

"She's not caged."

"Of course she is."

"Look," Victor said, "couldn't you at least try?" He finished Trina's omelet and set the plate back on the side-table. "She's not sincere about this, Warren. She's never been more than half-assed about anything."

"So you knew her. Before."

"Of course I knew her. I knew her boyfriend. He was the sort you don't want to know. One night he lost his temper, and this happened. So now I watch over her. She'd be on the street without me."

"You're a saint."

"No more or less than you," Victor said.

"I'm a little uneasy about talking with her here. We should at least go to her apartment. She'll feel safer there."

"Warren," Victor said, "this is her apartment."

The toilet flushed and Trina walked back into the room looking utterly revolted. "Victor," she said, "your friend has defiled our bathroom." She sat on the couch and picked up her empty plate with disbelief, holding it under Victor's nose. "And what happened to this?"

"Sorry, doll-face," Victor said. "And I'm off." He stood up and pulled a heavy wool sweater over his head.

"Should I come?" she asked.

"I was just leaving," Warren said.

"No, no," Victor said. "Warren said he'd talk with you about things, Trina. I'll leave you two alone, as I have some details to fine-tune before I wing off to Atlanta. I'll be back tomorrow about noon." He gave Trina a chaste kiss and winked at Warren. "Now don't be hypnotizing her or anything like that, Warren," he said, and left, locking the door behind him.

"Well," she said, "I'm still hungry. You want any more?" She picked up the two dishes from the side-table, and balanced Warren's plate on top of them.

"I'll pass," Warren said. "I really do have to be going."

She placed the dishes in the sink and walked back into the bedroom and sat on the arm of Warren's chair. "Victor says you're a junkie because you were burned."

The fabric of her skirt rubbed against the back of his hand. "I was," he said. "Although I don't remember much of it."

"What do you remember?"

"I had just finished breakfast. I was still in my pajamas and I was about to go to the hospital to scrub in on a rotator cuff when the phone rang. The neighbor said my dad's place was on fire—" he trailed off. He doubted that she would understand. "But that's sort of where the memory ends for me, too. I go straight from breakfast to the grafts."

"Couldn't you ask your wife what happened?"

"My wife's gone," he said. "A long long time."

"You and Victor," she said. "You really are one in the same. Truly a pair."

"How do you mean?"

"He lost his wife too. Years back in a car accident on the Expressway. I suppose he told you he was still married. He tells everyone that."

"Then why does he stay here?"

"Well," she said, moving fractionally closer to him, "everyone likes to forget a little bit every now and then, don't you think?"

Warren said that he supposed everyone did.

"Victor gets lonely," she explained. "Case in point, his work. Bottled up in an airborne steel tube with two hundred strangers. For three hours. And he loves it. What sort of person would want a job like that? I'll tell you who. A person who finds the world flat and needs to be reminded that it's not. Victor. He's afraid of being alone so he finds a job that guarantees he won't be. At least three days a week. And I fill in the gaps."

"You don't—" he searched for the right word, "—you don't work for him?"

She shook her hair. "Nothing like that. I'm just a friend who helps him forget. And he helps me out with the rent."

"So this is your place?"

"Now you've got it," she said. She studied him closely. "You're sort of cute, for an old guy."

"I don't feel so cute."

"Well I guess that's up to me, isn't it?"

"That hardly seems fair."

"That's the nice thing about being a woman," she said. "You get to decide what's fair and what's not."

She hadn't decided, Warren thought, about that knock on her head.

She slid off the arm of the chair and crouched in front of him.

"Trina," he said, "I think you've got the wrong idea."

"No," she said. "It's you who's got it all wrong. I understand perfectly. Victor says you're going to help me. And where I come from you don't get something for nothing." She undid his belt buckle and pulled his pants and underwear down to his knees. His exposed cock looked orphaned on its bed of graying pubic hair. He had every intention of resisting.

"There's no point," he explained. "It doesn't work any longer."

"We'll see," she said. She slid forward and swallowed him whole. He felt her teeth outlined against his skin, and realized that she could unsex him with a single savage bite. Although, he supposed, I've already done that to myself, haven't I?

It was no use; they waited but nothing happened.

"I'm sorry," he said. She sat back on the couch, confused. He pulled his zipper up and buckled his belt. "I can't anymore. I haven't got it in me."

We've both been had, he thought. Victor knew this was how we'd end up. That's why he left us alone. He wanted you to think I'd help you, but Trina, I can't even help myself.

"You junkies," she said. She shook her head. "I don't understand why. You really are missing out."

He stood up to look for his hat. He was about to cry, and he didn't want her to see. It would only make her understand less.

TWO

Thirteen

Ben was in the barn, cleaning the needle valve of the Sahid's MG with a can of pressurized air, when he heard the phone ring in the kitchen. He raised his head and listened to the second ring. "Somebody get that!" he shouted, but heard no reply.

They weren't back yet.

His honeymoon, he guessed, was over. Emma and the girls had been skulking about the house for two days, chastened and attentive, but that morning they had gone to the mall and left him alone with this damn needle valve. And no lunch. It was so cold in the barn the aluminum can ached in his grip. He had, he recalled, fixed the Sahid's needle valve three times. Some things, he'd told them the last time, just stay broken. But the Sahids had a stubborn, austere Brahmin streak, and had he fixed it a hundred or a thousand times, the car still would have been their smiling, flawless baby. Or their second one, anyway, considering their chubby ten-year-old, with his enrichment-class pedigree.

For God's sake, Ben, he thought as he jogged to the house. What the hell's with you? It's business. It's money you need.

It was the Zoloft. It was the craving for alcohol. No—it was the Zoloft. Since his release, he had swallowed the fifty milligram pill every morning after brushing his teeth. He'd waited and waited for that sea-change he'd been promised, that beautiful flood of inner calmness that was supposed to follow, but with each ingested pill he felt slightly more unhinged. The drug piqued his senses in a way he'd never experienced. At night—sometimes after waiting as much as two hours for sleep to come—the slightest noise woke him. He'd begun to feel like one of those cowardly foils in the old black and white war films: the spineless kid from Connecticut who won't go over the top, his rifle barrel plugged with muck, wide-eyed and blubbering, wincing at every bullet zipping by. It was true that he felt less depressed. He felt—well, you could say he felt *evened out*. But every time a pine knot exploded in the stove, he nearly had a stroke.

What irritated him was that as he'd crossed the invisible line that separated his twenties from his thirties, things had been going *well*. If he'd sprung from his mother's loins this way—unmediated by even temperament, incapable of directing his thoughts where he wanted them to go, addicted, dependent, slack, and impotent—that would have been one thing. At least that way he wouldn't have known any better; he wouldn't have suspected that life could be enjoyable. But for years he and Emma had been doing well—no, *very* well. At twenty-eight, he bought a house that cost twice what his friends could afford, with money left over to furnish the place. Although he hadn't made peace with his mother's death—because that would have been impossible, as vivid as the image of her swallowing a fistful of pills was in his mind— although he hadn't made peace with it, he had *accommodated* it, given it its own shelf, its own private stratum of his personal history. Nina was a beautiful baby, and she sometimes slept for six or even eight hours at a stretch. They had money. They made love often, sometimes twice in a night. They'd had plenty of friends. Choices. And now there was that damned *photograph* in the front hall, the photograph taken the night they went to see the tree at Rockefeller Center that *reminded* him of all of this happiness that had bled away. He wanted to rip the thing off the wall, to burn it, to hack it apart with the hatchet—because they'd been happy and now they weren't.

What do you do—what is it that you do, when you want to be happy but cannot?

You could not, he reflected, prepare for something like this: for the sudden arrival of a deep and humiliating secret; for the mixed message insisting you couldn't drink but could mask your depression with a pill that was, as far as he could tell, the prescribed equivalent of coke-laced tequila; for the schoolboyish explanations that followed your daughters' bedtime questions about your recent stay on a locked ward of the hospital; for the fucking needle valves that stuck, no matter how many times you cleaned them; for the soul-sucking need for a drink. For the absolute sheer fuckall-of-it-ness.

Nor could you prepare for your wife leaving you in the hospital, nor for her sudden return; nor for the telegraphed understanding that she came back not because she loved you too much to stay away, but because she had an agenda to satisfy; nor for the willingness with which you took her back, without explanation or apology, because you were just grateful to have someone, *anyone* next to you when a pine knot exploded during the night and you were snapped awake in the dark, your heart standing in your throat.

You couldn't prepare for any of it. It was one of those matters that fell squarely in the land of *Do or Do Not*. You either managed it or you did not. What was preparation, after all? You might well prepare for a skydive—sure, you could go over it in your mind, but when the airplane hatch was opened, the long drop revealed, it became a matter of *Do or Do Not*.

He'd felt exactly that way—faced with a *Do or Do Not*—when he found the silver missing three nights ago. Emma had phoned to tell him she would be coming home with the girls tomorrow. After he hung up the phone, he remembered about the silver and walked out to the barn to retrieve it. *This could have given us four or five mortgage payments,* he thought, as, without turning on the overhead light, he pulled the wood-tarp aside. With a great deal of effort, he slid his arm in between the stacks of wood to pull out the wrapped wood box that held the silver. *Instead, it'll sit on the shelf and we'll use it twice a year, once for Thanksgiving dinner and once for Christmas dinner, and it'll look lovely and yet be absolutely worthless, and if this keeps up we'll have no table to put it on. That's what we'll have, Emma. Beautiful silver but no roof over our heads. Because you refused to stick by me on a simple phone call.*

But the silver wasn't there. The painting, *Study for Siege of the Round-House,* was there. He could feel it with the tips of his fingers, still wrapped in an old wool blanket bound with duct tape, but the wood box was gone.

A rat squeezed between his boots suddenly and skittered out through the open door. Ben experienced another almost-stroke.

"Impossible," he said. "Of course it's there."

He reached in again to see if he was mistaken but understood immediately that he was not. It was gone. As he realized why, he began pulling logs off the top of the stack, bellowing Warren's name. In rage and frustration, he threw his full weight against the wood pile, a half-cord that had taken him hours to stack. The pile tilted neatly and gracefully at first, and then overbalanced suddenly and crashed down, exploding into an impossible jumble of logs. He went to the door and snapped on the overhead light.

The painting sat there, wrapped, exactly where he expected it to be. But the case that held the silver was gone. For a moment he watched the empty space in disbelief, then walked out through the barn door and climbed into his truck. The thought occurred to him, as he started the truck, that he might possibly lose his temper—that in his current state of mind, he might lose it all the way, might fall right off the map— and this seemed all right with him. A small part of him wanted it to happen. As he drove through town toward Lasting Drive, he reflected on the similarities between this short drive and his grandfather's short drive to Haskell Electric. He reflected on the usefulness of rage.

He stopped at the curb outside Warren's house. The front door opened suddenly and Warren walked out, carrying a full garbage bag. Ben put the truck in park, stepped out onto the lawn, and walked deliberately toward his father, not bothering to shut the car door. "Hi, Warren," he said. "Let's talk about the silver."

Warren dropped the trash bag and turned and stepped inside the front hall and pushed the door shut. Ben heard him string the chain across, and then the door cautiously opened three inches, the chain taut across the opening. Half of Warren's face appeared in the gap. "I had to do it, Ben," he said. "Hear me out on this one first."

Without hesitating, Ben threw himself at the door and reached through the gap up to his armpit as Warren pulled back. He gripped Warren's throat just beneath the jawbone, felt the birdlike muscles, the scrape of his unshaven chin. Not long ago, he recalled, Warren had been the bigger one, the stronger one, the more aggressive one. For a moment, his father beat feebly at his wrist. "Give me the silver," Ben said calmly, "or I swear I'll break this door down and snap your neck."

He released his grip and was about to pull his arm back through the gap when Warren suddenly threw his weight against the door and pinned Ben's arm. Warren grasped his trapped arm firmly by the wrist. "Listen to me, sonny boy," he said through the door. "I've got a steak knife here in my fist. I keep it in the mail slot for just this sort of occasion. A little piece of Victor's advice I decided to follow."

"All right," Ben said. The back of his neck had gone cold with sweat.

"If I wanted to," Warren said, "I could nail your hand to the wall. Right?"

"I understand," Ben said. It seemed possible that Warren was bluffing, but he didn't want to find out.

"I sold the silver," Warren said patiently, "because it was the only way I could pacify Victor. We both still need him. And you'll recall that you owe him, too, yes?"

"Yes," Ben said. When your arm was pinned in a doorway, he reflected, it was easy to be agreeable.

"So then take your fucking arm out of my fucking door, then climb back into your fucking shitkicker truck and drive the fuck across town to your fucking house, and be thankful I didn't sell the fucking painting, too. Understand?"

"I understand," he said, his mouth dry. The pressure on the door relaxed slightly, and he drew his arm back. All the rage he'd felt had been replaced, in an instant, by fear. Now that the moment had passed, he felt queasy, adrenaline-sick. He wanted to fight, but could not.

With his arm removed, the door closed tightly. As Ben walked back to his truck, he heard Warren throw the bolt across. He drove back across town, massaging his sore bicep where the edge of the door had pressed against it. It took two hours to restack the wood.

"What!" he shouted into the phone. He'd jammed his index finger opening the kitchen door and he stuck it sorrowfully in his mouth, sucking away at the pain. It reminded him of sucking on his Aquavit-stained index finger in the hospital. He wanted a drink.

"Ben?"

It was Jane Rhoden's husband, Mick. "Sorry," Ben said.

"Bad time?"

"Well," he said. He didn't know how to answer that.

"You're busy?"

"The Sahid's—" he said, then dropped it. He occasionally fixed parking-lot dings on Mick's Jag, and he didn't want Mick to know how much the work irritated him. He couldn't afford it.

"Right," Mick said. "You free for lunch?"

"Well," Ben said. Lunch? "Of course."

"One o'clock? Why don't you meet me in the bar at the club?" Rhoden was on the board of directors for the Lansing Country Club, and he ate lunch there almost every weekday.

"All right."

"Wear a tie."

Ben said that he would and then hung up, dizzy with the suddenness of the exchange. He didn't know Mick well, and he certainly didn't like him much. Mick didn't like him either, as far as he could remember, at least not well enough for them to have lunch together. They spoke often at dinner parties, but they had never advanced their relationship beyond the fun-loving mistrust that Ben had seen Mick share with most other men. Mick seemed to believe that every man on earth wanted to sleep with his wife. Which was nearly true. He was, Ben reflected, a man's man, insofar as his closest acquaintances were the men he mistrusted most.

It had been at least a year since he last wore a tie. He buttoned up a clean blue oxford shirt and then selected a yellow tie, rumpled and worn, from the back of his sock drawer. On his third attempt, he managed a reasonably presentable knot. As he walked downstairs, pausing to check his knot in the landing mirror, he realized that Emma had taken her car and he'd have to drive the truck, which would look ridiculous in the country club parking lot. He dared himself to take the Sahid's MG, but didn't only out of fear that in his state he'd get in an accident. The shirt pinched at his Adam's Apple, and the tie seemed to be gently strangling him. As he passed the Rialto he drove with one hand and with his free hand loosened the tie and unbuttoned his shirt at the throat. Mick would understand. Everyone knew who Ben was, and there was no need to affect the illusion of a business lunch. If Mick wanted to meet for lunch, it was certainly about money. Something big. A fixer-upper. He'd present it as Ben doing a real favor for him, when they would both know that the favor was coming from Mick. Most of Ben's business came from a sort of pity. That he was good at what he did and charged less than the shops by Nina's school was beside the point. People went to him because they knew he was in trouble. At first he had been grateful for the money, a real hand-kisser, but slowly he had come to resent being thought of as a charity case.

At the country club, he parked between a black Cadillac and a silver five-series BMW. Stepping back to examine his parking job, he saw that the truck looked even more incongruous than he thought it would. As he wandered in through the front entrance, he wondered if someone would ask if he was the help. He wanted a drink.

Mick was waiting in the nearly empty bar. Tie my ass, Ben thought. Who would notice? Rhoden had chosen a table beside the windows. As Ben shook his hand and sat across from him, the sight of the leafless trees in the wide expanse of the golf course depressed him. It looked like a rich man's wasteland, lush and perfectly mown and entirely vacant. He had once been a member here. Warren had taken care of that.

"Be a bad winter this year," Mick said. He was drinking ice water. Why the bar?

"What's good here?" Ben asked. "I've forgotten."

"Club sandwich," Mick said. "How's Emma?"

"She's fine," Ben said. "Just got back from visiting her mom and dad."

"I saw your dad the other day. Out by your place. Muddy as hell."

"He was, ah, out in the garden."

"Warren gardens?"

"He does now." He massaged his sore bicep.

"In December?"

The waitress, an attractive college girl with a pierced eyebrow, arrived at their table and asked if they wanted to hear the specials. Mick ordered them two club sandwiches and two cokes without asking Ben what he wanted. He seemed distracted and nervous, and Ben wondered if that was something between them or if he was on the wagon. Emma had told Ben about Mick's affair, and he wondered how rough Jane was making life for him right now.

"I want to make you an offer," Mick said. The waitress set a sandwich before each of them, and Ben waded in. He had skipped breakfast, and was starved.

"What sort of offer? You got an old Jag or something?"

"Nothing like that," Mick said. "It's something here."

Ben forced himself to act only slightly interested. "That so?"

"Our second in line on the business side got an offer at a course in the Keys. He's moving in a month."

"And you want me to fix his car." Only half joking. You can't be serious, Mick, he thought.

Mick smiled. "If you want. But we've been kicking around asking you to take his place."

Ben swallowed.

"It's not anything like what you had," he said, "but it's a good thing. Trust me. Lots of perks." His eyes flicked to the waitress and back.

That sort of perk, Ben thought, is the last thing I need right now. "What sort of work?"

"Payroll. Hiring and firing. Oversight."

"I don't know anything about golf. Or golf courses."

"We've got a course manager."

"How large is the staff?"

"The restaurant's separate, so you'd just have the club staff. Maybe thirty, thirty-five, including the maintenance crew. Summers we have a lot more. Winters you'd have to scare up business."

"Christmas parties? That sort of thing?"

"That sort of thing," Mick said. "Like I said, it's not as glamorous as what you had, but it's something."

"How much?"

"Maybe seventy to start. Club membership for your family."

Ben sat back in his chair and passed a hand over his mouth. It was a lot of money. It was enough. "Listen," he said, "you know what happened to the last company I ran."

"You went belly-up in the recession."

"I did."

"So did a lot of people."

"Not like that."

"It doesn't come and go, here."

"I'd think it would."

"The rich," Mick said, "tend to stay rich."

"It must be up and down some."

"Not really. You scramble in the summertime. Winters you brood."

That shouldn't be a problem, Ben thought. He chewed his thumbnail for a moment. "How'd my name come up?"

"I spoke up for you."

"Why?"

Mick picked up his fork and tapped it against the table. "Can I talk to you about something?"

A muscle began to spasm in Ben's leg. "Shoot."

"Jane's got a lawyer," Mick said. "I've been sleeping on the couch for three weeks. She says she's had enough."

"I'm sorry to hear that."

Mick shrugged. "Things have gotten complicated."

"Jane seems complicated."

"Listen," Mick said, "I know Emma and Jane talk a lot."

Ben watched him. "I didn't think they were all that close."

"Maybe," he said. "But Jane trusts her. You know?"

"I guess," Ben said. "Most people think Emma has it together."

"If you could just have Emma talk to her." Mick set down his fork.

"And say what, Mick?"

"Emma could tell her I'm turning myself around. And I am. No joke. I stopped drinking. I'm home every night. It should be enough. But Jane doesn't trust me. Whatever I do, it isn't enough."

"You think Emma could convince her?"

"I can't handle a divorce," he said. He looked out at the golf course.

"Mick," Ben said.

Mick looked back at him.

"What if she can't, Mick?"

"Really," he said, "I think she could. I mean, Jane's wide open right now." He rubbed at a spot on the table with his finger. "It's not as bad as it sounds."

Ben said nothing.

"I really have turned myself around," Mick explained.

"Is that—" Ben searched for the right words, "—is the, uh, is the job—"

"Look," Mick said, "just talk to her."

"It may not be so easy," Ben said. He wanted a drink. It seemed odd to be in a bar and not have one.

"I'll let you know," Mick said. He raised his hand to signal for the check.

Fourteen

Emma lay beside Ben in bed and watched the ceiling. The sheets were damp with sweat. He said it was the Zoloft. They had never had a problem with that happening to him before, at least not when he wasn't drinking. It seemed strange that now, after ten years together, sex could so quickly become a mystery.

She turned on her stomach and rested her chin on his shoulder.

"It's better if we don't talk," he said. He lay with his arm thrown over his face. He had tried for half an hour, and he was trembling, exhausted. "Let's just go to sleep."

"Are we still in love?"

He lifted his arm and looked squarely at her. "Well—of course. Right?"

"I don't want the answer you think you should give. I mean we haven't really had a serious talk about what happened."

"I think we're in a tough spot," he said, and dropped his arm over his eyes again. "I think I'm angry that you left."

A slight thrill of terror moved through her. Whether he was angry at her or not, at least she knew that he felt something. "We've had tough years before," she said. She thought of his drinking three years ago. They hadn't made love then, either. "But we've gotten through them."

"Well, yes," he said. "But not with everything intact."

That was true. The affairs had only made things worse. "I don't think we can expect this to be easy."

He sat up. "I can't sit still," he said. He didn't seem to be listening to her. "It's like I had too much coffee, but I haven't had any all day. I haven't had any all week." He got out of bed and paced around the room with his arms crossed around him for warmth. He was limping slightly, favoring his uninjured leg. He wore no bandage even though the wound hadn't yet healed entirely. The skin around the exit wound was, she noticed, hideously bruised. Other than that slight patch of color, he was so uniformly pale that he seemed almost luminescent in the moonlight.

He stopped pacing the room and stood before her. "I need to know something," he said.

She sat up and wrapped herself in the blanket. "Ask me."

"Were you," he asked—and for a moment he seemed unwilling to continue, as if he didn't want to know her answer. "Were you with anyone in Boston?"

"Of course not."

"Because I would almost understand. Almost. I mean it would make sense."

"Ben," she said, "that's the last thing I need right now."

"But it's happened before."

She didn't answer. Of course it had, and he knew that.

He was shivering. "Only when I was drinking?"

She nodded. He sat down beside her, and she pressed her mouth against his shoulder.

"Good," he said. "At least I have an excuse for not noticing."

"Do you hate me?"

"I don't seem capable," he said, "of feeling much of anything right now."

"You did it, too. You told me about it. Every detail."

"Emma," he said, "I made all that up."

"Don't say that."

"It's true. For Christ's sake. I was drunk all the time. I couldn't have been with anyone. Who would've had me?"

He was telling the truth. Who would've had him? It had been her and only her. So, she thought, I was the one who failed to rise above it. No, I wasn't. The hell with him. He was the one who was drinking. He was the one feeling sorry for himself.

"I was jealous," he said. "I wanted to hurt you. But I couldn't possibly have been with anyone. I was a drunk."

"So you've been holding this over me?" She was suddenly furious, the blanket gathered in her fists. "It wasn't enough to be the saint. You had to be smug about it. You had to hold it over me without me knowing. Next you'll tell me that you never even wanted anyone else."

"I didn't," he said.

"Really? What did you want?"

"I think," he said, "I wanted to be dead."

The fury left her all at once. They were both silent for a moment. "What about now?" she asked.

He lay down and looked at the ceiling. "Sometimes I feel better. But now I feel worse than ever. I don't see how this helps."

"We can work through this part."

"I feel confused all the time. I hear things. Sirens. Echoes. Like I'm living in the bottom of a well. And I can't sit still. I worked fifteen hours yesterday, trying to catch up, and then I went to bed and stared at the ceiling for five hours. It's as bad as drinking. You just go and go and go until you drop."

"The nurse said you drank on your last night."

He pulled the blanket up to his chin. "I did."

"What happened?"

"I stopped myself. It was a miracle that I did."

"Have you had anything since then?"

"No. I don't know how, but no. I've been sober all week. Three years of it for nothing."

"Not for nothing. If you hadn't stopped I would have left you."

"But you did leave me."

"I came back," she said quietly.

"Well that was generous of you."

"We have to talk about this."

"I'll bet Carl had some things to say."

"He didn't say a word."

"I'll bet he was a real prince."

"Ben," she said.

He sighed. "So what now? It has to get better than this."

"What are you going to do about Warren and his friend?"

"I'm through with him."

"Since when?"

"Since I learned that I don't handle confinement well."

"What do you do for them?"

"Nothing," he said. "It's nothing, Em. I mean it."

"But it's enough to get you in trouble. All of us in trouble."

"Yes," he said, "but not anymore."

"What'll we do for money?"

He thought for a moment. "I had lunch with Mick today," Ben said. "He offered me a job."

"At the club?"

"Business manager."

"Did you take it?"

"I think the idea," he said, "is that you have to talk Jane out of divorcing him first."

Emma was silent for a moment. "They're getting a divorce?"

"I guess."

"He wasn't serious."

"That's the way it seemed."

"Jane's better off without him."

"It's a way out. It could get us back on our feet."

"I'm not going to convince Jane to stay with him."

"Better that than go broke."

She didn't answer.

"You know we're in trouble."

"I know. We've *been* in trouble. I live here, too."

"You have any better ideas?"

"We could sell the house."

"Do you really want that?"

"No. But we don't have a choice, Ben."

"Of course we do."

"You know what'll happen if we don't sell it."

"What do you think will happen?"

"We'll lose it anyway," she said. "We'll have to move in with my parents."

"I don't want to move in with your parents," he said.

"I don't either," she said. "But it doesn't matter. We'll have to."

"I'm not selling the house. We're not selling the house."

"Ben," she said, "it's one or the other. Why am I the only one who sees that?"

"Talk to Jane. Make that work."

"And what then? What about the next time he sleeps with someone? Because he will."

"Well, what if he does, Emma? That's up to him. It's their problem."

"You'll owe him, Ben. And then next time it happens he'll expect the same thing, and the next, and the next. And sooner or later she'll see him for what he is, and nothing will convince her to stay, and he'll ditch you, and we'll be back where we were. Where we are now."

Ben got out of bed and went downstairs and into the laundry room. He searched around on the floor for clothes and found a pair of khakis and cotton shirt. After he was dressed, he went to the front hall and pulled on a pair of work boots and a heavy jacket and gloves and then went outside. The night air was very cold and the stars were blurred by a spectral sheen of clouds. As he walked across the driveway a rabbit bolted across the lawn to the back field, startling him. He watched it run into the back field, his heart beating quickly.

He had to convince her. It was a good opportunity, and if they had to take a detour through Rhodenland to get to it, well, that was too bad. Sometimes you had to do unpleasant things to get back on your feet.

The barn door, he saw, was slightly open. He was almost certain that he'd closed it and had hung the lock in the latch before dinner. Hadn't he? He couldn't remember. Fucking Zoloft. Fucking sertraline. He opened the barn door and turned on the overhead light and immediately saw an envelope clamped in the vise, standing straight up like a white exclamation point. *Warren,* the face of the envelope said, *make sure Ben gets this.* Ben loosened the vise and opened the letter and immediately recognized Victor's neat handwriting.

Welcome home, Westchester!

My sources tell me you had a bit of a *cañadir* your last night in the hospital. Please advise as it was my understanding you were a fall-down drunk not three years ago. If you've started up again, remember to hide your car keys from yourself or you'll end up as a smear on the road. And of course I value your services so it would be a shame to lose you.

While we're on that subject

He folded the letter and then placed it back in the envelope. There was no need to read the rest. He knew what it said. It said I am Victor and you are My Westchester. There would be witticisms and Victor's unique way of folding serious threats into lighthearted jokes. Sorry, Victor, he thought. I took one look at the long drop and lost my nerve.

Work was out of the question now, as out of the question as sleep. He turned out the light and closed the barn door and deliberately hung the lock in the latch. As he was walking back to the house, he thought, Where are you going? You can't sleep. You can't work and you certainly, certainly can't fuck. You're a little stingless medicated moth. So what are you going inside for? What are you going to do once you get there?

He knew what he was going inside for: he was going inside to have a drink. For three exhausting days he'd outrun it, and it had finally caught up to him. Having a drink would be the first relief he'd granted himself since leaving the hospital. He was going to have a drink, because life without alcohol—and there was simply no other way to explain it—life without alcohol was just life. It was soul-killing white noise.

In the living room, he went to the bookcase without turning on the light and pulled down Emma's copy of *Nostromo* from the highest shelf. Behind it was an unopened bottle of bourbon. The bottle had sat there, behind the book, untouched for three years. It was dusty, and the seal had yellowed slightly with age. He opened the bottle and placed it to his lips and paused for a moment. If Emma had appeared in the doorway, he might have stopped himself; but then he tipped the bottle up and drank deeply, watching the bubbles roll behind the glass. The bourbon stung his mouth and a single tear rolled down his cheek. It was a relief to have the first drink behind him. The tactile sensation of gripping a glass bottle by the neck caused him to shiver. He lowered the bottle and capped it and hid it on the shelf again.

Have to start drinking vodka again or she'll know, he thought. She'll know anyway eventually, but it'll take longer if I'm drinking vodka. Hate vodka. Hate Zoloft. Hate night-time. Love drinking. Love bourbon. Lovely bourbon. One more. Christ. That hurts. Hurts going down, but better once it's there. Opposite of the Zoloft. That's easy going down, but it hurts when it's there. Bourbon's much better. Impotent but so what. Impotent anyway on the Zoloft. Would be nice if I could keep it under control. Feels good, and if I could control it, I could have that again. Can't keep it under control, of course, but nice to think so. He had another drink and then another and then didn't bother to put the bottle back.

When daylight began to show through the trees, he was standing at the window watching the road. It was time to sleep. He could sleep on the couch in the basement, and Emma would think he was angry with her and wouldn't bother him. His mind, blunted by the first drink, had cleared remarkably toward dawn. Now he saw, sharply and clearly, how things would be. His best intentions had been overrun. He hid the bottle, half empty now, behind the copy of *Nostromo,* checking to see that it was hidden well, and then took off his work boots and went down to the basement and lay heavily on the couch with the pale gray light coming down the stairs. He pulled the blanket over him. It would be a long time until sleep came, and when it came he would dream of Victor, and worse.

It doesn't end with me, Victor had said.

What did that mean—what did it mean, when Victor wasn't the worst you were up against?

He went back upstairs and pulled on his boots. Outside, the black lines of the birches in the back field were clearly visible now. In the barn he turned on the light and went to the work table, where he searched through the drawers until he found the eight-inch locking buck knife he bought last summer. He remembered that when he bought it he'd asked the clerk if it was sharp. The boy thought for a moment and then replied that what was sharp for one was blunt for another, but that as far as he was concerned it was sharp enough to castrate a mosquito. Ben answered that he expected that would do the trick.

He went back inside, and as he was taking off his boots downstairs, he remembered that he'd forgotten to close the barn door. The hell with it, he thought. He lay on the couch and placed the knife under the cushion and listened to the tick of the grandfather clock at the top of the stairs.

The next night Jane telephoned Emma and asked if she wanted to meet to go Christmas shopping. Ben had looked haggard and exhausted all day. When she asked if he would make dinner for the girls, she realized that he had probably not slept at all last night. "I heard you in the barn," she said. "You were working?"

"All night," he said.

"I'm not going to tell her to stay with him."

He said that she could do whatever she wanted.

"Would you really want to work for someone who would ask you to do something like that?"

He said that he guessed he wouldn't.

She gave him a light kiss on his unshaven cheek and then pulled on her coat and drove downtown. Jane was mercifully light on the subject of their absence. It surprised Emma that Jane didn't know that Ben had been held in the hospital. Somehow they'd been spared. She listened as

Jane told the story of how she had been thrown out of the Brookstone in Faneuil Hall for making obscene noises while sitting in the massage chair. Jane mentioned nothing about a divorce. Emma finished two drinks as she listened. When the Faneuil Hall story was finished, she realized that she felt happy for the first time in weeks. After the drinks, the situation seemed less terrible. The money, she now believed, would work itself out. They would have enough. She had been looking at things all wrong. After they had paid off the house, without the mortgage to battle, they would have plenty of money and a nice house besides where they could live and where they would have everything they needed. Until then, if they got in trouble they could borrow money from her parents to get by. Ben could see his doctor and adjust the medication. They would be able to make love again, and everything would be different.

They did no shopping—they had never intended to, of course—and agreed to meet downtown again on Saturday.

On her way home, long after dark, Emma stopped at the mailbox to pick up the mail and saw a car she didn't recognize parked in the driveway. She walked halfway up the drive. A younger man she understood to be a friend of Warren's was standing before Ben on the front walk beneath the spotlight. She had seen him, she realized, a few times before, with Warren. The younger man was pointing at Ben's chest with his index finger. Ben's hands were spread in front of him, palms up, in a gesture of helplessness. She couldn't hear exactly what was being said, but the tone of their voices and the way they were standing made it clear. Another man was sitting in the car's driver's seat, holding a cigarette out through the open window.

She walked quickly back to the car and drove fifty yards down the road and parked on the shoulder. In a few minutes, the car came up the driveway and turned onto Skylark Drive, the rear wheels spinning and kicking up stones. She ducked down as the car accelerated past. He had, she guessed, just told them he was finished with them—how she hoped that was what he said. She started the car and drove back home and parked in the driveway, sick with fear, but also happy that he sent them away.

Inside, she found him standing at the living room window looking out at the street. It was clear that he knew she was there, that he saw her reflection in the glass; she realized he was waiting to see if she would come to him, or if she would move upstairs. He seemed to be silently pleading with her.

She went to him and put her arms around him and pressed her nose into the back of his neck. "Don't sleep downstairs tonight," she said. "I don't know the answers. But please don't." She hadn't gone to him to satisfy the instinctive need-to-comfort; she went to him because she didn't want to sleep alone or lie awake in silent meditation.

"I don't want to," he said. "I really don't."

Fifteen

Warren was moving his remaining ampoules of Dilaudid to the water tank of the downstairs toilet when there was a loud knock on the door. He always waited until after he had moved them for his fix, because he had once moved the ampoules at the zenith of his high and had promptly forgotten where they were. It had taken him seven hours and a crowbar to find them again.

He had been visited by the police before. If they had had a search warrant they wouldn't have knocked, so this was probably a routine tip-off by one of his neighbors. And he wasn't afraid of his junkie neighbors. If a neighbor got wise or threatened him, he had the loaded .38 in his desk. He had never fired it, but he was sure that waving it around would get the point across. Neighbors and police he could handle. What he was afraid of was breaking the ampoules as he moved them. If he had lost them, they could be found, but if they were broken they were gone forever. One had been broken last winter, and oh, how he cried for it—how he wept with a drunk poet's grief. He knelt before the remains on the frozen garage floor and cried so tenderly that the broken shell of glass may as well have been his wife's fractured skull. Bent to the floor, in a posture of contrition, he licked up whatever bitter Dilaudid hadn't already been absorbed into the pores of the cement.

The hammering on the door now was louder. Dank water slopped onto the tile floor. The tiny cuts he had gotten while digging began to sting. He was reminded, strangely, of the bowl of holy water at the hospital chapel.

He chained the door and had opened it just a fraction of an inch when it was kicked inward from the outside, splintering the wood where the chain was anchored to the door, the edge striking him in the forehead. He was on his hands and knees in the hallway. A single drop of blood fell to the tan carpet. He touched his forehead and his fingers came away wet with blood. He reflected that at least the door hadn't broken his nose and was about to stand up when he was hauled to his feet by his collar and thrown back against the wall. A pale-skinned man whose features were sharpened by a pair of wraparound sunglasses seized him by the belt buckle, pulled him into the dining room, and forced him down into a chair. His hairless forearms were tattooed with geometric symbols. Victor firmly closed the front door and walked into the kitchen.

The tattooed man accompanying him moved about the room, drawing the shades on the windows.

"Warren," Victor said, "we've driven up from Queens for the second day in a row, because we have two distinct problems. I've decided that we're going to deal with them separately. Is that all right with you?"

"That sounds like a plan," Warren said. A drop of blood fell to his thigh and was absorbed into the fabric of his khakis. He found the sight of his blood strangely fascinating and realized that he was about to see much more of it. When the large man had finished lowering the blinds, he came around the table and lifted Warren to his feet by his belt buckle. He began to strip Warren methodically. After he had removed his shirt, he recoiled at the sight of Warren's scarred and hairless skin. "Shit, Victor," he said, "you didn't tell me he was burned up already." Victor shrugged. After Warren had been stripped to his tattered boxer shorts, he was turned around and his hands were fixed together behind his back with what felt and sounded like duct tape. He was forced back down into the chair and strips of silver tape were looped around his neck and the rungs of the chair, holding him firmly against the back. Although he was cold, his body began to run with sweat and the cuts on his palms stung even more. He wanted a hit very badly and wished that he had fixed before moving the ampoules.

"Theo," Victor said, "see what he has in the kitchen."

Warren heard Theo begin to search through the kitchen drawers behind him. Occasionally Theo made a sound in his throat and set something on the counter with a clatter. Warren strained his head to the left to see what was being prepared, but the tape noose was too tight and turning his head neatly siphoned off the blood supply to his brain. The edges of his vision began to sparkle.

He heard a rapid *tak-tak-tak-tak* from the kitchen.

That's the pilot light on the stove, he thought. Isn't that the pilot light on the stove?

Theo turned on the kitchen radio and slipped up and down the band.

That was the pilot light on the stove, Warren thought. A cold drop of sweat rolled down his ribcage.

"Find me something athletic," Victor said. Theo slipped across the band again and stopped at a jazz piece with a walking bass and a frenzied uptempo pace. *Dolores,* Warren thought. No. *Gingerbread Boy.* Theo turned the volume up high, and the room assumed a kinetic sort of momentum. Victor pulled out a chair out and sat across from Warren, grinning like a carved Halloween pumpkin. He bent and pulled Warren's boxer shorts down to his knees. Miles Davis was shrieking through his trumpet.

Warren realized what was about to happen and strained against the tape noose, hoping to knock himself out, but Theo circled his neck with his arm and held his head fast. Warren could smell Theo's floral cologne. Victor stood up and walked into the kitchen. When he returned he was carrying the matching knife and fork set that Warren had, in another lifetime, used to carve the holiday roasts. The blade of the knife and the twin tines of the fork glowed a dull red. Warren believed that he could feel their heat. Theo slapped a strip of duct tape over Warren's mouth, and Victor suddenly bent over Warren's exposed crotch, just as Trina had. His black hair obscured the details. When the pain came, it was huge and white and unbearable. Warren strained against Theo's grip like a snared rabbit. The skin of his face seemed about to split open from the pressure. Theo grasped his hair with his free hand and held him fast as Warren screamed into the duct tape. A wisp of smoke slipped upward, and Warren smelled his burning flesh mixed with Theo's flowery cologne and the ozone smell of the superheated steel. Herbie Hancock's right hand stumbled across the keyboard. Warren was still screaming into the tape as the quintet surged together into the song's hook and then receded behind Tony Williams's closing groove.

"Teo," Miles Davis said over the fading quintet. "Play that. Teo. Teo."

"You hear that?" Theo said. "He's talking to me."

"He was talking to Teo Macero, shithead," Victor said. "The producer."

"I was just kidding," Theo said sullenly in Warren's ear. He sounded as if Victor had hurt his feelings. Warren nodded and tears dripped onto his collarbone. He wanted Theo to know that he understood.

Tony Williams began a groove that Warren recognized as the opening to *Freedom Jazz Dance*. Victor went into the kitchen again and then returned and sat down and bent over him and time fell inward. At the peak of Cannonball Adderley's solo, Warren's vision began to sparkle again. Then he was awake without having realized he had nodded off. Someone had thrown cold water on him because he was dripping wet. Theo and Warren were somewhere behind him in the kitchen. Warren strained forward, trying to drip some of the cold water from his chin onto his seared scrotum. John Coltrane had just finished his solo and Paul Chambers began repairing the structure of the song with his bass. Theo suddenly cut Warren's hands free and Warren tore the noose from his neck and scrambled under the kitchen table. Theo seized him by the ankle and dragged him across the tiles into the kitchen. He was lifted suddenly and laid on his back on the cold Formica counter beside the stove. The shriek of Miles's trumpet sounded like a plea for mercy. Theo held him down by the neck. Victor grasped Warren's right ankle with both hands. One of them had removed the trivets that covered each burner. Blue, teardrop-shaped flames wavered gently. "This," Victor said, shouting to be heard over the music, "is for fucking my girlfriend, Warren." He pressed Warren's heel firmly down onto the flames. Warren screamed into the tape. He couldn't seem to get free. When he had finally torn his ankle from Victor's grasp, he rolled in under the overhead cabinets. The skin that had stuck to the face of the burner began to smoke. As he struggled with Theo, the fire alarm over the stove emitted a piercing alarm that was oddly consonant with the music. Theo reached up and smashed the plastic cover with his fist and the alarm went silent; he clubbed Warren twice in the back of the neck and dragged him off the counter. Warren struck his forehead on the tile floor and blood began to run freely from the cut. The light began to sparkle again but cleared as another bowl of cold water was thrown over him.

Victor turned the music low and knelt down beside him. "Now," he said, "we've gotten the first part out of the way. I'm thinking the next part will be easier."

Warren nodded. He agreed wholeheartedly. His tears stung in the cut on his forehead.

"I'll explain the situation," Victor said, "and you'll offer solutions. Okay?"

Warren nodded again. The burner was still smoking gently. He reflected that the skin he had lost had been scar tissue and not real skin, so it hadn't been his anyway. The smell of the burner reminded him of a dinner from his honeymoon. He and Linda had been on the Big Island. A pig had been roasted whole in a covered pit. When they had lifted the cloak from the pit after the pig was ready, it had smelled exactly the way the kitchen did now. Theo pushed the blind aside and opened the kitchen window and the room swirled with December air.

"I spoke with your son last night," Victor said. "I explained that some people are very unhappy with me about our lost revenue. But get this, Warren. He was totally indifferent. Can you imagine that?"

Warren shook his head.

"Your son," Victor said, "seems to think that the work we've been doing at the airport is suddenly beneath him. Apparently, this job at the country club has restored his position as a respectable citizen."

Job at the country club? Warren thought. What, fixing carts? Fixing drinks?

"What's more," Victor said, "he suggested I take the balance I'm owed and shove it up my ass. Done enough for me already, et cetera. Taken all the risk, et cetera. He added, added forcefully, that any reassurance I've gotten from you that he'll share his settlement with the city are false. And he seems to think your habit is the root of all this evil, and as such you should bear the cost of this circus. You, Warren, are the only one getting a free ride. Now, ordinarily I would have visited him with Theo, but I happen to think that he's right. I've seen the light, Warren. The fact that you rooted about my girlfriend's perfumed crotch, and allowed her, I'm told, to root about yours, suggests a certain absence of loyalty, don't you think?"

Warren nodded.

"It suggests your infidelity has become inestimable. I also happen to think your son is unusually stubborn and that holding his heel to the flame would only complicate this process. You, on the other hand, seem to be able to reason with him." He reached up and took down the carving fork from the burner. It glowed a fiercer red this time then before. Warren thought he could hear the steel sing with heat. "So this is what I suggest. You agree to convince your son that paying one's debts is the gentlemanly thing to do, and I agree not to stick this fork in your eyeball."

Warren was weeping now. He wept, because if they hadn't put tape over his mouth, he could have stopped it by telling Victor that he'd never touched her, that she'd lied to get back at him, that whether she remembered or not, she *knew*. Or maybe telling him that would have made it worse. Either way, it was too late now. Victor saw the willingness in his eyes and handed the fork to Theo, who dropped it in the sink and turned on the faucet. A cloud of steam erupted. Victor opened his hands and smiled benevolently, as if he had just performed a magic trick by making the fork disappear. Warren thought again of those times when he had used the knife and fork set to carve the holiday roasts, his wife across the table with a smudge of gray at her temples. He tried to reconstruct the memory, to make it real in his mind, but he found he couldn't. It seemed impossible, now, that he had ever been happy without Dilaudid. The drug had widened his avenues of pleasure but had cruelly distorted his memory.

"As a little incentive," Victor said, tearing the tape from his mouth, "I've decided that our arrangement at the airport should be suspended. Until this is resolved."

"That sounds fair," Warren said. When you're being tortured, he decided, anything that's not torture sounds like a pretty fair deal.

From the quieted radio, Warren recognized the restrained opening melody of *Blue in Green*. The notes were as hushed as rain on water.

"Man, that's beautiful," Theo said. He removed his sunglasses, and Warren noticed that he had unusually sad, gray eyes. The music appeared to have moved him deeply. It showed in those eyes.

Sixteen

After Ben had gone out to the barn to start work for the day, Emma telephoned Sweet at the hospital, using the number Ben had added to the fire, police, and poison control numbers listed on the wall beside the phone. The phone rang four times before Sweet's answering service picked up.

Would she like to page him?

Yes she would.

Was the call regarding one of Dr. Sweet's patients?

Yes it was.

Was it urgent?

Of course not. It most certainly was not urgent.

Would she like to leave a number where Dr. Sweet could phone her back?

She thought about that. This was something she wanted to do without Ben's knowledge, so if Sweet took his time calling her back, there was the risk that she would be away and Ben would answer. Not likely, she thought. For the last few days he'd worked outside all morning, and had once even skipped lunch, trying to catch up on his backlogged work. It was a risk she'd have to take. If he found out about it, she'd deal with it. Some things just had be done. She gave her number and hung up the phone.

First you see it, she thought. Then you do it.

The phone rang suddenly and startled her. It was Sweet, apologetic as always. He asked if they could meet for lunch in an hour. "I know it's a little sudden," he said, "but it's my only free moment today. Is that all right?"

It wasn't all right, of course, because eating anything before mid-afternoon still nauseated her. The stomach flu had stubbornly held on and it seemed unfair that she had been the only one to get it. Yesterday, in a sudden fit of terror, she'd driven to the pharmacy and bought two pregnancy tests. To her immeasurable relief, both had come up negative. She hid the remains of the tests in the bottom of the trash and ignored the temptation to debate whether or not she would have had an abortion. "That sounds fine," she said. "Why don't we meet at Lab Street?" She would tell him she'd eaten a late breakfast and would have only coffee.

Upstairs, she undressed and stepped into the shower. The first touch of the warm water caused her to shiver pleasurably; she was grateful there was no need to hurry. In Boston, Nina and Sylva had monopolized nearly every waking moment of her day. To fit everything in, she'd had to hurry through showers, through washing her hair, through the money-saving home manicures. Through virtually everything that made her feel good about herself. Now, she was content to be alone. Not that she'd been able to make much of the time; she'd been sick almost every morning. Showering seemed to help, or maybe it just momentarily took her mind off it. She wondered if she'd picked up a parasite from the truck-stop food they'd eaten while traveling back and forth.

When she and Warren had been civil to each other, years ago, she recalled that he'd once told her a story about the time he'd picked up a parasite in Matadi. She asked how one got rid of a parasite in Africa, so far from a hospital or any conventional medicine, and he told her that out in the bush there had been only one known cure, a very unpleasant one. The patient, he said, didn't eat or drink for two days. On the morning of the third day, a single sugar cube was placed on the patient's tongue. When the first cube dissolved, it was replaced with another, and so on, until the parasite began to move upward from the intestine into the stomach, seeking the nourishment of the sugar cube. There, he'd said, it was involuntarily rejected.

Rejected? she'd asked.

Rejected, he'd said, and had grinned. She'd given him a puzzled look and he mimicked a person throwing up. The human body, he'd said, is like an art critic. Anything that slithers in off the barometer gets tossed out.

If that was the case, she should have gotten rid of it by now. As she stepped out of the shower and toweled herself dry, she thought more about Warren. He was full of those sorts of stories. While most of the stories were graphic or even slightly obscene, she found their genuine detail fascinating. Like the ringworm story. She always remembered that one. A broken pencil and two inches per day. It was an obscene story, but hearing it had given her a slight, familiar twinge of envy. Like most women she knew who had given their lives wholly to raising children, she was fiercely proud of her work and yet deeply suspicious that it had robbed her of a great deal of experience. She never doubted that what she did was important, but she sometimes regretted the sacrifices it required. Warren had seen so much, had been to so many places, while she had lived out most of her thirty-three years in this narrow corridor between Boston and New York. It seemed indecent that so much experience had been wasted on someone like him.

She chose to wear faded jeans and a blue top. For a few minutes she considered dressing up, but then decided that doing so would deliver a mixed message to Sweet. We are broke, she would tell him. And yet she'd look like someone ready to go out on the town? It wouldn't mesh. He'd decide right away that she was just another spoiled little rich girl, pouting over having to clip a buck here or there. We are broke, she would tell him. Tell me what I should do. He'd take in her sensible clothes and the worry lines around her eyes and the fact that she had eaten nothing with lunch, and he'd understand. She hated looking sensible but sometimes you had to look the part. She studied herself in the mirror. Sensible, all right. But it would have to do. She went downstairs and walked out to the barn to tell Ben she was going to lunch. Because he was working, he wouldn't ask questions, so she hadn't bothered to construct a plausible lie. Sometimes it bothered her, the way he could turn her on and off. Another paradox of womanhood. You hated the jealous types, but you resented the ones who were never jealous.

In the barn, she found Ben crouched down by the rear passenger-side tire of the Sahid's MG. He was hammering savagely at the end of the tire iron with the side of a wrench, trying, she guessed, to loosen a rusted lug nut. The image seemed incongruous. Almost as a rule, he was gentle with everyone and everything but himself. He didn't see her watching him and went on hammering for more than twenty seconds, the bolt refusing to loosen. Finally, he threw the wrench down.

"Cocksucker," he said. He was out of breath.

"That's a new one."

He looked up and, incredibly, smiled. It was the first smile she had seen out of him since the hospital, and it seemed to release a small amount of the tension between them. "I learned it from Nina," he said.

She uncrossed her arms. "I'll bet," Emma said. "She was working on her repertoire up in Boston." Was it safe to joke about that yet?

He shook his head, and his smile grew by a notch. Apparently it was. "I hope she didn't use that one."

"I know?" Emma said. "Imagine my mom trying to spell that one out for me. 'Emma, it began with a see-oh-see-kay.'"

"'Well what did it end with, Mom?'" Ben asked, mimicking Emma's faux dutiful-daughter voice.

"'Emma, it ended with an ess-you-see-kay-ee-are.'"

"Thing is," he said matter-of-factly, "she swears like a sailor when she's watching the Red Sox. Every fly ball she goes, Damnit, damnit, damnit."

"I hadn't noticed," Emma said. But he was right. "I guess she does."

He looked at the wrench. "Anyway," he said.

She was late, had to get going, but she was reluctant to let the moment pass. "Nina seems better," she said.

"She does," he said. "I think it's good that they're both back in school."

"The Ritalin's helping, too."

"I guess so," he said. He stood up, wiping his hands on a rag, and leaned against the fender of the MG, placing most of his weight on his good leg.

Had he wiped his hands off because he planned to touch her? It occurred to her that they hadn't yet made love. Tried, yes; consummated, no. Maybe tonight? If the Zoloft would let him. Would let them. It has to be us in this, she thought. She wanted to make love, but not necessarily to satisfy any immediate physical desire. It merely seemed important that they be close. "I'm wondering," she said. "How are you?"

"I'm okay," he said. He looked at her openly. "I mean—you know."

"Right," she said. She didn't want to press that line any further. If he wanted to talk, he'd talk. The worst thing she could do is corner him. "I'm meeting Jane for lunch," she said.

He raised an eyebrow. She expected some sort of dig, but he only said, "Good," and bent to retrieve his wrench, his mind already back on work. Apparently he'd decided not to argue that point with her anymore; it was up to her. Which of course made her feel more guilty about lying to him.

"I'll be back in an hour," she said. "You want anything from downtown?"

He waved her off and began hammering away at the tire iron. Whatever aperture she had pried open had snapped shut. She pulled the sliding door to the barn shut and walked to her car. He was still hammering as she started the car and drove away.

Sweet was already seated and eating when she walked into Lab Street. He made no apologies, nor did he acknowledge the possibility that starting without her had been rude. He signaled for the waiter to bring her a menu, but she stopped him and said she had just eaten a big breakfast.

"You want some water?" he asked. He didn't wait for her to answer, but only nodded to the waiter and tapped his glass with an index finger. As the waiter was filling her water glass from a pitcher, Sweet's beeper went off. He examined it and muttered an almost inaudible curse.

Emma wondered if they were going to have time to talk. "Are you sure this is okay?"

He looked up from his beeper and seemed to realize that he'd been rude. "You'll have to forgive me," he said. "I need to give my full attention to my patients, so when I'm not with them I compress my time a little."

"That makes sense." She wondered if having patients felt like having children. She wondered if Sweet hurried through the things that made him feel good.

"This place is strange," he said. He set down his fork and examined the dog photographs that covered every wall of the restaurant. "I've only been here once before and I don't remember all this."

"It is a little creepy," Emma said. "He did it last year after his dog died."

"I've heard he's a nice guy."

"He is," Emma said. She and Jane Rhoden often met here and drank at the bar. One night the owner had been tending the bar, and Jane, of course, had introduced herself. "If he wasn't so nice people would say he's crazy. But since he is they call him eccentric." She sighed. "Maybe that's the secret. You have to earn yourself a little slack."

"Maybe I should have a talk with him," Sweet said, and winked.

Apparently it was safe to joke about that, too. She decided that she liked the doctor, although she was slightly embarrassed that she'd been so forthright with him at their last meeting, the morning Ben had been shot. It seemed improvident to share so much of yourself with a stranger. After you had told the truth even once, there was nowhere to hide. She wondered how Ben had fared in their meetings. He'd probably, she reflected, closed down like an oyster. God knew he did with her, when he was pressed.

Sweet began to work on his club sandwich. A healthy eater, she noted. Ate an awful lot for someone his size. He probably didn't weigh much more than she. As she watched him eat it occurred to her, oddly, that this was the first time she had ever eaten a meal alone with a black person. It seemed a shameful fact of life that she should broach a first such as this so late in life. The walls, however invisible, however broken down by her liberal upbringing, were still there. He was black, and she was white, and they were having lunch together only by accident. "I think everyone could use a little time with you," she said.

"Imagine how busy I'd be," he said.

"You'd be rich."

"Believe me," he said, "and I don't mean to sound like an ass, but there comes a point when the money ceases to be worth it." He stabbed a forkful of greens from his plate.

"It works the other way, too," she said. "Sometimes not having it isn't worth it."

"Isn't worth what?"

"Isn't worth fighting the good fight."

"I was broke all through college," Sweet said. "It was all the rage. Everyone was doing it."

"It wasn't so bad when I was twenty-five," Emma said. "But I'm learning that it chips away at you. After a while you start to come unfastened from your ethics."

"How do the monks do it?" Sweet asked. "They say the poverty cleans them up."

"I don't know," she said. "Hawthorne had it all wrong. Puritan life's a drag. That's why his novels are so boring. The only interesting part is the sin."

"And you don't really get much of that," Sweet added. "It's all after the fact."

"Maybe that's the whole point. Although pornography would have helped his sales. Maybe he should have studied under Henry Miller." She thought for a moment. "Chekhov's pretty bad, too. He writes as if he had indigestion."

"I think the Bible's the worst," Sweet said. "No one ever has any fun. So you never have any fun while you're reading it."

"You read the Bible?"

Sweet yawned. "A bit," he said. He seemed slightly distracted.

"I've only read Revelations. Back when I was bored in church. It's better than a John Ford western."

"You read a lot."

"I used to," she said. "Before I had kids?"

"So it's true, is it?"

"It is," she said. "First you have the kids. Then they have you."

"Does having kids make things hard for you and Ben?"

She didn't answer.

"What I mean is, does it change how you deal with each other?"

"A little," she said. "We fight more, now that we have them. To control the fights you bargain. And after a while you become sort of like business partners."

"Sounds kind of dry."

"It's not so bad," she said. She thought of the conversation she had just had with Ben. "You have these little flashes of what's beneath. Of why you're together in the first place. You feel fun again. I think it's impossible to sustain that feeling all the time. But when you get that rare glimpse of it, it means that much more."

"I guess that sounds nice," he said. He seemed unconvinced.

She'd explained it poorly. But how could someone who had never been married understand? "Every day," she said. "You have to try every day. It's up to you." For instance, she thought, today? Entirely up to me. Which is sometimes nice, yes, but today it's overwhelming. I'm hoping you'll point me to where Ben wants to go, doctor.

Sweet set down his fork. "How are things with you now? Do you think the Zoloft is helping?"

Emma set her purse on the chair beside her and removed her jacket. "I'm not sure how much Ben has told you," she said.

"The truth is," he said, "what Ben and I have talked about has to stay between us. I don't mean to sound rude. But the confidentiality of it is half the reason it's so effective. It offers him a little shelter."

"I'm not asking about specifics," she said. "I'm just trying to figure out how much you know."

"Considering what I do know," Sweet said openly, "I'm a little stunned he was released."

"That wasn't you?"

"It was over my head," Sweet said.

"What is it that you know?"

Sweet rested his elbows on the table and opened his hands. He struggled for a moment, trying to form an acceptable answer. "Emma," he said, "maybe we should have Ben here."

"Please," she said. She wanted this to go on. "Please."

"He told me an awful lot."

"Why would he tell you so much?"

Sweet shrugged. "Hard to tell. Maybe he wanted to talk about it."

"But why not with me?"

"Sometimes," he said, "it's the people you're closest to that you talk to the least."

She watched him silently.

"They care about what you think about them," he explained.

She grimaced and pressed her fingertips against her eyes.

"He told you what he does on those Sunday nights?"

"You mean for Warren?"

"That. He told you where he goes?"

"He told me a little bit about it."

"What do you think about it?" she asked.

"I think it's inadvisable to do anything illegal. Ever."

So there it was. The thing she had known all along but had bargained away. Now that she knew, there was nowhere for her to hide. "You don't think it's a little more complicated than that?"

"No," he said, "I don't. The first step is to pull someone out of the cycles they've started." He sighed. "Sometimes it's too late, you know? Some people are so filled with rage or depression it's hard to help them. Those are the ones you feel for the most."

"I hope Ben's not one of them."

"He's not," Sweet said. "Not yet."

Emma took a sip of her water.

"What is it?" Sweet asked.

"I'm worried how you'll answer the question I'm about to ask."

He smiled. She still liked him, but to a small degree she also feared him. "Ben's had a job offer," she said. "A big one."

"Good. I think providing's important to him."

"There's a problem, though."

Sweet's beeper went off but he reached down and silenced it without looking at the number.

Am I the patient now? she wondered. "The offer came from a friend of ours. Or rather, from the husband of a friend of mine. The husband's kind of a snake. He's been having an affair, which isn't really anything new with him. I mean it's happened plenty of times before."

"Has she ever had one?"

"A few times. Not as much as him, if that means anything."

"Not really," Sweet said.

"She's decided to divorce him."

"And she's told you this?"

Emma took another sip of water. "She hasn't told me about it. But her husband called Ben the other day and they talked and he offered Ben a job. But as far as Ben can tell, his getting hired depends on whether or not I can talk her out of divorcing him."

"You think you have that kind of pull with her?"

"I don't know," Emma said. "I'm not sure I want to find out."

"Good," he said.

"But I wonder. It's a real opportunity for him. For us. I think he's going to worry himself into a heart attack in a few years, but I can't convince him to sell the house or the land. And her husband did say he's turned himself around. So I could be saving a marriage. I mean they have kids. This is fifteen years of marriage. I'm not even sure I could do it, but . . ." She trailed off. He got the point.

Sweet rubbed the back of his neck. "What does Ben think?"

"He asked me to do it."

"He thinks you should."

"He does. Said it was a way out. And that whatever happens between them is between them."

"Sounds like Ben's coming at things a different way than you."

"He's after the end. I'm a little confused about the means. I mean it's really possible this guy has turned himself around."

"I think," Sweet said, "you should be having lunch with your friend instead of with me."

"So does Ben," Emma said.

"You should be telling her these things. That's what friends do." He leaned back in his chair. "But you should know this, Emma. This isn't psychology, it's common sense. And we're getting ahead of ourselves by focusing on the mights and the maybes. The first thing we should do is help Ben understand his relationship with Warren. After that's taken care of, he can start thinking about what comes next." His beeper went off again. He ignored it. "There's got to be a better way. Any other way would be better."

"He told you it was for the money."

"He did."

"It is, and it isn't," Emma said. "I mean we do need it."

"There's more to it?"

"Do you know about Ben's mother? How she died?"

Sweet shook his head. "The subject never came up."

"She died about ten years ago. The year before he and I moved in together. She had breast cancer, and it really took its time. She decided that she didn't want to wait around for it. But Warren wouldn't help her. He kept her doped up in the bedroom for three months and refused to discuss the matter. Finally, Ben had to do it."

Sweet crossed his arms and looked at his plate.

"He never mentioned this?"

"I'm surprised I missed this," Sweet said. He seemed genuinely upset.

"For years afterward, he and Warren didn't speak. No words, but a lot of glares exchanged over highballs from opposite corners of parties. The air let out of a few sets of tires. Warren even got Ben's membership at the Country Club revoked. It went on like that for five years. And then it all changed when the business went bankrupt. Two years later, there was the fire at Ben's grandfather's house. And six months after that, somehow—I don't *know* how—all is forgiven. Or rather, the argument is put on the shelf. And they're talking again." She took a sip of water. "At the bottom of it all, I think Ben's not sure he did the right thing."

"About?"

"His mother. He broods. Terribly conflicted. But the farther Warren sinks down the drain, the surer he seems to be that he did the right thing. Warren's addiction marks him as the misguided one. Maybe what Ben wants is revenge. Or maybe he just wants relief."

"What about you?" Sweet asked. "What do you want?"

"I want him to put it all away," she said. "I want him to come back."

"Do you think he did the right thing?"

"Honestly?" she asked. "I'd want him to do that for me, too. If you love someone, you owe them that, at least." She doubted that Sweet, who'd never been married, could understand. She doubted that he'd ever given up anything for a woman in his life.

Sweet picked up his fork and began to tap it lightly against the edge of the table. "I need to think about this for a while," he said. "The next time I see Ben, I'll have to tell him that we talked."

"I know," she said.

"I think it'd be best if he heard that from you. If he doesn't, he'll mistrust us both. And then neither of us will be able to help him."

"I can't help him," she said flatly. "I'm in it, too."

"But you don't want to be," he said. "From what you've told me, I think Ben does. I think he's engineered a lot of this." Sweet's beeper went off and this time he looked down at the number. "I think he wants this to happen," he said, holding the beeper up to the light. His brow furrowed as he took in the number.

"Immoral," she said, "isn't it?" A bad joke about a bad subject. She wished she could take it back.

"Without a doubt," he said. He wasn't listening. He took a twenty-dollar bill from his wallet and set it on the table, weighing the bill down with his water glass.

"I think I'll stay for a moment," she said.

Sweet hesitated. "You're going to tell him that we met?"

"I will. I promise."

"And tell him I'd like him to call me."

Here she was, passing messages, like it was high school again. Never on the giving or receiving end, always in the middle. Always the conduit. "I will. I think he may want to talk with you about his medication."

Sweet nodded. He seemed to understand exactly what she meant.

There you go again, she thought as she watched him leave. You've been honest, and now there's nowhere to hide.

So Ben was, she reflected, pacifying all of them. He was employing the same euphemistic indirection as her father. They were *in a tough spot* because *money was tight*. But they would be *all right* because the work he was doing for Warren was *nothing, it's nothing Em*. There had been a time when his doublespeak would have enraged her, but now, after the slight connection she had felt with Ben that morning, it frightened her. She had allowed herself to believe that he was getting better. But now she saw that he was refusing help. He was slowly walling himself off.

It seemed plain enough that if Ben didn't get this job they would end up bankrupt, or he'd end up in jail. He'd begin to drink again. And how much of her own childhood—how much of that disgrace— would repeat itself for Nina and Sylva as the word spread of their drunk, jailed father? Of their family's bankruptcy? Of their mother, who'd failed to stop it from happening? Each of them would become *one of those women who*. They'd live their life out settling someone else's accounts. Serving the purpose of someone else's conscience.

At this point, she reflected, it was a question of who would pay. If Jane gave Mick one last shot and he blew it—what clearer evidence could she have? It would be whatever Mick made of it. Emma lifted her cell phone from her purse—it cost them an agonizing thirty dollars a month, but Emma insisted that she have it in case the girls ever needed to contact her—and pressed the first number on her speed dial.

Mick was deep into his backswing when his cell phone vibrated against his thigh. The descending stroke was distracted and poorly placed, and he hooked the ball—as he always did—into the birches. You shouldn't be out here anyway, he thought wearily, watching the ball rattle into the web of bare white branches. He dropped his driver and fished the cell phone from his pocket. It's mid December for Christ's sake. Everyone must think you're crazy.

The number on the phone's readout startled him: it said, BASCOMB, E, but Emma's number wasn't programmed into his phone. He examined the phone and realized immediately that he had accidentally picked up Jane's instead of his from the kitchen table that morning. They were so goddamn alike, how was he supposed to know? He considered answering the call to tell Emma his mistake and then realized that if he did, Jane would think he'd willfully stolen her phone that morning to monitor who called her. The truth was beside the point; he simply couldn't get through to her. It was like chipping at a glacier with a penknife.

Everyone had thought it funny when she built that bonfire in the front yard. He overheard her telling the story five or six times, and every time she had, it drew a sustained laugh, a head-shaking, isn't-that-like-our-little-Jane sort of laugh. The last time he heard her tell it, while coming out of the coat room at the country club Christmas party, he assumed such a feeling of despair that he carried his drink into the back parking lot, where he heaved his glass against the steel trash dumpster with such force that he frightened himself.

People thought the story was funny; but he had been there. He had seen what actually happened. As he placed the cell phone back in his pocket, he tried to recall exactly what she said. Whenever she told the story she knighted herself with wit, granted herself the ire that memory allows, but the truth was that her face, thrown into sharp relief by the firelight, had been slack and wasted. Her voice had quivered, and in its distinct, wounded register he sensed, for the first time, the way his indiscretions destroyed her.

Jane, he asked, nudging the fire with his foot, why are you burning our linens? He already knew the answer, but he wanted to grant her, at the very least, the small triumph of convicting him.

She stared him contemptuously for a full minute before speaking, her eyes dull and lifeless with drink, her hair unpinned. I'm burning our linens, she said, because that chippie who cuts your hair has given us the crabs.

He didn't answer.

Our home, she continued, is infested with an army that was born and raised in your girlfriend's cunt.

Jane, he said, forming his words carefully, frightened by the degree she had come unhinged, you're making a scene. He wanted to tell her that this woman he slept with meant nothing to him, that he thought her unattractive and uninteresting, and that she had simply been available, and that he had been selfish and weak. But of course it was folly to explain away pleasure.

Mick, Jane said, when I take the carving fork from the block tonight and bury it up to the tang in your black heart, that will be a scene. She went inside and left him alone to tend to the fire. It was his mess, anyway.

He was so certain she meant what she said about the fork, he took it from the block later that night and heaved it into the woods. There were, of course, thousands of other weapons in the house, but that particular one seemed charged with purpose. As he recalled, she even changed that part of the story, having him bury it instead of throw it. Thus allowing her the exit-punchline of explaining that she didn't like to garden.

It worked every time, for everyone but them. Somehow her poisonous wit, so welcome in the past, turned inward. He had done the worst thing anyone can ever do: he caused someone to change her base nature. His indiscretions, and his weaknesses, had killed off the part of her he always loved most.

He believed that he could be faithful to Jane. It seemed simple, really, now that he had made up his mind. If only he could get her to see that. He dropped his driver back into his bag and began to walk back toward the clubhouse. It was no use going on, now that he was thinking about her and about his dawning sense that his efforts were the stuff of futility. Emma's phone call left him feeling helpless. The bag's strap pinched painfully at his shoulder through his heavy jacket. It was a long walk from the third tee. He had come here this morning with the vague notion that time alone and exercise would make him feel happy, but he'd been reminded, as he always was when he found himself alone, that he wasn't cut out for silent meditation. Time revealed his limitations, and each time he found himself alone he accepted anew, without sadness, that he was not a particularly intellectual or philosophical man.

He succeeded among intellectuals, which was enough for him, but only because he understood them fully without understanding himself at all. From the time he was in college, he'd come to understand that his particular talent lay in his knack for convincing people to do things that frightened them. He employed that talent as leverage in seduction for so long; the fact that it aided him in his work as an investment banker always seemed secondary.

As he walked into the clubhouse, it occurred to him that, for all his earnest declarations of personal transformation, his most serious attempt at recovering Jane's trust had itself been deceptive. That was what sent him back to the clubhouse. Emma's call reminded him of what he had asked Ben to do. To that end, he realized, he hadn't changed a bit. It wasn't just his dealings with his wife that had to be reconsidered.

It was simple, he thought. As simple as being faithful. He would call Ben and withdraw his request and offer him the job. Ben had one stroke of bad luck, and he let it destroy him. In that sense, he wasn't really cut out for business. He was far too emotional about the numbers. But the board could keep their eye on him. If he did poorly, they could hold him to payroll and basic operations, and if he did well—they'd wait and see. For all his hardwired social ineptitude, Ben was a likeable person; or maybe he just felt sorry for him. Sometimes it was hard to tell the difference between the two. Mick had once heard that Bascomb helped his mother commit suicide. Mick himself had never, ever, lost anyone he loved, and he simply couldn't imagine this world without his parents living in it. He genuinely felt sorry for Ben.

As he came out of the clubhouse, adjusting his tie, one of the front desk clerks stopped him and said he had a visitor waiting for him in the bar. The clerk's raised eyebrow made it plain that the visitor was of the questionable sort.

Not her, Mick thought. Not her. We already burned the sheets for her.

"Someone named Bascomb?" the clerk said.

Better, he thought. He could do it now, in person. Apologize. And if Jane decided to leave him? At least he'd have the consolation of knowing he'd done the right thing. "In the bar?"

The clerk nodded, and Mick walked upstairs to the bar, thinking that he'd buy Ben lunch first and give him the news after they were finished. He hoped it would wash away the guilt he'd felt since Emma's phone call.

But it wasn't Ben; it was Warren, sitting beneath the window at the same table where he'd made that illicit offer to Ben. Mick observed him for a few moments, trying to guess the nature of his visit. He was drinking coffee and rending sugar packets to shreds. The blue paper placemat before him on the table was littered with the remnants of his work. He'd obviously been waiting anxiously for a long time. He was sitting askew on his chair, as if he'd recently injured a hip. With the life he lives, Mick thought, anything's possible. He recalled that until a few years ago, Warren had been a longtime member of the club. Handicap of nine.

"Warren," Mick said. "Kind of a surprise."

Warren twisted in his chair and looked up at Mick. He was pale. "You bet," Warren said.

"Here for lunch?"

"Just want to talk about something."

Mick sat across from him. Same chair he'd sat in across from Ben. He disliked the unpleasant suggestions that such parallelisms made. "I've got a few minutes," he said. He hoped he could shepherd Warren out and then return for lunch. Alone. Christ, he'd be swimming in despair by the time the check arrived. He wanted distraction, but not this sort of distraction.

Warren leaned forward and winced. He composed himself for a moment. "We have to talk about Ben."

"You think so?"

"It's important, Mick. It's something you should know about him."

"I'm listening." He yawned and made no effort to hide it. For weeks he'd been sleeping on the basement couch, and he never felt rested anymore.

"I've heard that he's been offered a spot here."

"That so?" Mick tried to affect disinterest. "Who told you that?"

Warren shrugged. "You want him to run things, right?"

"We're considering Ben for the assistant manager spot."

"Right," Warren said. He moved his coffee cup an inch to the left. "A lot of responsibility."

"I think he's up to it," Mick said.

"But a lot of responsibility, right?"

"I suppose."

"Payroll."

"Among other things."

"Watching the books."

"That would be secondary, really."

"And you'd only put someone in that position you could trust, right?"

"Warren," Mick said, already deciding what he'd have for lunch in a few minutes, "I'm really too busy for an interrogation."

Warren opened his hands in mock surrender. "I'm just saying that during the course of a year you've got hundreds of thousands of dollars moving in and out. And that a spot like that could be a problem for someone who isn't completely together."

"And you obviously think Ben isn't."

"No," Warren said, "I don't."

"Well, I guess you would know, Warren," Mick said. "You being family and all." Everyone knew that Ben and Warren could scarcely tolerate each other. Years ago, there had been an physical incident at the clubhouse on Christmas Eve that had gotten them both ejected, both their memberships revoked.

"I may be—" Warren thought for a moment, "—I may be less respectable than I once was, but I still know north from south."

"I think Ben does, too," Mick said. "I have a lot of faith in him. In fact I decided to offer him the job this morning."

Warren fixed his jaw. His fingers searched among the destruction he'd wrought on the placemat. "Listen," he said. "Do you know where Ben was the last few weeks?"

"He was in the hospital," Mick said. "Two nervous cops almost greased his ass, in case you hadn't heard. In his own home."

"He was in the hospital," Warren said. "You've got that right."

Mick theatrically checked his watch. The discussion was giving him a headache.

"He was in the psych ward," Warren said. "Locked in."

Mick rubbed his chin. He hadn't shaved well that morning. "That's a little hard to believe."

"Ask around," Warren said. "They admitted him on a court order because he was suicidal."

"And how do you know this?"

"I'm more a part of his life than you think. Than anyone thinks." He looked at Mick openly, his expression rife with subtext. "I'm just saying that there's more to Ben than meets the eye. He's got some things eating away at him."

"Seems like you do, too."

"I do. And Ben's got a lot to do with that."

Mick closed his eyes and tried to relax. His headache had ratcheted upward another notch. "Warren," he said, his eyes still closed, "it's all a little difficult to believe."

"You can check it out easily enough. And that's not the worst of it."

"I don't want to hear any more," he said. Hiring Ben was what he wanted to do. He didn't want to rethink this. He wanted to be very clear about what was the right thing to do.

"Ben's the one who keeps me supplied." He admitted this, an oblique reference to his alleged addiction, without any sign that it caused him shame.

"That's ridiculous."

"How do you think he pays that mortgage, Mick?"

Although Warren obviously had a motive for telling him these things, his designs didn't necessarily make them untrue. "I don't want to hear any more," he said. He could learn the rest of what he needed to know on his own. He could wade through fact and fiction without Warren's smug help.

Warren seemed to sense this and he stood up to go. "It is what it is," he said. He limped out of the bar.

Mick watched him go and then sat looking out at the fairway for a moment. Then he leaned forward and dipped his finger in the sugar piled on Warren's placemat and touched it to his tongue. Too late, with it already pressed to his tongue, he found that it was salt.

Seventeen

Raif gripped the fibers of the carpet tightly with his fists and grunted as he straightened his wrapped left leg and then lifted it six inches off the ground. The clock on the VCR said that it was eighteen minutes past ten. He forced himself to hold the leg in the air for a count of twenty. The physical therapist had warned him against working too hard, but he'd learned during the last week that only total physical exhaustion would drive the fear away. You have to be reasonable, she said. You have to be patient.

Being reasonable and patient, he thought, is exactly what got me here. I've treated every bigot I've met reasonably and patiently. I've deconstructed their prejudices calmly, even compassionately. I've never once allowed myself to show anger. But what I failed to realize was that bigots are, by their very nature, unreasonable. And they are impatient to reach to that state of unreason. Why is it, after they've broken my femur, that I'm the one being asked to be reasonable, to be patient? You cannot hope to combat unreason with reason, impatience with patience. If you do, you end up like this.

They had surrounded him, he recalled, as he walked along the unlighted footpath that led from his office to the parking lot. Because the attack happened in almost total darkness, he remembered the moment as an invisible composition of sounds and smells: the cheerful *clink* sound the aluminum bats made whenever they struck bone; the organic compost odor of the wet leaves beneath him as he lay on the ground; the deep thrum of the science building generator a few yards away.

He slept with a light on beside the bed every night now, but because that didn't quite do the trick, he also drank too much, beginning with a gin each night just before dinner, then a bottle of wine with dinner and more after. Always a heavy drinker, he knew that now he was slipping into something more withdrawn and more destructive than mere recreational use. He witnessed what was happening with a curious, clinical eye, but was unable to stop it.

Oh, fuck reasonable, he thought. Fuck resignation and patience, and fuck these crutches. I want to walk again. I want to feel that I'm able to defend myself, should someone decide to make another example of me for the local sodomites. But what have I done wrong? It must be the thought that's the sin, because God knows I haven't done it in so long. And won't for a long time. Who would have me, like this? He clenched his jaw and raised his leg again and promised himself he would recite all of Frost's *Design* before he lowered it, but made it only to *What brought the kindred spider to that height / Then steered the white moth thither in the night?* before the quadriceps muscles began to tremble violently and then fail. He lay back on the carpet and found that he had soaked his shirt through with sweat. Suddenly he was strangely near tears. That poem had always frightened him, and it seemed odd to him that he'd chosen it.

This was how events like this destroyed you.

They pulled you one way and another. And finally they pulled you in two.

There was a sharp *rap-rap* on the corner window. Raif sat up and peered at the dark glass. Through the reflection of the living room, he saw Ben looking in with those sad eyes, motioning to the front door—a translucent table-lamp perched on his left shoulder; a translucent wall-clock was suspended over his head. He wore a tie and an expensive suit. Raif gripped the arm of the sofa and raised himself to his feet, then gathered his crutches under him and passed through the kitchen to the front door.

His first thought when he opened the door was that Ben was drunk. He hadn't shaved and his tie was poorly-knotted and loosened. The suit was indeed an expensive one, a somber charcoal gray, but its creases were gone and it fit him badly. He had lost weight and clearly hadn't been sleeping much.

"What's the occasion?" Raif asked. He usually hated when people stopped by without warning, but tonight he was grateful for the company.

"I was in the neighborhood," Ben said. He ran his thumb down the inside of his lapel. "Got a beer?"

"Did you drive?"

"Well enough."

"Where were you?" Raif closed and bolted the front door.

"Me?" Ben asked. He sat at the kitchen table. "I was just getting flushed."

Raif took two beers from the refrigerator and the church key from the shelf above the sink and sat across from Ben. "What happened?"

"I had dinner with the city's lawyer. Nice fella. Very nice dinner at The New American in New Haven."

"I've never been," Raif said. "Can't afford it."

"Me neither. He bought."

"How'd you rig that?"

"I called him this afternoon. Said I wanted to talk about settling things with the city. He acts like I've asked if he'd mind sleeping with my wife."

"He must have been surprised that you called."

Ben picked at the label on his beer for a moment. "I had a job offer in the works. Thought it'd work out, but the guy called me today and said it wasn't happening. No explanation. Just wasn't happening. Why not? I ask. You're just not right for it, Ben, he says. So I'm shit out of luck on that and I've got medical bills you wouldn't believe. I mean thousands and thousands of dollars, and I can't even make the February mortgage, yet. So I'm thinking the city might want to do something quietly and quickly. And sure enough the guy says, Let's meet. Says he'll buy. I say buy away. Where, he wants to know. Let's try The New American. The place in New Haven? he asks. The very one, I say. All right, Bascomb. Whatever you want. I hop in the car and head south on ninety-five and roll past those nine exits with the radio going like hell, and I realize that, job or no job, I'm about to come into a lot of money. I mean a lot. So I beat him there, and I have a martini and say, On the tab, garçon. Lawyer arrives. Nice fella. Young like you. Says he wants the best for everyone. I know he's not on my side, but he's straight with me. Says he knows I have two daughters and a family to think about. Shows me picture of his own little girl. I have another drink and then another, and I notice he's not drinking. Just tap water. We both eat. Or rather I have the rack of lamb with some mustard thing and he just picks at his veal chop and we're eating in silence until he pushes his plate away and gets down to brass tacks.

"Listen Bascomb, he says. I've read the book on you. I know you've got debt. I know what happened to your business. I know you couldn't so much as take the wife to a ballgame right now, and you sure as hell can't pay the hospital bills. You could try and get something from us, he says. It's possible that in time you'd get a decent pile of cash. But then again, maybe you wouldn't. Maybe you'd wait five, six years while this dragged through court and get nothing for it but legal bills. I get wise and say, maybe I should give some interviews to the papers who keep calling and see what they think. Lawyer's not fazed by this. You're welcome to do this, he says. But of course we'd have to tell our side of things. Your hospitalization would come up. And we've got the tape of your call. You called and told the dispatcher there was a robbery, see? You said there was someone in the house. We've got the tape. The officers hear screaming, and they enter and see you bloody and your wife bloody, and they react to protect her. We've got the tape. The grand jury's not going to just roll over on that. A jury would find that very compelling. Five, six years of bills, and what if they decide that maybe you're not such a helpless guy? Maybe they back you, but maybe they don't. And then where are you? In a world of shit, I say. That's right, he says. Which is why we want what's best for everyone. So we would like you to consider an offer. We'll pay all of your hospital bills. We'll reimburse you for any time you've lost from your work. We'll even pay for some counseling for your wife and daughters to help them through what they had to see. We'll do all of this lavishly and gracefully and, most of all, quickly, as long as we can agree that this is behind us. And you'll get dinner tonight, I ask? That too, he says. As long as we can agree that this is behind us. You can pursue things further if you want. But like I said, a jury would find that tape very compelling. They might think you were up to something. Not such a helpless guy. Well, I say, I'd like to think about this. I'd like to run this by my wife. Of course you would, lawyer says. Here is my card and my home number on the back and you can use that any time, day or night, and let me know what you think. Good firm handshake in the gravel parking lot. And that's it."

"He's got a point," Raif said.

"He does."

"It rolls things back to zero."

"I suppose."

"Zero," Raif explained, "might be good for you right now."

Ben examined his soaked shirt. "What the hell have you been doing?"

Raif looked down at himself. "It is a little funny, isn't it?" It isn't funny at all, he thought. Or if it is it's only funny in a Flannery O'Connor way. "I'm doing leg lifts."

"With the pins and everything?"

"They start you early and you keep mobility."

"Mobility my ass," Ben said. "You're pinned like a debutante."

Raif looked at him.

"You're right. No jokes." They sat in silence for a moment. "What happened to all the get-well cards?"

"I threw them out."

"Too many?"

"The insincerity was getting to me."

"I thought they were nice."

"When I was a little kid," Raif said, "and it was someone's birthday at school, everyone in class had to draw a card for the kid who was having the birthday. Then the teacher would staple them all together and the kid would go home with this massive book to show his folks. For a day, even the most hopeless bully's got thirty, forty friends. Every so often I'd have to make a card for someone I didn't like. I didn't want to, but I had to, see? And I think that's what a lot of those cards were."

"That's a pretty cold way of looking at things."

"Six years of academia will do that to you. I'm guessing it's intellectually unfashionable not to care about me. I can only imagine what the talk is at the parties. The tenured sociologists saying, How ironic for these three to attack him for his sexual orientation, since their anger is itself an expression of displaced homoerotic rage, et cetera."

"Christ," Ben said. "No wonder you're hiding out."

Raif shrugged. "That's the way it is with academics. You interact all day with bored college kids. Out of the whole lot, you have maybe two or three good students who challenge you. Maybe just one. The rest are punching the clock. You become infected by their sloth. After a while you begin punching the clock, because, really, what's to keep you from doing that? It occurs to you that just about everyone on the staff is doing the same thing. You've got tenured professors who've taught the same lesson plans for a decade. Philosophers stalled on Bochenski. Cultural anthropologists who teach Margaret Mead as a modernist. Modern Lit professors who haven't read Philip Roth. Everyone knows it's a scam, and everyone feels guilty taking part in it, because he knows that he's never going to get caught with his hand in the honeypot. So this collective sense of intellectual inferiority develops. The tweedy types begin delivering soliloquies over their third drink. You know it's time to go home when you look around at a staff party and see everyone talking and no one listening."

"Still," Ben said, "it's not a bad life. Getting paid to think aloud."

Raif said that he supposed it wasn't.

"You mind if I have another one?"

"I'm not letting you drive if you do."

"I guess not then. I wouldn't want to get in the way."

"You wouldn't be in the way."

Ben sighed. "I suppose it's better than a DUI."

"A night in jail would sure top things off."

"More like a week. I don't think Emma would bail me out."

"Things are that bad?"

"I did something I shouldn't have done."

"Should I ask what it was?"

He didn't answer for a moment. "Anyway she's probably right. We should take what they offer."

"I think you should."

Ben took two more beers from the refrigerator and opened one with the church key. "I'm thinking," he said, "of doing some more work for that guy I was telling you about."

"I don't know, Ben. I think that might be a bad idea. It sounds pretty serious."

"What else can I do?"

"I could help you."

Ben looked at him levelly. "I don't see how you can help me, teachey. I don't need baby steps right now."

"How much do you need?"

"About two hundred thousand dollars."

Raif looked at him.

"And college money for the girls. And braces. Two prom dresses. Two weddings, I hope."

"Are you sorry you have them to take care of?"

"No," he said, "I'm sorry that I can't make it look easy."

"You think that's bad?"

"I think they're growing up with an idea that they live in a tough world. Nina's becoming difficult. Sylva's afraid."

"What about Emma?"

"Emma?" he asked. "I've turned her into an old woman." He yawned suddenly, expansively.

"I'm sorry to keep you up."

"It's not you," Ben said. "I didn't sleep much last night." He seemed suddenly upset. "I've been drinking a little bit too much."

"Maybe you shouldn't drink anymore."

"Not tonight," Ben qualified.

That sounds like a good plan, Raif thought. At least for tonight.

He made up the couch with sheets from the linen closet and loaned Ben a t-shirt and shorts to sleep in. Ben changed in the bathroom, and then walked back into the kitchen, where he carefully folded his suit jacket and pants. As he draped the pants over the back of one of the chairs, something fell heavily to the floor. Raif saw that it was a folded knife.

"What's that?"

"Think of it as a sleeping pill," Ben said. He seemed embarrassed as he put the knife back in his pants pocket. "It works the same way."

"Maybe I should get one." He felt sick for Ben, looking at the knife. He felt sick for both of them. That's how it starts for people like us, he thought. It starts with paranoia. Or maybe that's how it ends.

"I'm fine, Raif. Really."

"I shouldn't ask, should I?"

"No," he said.

Raif followed Ben into the living room. "You need anything else?"

Ben pulled the sheet up to his chin. "Nothing," he said. "Nothing but sleep."

"All right." He turned out the light and went upstairs and waited outside the bedroom door and listened. In a moment he heard Ben rise from the couch and walk quietly into the kitchen, where he searched through his clothes for a moment and then went back to the couch.

He can't sleep without it, thought Raif. He's that scared. Scared of what? Of the same things as me. Scared that a simple walk down a footpath will end in the hospital. Scared of not being able to defend himself. But suppose I'd had that knife. Suppose I'd had it there with me, as I was walking to my car. Would I have used it? I don't think I so much as raised a hand in my defense. What do you do—what *can* you do when they are three and you are one?

His parents had confronted him that way. The two of them and the invited priest, there in the hard white light of the kitchen eight years ago, three high-backed chairs opposing his; he'd arrived home from Yale after dark for the first day of Christmas break and found them waiting for him, the sink stacked full of dishes.

It is an unforgivable sin, Father Clelio had said, *one man with another.* The priest had been moved almost to tears. *Raif, you must consider what's at stake.*

Raif—then just a few days past his twenty-first birthday—had merely absorbed Clelio's steady gaze. His intellect had momentarily been bludgeoned to silence.

After Clelio left, his parents went to bed and left him alone at the kitchen table, where he watched the plate of food his mother had prepared for him turn cold. He stacked the plate in the sink and went upstairs to bed. Still dressed, he fell deeply asleep and dreamed his own suicide—the leap from the high terrace, the ecstasy of the fall. There in the dream, his afterlife was no harp-slung Eden, no drowsy Elysian oasis. Instead it seemed like an afterlife he'd read about once—his afterlife was a violet light and a hum.

Now, coldly enraged, he sat on the corner of the bed and reflected on the moral exile Clelio had bestowed upon him. In many ways, he had never returned from it. It felt very good to be angry, because while the fear went in the anger went out, and he felt the slow release as it went. It was the first time he had allowed himself to be angry, and he decided to be angry whenever he wished. Rage was a deadly sin, but that was no matter because it was already too late for him. Already, he thought, I've been turned away—at twenty-one, turned away for what I was made to be in this life.

We begin the afterlife in this life.

Ben woke in the dark later, and for a moment he couldn't remember where he was. Then he remembered that he had come to see Raif and had stayed because he was too drunk to drive and that he was on the couch in Raif's living room. He was frightened that he had drunk so much, because he had fully intended not to, and he was beginning to understand that he was powerless to stop himself. In the hospital, those first few drinks with Raif had made him feel joyful and unchained, drunk in the way a teenager feels drunk, euphoric and optimistic, but since that night the euphoria had slowly withered and had been replaced by a sense of isolation.

The light at the top of the stairs allowed him to make out the living room furniture around him and the doorway to the kitchen. By the clock on the VCR, he saw that it was half past midnight. The room was spinning lightly, and he wondered if he had finally poisoned his liver. He seemed to be more drunk now than he had been when he went to sleep. Overhead, he heard Raif talking on the phone. Ben stood up and wrapped the blanket around himself and quietly walked up the stairs. The wooden boards were sharply cold beneath his bare feet. At the top of the stairs he crouched down and listened.

He's all right, Raif said. He was silent as he listened to Emma speak.

I think so.

Maybe two hours or so.

I don't know. I don't think it went so well. At least it wasn't what he had wanted. They said they would pay the hospital bills and pay him back for the work he had missed. And something about counseling for the girls.

I don't know. If you want it, I guess. I thought he was already getting some.

Well he should.

I think so.

Yes.

I don't know him that well. But it does seem that way.

Maybe an hour. He went right out.

A lot. And then a few with me. He said he hadn't slept much last night.

Of course.

No, he's fine. I have his keys.

I promise I will. I'll check on him now.

It was nice to meet you, too. In person some time, I hope.

I promise. I'll check right now.

Ben walked down the stairs quickly and wrapped himself in the blanket and lay face down on the couch. He breathed slowly and rhythmically. At the edge of his vision he saw the light at the top of the stairs brighten and then darken all the way, and he heard Raif walk lightly down the steps. There was silence then, and Ben realized that Raif was standing beside the couch looking down at him. He was still wondering if Raif would reach down and smooth his hair—he wanted it to happen, *needed* it to happen, but not in a way that even resembled desire—when Raif walked into the kitchen and without turning on the light poured something into a glass and then quietly went back up the stairs. The light at the top of the stairs brightened again and then dimmed slightly as he pulled his bedroom door halfway closed. Ben rolled on his side and lay listening for a long time watching the dim light thrown across the far wall and the numbers on the VCR.

Eighteen

God bless the good pharmaceutical dope. God bless Demerol, Dolophine, Numorphan. God bless Tylox, Ultram, Percocet, Lortab. God bless the Peruvian opium farmers, with their slung Kalashnikov rifles and their unchallengeable ethics. God bless them, because thanks to them this ankle doesn't hurt at all. Can only imagine how it is for the street junkies. Shooting up with flour and talcum powder and whatever else the dealers cut it with in the ports. No wonder they overdose. Half of what comes through the spike is off the supermarket shelf. Have to take twice a lethal dose just to get a fix.

Wes taught me about all the tricks. Wanted my business. Wanted to impress me, even the first night I met him. Check this, Warren, he said, unfolding a small package onto the glass coffee table. See how it sparkles in the lamplight? Uncut coke doesn't sparkle. It's got a flat pale white color. And this sticks together. It's not supposed to do that. If it sticks it's got powdered laundry detergent in it. Can you believe this guy tried to pass this off as Peruvian? I'd be better off washing my clothes with it. Guy wants to sell me half a key. I say, how about I buy an eight-ball for kicks, and you get the fuck out. Thing is, you keep passing off stuff like this, someone's going to get hurt. And by someone I mean you. In this line of work, unhappy customers don't ask for a refund. They go straight to the manager, you know? Guy says, Why don't you take a sample and think it over? And I say, why don't you take your key and pound it up your ass?

Or wash your clothes with it, Warren said.

Wes laughed. Or that, he said. You're all right, Warren. I'm lucky I met you.

But you don't know luck, Wes. You wouldn't know luck if it took your pants down and got you off. Luck isn't who you meet. It's what you have. Luck, Wes, is having good pharmaceutical dope on hand after you've been cooked on the stove. It makes the whole experience seem so much less unpleasant.

Have to chip the skin off the face of the burner with a chisel or it'll set off the alarm next time, the next time the burner's on. No, it won't. He smashed it with his fist and what a fist that was.

Looks like it's getting infected and that will be something if it does.

Have to be careful. No more help from Victor. No more day-early handoffs and certainly no more rolling pharmacy. Bye-bye. Have to conserve, because it'll be harder now. Have to start thinking ahead. Ask around on the Drive and see if anyone knows someone who can dash off a script. Expensive that way. Have to consider cost now. Suppose I could sell her engagement ring. Had no idea when I asked them to take it off her that this was how I'd use it. Thought I'd take it out from time to time and remember her fondly. Never did, though.

Could have saved them the effort. Could have saved us all a great deal of unpleasantness. If you had waited a second longer to put the tape over my mouth, I would have told you that I didn't do anything with her. Couldn't have done anything with Trina because that part of me doesn't work any longer. Wonder what sort of treatment she got. Not so good, I bet. Nice girl. Mixed up with the wrong people.

Wouldn't be here if Lin hadn't gotten sick. None of this would have happened if she'd given up those cigarettes. She knew they were killers, but she never even tried to quit. Had them everywhere. In the car. In her beach bag. Kept her so thin. Coffee and cigarettes. How many times did I catch her in the bathroom, window open, waving the smoke out?

Damn it, Linda, can't you smoke outside? You're turning our home into an ashtray.

Wren, don't be such a yutz. You sawbones are all alike.

Do you know what your lungs look like, love?

Still fanning the smoke. What's that, Wren?

I'll show you a slide tonight at dinner. Not a pretty sight, love. And your heart.

What about my heart?

Those things give you an enlarged heart, Linda.

How large is my heart?

As big as a canned ham.

Wren, you're such a yutz. What should we have for dinner tonight, yutzy?

Let's have canned ham, Lin. Let me get my scalpel and we'll take it out of you.

You're going to eat my heart?

Of course. Should be some leftovers for lunch.

I'm going to shower first.

Can I watch?

Out. Out out. Later.

Kidded with her about it. But I always knew that someday it would kill her. Slowly and then suddenly. Dying and then dead. No, it was Ben who killed her. She had another three good months when he unlocked the drawer for her. She wasn't thinking right. Off her rocker from the Roxanol. Had another happy three months at least. And no pain. Never let you hurt. Three months more. If I had three months now. Three months. Three months at least. Three months more with you. Thank God she didn't use the .38. Same drawer. Under the box with her medication. Thank God, because imagine what I would have found then. Her brains all over the wall. But women never use guns.

The women never use guns, because even in suicide they find violence distasteful.

Warren sat up now and rubbed his eyes. Sleeping on the tile floor all night had left him feeling slow, but there was no sign of the stiffness that usually followed a bedless eight-hour nap.

After meeting with Mick yesterday, he fixed in his neck for the first time—ignoring the grim significance of that dubious, resigned first—and then fell asleep on the tile floor. In the morning, hungover to the point of stupefaction, he at first forgot what had happened with Victor. As he stood up, the first step sent a spike of pain up his leg and caused him to shout with pain. Then he saw the carving fork in the sink, the smashed fire alarm over the sink, and all at once remembered everything that had happened.

Now, in the bathroom, he sat on the edge of the tub and examined his ankle. The rectangular patch of skin over his Achilles tendon was gone, the edges of the wound charred and raw and pinkish. It would get infected for sure. And then there was the other burn. He hadn't looked at it, couldn't look at it. He would have to go to the hospital, and he could only imagine the reception he'd get there. Oh yes, you're the one who operated on that kid's knee while you were high. And your lovely son was here in The Box for two weeks.

And how *had* Ben gotten out? Probably antagonized everyone he met. The nurses and the doctors and even the other patients. Strickland refused to help. Lucky for me Ben's out, but maybe not the best thing for him. He is sick sick sick. That boy. If he doesn't get things right with Victor we're both out of luck. I'll be sober, and he'll be bankrupt. Maybe not so good for him to be out, but I need him. In Matadi we did what we needed to survive, and there was no problem. Everyone was a little off. Especially the doctors. Alcoholics. Bipolar philosophers. The trauma surgeon from Chicago who told me he came to Matadi to find The Thing In Itself. It seemed only natural that they were that way. You want doctors like that over there. The Congo River is a huge sink running to the Atlantic ocean, and Matadi is the drain. You need someone well acquainted with filth to clean out a drain like that. Someone unafraid to put his hands in it and smell it and see it and call it what it is.

He crawled to the dresser and took the first-aid kit from the bottom drawer. Cleaning the burn on his scrotum would hurt like hell, but if it became infected it would hurt a lot worse. He searched through the kit and found that he still had a bit of the Silver Sulfadiazine left from three years ago, although it seemed possible that its potency had diminished. So you get an infection, he thought. It's always going to be something. If it's not one disease, it's another.

Patients, nearly all patients, fall in love with their doctors. Warren found this to be true of every specialty, even the strange sort like neurosurgery or mycology. He remembered reading somewhere that Casanova had said anyone could be seduced if made grateful enough. This was the crucial point of your relationship with your patients; either you made them better, and therefore grateful, or you fucked them up more and were sued. You took their battered bodies, and you made them whole again, piece by piece—scapula, metacarpal, humerus. You repaired them and made them more grateful than they imagined they could be.

Occasionally there were embarrassing moments. People talked as the anesthetic was started—they held forth, as people often do after they've had too much wine. It was nearly always funny, though sometimes unwanted pieces of information were shared. Women—women *and* men—had pledged to sleep with Warren after they recovered. One old man, before a laborious hip replacement, had passionately, and wetly, kissed Warren's hand—he'd been unable to ignore the biblical suggestion of the act.

At Christmastime, he received so many cards he hadn't the time to open them all—many were swept, unread, into the trash. These cards, he'd found, often shared a sinister similarity, as if some local patient had conducted a class to establish rules for patient–doctor epistolae. All featured a photograph of the respective patient displaying the regained functionality or usefulness of the appendage or joint Warren had repaired—by the first week of December, his refrigerator and the adjacent walls began to look like a sad, eclectic sports-page: a flannel-shirted older man hurling a bowling ball down a lane toward blurred pins; a white-haired senior playing tennis in her ankle brace; a skier suspended over the long fall. And the note. Yes, the note. There was always the note.

> Dr Bascomb, I thank the LORD every DAY that I was shown the way to you and your TALENTS. I am better now and my medial meniscus is better than ever and THAT is because the LORD saw fit to give you such PROMETHEAN talent and the GIFT for healing the sick! Dr Bascomb, you are an ANGEL here looking after us on EARTH and the Lord KNOWS that. You are in our PRAYERS every NIGHT.

Their intent was to draw connections, but the relationship always remained the same; he felt separate from the sick. The letters deepened the rift. He felt that he lived outside their sphere of pain and convalescence. He began to believe that the notes were true. It is a destructive thing to believe everything said or written about you, good or bad, and if, by a certain age, you haven't learned that, you condemn yourself to a life of narcissism or of persecuted misanthropy.

The day after the fire, he woke in the burn unit. An old patient he'd seen through not just one but two knee replacements was sitting beside his bed, weeping.

Oh, you're dead, she said, and wept. You're dead.

For a long time, he simply lay and listened to the human sound of her tears, to the rhythmic, supermarket-checkout tone of the heart monitor. It occurred to him that he had fallen, permanently, from the impenetrable ivory tower of the surgeon. He wanted to move, to show her that he wasn't dead, but found that he could not; he was as drugged as a captured bear. There wasn't any pain—he was out, *all* the way out in a warm sea of Dilaudid, a black ocean of hydromorphone, surfing weightlessly far past the last marker, the last lighthouse, the last floating beacon—but the fear was there with him. The pain was ten fathoms gone, but the fear was all around him; it was in his cells and his synapses. It prowled his bloodstream.

He'd seen this woman splayed out before him on the slab, made unpretty by anesthesia, and then had peeled her knee open, precisely and deliberately—but now he was dead to her. He was someone to be mourned.

Oh, you're dead, she said, weeping, and for a moment he believed that he was.

He had been burned because of geographic proximity. He had been burned because his spite for his father was so strong he intentionally built his house just a quarter mile from William's, but in a slightly better neighborhood, so that William would be reminded, every time he drove past it, that he'd been bested. Close enough to see the smoke drifting over the trees, like a vent from some queer tectonic fissure; close enough to choose to ignore the car and run over; close enough to arrive at the weird Faulknerian scene before the firefighters had even begun to react. He saw his father appear in the upstairs window, looking like some sort of monied madman, and he thought: *I could have stopped this. I am responsible for this.*

From the moment he found himself in the kiln of the front hallway—the smoke wrapping him like an opaque caul—he was lost, disoriented. He encountered angular corners where he expected to find smooth walls, and tripped over unseen pieces of furniture. The walls were burning around him. He believed he could hear the foundations strain. He followed the sound of his father's shouting from the upstairs window. At the bottom of the stairs, he noted with clinical alarm that his sleeve was on fire. He beat at the flames with his hands. At the top of the stairs he discovered that he was on fire once again. He beat the flames back again and then tried to open the attic door but the knob seared his hand, so he stepped back, grasped the rail with both hands and kicked at the door with both feet. The fire-thinned wood collapsed inward and smoke boiled out into the hall and blinded him. He tried to run up the stairs but was stopped halfway by the heat. His father stood at the top of the steps, his profile bisecting the bright photosphere of window light. Warren shouted to him.

His father turned to look at him, took one step toward the stairs, and the roof collapsed over him.

Warren nearly lost his way trying to get out, but then he saw a curving haze of light through the smoke and lurched toward it and burst out the front door. He heard a human sound of pain and realized that that sound was coming from him. He was fully alight, a nimbus of flames around him. His hair was burning. Someone tackled him and the light was blotted out by a heavy blanket. Then he found himself in the ambulance, drifting in and out of himself. When he woke in the hospital, they were scrubbing at him like a dog that had rolled in something. There, in that diamond-hard point of a moment, he began doing penance for every sin of his life with that unthinkable, unthinkable pain.

Warren limped through the emergency room doors on the same crutches he had used during therapy, three years ago. He was, he reflected, still living this penance. At the front desk, he didn't bother with a story—lying was undignified, he had decided, at least when it didn't involve money or Dilaudid. He simply unwrapped the gauze circling his ankle and showed the nurse his burn. He had handled the burns on his scrotum an hour ago, scrubbing the burn clean while sitting on a chair in the shower, weeping from the pain. Then he had dressed the wound with Betadine and the aged Silver Sulfadiazine and had wrapped himself up, diaper-wise, with gauze. He looked down at the white fabric bunched about his crotch. Now, he had thought, I am truly, truly an old man.

Did he have an insurance card?

No he did not.

How did he intend to pay for the treatment?

Cash. Although he had hoped the cost would be reasonable. He had worked here not long ago.

Really? And where had he worked?

He had been a surgeon. A very good orthopedic surgeon.

There was a sudden ripple of recognition in her face. The line of her mouth went white and thin—perhaps she was friends with the mother of the boy whose knee he had compromised?—and she tersely asked him to take a seat.

He leaned the crutches against the wall and sat on one of the molded blue plastic chairs in the corner of the waiting room. He pulled his hat down low in the hope that he would not be recognized again. It had started to rain and the view of the ambulance bay through the window was blurred. After he re-wrapped his ankle, a candy-striper called his name and then led him to a room with four empty beds. Warren recalled that more than once he'd examined patients in this very room.

"The doctor will be here in just a moment," she said.

"Do you want me to unwrap this?"

"I think it would be best if you let her do that," the candy-striper said, and then pulled the curtain around his own bed.

A young woman whom Warren recognized immediately but was unable to name stepped through the narrow wedged opening in the curtain and gave him a brilliant smile. An earthy name, he recalled. A parents-at-Woodstock name. Sierra. He hadn't seen her for years. "Hi Warren," she said. "What happened to you?"

"Walking on hot coals again," Warren said, and winked. His crotch hurt like hell. He was flattered that she'd remembered his name.

Sierra winked back and put her hands in the pockets of her white coat. She was a good doctor, he reflected, in that she always knew what not to ask. "So," she said. "I understand that it's the right ankle?"

"On the heel," he said, flexing his right toes.

She pulled a stool beside the bed, propped his shin up on a pillow so that his ankle was slightly raised, and then began to unwrap the layers of clean gauze. The smell of her hair began to fill the small oval space within the curtain. Warren was suddenly very uncomfortable and realized that his discomfort was engendered by something other than his burn and its compromising circumstances. "A lot of pain?" she asked.

"Some," he said. He was afraid to invite too much sympathy. Any larger-than-average dose of painkiller would surely send him into arrest.

She looked down at his ankle for a moment and then up at his forehead. "I'm not supposed to ask, am I?" Sierra said.

"Not today," Warren said, feeling more artless with each moment. In a parallel universe, he thought. In another life. He recalled the moments—only four years ago?—when she'd consulted him in the hallways and offices, when he'd offered her the bits of wisdom that he reserved for his favorites. He'd believed, then, that his experience complemented her youthful shine; for years, he'd allowed himself to believe that something, someday, would happen between them—a drug-closet kiss, a suture clinch. It's not a parallel universe, he thought. It's this one. And that possibility had been neatly amputated.

"You've lost some skin," Sierra said. She was bent intently over his foot and as he studied her Warren noticed one long thin braided lock of hair behind her ear. I'll bet, he reflected, that she gets high every single night without guilt. Good pharmaceutical THC. "I wonder if this will re-epethialize? Since the quality of skin here was already poor."

"How long until we know?"

The quality of my skin, he thought, is poor.

"We'll point you toward a burn specialist," she said, "but offhand I'd say they'll simply clean and dress and watch for spontaneous skin growth. In eight or nine days. Outpatient for sure. You'll have to keep a close eye on this, Warren. Staph is really your biggest problem."

"We can clean and dress it here," Strickland said, standing in the slice of fluorescent light at the curtain's opening. He looked, Warren thought, angelic in his size and position. "No need to distract a specialist who's got critical patients. That burn's the size of a half-dollar."

Sierra, without looking up from Warren's ankle, said, "He's well over sixty, Ned. You know that."

"I also know that he survived partial- to-full-thickness burns on over forty percent of his body. Warren's tougher than he looks." He stepped through the opening in the curtain and suddenly the astringent quality of his aftershave cleaved sharply through the soap-and-flower smell of Sierra's hair.

"Why don't you let me handle this?" Ned asked. "I'd like to talk with Warren for a while."

She looked obliquely up at Warren, not with the disgust that he expected but rather in a sort of despair. "This is my patient, Ned," she said, but she was already standing. She looked down at Warren with her hands in her pockets. "Keep your eye on that, Warren," she said, and pushed passed Ned through the curtain opening.

Ned sat on the stool and crossed his arms over his chest.

"What now?" Warren asked.

Ned bent over Warren's ankle critically and gently flexed the joint.

"I can't believe," he said, "that she was going to send you to the burn unit. Can you believe that, Warren?"

"She always was a bit too thorough. But then again I must look awful."

"You certainly do," Ned said. He looked up from Warren's ankle and squinted at him. "We'll have to butterfly that knock on your forehead. Always sad to see an old man who took a knock on the head." Strickland tapped his temple. "Who did you piss off this time?"

"A friend of mine."

Strickland smiled. "Owe him money?"

"Actually, Ben owes him. I think my friend hoped that doing this to me would evoke some sort of sympathetic financial outpouring from Ben."

"Will it?"

"Ben," Warren said, "is out of reach. So I had to readjust things myself."

Strickland lowered Warren's ankle to the pillow. "He wants to reform you?"

"No," Warren said, "he's just broke."

Strickland walked the stool over to the bedside cabinet and lifted a roll of gauze, a pair of scissors, a small white tube, and two flat wrapped packages from the drawers. "I'm waiting for you to ask me why I agreed to discharge him," he said. He glanced over his shoulder at Warren.

"Tell me," Warren said. "Because I can't imagine why you did."

Strickland rolled the stool back over to the bed and placed the gauze, the scissors, and the tube on the steel tray. He tore open one of the flat white packages and the astringent smell of his aftershave was suddenly overtaken by the bleachy antiseptic odor of the white pad inside. Warren's nostrils stung. "I thought it was time I made amends."

"For what?"

"For the credentials committee meeting."

"Your vote," Warren said, "wouldn't have been enough to save me."

"But I didn't know that when I cast it," Strickland said. "While I was voting, I considered the possibility that mine could be the vote that saved you. But I knew that with you gone there wouldn't be anyone in my way. A small part of me feels responsible for what you've become. And I decided that this was the only way to give you something back." He looked levelly at Warren. "Even though I know that with Ben around, you'll never be anything but an addict."

It was true. He had fallen so far. From scalpels to picks and shovels.

Strickland took Warren's ankle firmly in his right hand and bent over it with one of the antiseptic pads in his left hand. "This is going to hurt," he said. "I'd give you something for the pain, but I can see by your pupils that you've already helped yourself. Tough luck."

Warren lay back on the bed and bit his lip to keep from screaming.

Ned stood in the ambulance bay watching Warren's taxi drive away. It began to rain harder, and he wondered if his roof was holding. He reminded himself to go to his office and phone Cindi and ask her to check that all the windows were closed. God help them if the roof began to leak again.

One of the new nurses, who hadn't yet learned to not disturb him when he was deep in thought, came up beside him. "We're taking bets," she said.

"Bets on what?" He hoped the tone of his voice would warn her off.

"On which one goes first. Warren or his kid."

Ned turned to look at her. "I think that's disgusting. Go home and come back tomorrow. I don't want to see you again for the rest of the day." He walked inside without waiting for her apology and went to his office, where he dialed home. The telephone rang four times before the machine picked up.

He hung up without leaving a message and then rose from his chair and began to pace around his office. He was too restless to sit idly, and yet he was unsure of how to occupy himself. The unanswered telephone had unnerved him. He knew Cindi was likely out shopping, or even just having a cup of coffee somewhere, reading one of those fat supermarket novels she loved; what unnerved him was the sudden collision of his old life and his new life, the insecurity he found threaded between them. When he first met Cindi, he was drowning in medical school debt, and he immediately recognized that this debt clashed with her silent conviction that love contained elements of commerce and commodity; in her mind, his debt meant that he was a somewhat incomplete mate. While some people might have seen her businesslike approach as cold or materialistic, he admired it for its simplicity and its directness. He solemnly promised himself that one day he would be free of debt, in a position of intellectual and social authority, and, as a result, entirely untouchable by the marital ruin that befell most men.

And yet now, surrounded by an office that seemed to be the summary of all he desired, he felt no less or more vulnerable than he had before. His careful planning had failed to insulate him; it seemed improvident that he devoted so much of his life to it.

Ned had been conditioned to plan. As a child, he'd been slightly overweight, sanctified by an outsized intellect, and almost irretrievably shy. The shyness was the result of his family's rootlessness; they moved an average of twice a year every year since he was born. They moved often because Ned's father, a physics luminary who designed surface-to-air missile systems for the military, possessed a sprawling genius ungraspable by other minds; it was necessary that he oversee each new missile site's development. Ned remembered those years as a riot of suitcases and airplanes, of schoolyard beatings and solitary lunches; he lived in so many different cities he was essentially from nowhere. It seemed sad that he never slept in the same room for more than six months, that he never developed so complete a familiarity with a home that he could navigate it in the dark.

At the heart of Ned's memories of those moves was Island 26B. By December first of 1951, the day ten-year-old Ned received the news that they would be moving to an island in the southwestern Pacific, Ned had already lived in seventeen different places. His immediate thought upon hearing the news was not that he'd be leaving the few halting friendships he managed to cultivate here, nor was it that he'd have to start over at a new school, nor was it a sense of wonder or anticipation or even fear. His first thought was simply, eighteen. And soon nineteen. He tried to feel sad about leaving, but the truth was that he felt no loss in leaving Nevada—they'd already moved three times that year—and it occurred to him that he'd never felt any sense of loss at leaving any of the places they'd lived. Although each city had a different name, although the landscapes and phone numbers and addresses were different, each new home was essentially the same in its disposable nature.

For as long as he could remember, he'd suffered a recurring nightmare in which he was catapulted miles through the air. He hurtled over meadows and streams and forests and then suddenly fell to earth and awoke upon impact. The dream was constantly at the forefront of his thoughts and often after he was awake the sensation of hurtling through space remained.

He and his father, as was their habit, spent the next day looking up the location of their new home in his father's atlas, a practice Ned understood was intended to fill him with a sense of place, but the two of them were unable to find it. Island 26B, they soon learned, wasn't listed in any index, nor was it described in any encyclopedia. The next day they enlisted Ned's school librarian for help, but after an exhaustive, week-long search she declared the island imaginary, and slunk away behind her stacks in utter defeat. The island's nonexistence was at first something of a joke, but as the day of the move approached, an uneasiness settled over their dinner table conversations. Ned understood that his father was involved in extremely secretive work, and he feared that this was how the government did away with families whose fathers were no longer needed. Their plane would find only empty ocean where Island 26B should have been. They would search and search and realize that the island was indeed imaginary, and then run out of fuel and crash during the fevered search for land.

The actual journey to Island 26B was fuzzy in his memory. He was awakened by his mother at some time around three in the morning. At her request, he dressed but then promptly fell asleep on his bed. When he woke he was being carried by a uniformed marine toward a jeep idling in their driveway. He woke again later while it was still not yet morning—he was being carried by the same marine across a tarmac prowling with the whining, low-slung, jet-fighter prototypes his father sometimes called *Grumman-killers*. His father and mother were ten steps behind. Ned's father, his face hidden by the lowered brim of his fedora, carried a suitcase in each hand; behind him, the desert horizon was a pale band of gray light. Ned twisted in the marine's arms and looked ahead. A massive army-green airplane, two propellers spinning on each sheltering wing, idled on the tarmac—the sight of the plane filled Neddie with dread. These planes were always carrying him away from something.

Miles out in the desert, a missile arrowed into the night sky. Ned watched it flame up into the darkness and vanish.

Inside the fuselage of the plane, he sank drowsily into his seat while the marine fixed his belt across his lap. The hatch was closed; the engines suddenly whined higher. The plane began to taxi. It described a single wide turn, then was still for a moment before it began to roll clumsily down the runway, moving faster and more roughly until, with a gentle goodbye kiss, it was gracefully aloft.

When Ned woke, the Pacific sun was a battering ram coming through the oval window to his left as the plane banked hard to the right. Beneath them was a green trapezoidal island that seemed orphaned amid a blue plain of ocean. Whitecaps paced the water's surface. Circumscribing the island was a thin band of the whitest sand Ned had ever seen in his life. We're going to land on that? he wondered. The plane banked harder and circled back over the ocean and all Ned could see now was blue ocean. The fuselage vibrated beneath his feet and whined pneumatically as the landing gear was lowered and fixed. Suddenly the plane seemed to fall through space and Ned clearly saw the debris littering the beach pass beneath and then the individual leaves of palm trees and then suddenly the pristine, onyx-black pavement of a new runway. The shadow of the plane danced across the sand and tall grass at the edge of the pavement, and then with a jolt the plane touched down, the engines roared higher, and Ned was pushed forward in his seat as the plane braked to a halt.

The heat and humidity were so strong that Ned's heart quailed as he stepped down the ladder to the tarmac. His mother collapsed halfway across the runway—they didn't yet know that she was pregnant with a baby that would miscarry during a beach-walk in another month—and as Ned and his father, still dressed in their traveling clothes, sat beneath the ceiling fan outside her hospital room, Ned's father turned and said to him, And you understand, Neddie, that these things I construct are designed to kill people. He said that sentence in the midst of a great silence—Ned's mother was sleeping sweetly on a bed inside the room, an IV seated firmly into the back of her hand—but he said it as if it were the answer to a pointed question. Ned nodded thoughtfully—he understood that the essential usefulness of his father's genius was that it aided in the creation of missiles that killed more expediently and successfully than the enemy's missiles—but he realized immediately that he knew absolutely nothing about the finality of death. And that the death of a thousand enemies would mean less to him than the shock of seeing the woman in the next room stumble and then collapse to the pavement outside the airplane. Having traveled to so many different homes, the only constants in Ned's life were his mother's engaging habits: the way she brushed her hair out of her face while rolling pastry; the way she slept every midafternoon on the couch with the newspaper draped over her face; the way she bumped her nose against his instead of kissing him goodnight.

The next day his father quit. Ned later learned, by listening to his mother's phone conversations, that his father had entered the base that morning, had walked to the receptionist desk and had announced loudly that he would compose no more missile systems. Given the chance, he added, he would create faulty and ineffective systems. Missiles that exploded harmlessly in beautiful displays of light. Missiles that drenched a city in a sweet vapor of maple syrup. Missiles that spread wildflower seeds.

His superiors were utterly baffled. Each day for the following week, two men, one wearing a suit, the other wearing a uniform bristling with metal, visited Ned's home at exactly three o'clock in the afternoon. Sitting across from Ned's silent, bathrobed father in the living room as Ned listened from his carpeted seat the top of the stairs, the suited man explained that it was not the place of one man to decide the fate of an entire nation. It was a crime against humanity, he said, to allow such prodigious gifts to lay fallow while dangerous forces were at work elsewhere. And abstaining from work, the uniformed man added at the close of their seventh visit, was also a criminal act, in light of the contract

Ned's father had signed. The next morning, as three uniformed marines handcuffed Ned's bathrobed father and led him out the front door, Ned's father looked down at him and said, I think I feel better now, Neddie. Three weeks later, while smoking and strolling innocently, happily, in the stockade yard, his father collapsed and was pronounced dead of a heart attack. Later that same day his mother miscarried on the beach after being told the news by the base commander.

That night, after the guard who was babysitting him fell asleep on the couch, Ned let himself out of the house through the basement window, and then jogged his bulk the half mile to the very beach where he had been told the incident had happened. He searched for a long time in the moonlight until he found a wide, orange-colored oval in the white sand just above the high-tide mark. He knelt down next to the oval, wetted his fingertip in his mouth, and dipped it in the amber sand. With a feeling that he was certain encapsulated all the sentiments that should have surrounded the word *home,* he pressed the fingertip to his tongue.

It tasted like ash.

That sensation of hurtling through the air was still with him—while walking down the hall, while sitting in his office composing a memo for the hospital staff. The slipping and gliding, the sense of being catapulted through life.

He had, in a small way, subdued that rootless sensation by building, from scratch, a home that was the summary of every home he had *not* had. He had paired himself with a mate who would never leave him. He had established a career path that would allow him to retire young. Yet despite his planning, despite the fact that he planned his life as carefully and as thoughtfully as one proceeds in a serious game of chess, he feared that one never achieved a true feeling of completeness. The protean nature of life was constantly in pursuit.

Warren. Warren was and always had been a variable. He had been a better doctor than Ned, the clear choice for Chief of Staff, and it had been a distressingly sweet, appalling relief when Warren destroyed that kid's knee. After casting his Credentials Committee vote to dismiss Warren, a vote he knew to be both unjustified and self-serving, Ned let himself into the staff locker room, checked the bathroom stalls to be certain that he was alone, and then locked himself in a stall, where he suffered a violent, five-minute hybrid of laughter and sobbing.

When he finished crying, he went to the row of white porcelain sinks and lowered his face into a cupped palmful of cold water, and then faced himself silently in the mirror.

I think I feel better now, Neddie.

We all do what we have to do, he thought. We do what we have to do to make this life tolerable. Addicts are not so different from the rest of us. But in one way they're very different, and very lucky. They understand there are punishments far worse than disgrace.

He went to his office window and looked out at the parking lot. Sleet fell obliquely through the arc–lights. He was caged by a chilly dampness that was neither fall nor winter. He was being held indoors. What he needed was the momentary absolution of the green's geometry. Inside, with the coming darkness turning the windows to mirrors, it seemed all too clear who and what he was.

Nineteen

Light snow rushed toward the windshield from out of the darkness. Emma drove slowly around the hairpin turns on Skylark while Ben dialed up and down the FM band. He couldn't find a single radio station that wasn't playing the usual saccharine Christmas Eve trash, but silence right now seemed too risky, so he found an AM news station and then sat back and looked straight ahead at the twin beams of the headlights and thought about the money they had just spent.

They had accepted the city's offer four days ago on the condition that the city reimburse them immediately for his lost work. Ben tapped Raif at the last minute to watch Nina and Sylva, and after dinner he and Emma drove downtown to elbow their way through the toy stores, the music stores, the clothing stores. Somehow they ended up being more lavish than usual. As he packed the trunk with armloads of shopping bags, Ben reflected that Sweet probably had some sort of word for what they had just done. *Overcompensation,* he would call it. *Substitution.* Or something like that.

After they finished the last of the shopping, they agreed that if they came up short for the February mortgage they'd borrow money from Emma's parents. January was all right but February wasn't and Ben's repair work always thinned during winter months.

Call me, Mick, he thought—he felt a bone-deep lassitude as he watched the car's headlights play over snowy banks, picket-fence birches, bent guardrails. Change your mind, Mick. He dug his fingernails into his palm. When I arrive home in a few moments, you will have called. You've reconsidered, decided that I'm perfect for the job. He felt like one of Mick's elfin girlfriends, hanging around the house all day in case the phone rang, checking the answering machine every time she stepped out for five seconds, replaying their conversations over and over, examining and re-examining each sentence for double and triple meaning. Had he been too aggressive, too passive, too confident, too unsure?

He needed Mick to reconsider because he would never, never agree to borrow money from Carl and Sarah. Well, actually he'd already agreed to do that—but he would never allow the actual borrowing to happen. He had agreed that he would simply because he and Emma had been getting along, and he'd been reluctant to allow such an enjoyable evening—maddening as the shopping had been, it *had* been enjoyably domestic, enjoyably *normal*—to spiral into a fight. He believed that a lot of being a good husband was knowing which moments to preserve.

They hadn't fought about his drinking, either, because he'd kept it slightly under control for the last few days, and because she understood as clearly as he that it was beyond him and beyond her. He'd either stop or he'd go forward, and they both knew that if he went forward for much longer she'd leave, and that would be it for them.

Anyway, he thought, watching her bite her lower lip as she concentrated on the road, she's still awfully young looking. Still very beautiful. I've never understood all this fuss about blondes. Give me that black hair and those green eyes any day. I'm betting that, equipped like that, she'd find the world much more receptive than she thinks. Sometimes when he had such thoughts, he imagined her in bed with other men, sometimes with *many* other men, imagined the things they would do to her and the things she'd do to them—it was a distasteful habit that he couldn't seem to shake. To forestall those images, he looked straight ahead at the snow rushing toward him and thought about nothing, while Emma, over across the seat, concentrated on driving. The disc jockey on the radio said that a low-pressure system was moving northeasterly toward them, bringing a severe blizzard up the coast. It would be here in two days, he said, but she wasn't really listening. She was thinking about how much he was drinking and how easily he had agreed to borrow money from her parents—it had always been such a fight in the past, but tonight it hadn't been at all— and she was thinking that something was wrong or that he wasn't being honest with her. He's got something else in mind, she thought. Since he's not getting this job at the club, I can only imagine what it is. I hope to God he's not thinking of going back with Warren.

She had, she felt, been duped. Used. First, she'd gone against her instincts and had convinced Jane to give Mick another chance. And then, Mick—that snake, that fucking reptile—had reneged on his offer to Ben. He'd used both of them.

Nina and Sylva were already in bed. Ben gave Raif a drink but had nothing himself. Raif helped them wrap some of the presents and then suddenly seemed to sense that he was intruding and said that he had to go. He gathered up his crutches and gave Emma a kiss on the cheek, and Ben saw how they looked at each other knowingly and sympathetically. That was for me, he thought. They talk about me and wonder what's going to happen. But I had nothing tonight, so why the bitchy, embattled looks? Why are you the ones sharing the nice telegraphed moment when I'm up to my neck in it, smelling it and tasting it? He was furious, and as Emma walked Raif out to his car, he went to the bookshelf and took the bottle down, then checked himself and replaced it. When Emma came back inside, dusting snow from her shoulders, he was wrapping presents again, and it was as if nothing had happened while she had been gone.

The next morning was cheerful and happy. The girls, chattery on the sugar cereal Emma allowed them to have only on holidays, seemed awed by the number of presents. The sky was a halcyon blue, and the bright sunlight that angled in had through the windows warmed the room. After Sylva opened the last present, Ben and Emma exchanged looks of sudden realization that they bought nothing for each other. She shrugged and he shrugged, and it was a small connection, and both of them laughed. They were happy that day, and he didn't drink anything that night.

After lunch the next day, Ben was sitting out on the wood bench beside the barn door in a blinding shaft of sunlight when Mick's Jaguar turned into the driveway. Emma and the girls had gone downtown to exchange some ill-fitting clothing. Ben had been sitting in the cold sunlight for twenty minutes, freezing his ass off as he sanded the sonofabitching contact points of the sparkplugs for the Sahid's MG. You had to sand both the underside and the topside of the contact points so the charge would be even, and the sonofabitching hangnail he'd developed during his, ha-ha, two days of sobriety kept catching on the sonofabitching rusty edge.

He was sitting outside, because a news report that morning had reminded him lack of exposure to sunlight sometimes deepened feelings of depression. The Zoloft certainly hadn't been doing the trick, so he'd decided to give sunlight a chance. He hadn't minded that he looked ridiculous, sitting outside in the cold, until Mick arrived; if you looked ridiculous when you were alone, it was like the proverbial tree falling in the forest. The fact that Mick had reneged just a few days ago only made getting caught worse. It felt, Ben thought, a little like being seen dining alone by an ex-girlfriend. He felt as if he'd made Mick's impression of him come true.

He set the sandpaper and the spark plug on the bench as Mick stepped from his car. Beside the Jag, the trash cans overflowed with the sad, torn remains of all the green and red wrapping paper they'd used. They certainly had overdone it.

"Having second thoughts, Mick?" Ben asked. He leaned back against the side of the barn and wished he'd combed his hair that morning.

Mick put his hands in his pockets as he crossed the yard. He ignored Ben's question. "That for the Sahids?"

"Almost done."

"Until next time." Mick had owned an MG in college and he knew how it was.

Ben sighed. Mick was right. It would go on and on. "I guess you're right."

"Don't look so down," Mick said. "It could be worse. There could be no next time."

"Sure," Ben said, "but what a relief that would be."

Mick said nothing.

"So how did it go?" Ben asked.

"What. Christmas?" He sat next to Ben, momentarily blinded by the sunlight. "It wasn't so bad."

"You think Leelee's got an idea what's going on?"

"Sure. She's a smart kid."

"No tough questions? 'How will Santa come if dad's down sleeping on the couch?' "

"The thing is," Mick said, sitting back, "I'm not anymore."

Ben picked up the sparkplug and began to sand at the contact point again. "You're working at it?"

"We're working at it," Mick said.

"Good for you."

"I think maybe I have you to thank for that. You and Emma."

"Mick," Ben said, "you could have thanked me another way. The way you told me you'd thank me."

"I couldn't, though," he said. "You know that. Not after you were in the hospital that way."

Ben felt blood warm his face. "It's a hell of thing, losing your marbles," he said. "Everyone suddenly loses their sense of humor."

"You can't expect anyone to joke about it."

Ben stopped sanding. "Funny," he said, "I thought nobody knew."

"No one does."

"But you do."

Mick said nothing. He shaded his eyes with one hand. He was looking across the yard at the brightly-colored trash.

Ben had watched him for a moment before he realized what had happened. He set the spark plug on the bench beside him. How stupid he'd been not to expect it. "It was Warren," he said. "Warren told you." A cold fury settled over him. Congratulations, Warren, he thought. We've both robbed each other of our last chance. I took yours away three years ago when I agreed to help with Victor, and now you've taken mine. I suppose this is the presentation of the bill.

Mick cleared his throat. "After I found out," he said, "it would've come back to me, you know? And the last thing I can have right now is a liability." He folded up his jacket collar. "I feel rotten about what went on, if you really want to know. It was wrong for me to ask you for that. I had every intention of giving you the job. I mean, it was *yours*, Ben. Whether she took me back or not. But then this happened."

"It certainly did," Ben said.

"I didn't cross you."

"Don't even think about it," Ben said. "Water under the bridge."

"The circumstances changed."

"Not a problem," Ben said. "It is what it is."

"You seem busy here, anyway."

"Sure," Ben said. "I've got more than I can handle."

Mick stood up to go. Ben squinted up at him. "You know," Mick said, "she won't do anything but kiss me? Says we have to date again first." He reddened and looked around at the back field. "She's not the same, you know? The old Jane would have withheld sex for the fun of it."

"Seems awfully adult of her."

"—To act like she's sixteen," Mick finished. "It doesn't make sense."

"What doesn't make sense?"

"None of it," Mick said. He cleared his throat again and then, incredibly, stuck out his hand. Ben shook it. "I'm sorry about this, Ben," he said.

"I guess it was bound to happen."

"You're, ah—" he searched for the right words, "—you're doing all right?"

"Mick," Ben said, "I'm sanding a goddamn spark plug here."

"Right," Mick said.

Ben watched his Jag roll up the driveway. After Mick's car was gone, Ben held the spark plug up to the light and began to sand the contact point and tried to obliterate himself with fierce concentration. For a few moments it was all right, at least in a Zen-workmanlike sort of way, but then all at once the rage came tumbling down on him from its great unseen height, and he gripped the spark plug so tightly in his fist that the cords of tendons stood out on his wrists. When he had finally relaxed his hand, there was a deep red indentation in his palm.

Ben parked his truck at the curb in front of Warren's house. As he stepped down onto Warren's lawn and shut the driver's-side door, he noticed that flecks of rust had begun to flower around the front and rear wheel-wells. Another expense he'd have to contend with before the inspection was due. He wrote the truck off every year as a business expense, but he still had to front the cash for repairs and wait until his next filing to get reimbursed.

He was about to rap on the front door when he heard Warren's voice come through an upstairs window.

"The silver's gone, Ben," he said. "Let it go."

Ben stepped back onto the lawn and squinted up at the second floor, shielding his eyes from the bright sun with one hand. Warren was a vague dark shape behind the window screen. It really was a beautiful day. He should have gone downtown with the girls. His fist ached where he had gripped the spark plug a few minutes ago. "I know it's gone," he said. "That's not why I'm here. Why don't you let me in so we can talk?" He forced himself to smile, a rictus of artificial chumminess. The back of his throat was painted with the sour tang of bile, and he swallowed it down. I should have snapped your neck, he thought, when I had the chance.

"Let you in," Warren said. He seemed amused. "So you can bounce me off the wall?"

Ben forced himself to widen his grin. "Come on, Warren. If that was what I really wanted, would I be standing here on your front steps?"

"As I recall," Warren said, "that's exactly where it happened last time."

"Warren," Ben said, "I'm here about Victor."

Warren didn't answer for a moment, and then Ben heard him coming down the stairs. He seemed to come down at half speed, in a sort of *clunk*-step, *clunk*-step. When he opened the door, the first thing Ben noticed was the scabrous butterfly above his left eyebrow, the purplish bruise around it. Then he noticed the crutches, the wrapped ankle.

"What the hell happened to you?" Ben asked.

"Oh, this little nothing?" Warren asked. He seemed furious. "This is what happens when you tell Victor to go fuck himself."

"I never told him that," Ben said. He was still grinning. The grin felt like a mask, like someone else's face superimposed over his own. He didn't think he could hold the grin for much longer. "I told him to take the money I *owe* him and shove it up his ass. Although that sounds a little strange, doesn't it? Telling someone to shove something they *don't* have up his ass?" He was pleased that Victor had acquainted Warren with consequence. Warren was, he reflected, going to learn a great deal about that subject in the next few days.

"Ben," Warren said, "what is it that you want?"

Ben let the grin fall away. Letting it fall away was a relief; every muscle in his face ached from the effort. His throat was still painted with bile. "I need a favor, Warren," he said.

An hour later, he watched from the living room window as Emma's car turned into the driveway. He held the nearly empty bottle of bourbon by the neck.

I need a favor, Warren.

Funny, Warren had replied, *I need one, too.*

How he'd wanted *hurt* him; how his hands had wanted to reach and maim and throttle him. To snap and tear. But the time for naked brutality had passed; each thing in its own time.

As the car rolled by the window he went to the bookshelves and hid the bottle behind the copy of *Nostromo,* and then walked into the bathroom, weaving slightly, to brush his teeth. He noticed that his leg no longer hurt. The bourbon had done its work, or perhaps he'd healed up. Either way, it was through-and-through. In and out, with nothing to show for it but the twin scars. A portal, a coil of gristle. Like it never happened.

Twenty

The snow was coming down hard now. It wasn't a storm yet, but it would be, soon.

He took Exit 1A off the expressway and detoured, at the bottom of the ramp, into the gutted trapezoidal parking lot of the Amoco station. Having stopped there so many times to piss, he could no longer pass it without feeling a sudden urge to urinate. As he crossed the parking lot, hopscotching around rainbowed pools of gasoline and wiper fluid, a flight passed by overhead. The running lights on its wings bored ahead through the darkness.

The bathroom was filthy, almost appropriately so; it was exactly as filthy as a bathroom at an Amoco station just off the expressway should be. He shook snow from his hair, closed the door with his foot and, with his elbow, felt on the wall for the light switch. It clicked up and down to no effect. In total darkness, he pissed without making any skin-to-skin contact, and then flushed the thunderous toilet with his heel. A gas station bathroom, he reflected, revealed just how well you could function without the use of your hands. As he crossed the parking lot to his car, a helical gust of wind snapped his jacket collar upright.

Ben drove the quarter mile to long-term parking and stopped at the entrance kiosk. The machine to his left opened its mouth and spat out a ticket. With the cardboard square between his teeth, he followed the rows of parked cars to the Southwest end of the lot. He stopped when his headlights settled on Anthony. Incredibly, Anthony was still dressed in his blue thrower's uniform. His reddish hair was laurelled with snow; he shielded his eyes with his right hand and gestured to an open parking spot down the row.

Ben plucked the ticket from his mouth and took the car out of gear. Careless, he thought. I don't care if he's Victor's knighted thief. This is how we get caught. We get overconfident. We think no one raises an eyebrow at a Thrower waiting at long-term parking. And then we get pinched.

He idled there for a moment, watched the individual snowflakes fall into his headlight beams and catch fire. With sudden panic, Ben sensed that this would be the night he would be caught, but when Anthony motioned again to the open parking space, he was helpless *not* to put the car in gear, because it occurred to him, as he turned into the open space, that this was how life worked. It was *always* the night you were to be caught—your number was always up. No one was ever comfortable with it, because no one, really, was ever a criminal—he was just unlucky. He had just been caught doing the same things everyone else does.

After he'd turned off the engine, he rubbed his palms on his thighs and stepped out of the car. The filth, he reflected, stayed with you for a while. For hours afterward, you felt as if you were the host of a thousand different forms of bacteria.

"You're a half-hour late," Anthony said. In the light of the vaulted halogen lamps, his features limned with their pale shine, it was impossible to judge his expression. Body language, instead: his bantamweight build seemed readied for a fight. He smelled of tobacco and mouthwash.

"Traffic's backed up for the weather. Have a heart, will you?" He remembered that Victor had asked the same of him while he was on the ward. Ben rubbed his palms on his thighs again and reflected that it was lucky that people like Anthony weren't interested in shaking hands. A simple handshake would have explained everything.

"You think I've got nothing better to do than to wait around for suits like you?"

"No," Ben said, and wiped his palms on his thighs again. "I don't."

Anthony showed his teeth in the darkness. "How much this time?"

"Three thousand."

"He lowballs me every time."

"The first time I did this, he told me you'd try to lowball me."

"Absolutely," Anthony said. "Get started and I'll bring it over."

Ben took the jack, the tire iron and the flashlight from the trunk. After he'd jacked up the car, he loosened one of the bolts and then set the tire iron on the pavement and waited. He crouched down beside the car out of the wind. The snow would begin to stick soon and the drive back would be bad.

When Anthony had brought the two suitcases back, he dragged them into the space between Ben's car and the next. "Victor's lucky there's a strike brewing," he said. He lay the suitcases on their sides. "After I give everyone their share back in cargo, there's hardly enough for a car payment."

"I know how that is," Ben said. He scanned the lot for the security van, crouched down beside Anthony and dragged the zipper around the suitcase's perimeter. With the lid propped open, he examined the six steel cases inside. Each case's face was stamped with a serial number and the U.N. insignia. "So twelve?" he asked.

"Eleven. One for Warren."

I haven't decided about that yet, he thought. He lifted one of the steel cases from the suitcase and placed it in the trunk. Anthony lifted a second case from the suitcase and placed it beside the first, and then leaned against the fender and watched for the security van as Ben placed the others in the trunk. Ben covered the cases with a blanket and then tightened the bolts on the jacked up tire. He lowered the jack and then put everything in the trunk on top of the blanket and slammed the trunk hatch. His palms were sweating so heavily that when a second *Air Singapore* plane passed overhead, the trunk reflected two palm prints in the plane's running lights.

They sat in the car, Ben in the driver's seat, Anthony opposite in the passenger seat. Ben lifted the envelope of twenties from under the seat and handed it to Anthony, who counted the stack twice. As he counted, his lips moved and his brow furrowed. Ben's palms sweated. He was grateful again when Anthony declined to shake to close the deal.

"It was a pleasure, Westchester," he said. He stepped out of the car and bent down before closing the door. "I'm sure I'll be seeing you soon. Victor likes you. I can't seem to figure out why."

A gust of wind angled snow in through the open door. "Can we work on a new nickname?" he asked. "I'm not from Westchester."

Anthony slammed the door and the overhead light went out. He bent down again and through the glass Ben saw his teeth in the darkness, the snowflakes in his hair. "I understand," he said, "that your old man calls you the Saint of Skylark when you're not around."

"That's not so bad," Ben said.

"Well," Anthony said, his voice muffled slightly by the glass, "I don't think he means it in a nice way." He lifted the two suitcases from the pavement and walked back to the shuttle bus.

The snow began to fall more heavily during the drive from Victor's apartment to Lansing. On I-95, near the Connecticut border, the sparse traffic prowled along at forty-five miles an hour. Although he had at least another hour to go to New Haven, and ten miles beyond that to Lansing, he would arrive home tonight much earlier than usual. Victor had insisted on coming with him to Garden City this time—the trust, apparently, hadn't yet been fully repaired—but when Ben had arrived in Queens, he'd learned that Wes had asked Victor to bring the morphine himself in the morning when the weather cleared.

"You're in luck, Westchester," Victor had said. "He's worried you'll have an accident on your way outbound. So I have to catch a train first thing tomorrow."

A thousand dollars for four hours work. That was only a tenth of what Wes would pay Victor, but it was still a great sum, almost half the February mortgage payment, and he expected to make as much in two weeks.

By the time he reached New Haven, he was exhausted. Blearily, he counted off the last ten miles. The Lansing exit hadn't been plowed, yet another example of his wasted tax dollars, along with the three blinking yellow lights the town council had voted to install last month. As he braked at the bottom of the exit ramp, his wheels locked and the car slid halfway into the intersection. He looked left and right, but found that he was entirely alone on the road. On any night but Sunday, he would have been hospitalized by a passing flatbed.

He piloted the car through a scimitar-shaped right turn and drove the quarter mile to Lasting Drive. His pulse was quick and light in his extremities, in his wrists, in his temples. The slide into the intersection had made him feel panicked again, out of control. To push the panic away, he thought coldly and clearly about what he wanted to do. He had no intention of giving Warren the case in his trunk, but he fully intended to let his father know that it was there, that relief was close and yet entirely out of reach.

I learned this from you, Warren, he thought. Mom learned this from you. You're an excellent teacher on the subject of need. *There is,* I've heard you say, *no close and almost in my world. You're either there or you aren't.* Forgive my amusement. You understand need, Warren, but only from the perspective of constant fulfillment. You only know half the story. There's an unpleasant side to need that the rest of us know about. That close and almost you've talked about. It's a side that you showed me. You showed me, and you showed mom, and now I think I'll show you.

Even as a fledgling chipper, Warren had possessed a seasoned junkie's ability to wrangle exactly what he needed from others. The arrangement with Victor had been established on the very day he'd lost his medical license. Warren was, Ben reflected, a zero-sum of moral bankruptcy, in that he maintained a steady, constant degree of vice. He raided the drug cabinet, Ben thought, until he lost his license. Then he raided me. I was hopelessly drunk that day, and I had hit bottom, and he knew that I was ripe for suggestion. Emma couldn't stand to be around me anymore. Drove into the city with Carl and Sarah and the girls that morning. What was it Carl said to me? *We came down to help sort things out.* But the fire had been out for months. We all knew they'd come down to sort me out.

Do you remember what you said to me that morning, Emma? Carl and Sarah were out in the car with the girls, and on your way out the door you detoured into the living room and said, *If you're going to drink today, Ben, get a hotel room. Think of your daughters. Think of what they see.*

I know what they see, Emma, thought Ben as he stopped at the curb outside Warren's house. They see that there are no criminals or alcoholics or addicts. They see that there are only the lucky and the unlucky.

We are the unlucky.

We came down to help sort things out, Carl had said. He lifted Sylva up and followed Nina and Sarah out to the car. Emma waited until the front door closed behind them, and said, If you're going to drink today, Ben, get a hotel room. Think of your daughters. Think of what they see, and Ben had replied, That's all I *can* fucking well think about, Emma. What they see.

He had gone to the living room window and had waved goodbye to them as they drove past, but no one waved back. He sensed that they were relieved to be free of him.

After they had gone, he remained at the window. The shadows of the trees lay motionless across the sunny expanse of snow-covered lawn. *His* lawn.

He resolved to take it slow. But later—and time *did* seem to pass that loosely when he drank, without the structure of minutes and hours, in a hazy succession of undifferentiated moments—later, as he watched Warren pilot his car slowly down the drive and park beside the house, he realized that he was a full three sheets to the wind and that he hadn't taken it slowly at all. He had no logical basis with which to confront the urge to drink. The urge to drink seemed as logical—no, *more* logical than so many other things in his life. Paying your taxes and cutting your lawn was something you did out of necessity; at least drinking had a *point*. At least it led somewhere.

Hunter Haskell owes us this, he thought. It would be nice if that were true, wouldn't it? It worked so well for grandfather when he said it. He crossed the room with the bottle of bourbon and hid it in its usual place on the bookshelf. Then he hid his glass between two cushions on the couch, snapped on the table lamp and the television, and sat gingerly on the couch with the newspaper open on his lap. He'd forgotten exactly how one presented signs that things were just fine, thanks.

I hope you kept all that stock, dad, he said as Warren opened the front door. Warren didn't answer. When he walked shakily into the room, balancing on the cane he'd used all through rehab, Ben noticed that he was pale, his eyes red-rimmed from sleeplessness. Something wrong? he asked.

His father sat on the edge of the rocker by the television with the cane across his lap. Where is it? he asked.

Where's what, dad? Ben asked. He recalled that he had neither combed his hair nor brushed his teeth that morning.

His father looked at him until Ben went to the bookshelf and pushed the copy of *Nostromo* aside. Ben handed him the bottle.

Do you want a clean glass? he asked. He wasn't sure if he was ashamed or relieved by his father's candidness.

His father shook his head. Ben fished the glass out between the cushions and picked a bit of lint off the rim before he handed it to Warren, who poured himself two fingers and drank it down. Then he poured another miserly drink into the glass and handed it back to Ben, who through a great deal of effort restrained himself to a small sip and sat on the couch, the glass between his palms.

Well, his father said wearily, that's that.

Yes, Ben said, and then realized suddenly that this wasn't just conversation; his father was talking about something Ben was intuitively supposed to understand. Today, he recalled, was the day the credentials committee was to release their decision. So, he asked, sounding, he thought, disproportionately hopeful, how did it go?

His father watched him in disbelief. Haven't you been listening to me? he asked.

Ben stood suddenly and walked to the window; the spineless winter sunlight irritated him and left him restless and eager for night to begin. He tipped his glass up and found it empty. What'd they say? he asked.

They made an example of me, he said. Ned didn't so much as open his mouth.

Wise man, Ben said. You never get in trouble for the things you don't say. What about the kid's knee? He walked across the room to Warren and took the bottle from him to pour himself another drink.

Good as new. Better than new, some say. He'll need rehab for a year.

Funny, Ben said, that with a little sacrifice you can actually improve on nature.

He tipped his glass back.

I need to use the bathroom, his father said.

Ben turned to look him. Do you need me to show you the way? he asked.

After his father was gone from the room Ben poured himself another drink and then hid the bottle on the shelf behind *Nostromo* again. He'd need to go easy or he'd run out around midnight, and Emma had long since learned to hide the car keys. A few weeks ago, during the thin slice of sobriety he cultivated each morning, Ben had conspired to make a copy of the key, or perhaps to fabricate a story in which he lost the key so that he could hide this one; but that plan had evaporated, along with the thousand other enterprises he entertained and then forgot each day.

Dad, he asked loudly, couldn't you just go into practice on your own?

Ben followed the trail of his unanswered question downstairs to the darkened cellar. The bathroom door was slightly open. A stripe of white light spilled onto the cement floor, bisecting the darkness. He moved quietly to the door and looked inside, at what was there, Warren there inside the bathroom, and then walked back upstairs.

When Warren came back into the room Ben was standing at the window watching for Emma's car in the dark. It occurred to him that the principle theme of the moment was unspoken mutual disgrace, and that this disgrace would continue unrelieved until one or both of them moved to stem it.

I've never seen anything like that before, Ben said shakily. A needle, like that.

It happens, Warren said, whether you see it or not.

What would granddad think? Ben asked.

They considered this in silence for a moment.

I'm an addict, Warren said, because of him, you know. Because I was trying to help him.

That poor man, Ben said, his breath fogging the window as he spoke. But he had bled himself dry of emotion during that last six months, and he found that those words had lost any genuine resonance. So why was he still drinking? He'd first started drinking to suppress any suspicions that he'd been responsible for William's death. But both the business and the charred timber of William's home were already razed; his grand-father's corpse had been rotting in the ground for six months. So why was he still drinking?

He was drinking because he couldn't think of a reason to stop.

If only, Warren said as he sat down on the rocker again. He grimaced. If only you could have seen the side of him that I saw.

I didn't, Ben said. But I'm guessing that has more to do with us than it does with him.

And you don't want to hear my side.

Seems silly to talk about it, Ben said. It's your side. Mine's over here.

So what should we talk about? Warren asked.

Emma should be back soon. You and Carl can talk shop. Saw this. Chisel that.

He wasn't cruel, Ben. I know that. But he had one idea about the direction the world was supposed to take. I didn't choose to be in medicine.

Well, Ben said, I suppose *that's* not a problem any longer.

He saw the slightest flicker of motion reflected in the glass and ducked. The cane passed over his head and impaled one of the small panes on the side window. Shards of glass spatted musically to the floor. Ben gingerly pulled the cane from the window, the cold air slipping in through the open space, and then went across the room and handed the cane to Warren. When he was back in front of the window again, the space where he was standing was noticeably colder, and he shivered. In the spirit of self-reliance, he removed his sweater and stuffed it in the jagged hole. Carl would, of course, fix it later without comment. The glass shards he kicked into the corner with his work boots. But of course that wouldn't do; the girls would want to watch television in their pajamas tonight.

Let me get this straightened out, he said. He walked down the front hall and let himself outside through front door. The still night air stung antiseptically against his bare arms and face. As he gathered the broom and pan from the corner of the barn, he began to shiver violently. Walking back to the house, he looked up. The cold points of the stars and the bare branches of the trees hung motionless in the windless night. It heartened him to think that the structure of the world had held together nicely despite all this human decay.

Warren was sleeping quietly when Ben walked, still shivering, back into the room. I think he came here tonight, he thought, to show me what he's become, to show me what he does to himself, although I can't imagine why. If that's what he does, maybe it's lucky that they fired him. Maybe it's for the best he loses his license. As he swept up the glass, he thought more about what he had seen.

I suppose he does it there so no one will see the marks. But still to see him that way. Mouth open. Eyes rolled back into the whites. Belt unbuckled and pants shoved down to his knees. The syringe resting on his thigh, the needle still seated in the vein.

He emptied the pan into the trash and then built a small fire. He somehow managed to burn his fingers badly, and he rewarded himself for it with another drink.

Later, when Warren woke, Ben was sitting cross-legged in front of the fire, the bottle in his lap, watching television. He'd achieved a sharply lucid mental state. For the last half hour, he had been doing math in his head, adding and subtracting columns of numbers and comparing them to the rising stack of bills on the desk.

Ouch, Warren said blearily, sitting up and looking about the room. That felt good, he said.

I'll bet, Ben said.

Warren sat forward and crossed his cane across his lap. Listen, he said. I didn't just come here to sleep.

On the television, a remarkably realistic cartoon ant was trapped, drowning, in a clear drop of water. He was straining to get out, pounding his cartoon fists at the walls of the droplet, but the surface tension was too great. His face was turning blue and he seemed to be weakening.

I came here to ask for your help with something, he said. To make you an offer.

Tell me more, Ben said. A slight thrill of terror went through him; the ant wasn't going to make it. He didn't have the strength. Ben identified.

I'm going to be out of money, soon, Warren said.

You're in good company.

We can help each other. I have a friend who needs someone like you.

What exactly, Ben asked, does he need?

Twice a month you drive from A to B, Warren said. Airport to apartment.

With what? he asked.

He has friends who are baggage handlers at the airport. A lot moves through and sometimes a few things get, ah, lost. They are misplaced and nothing can bring them back. And Victor picks it up and sells it and that's that.

How does this help us?

You get paid. And I get—I get what I need. You bring it to me.

It makes sense, he thought. First I brought her what she needed and killed her. Then I bring you what you need, and I kill you, too.

Now, outside Warren's house, his car idling and his brake lights reflecting a pale pink on the new snow, Ben remembered the paired horror and relief he had seen on Warren's face that night when he had agreed to the arrangement.

Funny, Warren said as Ben walked him to the door, I came here almost hoping you would say no. Then he gave a small nervous bark of a laugh and walked out into the cold.

I'll bet you did, he thought. But never, Warren, would I let you off so easily.

I think you like seeing him diseased like this.

I do, Emma. I do. But now it's right again. I make it right from this moment on. And if doing this—if denying him relief now, when he needs it the most—gives me a small thrill of pleasure, so what? If watching him suffer as he kicks gives me pleasure, so what? Didn't he cause so much suffering of his own? Didn't he make her suffer and rob her of the choice? Didn't he take away the last chance I had for a respectable life?

He put the car in gear and saw motion at the neighbor's window—the blind was pulled aside and a profile intruded in the bright framed square. Warren's neighbor, peering out through the glass. He had startled her with his sudden coming and going. She would be wondering who or what was disturbing her silent street, so deep in this winter night.

Suddenly he found himself near tears. He wished this hadn't gone on so long, and in this way. Act Five, he thought, should be over. We should be blinking up at the dawning house-lights from our seats, mourning our speared hero. We should be filing toward the exits. Those tricky exits.

Only the entrances are easy.

Twenty-One

W arren went to his front door and peered out through the glass eyehole. Petra, his neighbor, was there on his front steps, inches away in fish-eyed caricature. Through the warp of the biconvex lens, she was all Nordic bone structure and black dinner-plate pupils. Still beautiful, barely. Snowflakes fell around her in parenthetic arcs, like stars skirting an event horizon.

"Mr. Bascomb?" she asked.

"I saw him, Petra," he said. He wished that he'd repaired the door's latches. The Dexedrine sometimes made her violent.

"Your son was here, Mr. Bascomb."

"I know, Petra. I saw him."

She bounced from foot to foot, almost running in place. Warren sensed the norepinephrine cruising her plasma, the clench-release of her heart-muscle; he pictured interstate arteries and tunnel capillaries, the round-trip bloodwork. If he pricked her with a pin, she'd explode in a sticky red vapor. "I saw him parked out front for a few minutes. Do you think he had anything?"

"I saw him, too, Petra," he said, and placed his uninjured foot against the base of the door so she wouldn't be able to push her way in. "Go on home, sweet. I'll let you know if I hear from him. Thanks for telling me."

She was grinding her teeth again. He leaned hard against the door, expecting her to bash into it like a linebacker. She had done it before, after one of Ben's Sunday night visits, and it had taken him more than an hour to get her back out. If you lived on a street populated with junkies, you occasionally had to suffer through saturnine moments like this. *I have nothing for you. I haven't even anything for me.*

There was a light shove at the door. "Hey, what about it, Warren?" she asked.

He pulled a five dollar bill from his breast pocket—he'd had it ready there for five minutes—and slipped it under the door. "How about that?" he asked, shaking the bill so that it would catch her eye. "Thanks for keeping an eye out for me." There was a long pause, a moment of resistance as the Dexedrine had its say; then the bill was snapped from his fingers. Petra, one; Dexedrine, nil. Her footsteps receded through the snow.

Warren sighed and rested his forehead against the cool wood of the front door.

Time, he thought, turns nothing around, Ben. What time does is it takes what's true and makes it ten times truer. It advances every proposition. It narrows the aperture of possibility. First you use; then you become addicted; then you're an addict. Your wife is dying; then she's dead; and every year after that she becomes a little bit deader. Time cemented our arrangement; and then you tried to turn it around, tonight, to satisfy your own agenda. And time, sonny boy, doesn't give a shit about your agenda. It has other plans. Just ask the clock on the wall. Ask, and see what answer you get.

He searched through kitchen cabinets for a trash bag, then walked from room to room with it, picking up the old bills, the sprawling stacks of junk mail that seemed to have spilled down from a windblown height. When he was finished with the trash, he made a second pass, placing any sharp objects—anything he might use to harm himself—high up out of reach. Last year, he'd learned the hard way that this second pass was absolutely necessary, and he had the scar on his wrist to prove it. When things got bad, the mind redefined what forms of relief were acceptable. Eventually, as his cells began to scream for the narcotic, he would arrive at the same logic he had applied during Theo and Victor's morning visit: when you're being tortured, anything that is not torture sounds like a pretty fair deal. It didn't matter if it was knife thrust or a hollow-point bullet or a leap from a terrace. What was impossible became possible when adequate pressure was applied.

He poured four cans of soup into a steel mixing bowl. Food seemed to be a peripheral concern, now, but he knew that as he weakened he would need to eat something. Soup was the best thing to eat because you digested it faster, and if you got sick, it came up more easily. He stuffed the empty cans in the trash bag, then knotted the bag and heaved it out the front door toward the curb. Petra's footprints, he noted, were already filling in with snow.

It was so cold in the garage he could see his breath in the beams of streetlight that angled in obliquely through the windows. Warren windmilled blindly in the air until his hands encountered the naked bulb, hung from the ceiling by its black rubber cord. After he'd snapped the light on, he squinted around at the rectangular room; the light swung pendulum-wise on the cord, slipping his shadow from wall to floor and back. He found the plastic drop cloth in the far corner by the empty trash cans, and carried it into the living room, where he unfolded it over the rug and covered it with sheets that he could throw away after he was finished.

His last ampoule seemed orphaned in the toilet tank. He gently lifted it out of the dank water and held it under the sink tap for a few seconds. After he'd dried it carefully, he carried it into the living room. Beneath his feet, the plastic made an unpleasant sound that reminded him of the body bags they had stockpiled at the camp in Matadi. He snapped on the television and turned up the volume.

"You need to sand the end of the copper tubing to get a tight fit," the man with the flannel shirt on the television said.

Oh the clock has no sense of itself. How Lin would beseech it, plead with it—she'd pound it with her fist. Once she even threw it across the room.

Doesn't help, love, I told her, looking down at her snarled in the sheets. The clock smashed in the corner, speared plastic and glass. See, Lin? I said. You've accomplished nothing. It still moves forward. Tick tock.

Ah, but this way I don't know it, Wren. I'd rather not watch the minute hand creep.

It's not so unpleasant, is it? I asked.

She blinked twice. Well, no. But come on, Wren. What sort of answer do you expect from me? Us ladies are not supposed to get old. I don't like looking at it any more than I like looking at a stretch mark. It's a yardstick of desirability.

What's with you, Lin? It's just another morning.

You can't be so matter of fact about everything, Wren.

Of course I can, Lin. I'm a scientist, remember?

You're not a scientist, she said. You're too caught up in all that philosophy you read. I swear, Wren, you're an *ism* whore. The square of the hypotenuse is lost on people like you. Any day I'm going to come home and find you wearing a black turtleneck and chanting and sucking on a roach.

He walked into the kitchen and examined the contents of the steel bowl and decided he would eat later. On the way back into the living room he had to sit down on the floor and rest. She liked to joke about that. All that reading I did, that somber Schopenhauer. And let's face it, the Cessation of Desire was hard to read with a straight face. Victor was right. I lack restraint. It's not like you can fashion that out of twine and glue. All of the little components are there when you're born. Everything you'll be, decided from the start. What's that word? Preformation. Preformation. Everything there in miniature. The great oak, folded like a prone geisha into the seedling. As he rose from the floor he felt the vague arrhythmia in his chest, and he sat down again, his heart going like an excavation of his chest cavity. He waited for it to pass.

Waiting for the sickness to begin was a matter of suspense; it was an implacable *when,* not a vacillating *if.* It was like the feeling he'd had every time he stepped into the batter's box his senior year in high school. All the pitchers had begun to throw curveballs that year. Most of the curves had failed entirely and arrived at the plate as change-ups that hung high and inside that you could stroke easily over the left-field fence, but some of them went wild. A lot of kids were hit in the head that year, and of course after you were hit in the head once, you were never the same again. A lot of glory and a lot of fear that year. Waiting for withdrawal to begin was like stepping up to the plate and realizing your time was up, realizing you'd hit too many home runs and now there was nothing to do but take one in the head.

Three forty-six in the morning. Three forty-seven. Three forty-eight. You see, Lin? There's nothing you or I can do about it.

Of course I can. See that clocksprung mess? I smashed the little fucker good.

Lin, imagine how that poor clock feels. You killed the messenger. Imagine.

But the trail ended there, dissolved into abstraction, because the truth was that they'd never had that discussion. It was just another moment that he'd imagined so fully it had begun to seem real. A moment he'd wanted to have with her. Sometimes the daydreams did seem real. Funny how you could make what had happened seem as if it hadn't, and what hadn't seem as if it had. If you wanted to believe, you only had to get the details right, the tactile and the aural, the sleep-and-eucalyptus smell of the room, the softness of the carpet fibers beneath your bare feet, the tidal sound of the cars passing beneath the window. When the details had all been imagined fully enough, it was the same as if it had really happened. It was a nice trick, and he had gotten so good at it that sometimes it was hard to distinguish what was real from what wasn't.

Like the Grand Canyon thing, he thought. Still can't remember what happened and what I want to believe happened. It was so hot those two weeks. Stuck alone in the back of the car, a ten year-old with no one to talk to. Dad's girlfriend from the flower shop in the front seat.

Fay's going to come with us, Wren, his father said, a week before they left.

With us?

Yes, Warren. With us. On our trip. You like her, right?

Warren had never considered whether he did or not. Where will she sleep?

She'll have her own room. You and I will have one, and she'll have another. She's never seen the Grand Canyon, and she wants to go and. He stopped and nervously plucked at the lapel of his spring jacket for a moment. I'd like her to go. If that's okay with you.

I guess it is.

It is?

Yeah I guess it is.

Good. He looked relieved.

The morning they left it was sunny and suddenly spring all gone and summer upon them. Warren noticed that Fay had done her hair a new way. They had just crossed into Pennsylvania when Fay asked Warren if he wanted to play a game.

What game? Warren asked.

It's called Gramma's Attic. Do you know this one? she asked Warren's father.

William shook his head. He was whistling, driving with just one finger, his free arm slung over the seat. Warren had noticed, during the first few miles, the way the tips of his father's fingers occasionally brushed the fabric of her sweater.

Right, Fay said. You start with the letter A and go on from there. You have to remember or you're out. First I'd say, I was in gramma's attic and I saw an apple. Then, Warren, you'd say, I saw an apple and a bear. Then your dad would say, I saw an apple and a bear and a chair. And you keep going around, adding letters, until you forget, and then you're out. You see?

All right, Warren said. You forget and you're out.

Fine, Fay said. I was in gramma's attic and I saw an anthill. Now you go, Will.

I was in gramma's attic and I saw an anthill and a beautiful woman.

Fay laughed. That'll do, she said. That'll do just fine.

Warren watched her laugh for a moment. I was in gramma's attic, he said, and I spied an asshole and a bitch and a whore.

That was what he had *wanted* to say. But he couldn't remember now if he actually had, or if he'd simply granted himself the memory of saying it.

See? That's not so New Age, Lin. How's that for a cold scientific assessment: an asshole and a bitch and a whore. Three fifty-six AM. Three fifty-seven AM. Light in three hours. His heart had quieted, and he stood and walked into the living room, but what was in here? He couldn't remember why he'd come back in here. Oh yes, because he hadn't wanted to eat anything. It's impossible you feel this bad, he thought. You just think you feel this bad. It's only been six hours. You go six hours every night and then some. It's because you know the Dilaudid's all gone. With it all gone, there's nowhere to hide. There's no shelter, here, Warren. It's all bright sunlight and dry ravine. You'd better construct some shelter fast, sonny boy. Belay that. Ten-four, loud and clear. Zero interference.

The same flannel-shirted man was on the television. Six hours ago, tubes and framework had jutted upward, antennae-like, from the floor; now, the frame housed a finished kitchen. The seamlessness of the transformation was remarkable.

I hope you've enjoyed this series as much as I have, the man said. This was a labor of love.

Warren lay down on the sheets spread across the floor, rolled onto his left side, his right side, his back, his stomach. But there was no relief; no position offered him comfort. His skin began to itch, as if there were ants swarming over him, nested in the fibers of his clothing.

He stripped naked and found that the itch wasn't from his clothing; it was *inside* him, beneath his dermis. He'd have to tear through his skin to get at it. It was like the itch he'd felt as the grafts had healed, an itch that was worse than the burn itself.

Four o'clock.

The sheet had wound itself around his midsection. It was damp with sweat. The drop cloth, beneath him, was sticky.

You'd better construct some shelter, sonny boy.

He rolled onto his left side, then his right.

Sonny boy, you'd better construct some shelter. This is a high windy place, and you're about to topple off the rim.

I can't.

Well you'd better find a way that you can. You'd better construct some. Some shelter. Sonny boy, you'd better construct some shelter.

But there was no shelter; it was all bright sunlight and dry ravine. He was staked out on four points on an anthill. They were swarming all over him. They were swarming *inside* him. He began to cry. His tears were infantile, baroque; they were tears of outrage.

Couldn't you have done this three years ago, Ben? he thought. Couldn't you have turned on me then? Before I couldn't live without it. There's no shelter here. There's no shelter here. There's no shelter here. There's no shelter here, Ben. There's no shelter here.

It was morning. Skylark Drive was an unplowed path of white. Warren aimed the car between the twin lines of birches and dropped his speed to twenty-five. He wished he'd put chains on and then recalled that he hadn't intended to be out here. He was here only because his nerve and his resolve had failed him. Although for years he had lusted from afar after an abstract vision of sobriety, ultimately he loved himself too much to allow the suffering required to reach it.

First you use, he thought. Then you become addicted. Then you're an addict.

Two hundred yards from the house, at the hill above the Schecter place, the car seemed to disconnect suddenly from the road. The steering wheel went loose in Warren's hands, and the El Dorado drifted to the left and rumbled gracelessly off the road, plowing up spindthrift with the front fender as it listed onto the shoulder. It stopped violently, its nose buried in a shallow snow bank.

He turned off the ignition and leaned his forehead against the steering wheel. Just walk from here, Warren, he thought. Another one of those, and you'll go into arrest. His heart was hammering crazily beneath his sternum, and he tried to will it to slow. A heart attack, he knew, was a painful way to go. All that horseshit about having one in your sleep.

Believe me, he thought, they wake and they feel it, the rusty vise clamping their chest. Occlusion of the left circumflex artery. Left coronary thrombosis. Atrioventricular block. He was mildly impressed that even through the corrosive process of addiction he'd retained the infallibility of memory that was the defining quality of any great doctor.

When his heart had finally slowed, he lifted his head from the steering wheel. The house and barn, ahead through the birches, seemed framed by the windshield, presented with as much sinister understatement as a Wyeth composition. Somewhere within the scene, Dilaudid was hidden. It was always, reflected Warren as he opened his car door, the hidden information that mattered. The surface information, the first-glance datum—it was misinformation. Or worse, it was anti-information, because your first impression of anything was always the kindest, most forgiving, most wholesome, most *misleading* opinion you would have. You began with the delightful false impression, the charade, and then the truth intruded, and you went down from there. Perhaps that's why we spend so much time in that surface degree of ignorance. Our own little sphere of anti-information. It's so much less unpleasant there, where you don't know half of what's really *going on*.

He began to walk through the shin-high snow. The burn on his ankle was a screaming agony of nerve endings. His fingertips had gone numb in the cold, and he placed his hands deep into his jacket pockets. Occasionally a violent tremor overtook him, and he knelt down in the snow until it passed. At the end of each tremor, something forced its way upward from his chest and he spat it, yellow and solid, onto the snow. From the top of the driveway, he saw the sun fully up over the cloudless horizon. He thought that if he could fix he would be able to enjoy a fine sunny day at the kitchen window, where he would watch the plows cross back and forth with their yellow angled snouts. He would not worry about next month at all. He would not worry about next month. No, he wouldn't worry about next month at all. Next month would come and find him in its own time.

Ben's car was parked halfway under the barn overhang. The exposed trunk was layered with almost a foot of new snow, and the chrome and paint that peeked through glittered in the sunlight. He swept the snow away and tested the trunk latch. The fact that it was locked was sufficient evidence that the Dilaudid was inside. He walked into the barn and searched for something he could use to pry it open. Sunlight angled through the hayloft window onto the far wall. The same front-loader he and Victor had used to turn up the flowerbed waited in the corner. He found a pry bar on the workbench and carried it outside. The warm sun felt good on his face, and he decided that after he had liberated the case he would carry it back to his car before fixing. He could wait that long, at least. If a plow came along he would simply tell them he had pulled over and had fallen asleep because the snow was too deep to drive. He began to work at the trunk with the pry bar, but he had a hard time fitting the end of the bar into the seam. The steel buckled but the latch held.

"Come on," he said hoarsely. He restrained an urge to drop the bar and dig at the steel with his bare hands. He was sobbing. "Come on." He hacked and pried, but the trunk would not open. This was, he reflected, one of those strange moments of unbearable reality—one of those moments when he was startled to find that he was real and that all of this was *really happening*. He dropped the pry bar in the snow and rested his forehead on the fender of the car. The infantile tears had returned. They froze on his cheeks and salted his skin.

Is this, he wondered, the best that you had hoped for, Warren? Is this what you had wanted for yourself?

Of course it isn't. But I can't get out of this. I cannot get out of this.

Couldn't you just let it go, Warren? Couldn't you just go home and kick and let it all go? Couldn't you see it through?

To ask me that—to suggest that I might just snap out of it—is the summit of ignorance. Asking an addict to snap out of it is as ridiculous as imploring a dead person to wake up. Addiction is not something I've allowed to go on. It is a state of being. I am happy. I am sad. I am dead. I am addicted.

This is your state of being.

This is my state of being.

Think of the doctors over in Africa. There were addicts over there. They were both. They maintained two lives.

They did.

And you do not—you're nothing, really, but a fractured composition of regret. You've ceased to matter to anyone but yourself.

I don't care. I care only about this lock. I want this lock open.

But it won't open.

It will.

It won't. It's never going to open. And unless you make a change you'll always be right here, squatting in the cold, a bottom-feeding chipper who never quite manages to get by. You have to make a change. You know that. Think of what Lin would say to you. She would tell you to change, Warren.

I can't imagine what she would say.

You can. What did *she* say when she knew it was all over? What was it she said when she knew that she was finished?

He closed his eyes and felt the sun on the back of his neck and searched for the moment. It was there, immediately—a vision of Linda sitting in a shaft of sunlight, smoking a cigarette: as blamelessly—as blamelessly as Nero setting fire to Rome.

What do you think, Wren? she asked. He examined her in the memory, her watery gray eyes, her ash-colored hair and pale skin. He watched as she ran her hands down the length of her wasted body. *I'm going to burn it all down and rebuild it.*

Warren sat up. He lifted the pry bar from the snow and began to work at the lock but he knew that it would hold. He could go inside and threaten Ben; he could threaten to bludgeon one of the girls if he didn't open the trunk, but Ben would know—all of them would know—that he could never do that. He was an addict, not a criminal. He was this way only because he'd had what he required taken from him. Linda— Dilaudid. All of it taken. Taken. The arrangement was over. And when the arrangement is over, what do you do?

He dropped the pry bar and unsteadily lifted himself upright and thought, What do you do when the arrangement is over, Linda?

There was motion at the upstairs window of the house: he saw Sylva watching him through the pane, her blanket held to the side of her face. You should be in bed, baby girl, he thought. You don't want to see this. He raised his hand to signal for her to go back to bed.

Twenty-Two

*C*all it love.

That's what he said: *Call it love. That's what we have.*

There, on the very altar of her confession that she'd swallowed Warren whole, Victor's façade had fallen. He'd spoken the one word she waited for months to hear him say. *Love,* he'd said. *Call it love. That's what we have.*

With those words still dying in his throat, she'd answered, *Call it whatever you want.*

Trina rolled onto her side—Victor didn't wake, because Victor *never* woke; he slept as soundly, as defenselessly as an exhausted fieldworker. She propped her head up with one hand so she could watch him sleep. It was nearly daylight. She could smell the bakery trucks below on Queens Boulevard.

He helped her with her bills; he helped her manage her parents; he helped her with her acting. But help wasn't love. Lots of men helped her, and she certainly didn't love them. The list was growing, the list of men who helped her but had the sense to *not* call it love. Because she was bad with names, she remembered them by the nicknames she'd given each according to his performance in bed: there was The Delivery Boy, The Archaeologist, The Weeper. There was Mr. October, The Pool Cleaner, The Lazy Epileptic. All the men she had enlisted to help her find who she was. They came in and out of her life with varying frequency, and she'd begun to see that the nicknames often applied to their lives *outside* the bedroom. The Weeper became moody if his omelet was cold; over tepid coffee, The Archaeologist asked if she'd been abused as a child. The Weeper wept; The Archaeologist dug. They had earned their nicknames. But she'd always thought of Victor as Victor—nothing more, and certainly nothing less. That was what made him different. That and the fact that while the other men were the sort you wanted until you suddenly didn't want them—an instant after she'd achieved orgasm, she found them repellant—Victor was, in some ways, repellant to her *until* that moment.

He had never suspected that there might be others. A classic narcissist, Victor was unable to consider the possibility that she might find other men attractive. That was why the news about Warren had startled him so—the fact that it had been *Warren* had rattled his cage. Had she gone after someone more handsome, someone more together, someone younger—an equally matched opponent—he might have understood. At least that would have made sense.

That was exactly why she had chosen Warren: her instincts had told her—still told her, even now, with the bakery trucks slamming and stalling below her window—that some essential component of Victor's story about how they'd met was wrong, that it was artificial, or at least incomplete. Victor, she knew, perceived her as a sort of flesh and blood plaything, a consequenceless affair-of-the-moment—it had been entirely necessary for her to wound him at a basic, elemental level to make him understand that she was neither. Her intent had been to astonish—as such, she'd had to lie about the couch-clinch, to invent and create, because Warren was a junkie, and junkies just couldn't—well, they just *couldn't*. It had been an anti-event. Junkies, somehow, wanted something other than her. Which always surprised her, hurt her feelings, because she was a narcissist, too.

Victor says you're going to help me, she had told Warren. *And where I come from you don't get something for nothing.* What a meaningless line. What an absolute fabrication. As if she even remembered where she came from.

Victor had taken the news about Warren hard. She'd expected some sort of physical eruption, a chipped tooth or a black eye at the very least, but instead he'd simply closed down. For more than a minute, he'd stared at a spot on the carpet between her feet, his hands folded. When he lifted his head again, she immediately recognized not *scheming* Victor, not Victor the cheat, but instead the Victor she saw each night as he slept—defenseless, schemeless Victor. The Victor she *did,* regrettably, love.

Why? he asked.

I don't know, she said. *I have this feeling you're not telling me everything, Vic. I think you know why, even if I don't.*

Aren't you in love with me? he asked.

Love? she asked, her pulse quickening. *Is that what you just said?*

Call it love, he said. The corners of his mouth turned down in revulsion and fear. *Call it love. That's what we have.*

She opened her mouth to tell him that she loved him, too. For six terrifying months, she'd been searching for a pattern, for a constant about which she might orbit—for something, anything, around which she might form a foundation and begin to build upward. She was essentially a child again, a six-month-old, and love—really—is the only genuine currency of infancy. But somehow, that nagging suspicion of his story, the delicate impulse of her instinct, had checked her reply. Had *qualified* it. On its path from cerebrum to tongue, *I love you, too,* had somehow been cruelly distorted to, *Call it whatever you want.*

Things had been different since then, and different didn't always mean better. She was sure that Victor had extracted some sort of retribution from the world—that he had robbed some beggar of a handful of change, had broken someone's jaw with an aluminum bat. Someone, somewhere, had suffered for what she had done. Trina felt no immediate sense of responsibility or anguish, because people were hurt every day, and without reason. Herself included. People had things taken from them. But she did feel responsible for the change that had come over him. He seemed less *capable* now. Frail. Less at home in his life. Last night, when she'd come home from acting class and noted his suitcases by the door—packed, she'd guessed, for a trip to Garden City in the morning—she'd noticed a queer paleness in his look, a slight tremor in his touch. He'd reeked of the sort of fear that got people like him killed.

What happened with Ben? she had asked.

The weather, he answered. He walked to the window and stared out at the falling snow. *The fucking weather.* The tone of his voice caused her to shiver.

She would send him away soon, would take back her house key—she remembered exactly the moment she had given it to him, the sense of excitement that had accompanied her closed fist, outheld. The startled look on his face when her fingers had opened to reveal the shining, newly-carved silver key.

People like him, she thought now. They get killed. But they kill people like me a little bit every day.

Twenty-Three

Wͤe are the unlucky, he thought. And why do the unlucky sleep? To escape the misfortunes that occur during daylight, to dream of the assassination of enemies, to plan these hopeful mini-insurrections.

They sleep because they're not so much tired or exhausted as they are used up.

But at night, at night there's nothing to get away *from,* because nothing happens at night but other sleep. So we sleep during the daylight.

We are the unlucky, he thought. And because it was nearly daylight, he slept.

But not really. He soon found himself in that stratum of half-sleep in which you dream and simultaneously understand, with clinical awareness, that you are dreaming. This dream was like a war-film reel, the black and white Sam Fuller sort: *Fixed Bayonets. Steel Helmet.* It was deep night in the dream, and snowing heavily, fat flakes falling on a monochromatic mountainside. He lay on his belly in a snowbound thicket, the smooth wood stock of his rifle against his cheek, and he felt neither cold, nor hungry, nor lonely. He waited and looked down the barrel of his carbine at the snowy pass. He peered over the filed sights and wondered who was coming.

He might have happily dawdled there for hours if the dream hadn't been suddenly interrupted by the sharp odor of smoke—smoke in the waking world.

Smoke always brought him awake. He sat up and drew in a breath, testing the scent of the air. He'd been comprehensively conditioned to mistrust himself with fires—he was a sot-pyromaniac who stacked logs upward with abandon, and then promptly receded into drunken slumber without tending to them. On at least ten occasions he had woken on the living room couch and found the stack of burning logs collapsed and spilled out over the stones, wayward embers smoldering lazily on the fire-resistant rug.

He pulled on his boots and walked upstairs.

Miraculously, he'd remembered to place the screen in front of the fireplace before making his way, blind drunk, down the cellar stairs to bed an hour ago.

This was why he'd gotten drunk last night, and only this: after he'd returned from Warren's house, he'd locked the front door and hung his coat in the closet without turning on the hallway light and, entirely sober, had gone upstairs to bed. The house, hushed with night, had seemed unpleasantly lifeless and sterile—he was startled by his reflection in the landing window: well-dressed, trim and shaved, and surprisingly handsome in the kind landing light, as if he had momentarily crossed the border of some alternative life he might have lived. This was how he *would* have lived, alone, always returning much too late from some wayward lunge at life, burdened with mixed feelings about this or that choice he'd made or this or that thing he'd said, encountering his reflection everywhere—in black window-glass at night, in framed hall mirrors, in polished steel fixtures—as he made his way upstairs, toward the escape of sleep, because alone is always, always unlucky. Alone is *twice* as terrifying.

Upstairs, he found the bedroom door shut and locked. Twice, he gripped it and tested it to see if he was mistaken, and then rested his forehead against the wood for ten minutes. He wanted to speak to her through the barrier, to tell her that *This time, Emma*—that this time it was over for sure. He wanted to explain that he'd simply had one last task to complete, one unresolved piece of retribution. It then occurred to him, separated from her, that any sort of explanation was useless, because contrition had come too late. This was why he'd gotten drunk and stumbled down the cellar steps at daylight.

The smoke-smell—exactly like the odor of burning leaves you happily encounter during the fall—was stronger now. A flue-fire at the Schecters? He rubbed his neck and yawned and went to the window. His tie was still noosed about his collar.

Today he would drink again. He was sure of it.

A cloudlet of smoke drifted across the driveway. Perplexed, he leaned all the way over the couch so that he could look across the yard, where he saw, first, more smoke, and then, unbelievably, the burning barn, furiously alight.

He watched the flames dumbly. For a moment, the commands crowding his synapses seemed to cancel each other out. Then he turned and made for the front door at a sprint. He fell over the couch, picked himself up, ran to the hall, and burst out the front door into the strange, cold white world that had arrived overnight. Only after he'd gone halfway to the barn did he realize he was barefoot in the deep snow.

His first thought was to back the car from under the overhang. He'd gone a few steps toward it when he saw the scarred paint, the buckled lock of the trunk, the steel twinkling in the bright morning sunlight. The pry-bar was abandoned at the car's fender, a spidery black slash indented in the snow. In a single instant he understood what had happened. If he had spotted Warren in that instant, he would have silently picked up the pry-bar and struck him in the temple with it.

He climbed in the car and backed it twenty feet down the drive.

There would need to be room for the Sahid's MG. He stepped out of the car and addressed the conflagration.

You're really going in there, he thought.

He looked at the burning barn. The entire structure seemed alive with the motion of flame. Flame was in the gaps between the wood slats, beneath the eaves, curling and crisping the faded red paint. A portion of the roof had collapsed. Smoke boiled upward through the vent into the vaulted sky.

I'm really going in there.

I'm really going.

Four steps inside the door, he heard a cracking roar from overhead. He looked up and the light was blotted out. There was a slap of super-heated wind, a rain of embers. There was a crystalline moment of understanding. And then nothing.

Twenty-Four

The morning after Ben's drop, Victor packed the morphine into two suitcases and rode an early train out to Garden City. There was more than a foot of new snow, and the trains were running erratically. It took him more than an hour to make a trip that normally took forty-five minutes. Wes was waiting for him at the station, idling in the plowed drop-off zone in a flawless black four-door Mercedes with a dealer plate posted in the back window. Wes had a thing for cars, and he was clearly irritated when Victor didn't compliment him on his buy or on the fact that he had kept it clean during the overnight snowfall. During the drive to the baseball field, Wes said that he had lost some customers with the mid-month drought and that he hoped there wouldn't be any problems this month. Victor told him problems were part of the business and that there would certainly be more and if he didn't like it he could switch brands. His palms sweated into the fabric of his khakis.

"You know who stopped by this morning?" Wes asked. "Warren. Rang the doorbell, sweet as can be. Looked like a bit part from *Re-Animator*. Gave me the willies."

"That so?" Victor asked with posed disinterest. He studied Wes's expression. He imagined the plunge of poultry shears, the bright blood. That was how every end happened: when it came, it came that quickly and senselessly.

"Imagine. He said that Ben had stiffed him."

"Imagine."

"You know anything about it?"

"Not yet."

"But you'll let me know if there's something going on?"

"Of course," Victor said. "You send him away?"

"I gave him a couple hits for the ride," Wes said. "Like I said. He gave me the willies. Sometimes you don't know what people are capable of."

"He gives me the willies, too," Victor said. He imagined Warren parked somewhere nearby, deep into a nod. "I'll take care of it, okay?"

Wes drove to the deserted baseball field, his wheels spinning through the deep snow burying the access road. Wes inspected the cases while Victor stood watching with his arms wrapped around him for warmth. He would have to call Theo when he got back from Culebra. They would have to drive north and take care of things.

He took the train back to Trina's apartment, where he packed a small flight bag and then caught a taxi to JFK. There was no traffic, and the fare was half what he had expected to pay. From the expressway, he saw that the runways had already been plowed.

There were plenty of open standby seats on the first plane to San Juan. While he was waiting for boarding, he went to the bar and drank a weak Bloody Mary and telephoned Warren twice, Ben once. With every unanswered ring, he became more upset. He had a second drink, and half a third before he heard the last call for his flight.

Near the back of the plane he found four empty seats. After takeoff, he stretched out across the seats and fell asleep.

At the airport he caught the bus to Fajardo. Every seat on the bus was full, and he had to stand all the way in the back. They arrived at the ferry stop in Fajardo at nightfall. The next ferry was already sold out, so he bought a ticket for the last outbound ferry and walked into town, where he shopped for Christmas presents at the mall near the fast food stands. He bought a dress and a handmade hair pin for his mother, and he asked the salesgirl to wrap the presents for him. As he was walking back to the ferry with the presents, it occurred to him that he had paid for the dress and the hair pin and even the ferry with the money he had made that morning in Long Island. Although that might have bothered some people, driven them to an agony of conscience, to him the manner in which the money had been spent seemed just and perhaps even inevitable. It was all right to take people who should know better, he felt, especially if you did something good with the money.

His mother didn't know he was coming. More than anything, he loved coming for a visit without telling her. It was a dirty trick, not telling her, because it robbed her of something to look forward to, but the look on her face whenever he surprised her at the door was one of those small, good moments that always felt new, even if it had happened a hundred times.

There was no wind tonight, and the ferry barely rolled beneath him. The people with him on the deck of the ship were happy. Most of them were islanders, because there were very few hotels on Culebra, and the tourists usually only came in for the day. The ferries from the island to Puerto Rico continued for a few more hours. He scanned the horizon and saw one coming a quarter mile to his left traveling toward the mainland, the light on its prow blinking. It was almost fully dark now. With each blink he faintly saw the shape of the ferry and the upper deck full of people. That was a good sign. He hoped that business had been good for her today, but he also hoped that she hadn't worked too hard.

After the ferry had docked, he walked down the ramp with his bags slung over his shoulder. No one spoke. It was a beautiful night, and the two bars at the landing were overflowing with young people. He walked past the bars into town and bought a bottle of water and a bottle of rum and then hid both his bag for later. Then he walked down the steep hill next to the store, a street so familiar to him that he sometimes dreamed of it.

He knocked at the door for a long time. When his mother answered, looking tired and very gray-haired, there was that fractional moment of unrecognition, and then she put her hands on either side of his face and stood on her tiptoes, kissed him many times, and began to cry. As he hugged her he thought, My God, mama, you are short. Why are you always so short? She had closed an hour ago, she said, and had sent Hector home. He followed her into the kitchen and sat at the table. She brought him a bowl of black bean stew with rice and a glass of water with ice in it. While she was getting him a fork, he quickly brought out the rum and poured some into his water, and capped the bottle, then hid it again.

She sat across from him. She no longer looked tired. "So," she said in Spanish, "tell me about work." She had never flown in her life, because the thought of being airborne terrified her. She was awestruck that he flew sometimes more than once a day. In Culebra his job was an honorable one, and he wasn't about to take that away from her.

"The airlines are showing much care," he said. The Spanish felt strange and alien in his mouth. It frightened him to think that he had become distant from his own language.

"For this New Year." She knew the answers, but she liked to hear them from him, anyway.

"Yes," he said. "I have spoken of this?"

She shook her head. "How are they careful?"

"Flights are canceled for some. And they use the machine to check for bombs."

She said the *machina* was a thing of great interest. "And so," she asked, "you are able to stay for a week?"

"Yes. I will work, and you can have much rest."

She was overjoyed. "We will both work and have fun, and you can tell me all about your life. You are such a good boy, Victor. No one has such a good boy." She called him *hijito*. "You visit me, and you are so kind to me. My friends say their children never visit or call or write, and they are miserable without them."

"I visit because you make me happy," he said. It was true. He liked how clean she made him feel and how she required nothing of him but his presence. He liked who he was when he was around her, and there were times, when he was alone with her, when he understood why some men never married.

"How is it with money?"

"Money is very good," he said. "I have some for you."

"I did not mean it that way."

"Of course not. But I have some for you, and my money is very well, and there will be more and soon I will have enough to come back."

"You are such a good boy. But we will not talk about money tonight."

"Tomorrow," he said. "We have much time." He thought of the presents. "I have something for you." He took the presents out of his bag. She opened them slowly, and he could see by her face that she loved them. She went into her bedroom and put on the dress and when she came out he saw that she was beautiful and something that was both sorrow and love seemed to turn in him. Something about a beautiful woman, even his own mother, frightened him. "You look beautiful," he said.

"Do I?"

"Yes. You always look beautiful."

"I will wear this when we go to church Sunday."

Inwardly he felt sick at the thought of going to confession, but he smiled and said he thought that was a good idea. He would go out with his friends the night before, sleep late Sunday morning, tell her he was sick, and she would go without him. She would wear the dress, and everyone would ask where she had gotten it, and she would tell them and feel proud and happy.

"Now I have to sleep," she said. "I love my presents, and I love that I have you here with me." She put her hands on either side of his face and kissed him again. For a moment she seemed as if she might cry again and then she was better. "I will make your bed for you."

"Nothing," he said. "You sleep."

"You are such a good boy," she said, and he knew that he was. No one could take that away from him.

Twenty-Five

The roof had collapsed over him just inside the barn doorway. He had gone in, she guessed, for the MG, perhaps thinking of the financial stakes. Perhaps not. Perhaps he had thought he was safe. She hoped that he hadn't suffered, that he had fallen unconscious, or that one's brain shut down at the last moment to make whatever was happening bearable. But that was just more of the same after-the-fact anesthetic. In all likelihood, it had been horrible, and he had suffered, and there was nothing to be done about that. At least he'd gotten it over with.

The fire had first taken down the barn, and then, as she and the girls, wrapped in blankets, had watched, had taken their home. It was her life—it *couldn't* be her life. This was something one read about in a newspaper. This was something that happened to other people. Except it *wasn't*. Ben was gone. Their children were fatherless, and suddenly their foursome had been reduced to a threesome: subtraction had done its subtraction thing.

She encountered his absence everywhere she went, like a cold pocket of water you passed through while swimming in a warm lake. That was one of the new things she had learned during the last few days: that an absence was as physically real—as much *there*—as a presence.

Jane looked ravishing in black, and Mick was regarding every male present at the funeral wake with naked suspicion. He was drinking soda water with lots of ice.

"Warren," Jane said. For the last ten minutes Emma had been watching her prepare herself to speak. "It was—Emma, you know that. It must have happened because of Warren. Ben would never—never."

"Jane," Mick said.

"I'm saying—" She raised a hand to her mouth and pinched her lower lip, balanced for a moment between thought and counter-thought. "I'm just saying what ought to be said. About Warren."

"Jane," Mick said.

"Mick," she said flatly, "don't say my name again. I'm begging you."

"Jane," he said. His tone was desperate. "Will you please?"

Emma wanted to yank Jane's hair out by its dark roots. To break a plate and stick a porcelain point in one mascara-framed eye. To throw everyone out of the house—but this wasn't her house. They had been staying with the Schecters since the fire. Her home was the blackened pile of timber a few hundred yards away up the hill. And you couldn't throw people out of someone else's house.

Could you?

She wanted to throw them all out, because of course she knew that Warren had done it. And because knowing that explained nothing.

Nina and Sylva were upstairs with the coloring books Lila bought for them. They seemed strangely unaffected by what had happened. They had cried at the sight of the fire, wept at the noise and the red spectacle of the fire trucks, but they'd given no signs that what they had seen had remained with them. There had been no nightmares, no night-light requests.

Emma initially thought Ben had run across the field to the Schecters for help, but as the trucks began to arrive and he hadn't materialized, she realized, with a feeling like the summary of all the horror she'd felt in her life, that he had been inside the barn when it collapsed. It seemed plain that neither Nina nor Sylva understood the finality of his departure. Emma had explained death to them yesterday, but her words had seemed ineffective and abstract. She realized that they'd need to experience his absence for a while before it seemed real. All three of them would.

All that remained of Warren was his El Dorado and its worn title. He'd sold the car for half its value in a Brooklyn lot just hours after the fire. Emma had gone to the lot with the police yesterday. Warren's signature and address on the back of the title were ragged and hurried, the work of a man who was suffering and had places to go. The turbaned man who Warren sold the car to was loudly argumentative, worried that the police would impound the car.

Where do you think he went next? Emma asked one of the cops.

The cop tapped his nightstick against the El Dorado's hood. I'll bet you lunch at Peter Luger's he's in Hell's Kitchen right now, he said. We'll probably pick him up on a drug sweep. Or one of the DEA snitches might flip him.

A plane roared overhead, wings dipping in the still air, ailerons making the necessary corrections. I'll bet, Emma thought as she squinted at the sky to watch it pass, that he's a long way from Hell's Kitchen right now.

If they found him now, she wouldn't tear him apart with her teeth and nails. She would simply ask him what happened.

Grampa waved to me, Sylva had told her. *He had his coat on, and I wanted to sled, but he made me go back to bed.*

Emma pushed the contents of her plate around with a fork. She was hungry and yet she was unable to view eating as anything other than the process of devouring something that was dead. Why was it, she thought, that at funerals everyone plied you with food? Instead they should come to the door with an idea of why and how things had gone wrong. Perhaps hearing hundreds of points of view would help her develop her own. She had telephoned Sweet that morning to invite him, mostly for selfish reasons, but his answering service told her he was home for Christmas. Was her call urgent?

No, she thought. It's the opposite of urgent. It's over. With that thought the tears came, and because she was unwilling to explain she hung up without leaving a number.

His absence was everywhere. His antimatter. Grief was this, and only this: grief was the inability to reason with the *not there*-ness.

She excused herself and set her plate down. Someone spoke to her as she made her way through the murmurous groups toward the front hall, where she pulled her coat on and let herself out through the front door. Cars were double and triple parked in the drive. It was still bitingly cold and mercilessly sunny. She had overheard that they had needed to dynamite the ground at the cemetery to dig his grave. That seemed fitting to her, and she thought that perhaps her father would approve. She would have to tell him about that later, after everyone left and the dishes had been cleaned and put away.

Will you come back with us? her father asked her that morning, looking at her through the mirror, as she stood in the bathroom doorway.

She walked up the hill toward what remained of the house. Her low heels punched through the frozen crust, and the snow came up to just over her ankles. The heels certainly weren't cut out for the snow, but that couldn't be helped, and she didn't want to go back to the Schecters to change. She had begun to think that it was time to move into a hotel or a small apartment with a short lease. There were hundreds of options for them, but the options, she found, had to become real before you could consider them honestly. If only. If only the trees beside the barn hadn't caught fire. If only the trees hadn't caught the roof on fire. If only the roads had been plowed. If only I had been awake. If only the fire trucks hadn't been slowed so much. If only. She had wanted to be free of the house for so many years—

If only in a less horrible way.

Will you come back with us? he'd repeated, razor still in hand, a wicked nick at his throat just beginning to show blood, and again she didn't answer.

She stood in the driveway and looked up at the blackened branches of the trees. The fire had melted the earlier snowfall, but it had snowed heavily again in the two days since the fire and now a thin dusting of snow clung delicately to even the most slender branches. Emma walked over to the burned remains of the barn and stepped under the yellow police tape and found the spot near the door where Ben had collapsed. She kicked at the ash and snow and rubble. Something bright turned over, and she bent to retrieve it with numb fingertips.

She held the bright circle up and found that it was Ben's ring, the ring that William had given him. It had warped slightly in the heat of the fire. She wiped it clean of ash with her sleeve and examined it closely. There was a word stamped on its face but without her glasses she couldn't read it.

THREE

Twenty-Six

H e heard the plane before he saw it. It was a two-seat bush-hopper, the type the smugglers preferred because they were small and light and required little runway or fuel. It looped once around the airfield in the afternoon sunlight, the windows reflecting brightly. After the plane had circled the runway, the pilot turned far out over the canopy to line up for his approach. The plane skimmed the tall grass at the far end of the airfield as it drew close and then touched down, bumping and skipping along the runway. The motor throttled down until Warren could see the individual propeller blades. He walked out to meet the pilot, carrying his canvas bag and mopping the sweat from his face with a torn square of an old T-shirt. Months of use had given the cloth the earthy tint of the airfield's orange dust.

The pilot opened the side door and hopped down onto the dirt runway. He wore wraparound sunglasses and was deeply tanned, and appeared to be exquisitely hungover. Warren had never worked with him before.

"You're the doctor?" the pilot asked.

After a heartbeat's hesitation, he said that he was. He no longer felt the need to explain about his license.

"Where is everyone?"

"Inside," Warren said.

"I hope you don't mind sitting aft," the pilot said. "You have any Dramamine? Windy today."

"I never get sick," Warren said. "Done it too many times."

"Mind if I get something to eat, first?"

"That's fine," Warren said. "You might want to wash your hands first. There's fresh water in the chapel."

"You?"

"Already ate." He set his bag down and sat in the shade of the wing and leaned back against the gear. "Take your time. They radioed again a few minutes ago. I don't think it's urgent."

The pilot walked toward the cement-block headquarters at the edge of the airfield, lifting a lazy cloud of orange dust. The missionaries had built the headquarters just three months ago, and immediately painted a large red cross on the tin roof. As you flew in over the airfield, from a distance you saw the cross in the center of the blazing tin like a deep perpendicular rift. Warren had been in and out of the airfield too many times to count. Depending on his mood, he occasionally allowed himself to see the cross as a good omen. Most days he did not. He mentioned this once to one of the missionaries. The missionary thought for a moment, and then replied that a bad omen was his own bad trip. Since then, Warren spoke to the missionaries very little. He spent most of his free time in his cot working his way through the ragged detective novels that composed the bulk of the missionary library. Nights, he played chess with Father Petruzio.

That he had achieved the reputation of a loner seemed perfectly natural; there were times when, with startling authenticity of feeling, he wished to get away from even himself. It was as if he could not be alone enough. Alone, he found, at least you could control the frequency of the guilt. You knew, for instance, to put down a book the moment you read the word *fire*. If you put it down quickly enough, and asked yourself some sort of mindless, borrowed, absorbing question, something like, *I wonder if that cloud will cross the moon?*, there was the distinct chance you could distract yourself long enough to forget that you had read the word *fire*. Other words had achieved the same emblematic status: *thief, airport, been*. It was a list that seemed to be growing day by day; in time, *of* and *the* would be sufficient to send him reeling into a cold sweat.

The Dilaudid helped. As of yet, no one knew about his addiction. It was only a matter of time until they did. The missionaries would complain, and Father Petruzio would sigh his consecrated sigh, but no one would do anything about it. It was the same as the flap about his license. That had gone as far as the Global Aid office in Kinshasa, where the inquiry had stalled. No one cared.

The pilot came out of the headquarters. He wiped his hands on his shirt as he walked toward the plane. "Ready?" he asked.

Warren nodded and stepped aside to let him climb in first. He climbed in behind him and latched the door and then sat on the aft seat and fixed the belt tightly over his lap. The cockpit smelled sharply of rifle oil and JP-8 jet fuel. Warren noticed that his seat was slightly mangled, the stuffing spilling out.

"No headphones," the pilot said. "Hope you don't mind. Hyenas got in and ate them last night. Part of your seat, too." He did a quick check of his flaps and then turned the engine over. The exhaust coughed once and then the propeller, ahead through the window, began to spin until the individual blades blurred together into a single transparent disc. Warren fixed his sunglasses over his eyes and sat back. A drop of sweat rolled down his ribcage.

The pilot taxied around in a lazy circle so the plane faced with its nose down the runway. The throttle roared higher in a vibrating, dust-raising roar, so loud that Warren felt it in the fillings of his teeth. With a gentle shove, they began to roll down the runway, jolting and bumping, the plane rattling and skimming faster, the pockmarks beside them running together and smoothing out, until suddenly there was a final, light bump, and then they were flying steeply and smoothly up into the sky. The airfield fell away beneath them. Warren looked down to his right. The black shadow of the plane rippled along the tall grass and then over the flat canopy where the airfield gave way to the jungle.

"What's this one?" the pilot shouted over his shoulder.

Warren leaned forward. "Girl got mauled last night."

"Think she'll die?"

Warren thought about it. "Not today," he said.

Warren had come outside after dinner and was reading *Double Indemnity* beneath the halogen spotlight at the edge of the airfield. Rhazi's note, which had served as his bookmark for the last three months, had neared its retirement. After months of use, the penciled words were almost completely faded.

Heaven, Warren, is a place with no memory.

The missionaries' library was not limited to mysteries. In the shelves were *Crime and Punishment, Wise Blood,* and *The Fall.* In the shelves was *Purgatorio.* Reams of atonement, and all of it fiction. Dante's so very unfunny comedy: *"Poi s'ascose nel foco che gli affina,"* he had written; *Then hid him in the fire that purifies them. Fire*—the traps and tricks were everywhere.

He looked up from the book when Father Petruzio opened the front door to the headquarters. The missionaries were asleep in the bunkhouse. Petruzio had grown bored of them and had begun to eat his meals with Warren. He was in the midst of an astonishing winning streak at chess, a streak Warren believed was engendered by his fear of Petruzio's vestments.

"How's the girl?" Petruzio asked.

"Fine. They had the sense not to clean it in the river."

"That bad?" He slapped at a mosquito on his neck.

"They bathe ten yards from where they wash their dishes." He sighed. "Every time I go out there I'm afraid I'll find dust and bones."

Petruzio sighed. "I'll have to visit them. What did you do for her?"

Warren shrugged. "Cleaned it. Gave her some B-twelve and a Mars Bar."

"How was the trip?"

Warren thought about it.

"It was fun," he said.

"We're lucky to have you, Warren. I wish you'd let us make it more formal."

Warren said it didn't much matter to him.

"Game of chess?" Petruzio asked.

"Not tonight," Warren said.

He was, for some reason, frightened of Petruzio tonight. The innocent, he thought, do not understand the gift of innocence. Because you cannot understand it until you lose it. And you cannot debate innocence with a priest; you may as well debate romance with a whore. They know everything and yet they know nothing. "No, I don't think so." He held up his copy of *Double Indemnity* so that Petruzio's feelings wouldn't be hurt. "I'm just getting into it."

"Great last sentence," the Father said. He checked his watch. "Well," he said. "Better get your lamp if you want to keep going. Have to turn off the power in a few minutes."

"All right," Warren said. His mouth was dry. "Anything doing tomorrow?"

"I guess we'll find out," Petruzio said. He slapped at another mosquito. "Good night, Wren."

"Good night, Nick."

Petruzio went inside.

As Warren tried to regain his place in the book, the spotlight went blank overhead and the words vanished in darkness.

There in the night he watched the cold light of the stars.